Falling off the Wind

Martin and Lawrence Press
43 Nod Road
Groton, MA 01450
978-448-6651
<rmpm@charter.net>

Printed in the United States

ISBN-13: 978-0-9820732-8-3
ebook ISBN-13: 978-0-9820732-9-1

 Date and locale of Hurricane Hugo are factual. Similarity and fate of the schooner *Grace* are purposeful, in memory of a "graceful" ship once owned by Owen Stuart.

Falling off the Wind

A novel

by

Richard Meibers

Martin and Lawrence Press
Groton, MA
2012

Other books by Richard Meibers

The Fitchburg Watch

Steal Away Home

Tree Rings

To Pan

Falling off the wind: A sailboat falls off the wind when it points its bow further from the eye of the wind. The opposite of heading up into the wind.

Acknowledgements

I would like to thank all those who helped with the writing and editing of this book. David Brody, Bernadette Colley, Paul Eisenberg, Ted Grosch, Dwight Harshbarger, Alyssa Kvenvold, Katherine Liebowitz, Joyce Mannis, Taeve Neese, Sally Reed, Alice Rennie, Jo-Ann Wangh.

Y muchas gracias a la communidad de Culebra, Puerto Rico.

Chapter One

The schooner *Panacea* fell off the wind. In a slow, majestic turn, her tanbark-colored sails bellied out as she heeled slightly to starboard in a broad reach, a south-southeast breeze nudging her into the current where she seemed to pause for a breath and then glided forward on the white-caps.

Leaving Water Island to starboard, the current of the Drake Passage and a ten-knot breeze carried the boat west into the Caribbean, the first rays of the morning sun dancing directly in its wake. They did not need all the sail they had up for the short voyage planned, but it felt freeing to be moving so lightly across the surface of the water, especially after sitting so long moored at St. Thomas.

Clement Scheutz secured the foremast halyard on its pin on the port rail and stood a while, his hand on a ratline, to watch the island slide by, happy to be shed of St. Thomas, the gaudiness, the loud music, the noise that never stopped, tourists, hawkers, vacation homeowners, sailors on leave from Roosevelt Roads.

He looked up to view the luft of the foresail and then turned aft to where Samantha, wisps of blonde hair escaping from under her long-billed cap, also eyed the set of the sail as she tweaked the position of the helm. He saw, or imagined he saw, their disagreement about leaving St. Thomas showing itself in the set of her jaw and tension in her shoulders. She had argued fiercely that she enjoyed being where they were, for her on-going love affair with the place, its music and color, and the opportunity of picking up a little temporary work when they ran short of cash.

He placed his left foot on the rail and adjusted a loose strap on an over-worn Teva sandal, its sole, like its mate, without tread, the velcro straps just barely still doing the job. Like everything else he wore, t-shirt with stains and paint splotches, a small tear under one arm; and canvas work shorts, covered with paint, caulk and glue, frayed around the legs—they were like Scheutz, functional but a little worse for wear. That could also be said of the boat itself, a weather-worn sixty-five-foot, wooden-hulled schooner, originally built in the 1920s as a British racing boat.

At age fifty, Scheutz did not mind wasting time but was damned if he would waste it in a place where he did not feel comfortable—like St. Thomas. His skin had begun to wrinkle from so many years in the Caribbean sun, and his hands, from working this boat, were calloused like an old-time seaman's. His beard had begun to show flecks of gray but the hair on his head had remained a sandy shade, drained of color by the sun. He did not feel old, but felt the world was old. 1989. The America he'd left seven years earlier, not long after the presidential election, had grown as old as President Reagan, himself as old and senile as the Death Valley, whose television series he once hosted. The country's corpocracy seemed to be enjoying another economic slump if he believed the newspapers that reached the islands. The slump was like watching a weather report of what was going on far out at sea. But even if it did roll in it would barely touch them.

He grasped the ratline to steady himself against the movement of the schooner's deck as they left the island behind. Under him, the boat steadied in her tack. With a fair breeze off the port stern she should hold well with just the foresail, staysail, and jib. Below him, the engine still rumbled. Samantha, always concerned about being under-powered, needed the assurance of either a running diesel or billowing mainsail. With the present conditions of wind and current, as far as Scheutz was concerned, they needed neither. He scanned the surfaces of the raised sails, this time looking for possible beginning rips in the canvas. It had been close to a year since the *Panacea* had been under sail, the canvases each wrapped in their respective sail covers. But the canvas looked fine; unlike so many things on the wooden schooner that needed restoration.

In the bow, Asher, the brown-black-skinned crewman, neatened the coiled jib and staysail halyards on their pins on the starboard rail. Beyond Asher, in a direct line with the bowsprit, tiny Saba Island lay in their path. Scheutz turned aft to see if Samantha was compensating to leave Saba Island to starboard also. With their twelve-foot draft he didn't want to have to bother with navigating through the shallower water between Saba and the Flat Cays. The upper half of Samantha's tanned body, visible over the teak roof of the companionway to below decks, arched just slightly as she turned the hand spikes on the large wheel, shifting the ship's course more to the southwest. Over Samantha's head, the main boom with its mainsail furled and tied along its length, dipped slightly and then snapped to the end of its traveler line. The loose strands of Samantha's streaked blond hair lifted in the breeze and whipped her face.

Behind her, the afterdeck raked up slightly to the taffrail, out beyond which a heavy nylon cable, towing a thirty-foot sloop, slackened and then tightened as the schooner shifted its course, while the bow of the sloop surfed in and out of the schooner's wake. Harding, the owner of the sloop, was nowhere in sight, and must have been still below, sleeping off his last night's drunk. The sloop, *Gaga*, towed behind it a fourteen-foot Boston Whaler, which bounced on the waves. Behind the whaler was hitched Harding's inflatable dinghy. The string of boats, beginning with the schooner, looked like a momma duck with a trail of ducklings behind her. Scheutz shook his head, wondering again why he had let Harding talk him into towing the sloop from St. Thomas to Culebra. But with a seasonal southeast wind and the strong eastern current they should have no trouble with drag caused by the *Gaga* and the two smaller boats. They should make Culebra in less than four hours.

Thinking of Harding gave Scheutz the usual twinge of irritation. The man could never seem to do what you'd expect him to do. At the last minute Harding had insisted on taking the Boston Whaler and of course he was too drunk to haul his dinghy aboard so they ended up towing that one, too. Harding could have gotten the sloop's engine running or, at least, patched his torn mainsail enough to get the boat to

Culebra under its own power. But, no. With Harding there was always a problem with something, usually because of his failure to take proper care of the boat. Or proper care of anything else, for that matter. He let everything go till it was too late and then somebody, often Scheutz, had to help him out of whatever predicament he'd gotten himself into.

Harding hadn't even shown up to help get ready the night before, and when he did show up just before they were ready to cast off this morning, Samantha pitched a fit and started yelling that they should just leave Harding and his boats in Charlotte Amalie. "If we dragged a dead fish behind us, it'd smell better." Scheutz had at first agreed with her but she kept up her attack on Harding, his irresponsibility, his drunkenness, his clothes, his bad breath, his fantastic schemes for making money, and on and on. Scheutz finally had to switch over and begin defending Harding. In the early dawn he had turned to Asher to ask him what he thought of the idea of towing the Gaga, but Asher had only shrugged in his characteristic way. What did he care? That was the thing about Asher, one of the many reasons Scheutz liked having the man around; nothing seemed to faze him. He was like the ocean; he was just there, on the surface always moving, but below a depth of calm. Samantha finally gave in and he tied off the line to the boat's prow while Asher hopped ashore and undid the sloop's stern line. Scheutz and Asher had secured the smaller boats as Harding staggered up from below onto the deck of the sloop. He turned in the cockpit to giggle at Scheutz like a conspirator and point behind his upheld hand at Samantha at the rail of schooner glaring at him.

The *Panacea* cleared Saba Island, moving out into open water. Scheutz considered again whether they should raise the mainsail or stay with just the three sails already up. There was not a whole lot of wind, but it felt like they must be making at least six knots, even with the drag astern. The drag from the tow would keep the schooner's bow steady. They were all right without the mainsail, but they probably should let out the jib and the staysail a bit.

In the bow, Asher had finished coiling his lines and was standing by to adjust the sail trim. "Standing by" did not accurately describe what Asher did. He never seemed to stop moving, even when he was doing nothing but standing by. Now he was dancing to some rhythm going on in his head. He looked like a moon-walking stork with his bony knees and elbows going in all directions. Scheutz stood an extra moment, watching his crewman. No telling how old the man was; he could have been anywhere between thirty-five and sixty-five, but again, like the sea, he had the feel of having been around since the beginning of time.

Now that they were out of the harbor they certainly did not need the diesel power. Scheutz waved to get Samantha's attention and sliced his finger across his throat for her to cut the engine. She looked toward him, turned to look behind at the boats in tow. Instead of shutting off the engine, she readjusted her cap, balancing the wheel against her elbows to tuck her hair up into the cap and then pull it low onto her forehead.

Scheutz made his way to the stern and stood behind her. "Cut the engine, Samantha." She made an adjustment of the helm and only then reached her hand to the binnacle to pull the kill switch for the engine. It was always as if she wanted to retain, for a few more moments, the comforting murmur of the engine below her feet before being left to the will of the wind and the current. For Scheutz, the moment when the engine noise stopped held a tingle of magic. Even after all these years messing around on the ocean, he was transported each time by the stillness, broken only by the creak of the ship's timbers and splash of waves against the bow. For that moment, he could be anywhere, on any ocean, during any one of the thousands of years that people have gone to sea in ships.

They entered the strait with the sun full up and warm. Off to the northeast a dark thunderhead loomed over Tortolla. The Roosevelt Roads weather channel had reported no front moving in that morning, but this was the season for fast moving storms. The cloud on the horizon appeared menacing but shouldn't affect them unless the wind shifted from south-southeast, which was unlikely in late summer.

Samantha made hand signals to Asher who worked the handle of a winch controlling the jib sheet a notch at a time, his head tilted back to watch the luft of the sail. Scheutz, standing directly behind Samantha, put his hands on her hips and looked over her shoulder at the compass in the top of the binnacle. Her body relaxed back against his. This knee-jerk-like response happened whenever he touched her, as if her body, against her will, longed to touch his. But, other than the sudden relaxation, she did not acknowledge his nearness. Then, as always lately, the defensive reflex took hold and the muscles tightened in her bronzed back and neck. He backed away. This was going to be another of those long, drawn-out isolations she was so good at. She stood with her bare feet planted solidly on the teak deck and her long tight body in halter and running shorts braced against the pull of the helm.

Her reason for not wanting to leave St. Thomas had been limited pretty much to one sentence, "At least, not right now," with no further explanation. They had argued for weeks. They could not afford the mooring fees for a sixty-five-foot schooner, especially during the coming tourist season, not that many months away. But she didn't want to leave Charlotte Amalie, the activity, the nightlife, her friends. To her, moving the boat to Culebra was like stranding themselves in the north woods or the desert. Eventually, she gave in, but the argument flared again when they were getting ready to leave. After one particularly lengthy discussion that turned into a yellfest, she moved her things into the aft port cabin to sleep alone. She was going to Culebra but only under protest. If he wanted to leave a perfectly good life for a dry existence on a barren hunk of rock, she was going to let him know what that kind of existence felt like.

Scheutz moved to Samantha's left and studied the instruments on the binnacle. They were making better than three knots. With the usual three knot current in this part of the Drake Passage it meant they were actually moving about six knots. They would be fine as long as they had enough sail speed to keep the smaller boats behind them from drifting down on their stern.

"Steer a course of 270 until we can see the buoys."

She nodded.

"You see that weather behind us?"

"Yes." Her head tilted to look up at the billow of the foresail, then down to the compass, and then straight-ahead. He waited for her to say something else and, when she didn't, he left her to go below. He wedged his way through the main cabin, filled with the tools they had cleared from the main deck in preparation for this trip–table saw and a planer lashed to the permanent table in the center of the room, piles of lumber secured against the walls. On its shelf, the radio scanner flashed red signal lights across its face. Bracing himself against the list of the deck he made his way forward to the galley where he set a pot of water to boil for coffee on the gimballed propane stove. Back in the main cabin he unhooked the radio mike and tried to raise Harding in the *Gaga*. No answer. He switched to the weather channel. Partly cloudy, winds out of the southeast at ten to twelve knots, gusting up to fifteen. When the water boiled in the galley, he made three cups of coffee. He shouted for Asher through the forward hatch and put a coffee cup in the hand that extended down through the opening above his head.

"I thank you, Mr. Clement." Asher squatted on the deck above the open hatch and finished lighting his already half-smoked cigar. He flashed a smoky grin at Scheutz. "Look like weather coming."

"Radio says no." Scheutz squinted up at him. "Anyway, we should be there before it hits."

He hooked the fingers of one hand through the handles of the other two cups and carried them through the main cabin and up the gangway. Samantha took the mug he held out to her and used her knee to help her left hand hold the wheel. "Why don't you put on some music?" She sipped without turning her head.

"I'd rather not. If you don't mind." On St. Thomas it seemed the music never stopped, coming at you all day long from a hundred radios and CD players, from boats, from houses, from restaurants, bars, souvenir stores, from discos and dance joints that stayed open until dawn, the music amplified across the water in marinas and bays, country-western, rock, reggae, calypso, a confused, perpetual din, driving him out as much as the mooring fees. If the boat was finished, and if they had the money for a long voyage, he'd keep going right past Culebra, all the way across the Caribbean and Gulf of Mexico to the Panama Canal and then on to the South Pacific where he and Samantha had been planning to go ever since they bought the boat.

He moved to Samantha's side. "Would you like me to take the helm?"

For the first time that day, she looked directly at him, but then looked past him toward the stern.

"You still pissed about towing Harding?" he asked.

She shook her head and sipped the coffee. "No, but I'm still pissed."

"Listen, I'm sorry about this. You know we don't have a choice." He was sorry about it, about dragging her away from a place she enjoyed. Now that he'd won out and they'd left that damned tourist trap behind, he could afford to let himself feel what she must be feeling. She had chosen this life when she left New Hampshire with him, but for the last two years had done everything she could to influence all their decisions toward keeping them as close to mainstream civilization as living on a schooner would allow. But as hard as she pulled, the harder he pulled them away from it.

She looked up from the coffee cup. "Oh, really? We don't have a choice? Of course we don't have a choice. As long as we own this goddamned boat we don't have a choice in anything."

"That's not true. Once we get finished with the restoration we can go anywhere in the world we want."

Her mouth tightened and her eyes filled with tears. She gritted her teeth as if fighting the tears and then suddenly whipped the wheel to windward and walked away toward the starboard rail.

The spinning helm threw the bow to leeward and caused a flying jibe, the foresail boom swinging from starboard to port with a creaking strain. Shuddering at the length of its sheets, the sail popped as it filled again with wind on the opposite side. Both jib and staysail back-winded and the schooner heeled hard to port. Scheutz reached for the binnacle to keep from falling, spilled his coffee as he grabbed the wheel. The boat jibed again, back in the opposite direction and righted itself on course.

In the bow, the jibe sent Asher from his perch. He had grabbed the staysail sheet and swung himself first one way and then the other as the boat completed its second jibe. He held his cigar between his teeth and looked back toward the helm as if waiting for some sign to tell him what to do. Once back on course, Scheutz signaled to trim both the jib and the staysail. The wind was shifting as well as picking up.

Samantha tramped from the rail to the gangway, giving Scheutz her offended victim glare as she passed, and descended below decks. Up forward Asher fiddled with something on the bowsprit. Scheutz held the course and watched the companionway where Samantha had disappeared. Her moods had gotten worse in the last year. She had been enthusiastic about the restoration at first, back when they were in Soper's Hole in Tortolla. She'd grown bored of her job as a charter captain for Sunsail. Having to smile for tourists for days on end made her face crack, she said. All the money she made, and the money he had picked up working as a rigger in the boat yard, was spent on the *Panacea*. To please her, he agreed to move the boat to St. Thomas. She seemed happier there for the last six months, but he was miserable. And they were running out of money.

Culebra was an inexpensive alternative. It had a peaceful bay where they could anchor the *Panacea* for nothing, live cheaply, run the power tools off their own generator, and, with not much else to do, complete much of the boat's restoration in six months. Culebra had no glitz, no nightlife, few tourists. It attracted a few scuba divers, a handful of naturalists who didn't mind sitting up all night to catch a glimpse of the dark bulk of a leatherback turtle coming out of the sea to lay her eggs on the beach. Culebra and its sister island Vieques were a little out of the way for casual sailors touring the Virgin Islands. Plus, Vieques contained an active naval bombing range on its western half that kept tourists away. And the approach to Culebra had one narrow channel through the reefs surrounding the only inlet to its bay. On the Caribbean side of the island a ferry made two trips a day to the main island of Puerto Rico, where they could obtain any building materials they might need.

They had sailed into the mouth of Culebra's bay once before, seven years earlier, while he and Samantha crewed on some Dutchman's yawl. They had sailed jib and jigger directly into the setting sun and, after dropping anchor, rowed to shore in the dark. It was about the most romantic night he could remember. The little Spanish town at the end of the bay was having its summer carnival with a salsa band playing on a temporary platform while people danced on the paved basketball court outside the grade school. One booth sold beer in cans, another shots of rum to mix with pineapple juice, and another booth dispensed cuchifritos and deep-fried shark nuggets. Dancers crowded in front of the band platform and, at the edge of the court, children danced with their mothers and grandmothers.

The world was so new to Scheutz and Samantha then. They had only recently run away to sea together. They were in love. His two sons were grown and his ex-wife, Gerry, had bought out his half of the old farmhouse in New Hampshire. Samantha, eighteen years younger than him, had money from her parents who lived in the same town. Scheutz had no responsibility to anyone any longer.

It took a couple of years, but the world of no responsibility became wearying. He's seen so many people toss their life aside and come to the Caribbean for the life of fun and sun only to sink into a desperate state of drunkeness. Samantha seemed to handle it in a way he could not. He became lost without working, a habit that would not change for him. They crewed on people's boats. They each accrued enough sail time and passed the U.S. Coast Guard test granting them a license to captain a small boat with as many six passengers. They saved all the money they could until they bought the schooner.

But that night on Culebra five years earlier, for the first time in his life, at age forty-four, Scheutz had learned to dance. On the basketball court, he and Samantha danced to the salsa band. It felt as if the deep muscles that had held up his bones all his life just melted in the moist tropical heat and he found himself laughing, for the first time in his life, when there was really nothing to laugh at. But it all felt so funny—Samantha, the basketball court, Mies, the Dutchman who owned the boat. Funniest of all was the thought that, even though he did not deserve such earthly pleasure, he was taking it.

They made a friend that night, a woman from the island, named Migdala, who spent the evening dancing with old Mies. She looked to be only a few years older than Samantha, but with a child in tow, a girl about ten, who spent her time running between the dancers with a group of feral boys. Migdala danced as if she were born dancing, but at the same time kept an attentive eye on her daughter. She was a head shorter than Samantha, with black hair pulled straight back from her forehead, dark skinned, her hips and breasts rounder but just as taut. That someone could actually dance the way she did and still keep control over her apparently wild daughter at the same time had Scheutz in awe. And, of course, made him laugh.

Migdala and Samantha switched partners, she now dancing directly in front of Scheutz's chest until her daughter caused a ruckus in the middle of the dancers by dragging a boy bigger than her to the tarmac and beating with him her fists about the head and shoulders. Migdala dragged her daughter away as the girl kicked out, catching the boy on the side of the head. As she passed Scheutz with the girl, she glared at him for laughing at the scene. Scheutz laughed at her look and at the imitation of the same look by her daughter. And he loved them both, the same way he loved Mies, and the basketball court, and the salsa band. They were all part of Samantha and the island night.

The sound of drums from below the schooner's deck blasted away his reverie. From the companionway hatch the drums were followed by a throb of electric guitars. Scheutz stretched from the wheel to slam the hatch, but the music continued to pound through the deck under his feet. Up forward, Asher picked up the beat and did a gawky hiphop across the foredeck, his ragged, loose-fitting shirt flapping beside his elbows and his knees. Scheutz laughed, his dancing crewman making Samantha's music almost bearable.

When they were well past West Cay and into the Southwest Roads he had to tack from a port reach to a starboard reach. Culebra was now in view directly off the bow. The wind had shifted fully to east-northeast and pulled the dark heavy clouds over the schooner. Rain fell and the wind picked up to twenty knots. Scheutz yelled for Asher to take the helm so he could try again to reach the *Gaga* on the radio.

Below decks the sound of the rock and roll filled the space like the inside of an amplifier. Samantha was not in the main salon and her cabin door was closed. Scheutz flipped the switch shutting off the music and sat down next to the radio. Samantha swept out of her cabin as he picked up the mike. She flipped the tape back on and the blast of sound next to his head jarred his teeth.

He hit the off button again. "I've got to get hold of Harding; do you mind?" This mood was so unlike Samantha. Yes, she had argued her point about staying in St. Thomas but had finally agreed to leave, her agreement coming only with the stark reality of their dire financial straits. This was new to her, and he knew that. She had never in her life been faced with truly empty pockets and he could see that it scared her. He was used to living with little money and argued from the viewpoint of always having to make little adjustments to keep himself afloat. She had trusted him and helped him with plans for what to do, where to go so they could continue working on the schooner. But that had all been in the unreal world of making plans. This actual leaving, the hard reality of pulling up anchor and heading for what she considered the poor house, had put her in some kind of rigid state, as if she'd pulled up the drawbridge and was hunkering down behind her defense-works. An, of course, towing Harding along behind seemed like a manifestation that they'd sunk to his level.

She glared at him for a moment and then turned and stepped back into her cabin, slamming the door. He tried to reach the Gaga again but no answer. He switched to the weather channel and heard only that there were still ten to twelve knot southeasterly winds.

He tried channel 16 again. "Gaga, this is Panacea. Gaga, this is Panacea. Come in Gaga. WAKE UP, HARDING." Nothing. He replaced the mike and crossed the slanted deck to the companionway, but before stepping up the ladder, reached to knock on Samantha's door. "It's getting pretty rough up there. I can use you on deck." Samantha made no sound.

On deck, he made his way to the front of the boat to close the forward hatch. The music started up again below. The wind had picked up and rain came in large drops stinging his skin. Asher seemed to hold the wheel lightly even though the boat pitched in a forward rolling motion. The black cloud enclosed the schooner and they lost Culebra's silhouette. Each time the ship dipped into a trough it crashed into the wave ahead of it. Waves broke over the bow flooding the foredeck. Off the stern, in the direction of St. Thomas, the cloud ended and the sun still glinted off the waves in their wake.

Back in the cockpit, Scheutz took over the helm. "Could you go below and get Samantha up here?" If Scheutz told her to come up she would ignore him again. Asher had always had a calming effect on her. He grabbed the roof above the hatch with his long, thin fingers and swung himself down into the companionway. A few moments later he reappeared, shrugged and spread his hands, palms up as if catching raindrops.

"Too much sail, Mr. Clement."

"I know. If I could get Samantha on the helm, we could reef that foresail."

"I'll do it."

"No. Just drop the staysail. See how we fare." Scheutz was fully soaked by the rain, water running down his face and into his mouth as he talked.

Asher scrambled over the superstructure past the main mast. Samantha's face appeared in the companionway with a rain hat pulled low over her eyes. She climbed up wearing a bright yellow foul weather jacket and white sneakers. It was so easy to stub a toe in this kind of wind. Silently she took the helm from Scheutz and he went to help Asher haul the staysail and reef the foresail.

They came through the low cloud that had enveloped them and could see the blue shape of Culebra's low hills looming before them like another thunderhead. Once the sails were hauled in and tied, Scheutz and Asher kept watch for the buoys marking the channel between the reefs leading to the mouth of the bay. Asher's sharp eyes picked out the first one bobbing drunkenly in the current. The wind had picked up again and now blew a good thirty knots with gusts over thirty-five. Scheutz had the eerie feeling of being caught in a private little storm meant only for them. Behind them the sunlight shone over St. Thomas as well as off to port, over the island of Vieques. They ran with only a storm jib and a double-reefed foresail, close enough to the island to make out ragged trees fringing its silhouette. The surf smashed on a coral beach to starboard, and further out from shore waves broke over a line of reefs that lurked just beneath the surface of the water.

Asher scurried back and forth in the bow watching for anything that might present a danger. Scheutz worked his way amidship to relay any signals to the helm. Samantha held a steady course through the reefs. Whatever other problems he and Samantha had, as aggravating as she could be at times, there was one thing he could always say about her, she was a damned good sailor. Ahead, it looked as if they were being sucked into the mouth of a giant animal. A *culebra.* In Spanish the word meant a 'large snake'.

Asher indicated a landmark on a far hill for Samantha to point the bow. White-capped waves around the reefs pushed them off course while the *Gaga*, yawing crazily in their wake, pulled them from behind. Scheutz inched his way back to the helm, keeping his eyes on Asher, till he stood beside Samantha who fought the wheel to keep the ship on course.

"How the hell can anybody sleep through all that bouncing around?" Samantha jerked her head in the direction of the sloop behind them.

"Remember the story we heard about him passing out drunk in Jamaica and sleeping through a hurricane?"

Samantha nodded and opened her mouth wide in an explosive laugh. The gale that enshrouded the ship had pulled her out of her mood. She loved this. Her eyes shone with the excitement of steering a course through the reefs in bad weather. With her feet planted solidly and forming a tripod with the helm, she swayed in rhythm to both the waves of the following sea that hurried them through the channel and the satanic rock and roll percussion that pounded the deck they stood on.

"I just had a horrible thought." Scheutz yelled into her ear over the wind. "What if Harding isn't on his boat? What if he passed out in the cockpit and fell overboard back there?"

"Sounds good to me." She flexed her elbows and her knees in rhythm as if the wheel were her dancing partner. "I think we could use the engine going through here."

"We're all right." It thrilled him to see the way this old wooden schooner still handled so beautifully.

"Ho, boss. " Asher yelled into the wind, pointing behind them. The dinghy at the end of their tow train had broken loose and floated free in their wake, bouncing on the waves and turning side to side.

"Oh, shit." Scheutz ran below decks to see if he could raise Harding on the radio. But still no luck. Back on deck, he judged the width of the channel. "Turn the engine on, Samantha."

She gave him an appalled look. "We're not going after that dinghy."

"Yes, we are. The channel's wide enough for us to turn." He reached to the binnacle, flicked the ignition toggle switch and pushed the starter. The diesel whirred twice and caught.

"No, Clem. Let the damned thing go. We'll never make the turn."

"We can make it, I'm telling you. Hug the edge of the channel to starboard and then hard aport. We can bring her around."

"No way. I'm not doing it." She had stopped her dancing and now stood solid at the wheel, holding a course in the middle of the channel. "It's his dinghy, let him worry about it."

"That's an expensive Avon dinghy. We can't just let it drift off. Let me have the wheel." Scheutz moved to her left and took hold of the handspike just above the one she held. She pushed him with her hip and held tight to the wheel. He reached over her head and took hold of another spike at the top of the wheel. They stood immobile until Scheutz's strength slowly overpowered hers and he inched the wheel to starboard. His eyes locked with hers in a silent struggle that seemed to be recurring a little too often in the last couple of years.

Asher hooted from up forward. "Way off course, mon. You better..."

The hull thudded against something and then slowed with a shuddering jerk. From below came a crunching sound like tires on gravel. They moved forward for several feet and then slammed to a halt in the middle of the water, throwing Samantha and Scheutz against the helm.

"We on a reef, boss." Asher scrambled to release the foresail.

What felt like thirty knot winds pushed against the sails causing the ship to heel far over to port. With the foresail down, Asher released the jib and the boat righted itself somewhat. Samantha disentangled herself from Scheutz and pushed against him to stand on the sloping deck. Blood flowed from a cut on her lip. Scheutz braced himself and reached for the engine gearshift lever on the binnacle. He shoved it in reverse and kicked up the throttle. The schooner began to inch backward with the same crunching sound of broken coral it made going onto the reef.

"Oh, my God!" Samantha's voice came from behind him.

Scheutz turned to see the sloop bearing down on them from the rear, moved by its momentum and the current, leaving them with nothing they could do as the smaller boat raced up under the stern of the schooner and hit with a sickening crunch of fiberglass against wood planking. The metal forestay rigging connecting the top of the sloop's mast to the bow snapped. The mast, which was stepped on the deck, toppled backwards out of sight below the schooner's stern.

Scheutz turned back to the binnacle, his main concern getting the schooner off the reef. He eased up the throttle and the boat moved a short distance and stopped again. The engine stalled. With the gear in neutral he started the engine. Putting the gear in reverse only stalled the engine again. Twice more, putting the transmission in gear only stalled the engine.

Asher had finished doing a quick tie-off of the sails and now stood leaning over the taffrail staring down into the sloop nuzzled like a puppy under the stern of the schooner. "Sound like something down there holding the screw."

Scheutz left the helm and went to the rail. Samantha leaned over the rail next to Asher, nursing her torn lip. Off the stern lay a tangled mass of shroud lines draped over the sloop and into the water. The mast, half in the water, had bent where it hit the side of the deck and took out the lifeline on the starboard side. The Boston Whaler bobbed against the side of the sloop, entangled in the fallen rigging. In the center of the channel, Harding's dinghy floated past, as if making fun of them, the current carrying it into the mouth of Culebra's bay.

A dark mass of hair and beard with Harding's face in the middle appeared over the top of the *Gaga's* cabin. "What the fu..." Harding climbed onto the roof of the cabin. He wore only a pair of jeans cut off just above the knee. His black beard mingled with the hairs on his chest. He rubbed his eyes like a child waking from a nap and looked around at the mess on his deck. "What have you done to my boat?"

Asher and Samantha ignored him. Scheutz looked up in Harding's direction and saw something that scared him. He could not say for sure what it was, some kind of aura Harding carried with him, something nasty and evil, as if his laziness and slovenly drunkenness was really just a cover-up for what lay beneath the surface, the kid of thing you might only see when he was in an unguarded state. Scheutz pulled his attention away and back to the problem of getting off the reef. He asked Samantha to go below to see if they might be taking on water. The rain had slowed but the choppiness of the sea made it impossible to see what they were resting on, most likely the reef. Also, it seemed like the engine may be dying because the screw would not turn in gear. They needed to find out what could be impeding the screw.

Samantha came back to the rail. "No water. And the bilge pump hasn't turned on."

The wind and the current scraped the hull against the reef, which would cause who knew what kind of damage. Harding continued to rant from the deck of the sloop. His words, one more noise garbled by the wind, mingling with the slap of the waves, and the scrape of the hull on the reef. From a locker just forward of the doghouse, Scheutz and Asher pulled out a safety harness, snorkel mask and fins. Scheutz buckled himself into the harness and strapped on the mask. Asher wrapped the harness leash around a winch. Scheutz climbed over the rail and lowered himself down the starboard side of the schooner's hull into the frothy water.

The hull of the sloop nosed under the upswept stern of the schooner. Fortunately, the current had pushed it around to the port side so there was little danger of Scheutz getting smashed between the two boats, but the sloop had caught and held, slamming back and forth against the schooner's wooden transom like a wild animal tugging at a leash. Waves slapped Scheutz against the hull until he got low enough to grab the rudder and hold himself to it. He hand-walked down under the water till he could reach the propeller screw just forward of the rudder. He tried turning the screw while holding the rudder with one hand, but it would not budge, even though, with the transmission in neutral, it should turn freely.

At the end of his breath, Scheutz climbed hand over hand up the rudder to fill his lungs with air. Back under water, at the hub of the three-foot screw blades, he could see the problem; the metal cable of the sloop's mast had become tangled, holding the screw in place. He climbed back to the surface of the water and yelled up to Asher to send him down a bolt-cutter. Hanging onto the rudder, waiting for the bolt-cutter, his face barely above the chop of the water, he could see the reef that held his boat. The sloop banged against the transom of the schooner, the wind blew across the choppy water, above him Harding screamed unheeded words at Samantha, whose face hung over the stern of the ship smiling serenely at his insanity. Scheutz had the oddest sensation that resting here on this friendly rudder, hanging over the edge of a coral reef, was about the most peaceful place he could think of.

Asher lowered the bolt-cutter, attached to a nylon line, and Scheutz made his way back down to the screw, held himself in place with his legs scissoring a screw blade and worked the bolt-cutter on three sections of the cable until he was able to untangle it and pull the cut strands of the wire away from the screw. Back above water, he signaled to Asher who pulled up the line, retrieving the bolt-cutter. The sloop, now freed, drifted with the current away from the stern around to the side of the schooner's hull. Scheutz let go of the rudder and hung onto his leash-line, hesitating for a last moment before signaling to Asher to winch him aboard.

Harding continued to yell at them from atop the sloop's superstructure. "What's going on up there? Where's my dinghy?" Samantha started the engine as Asher winched in the sloop's towline to keep it from fouling the screw. On Scheutz's signal, Samantha shifted into reverse and with much scraping and jerking the schooner eased off the reef.

Harding escalated from his rant to jumping up and down on the sloop's deck. "What the fuck are you doing?"

"Oh, shut up." Samantha said the words calmly into the wind, as if to herself. Once free of the reef, she pushed the gear lever to its forward position and set the throttle for slow forward. Asher let out the towline as the sloop drifted back in their wake, its mast and rigging dragging in the water and still entangled with the Boston Whaler. Harding continued his complaints as the schooner pulled forward, the sound of his swearing retreating into the static of the wind as if someone turned the dial on a radio. On the last stretch of reef just before entering the bay itself, Harding's dinghy hung, grounded on rough coral that showed above the waterline.

Chapter 2

Scheutz hoisted himself out of the water onto the work raft that tilted slightly with his weight and then righted itself and bumped gently against the hull of the schooner, riding lighter than the boat on the unruffled water of the bay. He brushed the water from his face and shook his hair, scattering drops to the left and right. Stacks of various widths and lengths of lumber formed barricades on two sides of the raft, and inside the barrier were scattered pieces of brass hardware, gas cans, half-used tubes of caulking and loops of emery for a belt sander. Fins and a snorkel mask lay on top a wooden bin of nuts, bolts, screws and other miscellaneous fasteners.

Culebra was turning out to be everything he had hoped for, which was good for him, but not so good for Samantha. The previous time they had been here was during a carnival and the place had been filled with people enjoying themselves, but now when he looked close and could see beyond the little town and the calypso band he realized that the rest of the island was no different than any other quiet rural area where not much happened. In the three months they had been moored here he had fallen into the same country-side rhythm he had so enjoyed in his old farmhouse in New Hampshire. Even the little town, with no carnival happening, was no different than a small town found in the center of the main island of Puerto Rico or any other Caribbean island. Nothing happened here.

They had anchored the schooner away from the town on the north shore of the large bay and constructed the work raft from scrap lumber, floating it on empty fifty-gallon drums they found at the site of an old abandoned naval base. The raft extended a third of the length of the schooner and could easily be moved to whatever part of the hull they worked on.

Before they had even finished the raft Harding tied up his sloop to it and the next day disappeared for a month, taking the ferry to the main island. One of the first tasks they had to take care of when they came to the island was to remove the sloop's mast and rigging that had been dragged into the bay. Scheutz, Asher and Harding worked together to float the mast ashore and deposit near a parking area at the abandoned naval sight ashore. They rolled up the metal rigging and stowed on the foredeck of the sloop. Some of the cable might still be usable when and if Harding ever got around to re-rigging the boat. Now he was off, no one knew where or for how long. This apparently was a pattern of Harding's they had noticed back in St. Thomas. Every few months he would be gone for a month or so. Samantha surmised that he probably needed to go off and visit Hell, both to see his parents and get new instructions from his boss, Satan. Asher thought this was very funny but disagreed, saying it was more likely that Harding went to see the *mayombero*, the mischief-making witch doctor of the Santeria. After a few days, since it looked like Harding wasn't coming back for a while, Scheutz and Asher moved the sloop away from the raft, anchoring it at a fifty-yard distance and closer to shore. When Harding returned he didn't bother to move it back, so it rode at anchor with the Boston Whaler and the recovered dinghy tied to its stern.

Scheutz climbed the ladder made from two-by-fours extending from the raft to the gunwale opening on the deck of the schooner. On deck, he splashed fresh water from a pail onto his head and body to rinse off the salt water. The water was almost hot from sitting in the sun all day. The ever-so-slight stirring of a breeze on his wet body cooled him and he put on a t-shirt left hanging from a ratline near him on the rigging. With so little wind and no current in this cove of the bay the schooner sat rock steady in the water. Asher had one of Samantha's lilting calypso-beat tapes playing below in the main cabin, but other than that the world was quiet at the end of the day. Quiet that is, except for the occasional noise of a banging pot coming up through the forward hatch. Scheutz leaned his head down into the hatch and asked Asher to hand him up a beer, and then went to sit in his lawn chair with his feet on the starboard bulwark. He was tired, but nicely so. They'd gotten a lot done that day. For the past week, he and Asher, working in tandem, had been repairing chain plates that held the ends of the rigging to the hull, removing each one, looking for wood rot, and then if needed, scabbing on new pieces of oak to the underlying rib before rebolting and recaulking the chain plate.

In mid-summer the hills surrounding the bay were brown from lack of water. The scene from the deck of the schooner in late afternoon looked like an abstract painting with large bands of color. The deep water of Culebra's bay, a crater of an ancient volcano, shone a rich blue-green in the evening sunlight. Above that, the dark green mangrove banded the water's edge and above the mangrove, the serrated hills were a swathe of beige and sienna. Above that the wide blue of a cloudless sky reflected the color of the bay. The picture was broken only here and there by a splashed dot of white house or a shapeless outcrop of brown-red volcanic rock.

The eastern Caribbean trade wind had switched from northeast to its usual southeast bringing in hot dry air with no clouds for days on end. That is, when the wind bothered to come at all. Many days, like this one, sat on a becalmed sea. Few sailboats came into Culebra on days like this. The little two-man fishing boats still went out in the morning and came back in the early afternoon, and every day at noon the DEA narcs blasted in with their cigarette boats, did a tour of the bay and left again, just to let people know the law was still here and they better not try any funny stuff.

The DEA boats were enough to remind Scheutz of everything he missed but did not miss about that world going on beyond the horizon. He had known several drug-runners over the years, "mules" they were called; it was hard to live in the Caribbean without meeting drug runners. Harding had been one, he knew, probably still was, Scheutz would guess. But the drug-runner's life was merely a microcosm of what went on in the bigger world—a man driving himself to make the big bucks in order to buy what Scheutz had for nothing just sitting here on the deck of his boat watching the sun set over Cerro Sagrado.

"Supper ready, Mr. Clement." Asher's head popped up through the open forward hatch.

"We ought to wait for Samantha." Scheutz turned to look off across the bay toward the town where he could make out their red dinghy leaving the dock.

Asher climbed up through the hatch and set a bag of tortilla chips and a dish of salsa on the deck next to Scheutz's chair. He unfolded another of the lawn chairs stacked against the capstan and dropped into it. As he did so, the calypso tape playing below decks ended and Asher made to jump up again. Scheutz put a hand on Asher's arm. "Let it be."

Asher tilted his head and grinned at Scheutz, then settled himself into the chair and pulled a cigar from the breast pocket of his ragged, blue striped, dress shirt. He lit the cigar. "Supper gointo get cold."

Scheutz pointed with a tortilla chip to the small boat moving toward them across the bay, close enough now for him to be sure it was their dinghy with Samantha in it.

Asher puffed on his cigar. "Hope she remember the rum."

They sat in silence, Scheutz dipping chips into the salsa and crunching them in his teeth, Asher savoring his claro before extruding a thin stream of white smoke that lingered in a haze above his head. The sun, before leaving for the day, highlighted a white mast at a forty-five degree angle out on the reefs at the entrance to the bay. Asher pointed his line of smoke toward the mast and when it was finished shook his head. "Shame about that boat."

"Too nice a boat to be wrecked like that."

"It was a nice boat." Asher sat still for a moment. "But I seen my lady friend out there in the sea claim better boats than that."

"I'm sure you have." Scheutz threw in quickly, hoping to stave off another one of Asher's sermons on Yemaya, the orisha of the sea, and on the rest of the unseen spirits of the sky and the rocks and every other damned thing under the sun.

"I told the man the day he was in town there." Asher rose from his seat and moved to the rail. "I told the man his boat was marked. He said for me to get away from him. Said don't bother him with that voodoo bullshit. I said don't got nothing to do with voodoo and he said get away from him, anyhow."

Scheutz laughed with a mouthful of chips. "That wasn't very nice of him."

"People don't like to hear bad news coming." Asher shrugged. "If I had notta been drunk that night I wouldn'tna said nothing to the man."

The tilted mast was the only one remaining on a ketch smashed on the reef outside the bay. What had only a few weeks before been a pretty 46-foot cruising boat belonging to a dentist from the states now sat at a forty-five degree angle, wedged onto a reef with half its bow missing. The story went that the dentist, on vacation with his family, had not read the charts correctly and lost his rudder on a shoal at the south end of the island and then, unable to steer, was escorted by the current and the wind through the surf onto the reef. What had that morning been a gleaming family treasure became that afternoon a totaled insurance claim. But before the insurance adjuster could even reach the wreck four days later, the island fishermen and migrant sailboat tramps had stripped it of anything remotely useful, including its six-cylinder Volvo engine. Scheutz and Asher themselves had carried off two lovely self-tailing winches, several lengths of half-inch line and two dacron sails that didn't fit any mast they had but could always be bartered for something that did.

"Well, the dentist'll get a better boat with the insurance money."

Asher blew another thin line of smoke. "What I mean when I say it's a shame about that boat, is we coulda got more stuff off it if we'da moved quicker."

"We can still get that mast. There's a guy I know over in Tortolla I bet would buy it."

The dinghy, with Samantha handling the outboard, planed over the still water just beyond the work raft. She cut the engine and let it touch the side of the raft before hopping out. Except for her Teva sandals, she looked like a girls' high-school basketball coach with her usual athletic shorts, one of many t-shirts, this one yellow, and her long-billed cap. She moved like an athlete also, springing from the dinghy to the raft, arms full of packages. Asher descended the ladder to help her unload the cans of diesel fuel, and to hand bags of groceries up to Scheutz who took them at the top of the ladder.

"Did that oil filter for the Yan Mar come in yet?" Scheutz yelled down to her as she stowed the five-gallon diesel fuel cans against the lumber on the work raft.

"No, but I found something better. The guy at the dive shop told me that the oil filter from a Honda car is the same as one for a Yan Mar diesel. So I got one from the gas station in town. It's about a third of the price."

"No shit?"

"Here. See if it fits." She threw the box containing the oil filter up to him. Scheutz opened the engine room hatch and climbed down the steel-runged ladder to the side of a large plastic tarp that covered the six-cylinder Navy diesel engine, the schooner's main power. The engine had sat half-rebuilt for the last two months awaiting parts he had ordered from Jamestown Marine Supply in Rhode Island. Near the bulkhead, the little Japanese-made, three-cylinder Yan Mar diesel engine that ran the generator and compressor, sat idle. To conserve fuel, when the workday was done, they shut off the engine and existed with kerosene lamps and storage batteries, recharged every day while the generator ran. When the Yan Mar was running it dripped oil from a small rust hole in the oil filter. Scheutz changed the filter and came back on deck.

"You're right. It's the same filter."

She smiled up at him, pleased with herself. Up near the forward hatch she sat in the lawn chair Scheutz had occupied previously and dipped a chip into the salsa.

"Take the pot." Asher's voice came up from the hatch. Scheutz reached down with both hands and brought up the soup pot Asher handed him. Asher followed with a loaf of bread, bowls and spoons. Scheutz ladled out the soup.

Samantha picked up a spoon and dipped it into her bowl. "It's nice to have soup for a change. What does this make, thirty-two days in a row now with the same soup for supper? Is this meat from the same shark or did you catch another one?"

"This not all shark." Asher sat with his own bowl. "Different fish every night."

"It all tastes the same to me."

Scheutz slurped. "I like it."

The sun had dropped to just above the horizon, splashing red streaks across the bay. Samantha emptied the rest of her bowl over the side. "You want to hear the latest news from town?"

"I didn't know they had news in that town."

Asher chuckled. "People always got news." The smoke from his relit cigar lingered just above his head with no breeze to nudge it along.

"Well, Colwin's gone." Samantha sounded like this should be an issue of major concern.

"Which one is Colwin?" Scheutz was sure he'd met someone of that name in town but could not remember what he looked like.

"He's young, short blonde hair, a little balding, glasses. Looks like a student or a computer guy. You remember, he bought that little two-story house next to the gas station on the malecón, the wharf? He said he was planning to open a guest house?"

"I knew when I heard about it that it won't going to happen." Asher blew on the lighted tip of his cigar making little sparks fly.

"Why do you say that? Mark is a pretty smart guy."

"Mark?" So that was who she had been going with over to the main island. She had mentioned someone named Mark who also needed supplies and had a small Mazda pickup truck he took on the ferry.

"The mon does not know what he is doing," Asher said.

"Well, he does know what he is doing. He's a good businessman. And he knows a lot about computers."

"What that got to do with a guesthouse on the island?"

"I don't even want to go into it. Anyhow, that's got nothing to do with why the guesthouse might not happen. He left on the ferry this morning and might not be coming back. They beat him up pretty bad."

"Who beat him?" Asher wanted to know.

"That bunch that hang out down there in front of the liquor store."

"What for they do that?"

"They say it's his own fault. You know the inlet that runs under the bridge and goes behind that house he bought? There's a little dock where people tie up. So, he decided he didn't want people tying up there anymore."

"And somebody beat him for that?"

"No, not for that. You know that old guy they call Sharky? He tied up there. Colwin told him not to. Sharky said he's been tying up there for fifty years. Colwin said it was his dock now and he had the right to keep people from tying up. He went to untie the boat and Sharky hit him, and so he knocked the old man down."

Asher snorted from the back of his throat. "He hit the old man? He ought to be spanked."

"All those Puerto Rican guys that hang around in front of the liquor store and the gas station, they all got sticks and went after Colwin last night and beat him. So, Colwin left this morning."

Scheutz studied her profile. "You sound like it bothers you. What do you care?"

She looked down into her lap. "It pisses me off a little. I like Colwin." But her voice did not sound angry. If anything, it softened when she talked about Colwin, softened to a tone she often used talking about children, or the dog Harding had for a few months on his boat and then abandoned out near the airport on St. Thomas before leaving on one of his disapperances. "He's one of the few civilized people I've met in this hellhole. Besides, it's Colwin's property. He should be able to keep people off if he wants to."

"Yeah, but..." Scheutz did not care one way or the other, and it certainly was not worth arguing over, but he found himself wanting to argue over this Colwin character, using any tidbit to point out that Colwin was not somebody she should be consorting with. 'Consorting' was her word, a word she used often when referring to some of the 'riff raff' whose company they often found themselves in. He did not trust that soft tone she used talking about Colwin. There was a time she used that soft tone on him but certainly not in the last year or so.

"What if they all decide to come out here and tie up to our boat?" Samantha's voice stabbed the quiet air. "What are we supposed to do, just say, 'Oh, welcome aboard, do whatever you goddamned please, and excuse us for being intruders on your shit-hole little island?'"

"Oh, they wouldn't do that." Asher answered her as if her rant was a perfectly logical question.

"What the hell do you know?"

There she went picking on Asher again. Normally, she and Asher were the best of friends, but whenever she got snippy, like now, she would pick on him. Scheutz's impulse was always to jump in and buffer Asher; not that he needed defending. But Scheutz's saying anything at this point would only make it worse. Things had been fine for the last couple of weeks. Samantha had seemed content and relatively cheerful. She had made friends in town and on some of the other boats anchored in the bay. Since coming to Culebra, her occasional overnight jaunts to the main island, to San Juan, to get supplies or materials, always eased her temperament considerably. She mentioned on two occasions when she stayed overnight in San Juan, going to dance clubs with her friend Mark.

Those two different nights in San Juan seemed like an aphrodisiac to her. The next night after she came back, he awoke to find her slipping under the mosquito net into his berth. They did not talk about the jaunts to the main island, nor much of anything else, for that matter. She seemed to make a point of not bringing up her dissatisfaction with where they had moored the boat in Culebra, and never the fact that they were in Culebra at all. That subject had worn down to nothing more than their each knowing how the other felt. He thought her trips to town and to the main island were unnecessary. She seemed to spend as little time as possible on the boat, and in fact, completely abandoned any semblance of helping out. While they were still in St. Thomas, the running sore of their argument felt as if it at least had some hope of healing by being exposed to the open air, but since coming to Culebra, the sore had scabbed over and lay festering below the surface.

"I knows lots of things." Asher answered her, his voice low, with an ominous ring he put on whenever he wanted to sound dramatic.

"Oh, bullshit," Samantha said. "You and your voodoo prophecies."

"Got nothing to do with voodoo."

"Or what d'you call it, santeria?"

"Not the same thing."

"Different bull, same shit."

The conversation drifted away. Scheutz did not want to talk about Asher's religion. She was right, people were willing to believe all kinds of crap just to keep whatever culture they belonged to intact, but he did not want to agree with her out loud, against Asher. What difference did it make whether he made predictions or whether he had some pantheon of gods that ruled over the wind and the sea, it all came out to the same thing.

"And you." Her voice swung from Asher to score a direct hit on Scheutz. "You're so spaced out these days, you probably wouldn't even notice if somebody did tie up here."

"I'm sorry. What were you saying?"

"Hah." Asher's laugh blew another small shower of sparks from his cigar.

Samantha slapped her bare skin with a loud smack in the darkness. "Here come the mosquitoes." With no wind, the mosquitoes found their way out to the boats in the bay as the sun went down. Some nights were worse than others. The dry weather kept down the population of land mosquitoes but the little ones that bred in the mangrove could be vicious. On some nights the only way to get relief from them was to go to bed inside the mosquito netting as soon as it got dark. Her chair scraped the deck and her silhouette rose against the sky as she stood. "I'm going back into town. They're showing a movie on the VCR at Chuck's Pizza tonight."

"What's the movie?"

"I don't know, probably some stupid army movie. 'Let's all dress alike and follow each other around.' But it's better than sitting out here listening to the great prophet."

A deep chuckle gurgled from Asher behind his glowing cigar tip. "I predict you won't like the movie."

Maybe it would be nice to sit in a bar and watch a movie. Scheutz hadn't been away from this boat in over a week. "I'll come with you, okay?"

She moved toward the rear of the boat, stopped then continued. "Well, if you're coming, let's go."

"Come on, Asher, I'll buy you a beer." He'd make it up to Asher for Samantha being so snarky with him.

The fiberglass dinghy was shaped like an old Swampscott fishing dory, but with a transom for mounting an outboard. It could be sailed and had a slot for accepting a centerboard and a mount for a single mast that held a gaff-rigged sail. The mast, centerboard and a pair of oars were stowed in the bottom of the boat to be used on those occasions, more often than Scheutz liked, when they did not have even enough money for gas for the outboard. Scheutz started the motor as Asher let go the painter and stepped aboard. The bow lifted slightly as Scheutz turned the throttle and steered away from the work raft.

They passed close to where Harding's sloop rode silently at anchor. Scheutz hadn't seen him around for a few days. Further down the shore, on the site of the old naval base, the lights around the perimeter of the small desalination plant, which supplied fresh water for the island, showed in the gathering dusk. On the bank an ocean-going catamaran had been hauled ashore and de-masted. Paul and Joanna—Scheutz never could remember the couple's last name—who owned it had been for the past three weeks re-fiberglassing the hull in preparation for a trip down islands to Trinidad.

"Where are you going?" Samantha shouted at him from the bow, pointing toward the lights of the town showing now directly across the bay. He turned the boat to port and opened the throttle all the way. The bow lifted again and they sliced through the placid water. Moving through the evening air cooled his face and woke him from his after-supper lethargy.

Several dinghies lay nosed into the dock behind the gas station like cows at a feeding trough. Scheutz cut the outboard and let the momentum of the bow inch its way between two boats. Samantha hopped ashore with the painter before the prow touched the dock. Asher followed, and then Scheutz, after he shut off the engine and tilted the rudder out of the water. They strolled through the parking lot of the gas station out onto the malecon where two small groups, one of four Puerto Rican men, and another of three gringos, lingered, drinking beer, laughing and talking, the Spanish and English voices mingling and floating like cigar smoke above their heads. At the far end of the malecon, beyond the ferry ramp, a group of teenagers lounged on the benches of the small park.

The gas station, the liquor store, and the colmado were all closed at this hour so the only lights showing were the few along the malecon and the open doorway of Chuck's Bar and Pizza Shop. Anchored fifty yards off the malecon was a small, rusty tramp freighter of the style known in the Caribbean as an Island Trader. It showed no anchor lights and only one lighted porthole in an aft cabin.

Samantha paused for a moment to look up into the dark second floor windows of Colwin's guesthouse-to-be and then continued on. Scheutz walked behind her, stopped when she stopped, but could not continue on, the sense of abandonment heavy in the air between them. He turned to Asher behind him but Asher had left them to talk with the Puerto Rican group in front of the closed liquor store, probably the same men who beat Samantha's friend Colwin the night before. Scheutz followed Samantha inside the door of Chuck's where warm air and cigarette smoke moved sluggishly between two fans mounted on the wall at each end of the square, windowless room. The place reminded Scheutz of the classic cantina in cowboy movies he had seen as a kid. A bar ran along the right to an opening in the rear wall bearing a sign that said, "Order Pizza Here." In the middle of the room, tables were scattered in a haphazard pattern. In the corner near the ceiling on the back wall a television monitor showed a kung fu movie. The Chinese actors' words had been dubbed into English with Spanish subtitles running across the bottom of the screen. The bar was roughly half-filled, many of the customers tilting their heads back to watch the television screen between bites of pizza and sips of beer.

Samantha waved or nodded to several people inside the bar and sat at an empty table not far from the door. Without turning to see if Scheutz sat with her, she faced the video screen. Scheutz picked a chair at the table looking directly out the open doorway just in case a breeze might come skipping across the water looking for him. Almost immediately, the man they called the Junkman sat down next to

Samantha and said something in a voice too low for Scheutz to catch anything but the words "your friend, Colwin."

"Good evening," the Junkman said to Scheutz in his thick German accent, extending his hand in exaggerated formality.

Scheutz nodded and shook the German's hand. It was clear that the Junkman was Samantha's friend; Scheutz being treated, as always by him, like a guest in their house. The Junkman was fifty-ish and built like a professional wrestler, stocky and bald. His name was actually Karl von Fritzinger, his boat had the name Junker painted on the hull. He claimed to be descended from a German royal Junker family, but was known as the Junkman throughout the islands, except for the French islands like Dominique where he was known as Le Fritz. He was usually seen this far north only about once a year. This year he showed up on Culebra at the beginning of July, saying he would ride out the hurricane season here.

Samantha listened to what the Junkman was saying while watching the television monitor across the room. Scheutz was not any more interested in what the Junkman had to say than the Junkman was in including him in the conversation. "I'll get some beer." Scheutz stood. "You want one?" He pointed at the Junkman's bottle.

"No, I'm fine."

Chuck's was mostly patronized by the English-speaking community on the island, but tonight there were several Puerto Ricans as always on nights when a new movie came in for the VCR. Most of the Puerto Ricans sat at the bar while the gringos sat at tables. Billy the bartender, with a fat, round, flushed face, looked like a Puerto Rican but spoke no Spanish. Having grown up in New York he'd never bothered to learn it, he'd told Scheutz once, even though he was constantly harassed by other Culebrans for not speaking it.

"Ey, Scheutz. Harding was in here looking for you, man," Billy said with his Bronx accent as he handed Scheutz three bottles of beer.

"Why didn't he come out to the boat? He knows that's where I am."

Billy spread his hands and shrugged as if to say, "Why ask me?"

Scheutz set one bottle on the table in front of Samantha who, in the midst of making an animated point to the Junkman, picked up the bottle without acknowledging that Scheutz had set it in front of her.

He sat with the other two bottles but then remembered he had bought one of them for Asher and stood immediately. He waited for Samantha to pause for a breath but then turned and walked out the door. Asher stood in the midst of the men in front of the liquor store, where one, in a sleeveless undershirt showing his thin arms as dark as Asher's, spoke in rapid Spanish punctuating his monologue with short jabs of his left fist. Asher listened, his head moving left to right, up and down as if in rhythm to the man's fist. Another man laughed and interjected short quick phrases.

Asher accepted a beer from Scheutz and stopped his head bobbing only to sip from the bottle. He too laughed and threw in a few Spanish words. The man telling the story made no move to include Scheutz or even indicate that Scheutz had joined them. Scheutz stood outside the circle and watched the moving lights of a ship far out on the horizon. Asher never stopped being a source of amazement. He spoke fluent Spanish and, at different times, Scheutz had heard him talking with both French and Brazilian sailors in St. Thomas. His English was spoken with an odd accent that contained both a Caribbean lilt and something else that sounded vaguely African or Middle Eastern. There didn't seem to be much of anything that Asher couldn't do; he was a mechanic, carpenter, cook, master seaman, a wonderful dancer and possessed a beautiful singing voice. What the hell was he doing working as a crewman for people like Samantha and Scheutz for pay that often was no more than room and board? It made no sense, but Scheutz sure loved having him around.

Scheutz stood next to the group for a while, but, not being able to understand much, wandered away. No sense going back inside just to be left out of another conversation between Samantha and the Junkman, and the movie on the VCR looked to be truly inane with all those Chinese guys running around kicking each other in the face. He strolled down the ferry ramp and stood at the edge with his feet in the water. Darkness had completely fallen. The ship lights on the horizon moved slowly off to the edge of his vision. How nice to be on a ship like the one out there, except that on such a large boat you had no sense of the hull moving through water, so it was not much different than standing on shore. No, what he really wanted was to be out at sea on the *Panacea*, to feel the pull of the wind and the roll of the waves. The way he and Samantha had dreamed it would be two years ago when they bought the boat.

Did Samantha still have that same dream? It didn't seem like it, though it was hard tell since they did not talk about it any more. She didn't know what she wanted, she had said recently, but whatever it was, this was not it.

"Hey, Mr. Clement." Asher called him from the doorway of the bar. He turned to Harding who stood next to him and pointed at Scheutz. "He's over there."

"Scheutz, come here." Harding waved his arm. "Got to talk to you."

"What do you want?"

"C'mere. C'mere. Big doings. Hurry up."

When Scheutz reached him, Harding put his arm around his shoulder, giving him a whiff of foul breath that stunk of alcohol and something else faint and hard to pinpoint, like seaweed washed ashore and rotting in the sun. "Got somebody needs to talk to you." Harding waved a hand with a lit cigarette toward the center of town.

"What's going on?"

Harding led him away from the bar. "You wait. You'll love it."

As they turned the corner of the street leading uphill to the town hall, the island's police cruiser passed them, the driver nodding to Scheutz's wave. Next to the government building on the little rise a white Toyota minivan with its engine idling sat directly under the halo of a floodlight in an otherwise empty parking lot. Harding escorted Scheutz around to the passenger side and opened both the front and rear door. He got in the front and motioned for Scheutz to get in the back. The man in the driver's seat turned to look at Scheutz and said to Harding in a voice heavy with Puerto Rican accent, "Who is this?"

"This is my partner." Harding half-turned in his seat and pointed a finger at Scheutz. "We work real good together."

Partner? Since when was he Harding's partner? If Scheutz ever thought of himself as being anyone's partner, it certainly wouldn't be Harding. That would be like hooking up with the town drunk. In fact, he had often wondered why he put up with Harding at all. Even Asher would not try to predict what this idiot would do next. Like right now, what the hell was he up to? Scheutz let his hand lie slack on the inside door handle, nothing but curiosity holding him inside the vehicle. The air conditioning in the van made him shiver.

The Puerto Rican turned again to him, his face in shadow with the outside light shining directly down on the van. A slightly paunchy middle-aged man wearing gold-rimmed glasses, Harding introduced him as Juaquin. Scheutz was sure he'd never seen him on the island before.

"Are you a religious man, Mr Scheutz?" Joaquin twisted in his seat, adjusted his glasses. The question was not demanding at all, and not supplicating. It sounded seductive; the man could be either a Jehovah's Witness or gay.

Harding, twisted around fully in the passenger seat and leaned back toward the windshield so the man couldn't see him, nodding his head rapidly and signaling for Scheutz to say "yes" to the question. Whatever Juaquin was after, Scheutz automatically was not interested. "My religion is my own business." He pushed the door handle.

"No, wait." Harding reached a hand to lay on Scheutz's arm. "This could be a good deal."

"I would like to hire your boat, Mr. Scheutz." Juaquin put his hands together as if in prayer and pointed his fingertips in Scheutz's direction.

"For what?"

"Cargo."

"I don't have anything to do with drugs."

"I don't either. That's why I asked you if you were a religious man. Mr. Harding here has told me that he has accepted Jesus as his personal savior." Harding grinned at Scheutz and wagged his eyebrows up and down. "I have certain shipping needs." Juaquin paused and leveled his gaze, spreading his hands, palms upward. "Needs requiring, first a captain of good morals, and second a pleasure boat that is captained by a gringo, if you will excuse the term. And one that is registered in a country other than the United States."

"To carry what?"

"Mr. Harding tells me that your boat is registered in the British Virgin Islands."

"In Tortolla, yes. It's a British built schooner so I can't register it in the states. But what needs to be carried and where?"

"Where? To Cuba. What? Legitimate items that Cuban people cannot get with the American embargo. But items they need to have."

"But why a pleasure boat? Why don't you just hire a freighter registered in Liberia. They're all over the place."

"There are high Cuban tariffs."

"So you're talking about smuggling."

Juaquin turned his head to look at Harding and then continued to turn his head so that he looked at the white blank wall of the building in front of the windshield. "Do you believe, Mr. Scheutz, that the Holy Bible is the word of God?"

"No."

"Do you believe that the Lord God is the father of us all?"

"No."

"Yes, he does." Harding blurted. "I know I do. And I can vouch for Scheutz. He's a real good Christian. Aren't you, Clem?" Harding grimaced at him, urging him to agree with the God scenario.

No, this wasn't a God scenario, it was more like the Santa Claus syndrome. "No, Senor Juaquin, I don't mind a little smuggling." Nothing wrong with making a few dollars on a few harmless presents. "I don't have to tell myself it's for God's love, or for the greater good of the Cuban people. But I might consider calling it what it is and doing it just for the money."

Chapter 3

Scheutz cut the engine on the dinghy, let it drift in toward the small wooden dock jutting out from the mangrove. When bow bumped he stepped onto the planks, and tied the boat off to a wooden cleat nailed to the end of the dock. Harding's Avon dinghy, the only other boat there, lay motionless in the languid water at the end of the bay. Already as hot as midday, an early morning sun beat down from a cloudless sky with only a tiny breath of wind, unusual for this time of year. The heavy air, hard to move through, felt more like the inside of a forest than the edge of open water.

Out in the bay, more boats than usual rode silently at anchor, their bows pointed generally eastward in the merest stirring of a breeze. Various sizes of sailboats, sloops mostly, but here and there a two-masted yawl or ketch, plus a good proportion of motor-powered craft of varying sizes, even a few powered houseboats increased the population of those boats normally found here. There had been talk since the day before of Hurricane Gabrielle heading west across the Atlantic, but so far no one predicted where it might make landfall. Newscasts of a hurricane always prompted people to head for Culebra, with its hills completely surrounding the bay, reputed to be just about the best hurricane hole in the Caribbean. Everything, the boats, the water, the cloudless sky, even the slow-rising sun seemed to be holding its breath, waiting for something to happen.

Since shutting off the outboard engine he heard the silence of the morning. No bird sounds, no other motors or shore sounds drifted across the water. He stood for a moment on the dock and listened, feeling an odd sense of anticipation, an ambiguous foreboding of something to come that he both feared and looked forward to. Nothing big, but an unease nonetheless, like the feeling he remembered getting when he was a young paratrooper just before a jump. He walked to the shore edge of the dock and onto a narrow plank that led down to the muddy bank and connected to a slightly wider plank running into the mangrove.

The mangrove gave off the fetid odor of still air. He stepped onto a path on slightly higher ground, where his Tevas squished on mud for a few yards until he came out near the paved road. Had he come on the right day? Was it Tuesday, the day Harding said they were to meet Juaquin? Living on an old schooner moored in the bay of a Caribbean island, they measured time only in the difference between light and dark. Nothing changed from one day to the next, the ferry ran from the main island of Puerto Rico every day at the same time, the few stores and restaurants opened and closed at the same time. Occasionally, voices raised in song inside the one church in the center of town marked that day as Sunday. And some days the hardware store and the chandler's shop at the boatyard closed. School must have opened because now and then children with book bags, wearing blue and white uniforms, walked along the road.

Samantha had accompanied her friend Colwin on the ferry to the main island last Saturday, so if Scheutz's calculation was correct, today must be Tuesday. Colwin paid her for helping him with his business, overseeing the project of setting up his guesthouse. They needed the money, which was why he himself might soon be "doing things" for Juaquin, that character Harding had come up with. Scheutz remembered that his break-up with his former wife, Gerry, years ago, had started like that, with her going off on weekends and then disappearing altogether. He and Samantha were having it difficult right now, with no money and all, but he was determined the same thing would not happen again and they would make things better.

The paved road ran along a chain-link fence on the right, parallel to the island's single airstrip on the other side of the fence, with its tiny terminal building. The road branched off through the barrio that spread roughly halfway up the hillside. The morning plane from San Juan, a six-seater with wings over the cabin, buzzed in with a noise he imagined might be made by a two-thousand-pound wasp. It skimmed the top of the tree-lined hill to make a landing on the strip all but drowning out other morning noises in the barrio. When the plane landed the noises took up again, men shouting to each other outside the terminal building, a truck rumbling on the road, a dog in the barrio, a late-rising rooster, the voices of two older women walking in the opposite direction from Scheutz on the road.

The road turned away from the airport, past a grocery store and a few houses on each side, some with small yards in front, others with front porches close to the road with no sidewalk in between. Two blocks up on the left, he saw the words El Tapon, painted black on a flamingo-pink ship-lapped wooden wall, the site of the restaurant he had come looking for. A sandy yard between the wall and the pavement contained a rusted anchor set up on its side, several large conch shells, and three glass balls, the kind used as floats for fishing nets. As he entered the yard, three young men, two in t-shirts and one in a sleeveless undershirt, all wearing dusty pants and construction boots, burst out of the front door, laughing and talking, passed him and climbed into a tool-laden pick-up truck that started with a muffler-less roar and blasted off down the hill.

Inside, six long rectangular tables, each covered by a flower-patterned oilskin tablecloth, sat in two rows, each with eight mismatched metal and wooden chairs. Juaquin and Harding sat across from each other at the end of one table, another gringo in a gray suit and tie sat next to Juaquin. Three old Puerto Rican men huddled together in a similar pattern at a table on the other side of the room, and a woman and her daughter in a school uniform occupied the end of the table next to them. To the right, a counter separated the room from the kitchen behind it, and against the left wall a tall cooler with glass doors showed cans of different brands of soda, plastic bottles of drinking water, half-pint cartons of milk, and cans of beer. Bright yellow light poured through the screened doorway and, through a red and blue loosely woven cloth shade covering a small window, the sun's beams came directly from where it had risen over the reefs at the mouth of the bay. Light beams bounced off a low cloud of cigarette smoke donated by the three old men, with Juaquin contributing his share, clamping a cigarette holder in his teeth. The light on the lazily swirling smoke, undisturbed by the idled electric fan on a pole in one corner of the room, lent an other-worldly aura to the room.

The planked floor, traces of dark red paint in the cracks, was worn to bare wood between the tables. One pale green-painted wall sported a crudely painted image of Saint Catherine with her sword, doubling as Chango, the image that Scheutz recognized as one of the leaders of Asher's Santeria religion. On another wall hung a large crucifix and, just to the left of the door, was attached a three-foot square bulletin board with notices, all in Spanish, pinned in haphazard fashion. The place, like many others he could think of, had what he always thought of as the religious significance of the early-morning coffee shop.

A mixture of food smells filled the restaurant, stirring his hunger. Small noises floated with the cigarette smoke: the three old men arguing softly, the child's mother at the next table admonishing her, Harding spinning his usual speed rap, the drink cooler against the wall humming, and dishes rattling somewhere behind the counter. Harding forked a large mouthful of rice and beans, chewed and talked at once, interrupting himself with a drink from a can of Medalia beer. Juaquin looked up and raised his eyebrows at Scheutz, at which point Harding turned and waved him to the table. He dropped his fork and extended his hand for Scheutz to shake, and then motioned him to sit down next to him.

The third man at the table, an unlit pipe clamped in his white teeth, showed Scheutz a friendly smile, his long, angular face open but sterile as if frozen by a cartoonist. Before Scheutz could sit, the man extended his hand. "Hi, I'm J. R. Dobbs. You can call me Bob." He talked through the teeth that clenched his pipe.

Scheutz shook the man's hand, slack and sterile like his voice. "So what are we doing here?" he asked the man, and then included the two others in the question.

Harding, still chewing, waved his fork in Juaquin's direction.

Juaquin fingered the cigarette holder, the ring on his pinky finger flashing in the sunlight, one point in his display of gold, the rims of his glasses, the band around the cigarette holder, the cross on the chain around his neck, the larger ring on his other hand. He ignored Scheutz and spoke to Harding. "You have food in your beard." He pointed to the two pieces of rice floating among the hair on Harding's chin and then turned to Scheutz. "So." He nodded and smiled. "Are we ready to do a little business?"

Harding blurted something through his mouthful of food that sounded like, "Mumph mumph."

Scheutz slid his eyes toward the three old men. "I'm not real comfortable talking about it in a public place like this."

Juaquin smirked and waved a hand toward the old men. "No problema. The viejo facing us is my father." The man he referred to seemed taller than the other two, and more dignified, with a dark, narrow, lined face and white close-cropped hair. He wore a light blue guyaberra, the kind more often seen in the city than on an outlying island, but his talk and his laughter matched his two companions in its enthusiasm. "He's the one called Tapon, and this is his restaurant?" He spoke slowly and deliberately, his manner, the same as when they had met before, like that of a patrician, an assuring, understanding father.

"What about…?" Scheutz nodded toward the woman and child at the next table.

Juaquin nodded, raised his eyebrows, signaling that they probably should wait until the woman left. "Do you want anything to eat?"

Scheutz looked at the food on Harding's plate, "Well, I could eat. You buying?"

Bob spoke. "I'll buy...."

Juaquin interrupted him. "Anything you want. My niece is a good cook." He lifted his voice toward the kitchen area. "Migdala."

"¿Que quieres?" A woman's voice came from around the corner of the kitchen.

"You have a customer." He removed the cigarette holder and blew smoke in a sideways fashion away from the table.

"Uno momento."

"There's beer in the cooler over there." Harding poked him with his fork and then pointed to the glass cooler. "You have to help yourself. Get me another one while you're up."

"You want something to drink?" Scheutz looked at Juaquin, getting up from the table.

"No, thank you."

He pointed at Bob. "You?"

Bob shook his head slightly without changing his expression.

Migdala walked out from behind the counter as he came back from the cooler carrying a can of cold Medalia for Harding and a root beer for himself. She looked so familiar, with a dark, pretty face he'd seen somewhere before. It made sense he might have seen her here and there around the island, but her face stirred something more than casual recognition. She wore a white, bibbed apron over a red t-shirt and khaki shorts. Her body, small and tight, moved fluidly but in a start and stop fashion, thick black hair threatening to escape from a severe pony-tail. Her head turned less fluidly, her focus reminding him of a small bird. She looked directly into his eyes, hers narrowing and then widening quickly as if recognizing him, but only for a moment until she turned back to Juaquin. In the movement of her head he remembered where he had seen her—he had danced with her five years before during the visit on the Dutchman's boat. She had aged, but not too much, a touch of solemnity to her face. Yes, it was her, the sharply defined nose and cheekbones, like the sculpted face of some Incan princess he's seen once. And there was something, too, about her daughter that had happened that night, but he could not remember what it was.

"Hello again," he said.

"Hello?" She gave him a questioning look "But what do you mean 'again'? I don't think we have ever met. I would remember."

"Long time ago. At a festival over on the basketball court. We were dancing. You don't remember?"

She shook her head and gave him a half smile, half frown, as if he'd said something really dumb. "You remember everyone you dance with at a festival?"

"No, but you, I remember."

She seemed so much more relaxed that night than she did now. She arched her eyebrows at him and turned to look again at Juaquin, waggling her fingers. "Ooh, what a smooth talker. Where did you find him?"

"Never mind. We have business. Just bring him whatever he wants." Juaqüin's manner was curt, almost surly.

"What does he want?"

"Ask him."

Harding laughed. Bob nodded.

Migdala, startled, slighted at Harding's laugh, and backed away from his chair as if he might be contagious in some way. She did not look in Harding's direction and actually seemed to be avoiding looking at him. She moved around to the other side of the table and looked directly at Scheutz again. "What do you want?"

"Coffee. And some eggs and fried potatoes, por favor."

"We don't have potatoes. I'll give you plantanos."

"You had a little girl with you, your daughter. She was about nine or ten years old then."

"Blanca?" Her eyes darted to Harding and then back to Scheutz. "Five years ago? That would be possible. Before I went to New York. Oh, yes, I remember that carnival. That was a fun night. But I don't remember you."

"Your daughter got in a fight and beat up some boy."

She shook her head. "My daughter is always beating up boys."

Juaquin cleared his throat. "Can we get down to business now?"

Scheutz sat down at the table and looked up at her. "Your daughter must be big now, huh?"

"Oh, yes." Migdala raised her eyes in a look of exasperation. "All she can think of is boys. I can get no work out of her. And school…"

"Por favor." Juaquin slapped the table with his palm.

She frowned at Juaquin and shook her head before turning back to Scheutz. "Don't do business with him. He is not a very nice person."

Harding laughed again. Bob said to her. "Give him a little slack."

Juaquin slammed his palm on the table. "Go and bring his food. I do not have time to sit here all day and listen to this."

Migdala gave him the same half frown, half smile as if he had also just said something really dumb. "If you do not like the way I run this restaurant, you can go and meet someplace else. In fact, you can go and meet someplace whether you like it or not."

Harding again found all this very funny.

"Just go and leave us alone." Juaquin let her have a thick spate of Spanish too rapid for Scheutz to catch.

Migdala, behind Juaquin, gave Scheutz an exaggerated ogre look that made him laugh. She then pointed at him and said, "Coffee?"

He nodded.

She turned to the woman and child at the table across from them. "Maricarmen…" She lifted her left wrist and pointed as if to a watch. "Van tarde."

"Oh, Dios mio." The woman left off talking to the child and jumped up from the table, making flapping movements in front of the little girl. "Vamonos. Vamonos. Estamos tarde para la escuela." The girl, who looked to be about eight-years-old, finished a glass of milk while climbing off her chair. The woman picked a pink school bag off the floor, grabbed the girl's hand and pulled her out the door.

Juaquin watched the woman and child leave and then waited for Migdala to reach the kitchen counter before he spoke. "We have a shipment ready to go in two days." He put on such a serious, down-to-business look that it made Scheutz smile. "I will give you the location in Cuba where the goods will be off-loaded. They will be expecting you at night, three days after you leave Culebra."

"And what is in the shipment?" Scheutz wanted to know.

Juaquin shrugged. "You do not need to know that."

"Yes, I do. I don't carry anything in my boat unless I know exactly what it is. I don't have anything to do with carrying drugs."

Harding put down his beer can. "Clem, I told you, this has nothing to do with drugs. You don't have to worry about that."

"Well, I still want to know what I'm carrying."

Bob spoke again in a voice that seemed to be saying, "Oh, what the hell." He said aloud, "Go ahead, tell him."

Juaquin spread his hands and spoke slowly. "It is nothing more than an item that the people in Cuba cannot obtain easily."

"Like what?"

"Like mini-computers--…" Juaquin broke off as Migdala appeared with a cup of coffee for Scheutz, and stopped talking till she left.

Scheutz sipped his coffee. "Mini what?"

"Mini-computers."

"What the hell is that?"

Juaquin turned to Bob and opened his palm. Bob took his pipe from his mouth. "You have heard of computers? No? Well, they compute."

"Compute what?"

Bob cracked his face in what might be translated as a smile. "Anything you want. They are like complicated adding machines. Anyway, there is a big company in New England, in Massachusetts, that has a plant here in Puerto Rico, in Mayaguez. Last January they developed a new mini-computer called the DEC model 3100. It is already obsolete. It's being replaced in October by their new VAX 9000."

"Whatever the hell that means."

"They're called mini-computers because they're small enough to sit on some scientist's lab table. But Russia doesn't have them. Which is why Cuba doesn't have them."

Scheutz sipped and nodded. "And the US has a trade embargo on with Cuba, and besides, they don't want the Russians getting them."

"Well, the 3100 is out of date, so the US doesn't really care. Except they don't want them, or anything else, going to Cuba."

"And let me guess. You have somebody in Mayaguez who can lay his hands on all these obsolete mini…as you call them…computers. And you want me to carry them to Cuba."

Bob sat back, folded his arms, replaced his pipe and nodded

solemnly. "We just want to cut the Cubans a little slack. They have not done anything to us."

Migdala set the plate of food on the table for Scheutz. Harding poked Scheutz's arm and pointed to the three old guys at the other table. "See that guy next to Juaquin's father? They call him Sharkie. 'Cause he's a real good shark hunter. Well, he's Cuban. And he's the nicest guy."

"Isn't that the guy Colwin pushed down and got beat up for?"

Bob took his pipe out again. "Yes. He should have given Sharkie a little slack, being an old man and all."

Scheutz ate in silence, thinking over what he was being told. Mini-computers. No harm in them And this Bob character was right, what did the Cubans ever do to deserve the embargo? If they could get around the Cuban Coastal Patrol it was an easy way to make some money. He swallowed a mouthful of eggs. "Well, I don't think I can be ready to sail in two days."

"Come on, Clem," Harding said. "That was the deal we made."

"The deal you made."

"Okay, the deal I made. But you said you'd back me up. We need to be ready to go whenever the cargo is ready. Otherwise it doesn't work."

"Samantha isn't even here. She's in San Juan with Colwin. And I can't sail without her."

"I'll fill in."

"Nothing personal, but you ain't half the sailor Samantha is."

"I hope you are not going to let me down, Senior Scheutz." Juaquin's voice carried a slightly menacing tone.

"I'm not letting you down, but I need my helmsman. I'll try to get hold of her in San Juan, but we might have to put this off for a day or so until she's back."

"That is not good."

"Well, it might have to be. Besides, you ought to know better than anyone; you grew up here. Everybody around here works on 'island time'; it gets done when it gets done."

"Not in my business. You must understand, Mister Scheutz, we have certain, how do you say, windows of opportunity. Certain people are on duty and only those people will leave the window open."

"He's talking about the Cuban Coast Guard," Harding put in. "I'm not leaving without Samantha. That's all there is to it."

Juaquin stood and turned to look at Bob, who shrugged without changing his facial expression. Juaquin picked up a briefcase that sat on an empty chair at the end of the table. He spoke to Harding. "We'll see. I will also talk to one of my other shippers."

"Not just yet." Harding reached a hand across the table to lay it on Juaquin's arm. "Give me a few hours. Till this afternoon. I will convince my friend here." He nodded his head at Juaquin and then at Bob as if to say, "Okay? Okay?"

Juaquin shook the hand off his arm, stared at Harding without saying anything, then shook his head and turned to go. Bob smiled in Scheutz's direction and stood to follow Juaquin.

"Wait." Harding stood to follow Juaquin and Bob to the door, turning back to Scheutz for one last comment. "Goddammit, Clem." Then he turned and spoke to Juaquin as he went out the door, his prattling, insistent voice carrying back through the screen.

Scheutz finished his coffee as Migdala bought more coffee. "I'm afraid my meal ticket has just run out the door."

"That's okay. I'll still charge him for it. And for his friend. What is his name?"

"You mean Harding or Bob?"

"Not Bob. The other one. Is that it, Harding? I do not like that man. I have seen him talking to my daughter, and…" She shook her head. "You can see he is no good just looking at him."

"A lot of people feel that way about Harding."

"Is he your friend?" She seemed a little less nervous now that Juaquin and Harding had left, but still allowed no apparent softening or loss of directness in the way she asked questions.

"No, not really. I help him out sometimes, but he is kind of a bum."

"Are you kind of a bum, too? You don't have any money for food?"

"No, I'm not a bum. I'm just at a low point right now."

She sat down across from him. Looking toward the door where Juaquin and Harding just left, and then glancing at the three old men on the other side of the room, she leaned in toward Scheutz, lowering her voice. "Is that why you are going to do work for my Tio Juaquin?"

"And what about the other one, Bob?"

"I do not know who he is. I have seen him around, but…."

"Well, yes, I was going to do a job for your uncle. Why?"

She glanced again at the door. "I should not say anything. He is my uncle. But, you look like a nice person, so I will tell you. Do not work for him."

"He seems like a nice enough guy. So does Bob."

"You do not know who you have just met."

"It's only one trip."

"Did Tio Juaquin ask you to bring anything back?"

"No."

"He will. Sending stuff to Cuba is only an excuse. What you will bring back is the real reason he wants to hire you. Do not do it."

"We really need money."

Migdala sat back in her chair and gazed at him, squinting her eyes again. "I know who you are." So, did she finally remember him from the carnival? "You live in that big wooden boat out there. Your wife comes into town a lot. I talk to her sometimes at night in Chuck's Pizza Bar. She is a nice person."

"Did she tell you we have no money left?"

"Yes. That is why she works for that Colwin person. She cannot trust Colwin. And do not trust Tio Juaquin."

"Well, what else can I do right now? We have to eat. And there are not a lot of jobs around here."

She squinted her eyes at him, looked down and then back. And then, suddenly, by a softening in her eyes, she seemed to be letting her guard down a little. She looked around the room, at the old men, at the kitchen counter, at the portrait of Chango, at the few tables that had not yet been cleared of cups and dishes, at the sunlight coming in the screen door. Then she shrugged. "I'll tell you what. I will make a deal with you."

"What?"

"How about this? You need food, I need help. Not much help, not all the time, but sometimes I cannot do it all. My grandfather…" She motioned toward the old men at the table. "…is too old to do anything anymore. This was his restaurant, but…" She waved her hand upwards in the direction of the town. "My daughter, I cannot get to do anything. So I need some help sometimes, but I cannot pay for it. I have to feed those two, but there is still food left over at the end of the day. So…"

Scheutz nodded his head. That seemed simple enough. But why was she making an offer like that to him? There must have been any number of people on this island who could do the same job and needed work. How many people anywhere were willing to work for leftovers? He nodded again and finished the last of the eggs and plantanos. "That sounds interesting. You'll pay me with food."

"I cannot give you money, but…at the end of every day there is food left over that I just throw out. In exchange for a couple of hours, I can give the food to you. And believe me, there is more food than you could ever eat in a day."

"Enough for three of us?"

"Oh." She gave him another of those half frown, half smile looks. "Some days enough for six of you."

"Does that include beers and sodas?"

She laughed. "Nice try, but no. Only what will not keep. Sometimes milk. Or jugo de china. But nothing in a can." She shook her head. "I cannot afford it. You want to try for a couple of weeks, to see how it goes?"

He nodded. "Yeah, why not. It won't buy hardware for the boat, but if we can eat…Okay, it's a deal. What do I have to do?"

"Well, today we can start. If you have time. I have to drive the station wagon to meet the ferry to pick up groceries, produce, things like that. You can help."

As he finished his meal, she waved her finger at his dish and cup and then the others left on the table by Juaquin and Harding, telling him in her all-business-like manner to carry them behind the counter. Once there, she showed him the sink piled with dishes, utensils, and cups, the grill that needed cleaning, the plate scrapings that needed to be disposed of. The floor in the kitchen as well as the dining area needed sweeping and mopping, the oil cloths on the tables needed a thorough washing, food had to be put away, pots scrubbed, soda and beer cans crushed and dumped, the coffee maker scrubbed. She expected nothing new or difficult, certainly nothing he had not done in one place or another all his life, even still took turns doing aboard the schooner. The idea of receiving well-cooked meals for something so simple and easy, after eating so many of Asher's shark stews, felt a little like ascending bodily into Nirvana.

They worked together, exchanging only a few simple phrases. He swept food scraps from the kitchen area into the dining area and then added the crumbs from under the tables, motioning for the three old men to raise their feet. She mopped the kitchen floor while he pushed his pile of food scraps out the front door into the sandy yard for the seagulls to feast on. When she finished the kitchen, she handed him the mop to do the dining area.

From what he could understand of the conversation in Spanish she had with her grandfather, the man wanted to know what Scheutz was doing there helping her. No, he was not her new boy friend, she told the old man, he was just helping out, and why didn't he, Tapon, mind his own business since she was running the place now. The third man at the table, who they called Arturo, a gnarly old guy whose grin showed how few teeth he had left, picked a box of dominos off the chair next to him and turned it over to empty onto the table.

Migdala refilled the coffee maker to make fresh cups for the three old men. Standing next to Scheutz, who stood at the sink wringing out the mop before making another pass at the dining area, she shook her head and rolled her eyes. "Those dominos will eat up the rest of the morning." She heated the milk and brought the cups to the men's table, then stopped to open the window and roll up the cloth curtain. The sun had moved away and a light breeze had picked up from across the bay.

This would be easy enough. He could do this for an hour or so every day. The prospect of being able to provide enough for Samantha, Asher and himself to eat, with such little effort on his part, gave him a tickle of glee, as if he were getting away with something. It may not work out for long, but what the hell, give it a shot for now. And maybe he and Asher could trade off days helping in the restaurant. The woman, Migdala, seemed easy-going enough. She would certainly not mind such a trade-off. But if he did make this deal with her, there was still the problem of what to do about the other arrangement with Harding and Juaquin.

He wrung out the mop and put it into the niche she showed him behind the refrigerator. Then he leaned against the counter watching her, the way she did things, her short, direct, purposeful movements, much more relaxed now than how she seemed an hour ago. No music played in the restaurant, which seemed unusual for a public place anywhere in Puerto Rico, and unlike most women he had seen so far on this island, she never smiled or engaged in a running chatter. Maybe she was not comfortable with having some gringo she did not know working next to her. But she did say she'd lived in New York, and with the office-manager style she ran things in this place, he could almost picture her wearing a smartly cut suit and carrying a briefcase as she strode toward a morning rush-hour elevator.

She took off her apron, hung it near the broom and mop, and opened a door to the back of the building. "I'll be right back." She disappeared through the door. Tapon looked up at him and frowned, his gaze lingering until Arturo poked him to tell him it was his turn. Did he know that Scheutz had just signed himself on as cabin boy, getting paid with what would normally be thrown away? He had once heard someone described as a lunch whore—do anything for a free lunch. Well, too bad.

Migdala came through the door carrying a purse. He spread his hands to indicate the state of the kitchen. "Ship shape?" She looked around, nodded, and, without as much as a smile, pointed to the front door before leading the way out.

A rusted, once blue, Volvo station wagon sat in an unpaved driveway behind the building. She motioned for him to get in, then got in herself, backed the car out to the road, and drove down the hill to the main road running along the bay, neither of them saying a word. Finally, without taking her eyes off the road, she asked in a business-like voice, "Do you and Samantha have children?"

"No. We're not married." He opened his mouth to continue but found he could not. What the hell would he say? This was not the kind of person he would tell the story of how he and Samantha had been together for over seven years, doing nothing more than not much of anything except enjoying themselves. Even to himself, the story was getting a little embarrassing. Seven years of bumming around the Caribbean could leave a person feeling as vacuous as the open sea, as useless as that ketch washed up on the reefs outside the entrance to the bay. It was no wonder one found so many drunks in the many islands' beach bars, like so much human flotsam. "But I do have children. They're both grown." He told her about his sons, Dan and Marty, who he had raised in the house in New Hampshire. Telling her about them gave him a small lift, especially when she turned her head and allowed him a faint smile. But the lift was just that, a momentary dis traction, replaced by what was becoming an almost daily question to himself—okay, so what have you done lately?

"And did you have trouble controlling them?"

What an odd question. "No, not really. I mean…they were always so full of everything, into anything they could imagine. And a lot of times they would go too far. Mostly, I had fun watching what they might come up with next. You know how teenagers are."

"And their mother?"

"What about her?"

"Did she have trouble controlling them?"

"Yeah, I think she had some problems with that. That's why she sent them to live with me."

Migdala raised her eyebrows but kept her eyes on the road. "Did she miss them?"

"Very much."

"Then why did she send them away?"

"She didn't send them away. She sent them to me. They would still go down to New York to stay with her in the summer when school was out, and at Christmas. But she had a hard time with them in the city, and I lived in the country. She couldn't live in the country, it drove her nuts."

Migdala grinned now for the first time and nodded her head in recognition.

"You got that problem too, huh?"

She took her eyes off the road for the first time, slid them over at him and then back. "How long does it last?"

"Does what last? The adolescence or the going nuts in the country?"

She laughed for the first time. "Which one comes first?"

"Well, according to the kids' mother, it's a dead heat."

They branched off the bay road and up into the town. "I think I will go crazy first. Between living on this island and my daughter's determination, she will probably have to finish growing up with me locked up in a crazy house."

"She can't be that bad."

"You don't know. She fights. Me, her friends, her teachers. She swears at everybody. And now she is fifteen and the thing with the boys...Dios mio, tan bellaca. ¿Como se dice en ingles?...um...muy horny, you know?"

"What about her father?"

She shook her head. "She has no father. Tio Juaquin has tried to be a father to her but she swears at him and calls him nasty names."

They parked beside other cars lined up facing the ocean on the malecon. The ferry churned in, still about a mile out. Migdala opened the back of the station wagon and Scheutz helped her pull out a hand truck which she wheeled across the cement surface to join a group of other merchants waiting for the trucks to come up the ramp off the ferry once it landed.

He wandered over to the two-story house at the end of the strip of buildings facing the water, the house owned by Colwin with the tiny take-out storefront on the bottom floor. The place was open already with the odor of chuchifritos drifting along the street. Beyond Colwin's house and its small yard, two dinghies bobbed ever so lightly at the dock to the inlet that came off the ocean.

The ferry finally docked, lowering its forward ramp onto the cement incline running up from the water's edge. The first truck off the boat looked like a produce vendor, and by the time Scheutz got to where Migdala stood with the hand truck, she had already unloaded two cartons of vegetables. He stood among the other restaurant and groceria owners helping to fill a third carton with plantanos, peppers, tomatoes, mangoes, papayas, guanabanas, and other types of vegetables he had seen only in Puerto Rico. As he wheeled the hand truck toward the station wagon, Migdala moved with the small crowd of buyers to the next truck with its refrigerated meats. Coming back with the hand truck after unloading the produce, he could see her in a huddle with two other women, both of whom occasionally looked up in his direction. Well, if they were wondering what Migdala was doing with the likes of him, he was wondering the same thing.

While waiting for their turn behind the refrigerator van, he saw Samantha walking up the incline from the ferry, the last passenger to get off. Good. As difficult a time as they were having, he was still glad to see her, the easy, relaxed way she had of carrying herself, the alert gaze behind her sunglasses that, he knew, missed nothing. But her arrival threw him back into the dilemma of whether to sail to Cuba, to put her and himself into an arena of crime that always beckoned for anyone like themselves who lived the life they did. As long as she was gone he had a good excuse not to take Juaquin up on his offer, but now that she was back.... He turned to help Migdala lift a box of frozen meats off the van and onto the hand truck, and then stood, looking out to sea, waiting for the next box.

Chapter 4

"Samantha." Scheutz knocked on the door of her cabin.

A muffled, "What?"

"Supper."

"Not hungry. I'll eat in town."

"Well, come sit with us anyhow. We've got something important to talk about."

"What?"

"Just come on, will you?`"

"What is so important we have to talk about?"

"About maybe getting paid for hauling some cargo. Come on."

"Oh, Jesus. Go on, I'll be right up."

He climbed up on deck and made his way to the forward hatch. Asher handed up plates of warmed-over food from El Tapon. "Samantha says she doesn't want to eat."

"I'll leave her plate here just in case."

Scheutz settled himself in his favorite lawn chair, facing the low western sun. The breeze that had picked up during the afternoon had abated somewhat but not altogether, cooling the approaching evening and chasing the mosquitoes inland. He set the plate on his lap and poured water from a gallon plastic jug into an empty coffee cup. Asher joined him in his usual lawn chair. Just like at a family dinner table, members always ended up in the same seating pattern. Out in the bay, a trim white-hulled sloop left the opening in the reef, heading along the southern shore, sailing wing-on-wing to catch whatever little breeze its crew could garner. Behind it came an island fishing boat, the head of the boy in the elevated prow higher than his father's at the outboard in the stern. Asher waved at the father who waved back.

"Hey, this stuff smells pretty good for a change." Samantha's voice rose from the forward hatch. "What is it?"

"Come from the restaurant in town." Asher tossed his words over his shoulder.

Samantha climbed up through the hatch carrying the plate set aside for her, with an empty coffee cup dangling from a finger. She set the plate and the cup on the deck, retrieved her lawn chair, opened it and placed it in her spot between Scheutz and Asher.

Scheutz waited till she filled her cup from the jug and settled to eat. "So, we have a chance to carry some items to Cuba, if we want."

Samantha took a first mouthful. "Wow, this is really good."

"Did you hear what I said?"

"Yeah." She turned to Asher. "Where did it come from?"

"El Tapon."

"Oh. Isn't that…um…what's her name? I talked to her in Chuck's a few times. What the hell is her name?"

"Migdala."

"Right."

"So, about this boat trip."

"What boat trip?"

"I just asked if you heard what I said and you said, 'yeah'."

"Oh, okay. So tell me."

"The woman you just mentioned, her Uncle Juaquin wants to hire us to transport some stuff to Cuba."

"Why?"

"Because that's the only way they can get them there."

"Why us?"

"Because it's illegal," Asher said.

"Oh." She held her fork in mid-air.

Scheutz sipped his water. "Well, what do you think?"

"I think this food is damned good."

"That's not what I'm asking."

"I don't want to get involved with anything illegal."

"We need money."

"Which is why we should have stayed in St. Thomas."

"Will you get off it? Jesus, I'm going to hear about this for the rest of my life."

"As you well should."

"It is not illegal in Cuba." Asher leaned forward to look around Samantha at Scheutz.

Samantha grunted a short laugh. "No, not as long as you pay import duties."

"Not our problem." Asher made one of his Caribbean gestures, his hands spread as if each held a balance on the scale of justice. "We off-load the goods to another boat and go home."

"What Asher means is that the United States embargo is not illegal in Cuba. Which means…as long as we are in international waters, we are not taking anything to Cuba. So we could be just sailing anywhere with a bunch of what they call mini-computers aboard. Mini-computers are those…"

"I know what a mini-computer is." Samantha snorted. "So, if you work at it you can rationalize anything."

"So, come on." Scheutz laid his hand on the nape of her neck, a place she had, until recently, always liked him touching her. "This could be fun. It's a great sail. We'd have the wind at our back the whole way. Plus we'd make a nice piece of change for the delivery." He gazed into her eyes, hoping, but also expecting her to shake his hand from her back.

Her eyes remained expressionless as she returned his gaze, but then, slowly, one small increment of feeling at a time, her face softened until she actually smiled at him. "Okay." She nodded once, and then again. "We'll do it."

"All right."

She laughed. "This could be fun. God knows, I haven't seen you this animated in a while. You've turned into such a slug lately."

"How does that song go? 'Sometimes I'm happy, sometimes I'm blue, oo. My disposition depends on you, oo'."

"Spare me."

Two days later, anchored off the southern coast of the main island of Puerto Rico, Juaquin's people lashed their Island Trader to their port side. Harding stepped aboard with a 'big surprise' grin and announced he was overseeing the transfer of cargo.

"Wonderful." Samantha shook her head, giving Scheutz her most baleful look. "Always something to ruin a good trip."

Two men, with Harding giving orders and Asher translating, began transferring cartons wrapped in cellophane, from below the iron boat's deck onto the deck of the *Panacea.* Asher helped carry one of the cartons, then stayed below to tell the laders where to stow the rest. The main cabin had been cleared of tools and building supplies. Samantha suggested she and Scheutz go ashore and get a bite to eat instead of watching all this, and when he demurred, she said she would lower the dinghy and go in alone, so he gave in and said he'd go with her.

She handled the outboard on the dinghy, maneuvering alongside several large sailboats, a schooner, a couple of ketches, a yawl, a double-ender sloop, and one nicely restored wooden two-master that resembled the kind of caravel Columbus might have used in one of his voyages to this part of the world. Boat-watching had always been one of her favorite pastimes, in the same way people-watching in various yacht clubs throughout the Caribbean never failed to keep her amused for entire evenings. He had shared, in a diminished way, her enthusiasm for the many different styles of boats, but the comings and goings of vacationing sailboat people bored him. He sat on the center seat of the dinghy, facing her, as she chatted idly about this or that feature of some boat, as if they themselves were on vacation.

Even here, their interests did not jibe, hers being how some feature might affect the ease of sailing, while he invariably focused on the actual mechanical way a particular piece of rigging might be attached to the hull, or, on a wooden hull, the width of the ship-lap boards, or the shape of the transom and how the rudder was attached. But he did not talk about these things, merely noticing them while enjoying comparing sailing features with her. How long had it been since they had just relaxed and chatted this way?

They tied up at a pier under a sign that read, "Ponce Yacht Club." The yacht club's restaurant and attached bar looked to be full almost to capacity but the hostess found them a table in the rear, away from the water. Two-thirds of the patrons were obviously gringos and the restaurant's décor would not have been out of place in Newport, Rhode Island. Samantha ordered a Cuba Libra and chose an entrée from the menu. Scheutz ordered a beer and a sandwich. How many times over the last seven years had they sat in a place like this on some resort island in the Caribbean? She watched the faces of the people around them, making little comments about who she thought they might be in real life, what kind of work they did, where they might live the rest of the year, saying things out of the corner of her mouth like, "Des Moines. Insurance salesman."

He watched her face, and wondered who she was in real life. If they were not on this life-long vacation; if, say, they lived in New Hampshire still, married—or not—and had a child and jobs—or even careers—what would she be like? What would she do if not sailing and partying? She could do anything; she was smart, capable, poised, full of self-confidence, certainly beautiful, good with people. As they say, she went to weather like a trim sail racer. Working for different charter companies in the Caribbean, she had shown many times over the last few years her ability to easily handle the responsibility of captaining a ship. She had studied for and gotten her sailing captain's license right around the same time they had acquired the Panacea, and then later coached him through getting his license.

Come to think of it, right around the time she got her license they started having trouble between them. It all happened at once; she registered her captain's license in Charlotte Amalie, and the same day took over a charter to captain a small sloop from St. Thomas to Bermuda. He went along as crew. That trip went fine, and it was in Bermuda they found the old schooner, the British-built Panacea. Two days after taking possession of the boat, they took the chance of sailing it without a radio, heading south toward the Bahamas, and ran smack into Hurricane Dorothy. They could read the signs for heavy weather coming, the mare's tail wispy clouds, the red sunrises, but never expected anything like what they got. Asher, who had been a crewman under the previous owner, made a joke of their encounter with Dorothy, saying every time his boat changed hands a hurricane came along to seal the deal. While taking emergency steps to cope with the weather, Scheutz and Samantha had their first serious argument, over who actually was in charge of the ship. Sharing responsibility in fair weather was all fine and good, but when the bad winds blew only a single head, with no arguments, could carry them through.

In the end, Asher's advice that they heave to brought them through the hurricane. Asher laughed. "This just like the Wizard of Oz. Dorothy going to blow this boat all the way to Kansas." Scheutz and Samantha were so angry with each other by that time, they did not find Asher funny in the least.

Everything changed after that trip. He chalked it up to how different it felt having their own boat, but as time went by it seemed like something more. While he was trying for his own license they argued more than he felt appropriate to the minor differences of opinion they had.

After finishing their meal they lolled around the yacht club. Near midnight they returned to the schooner, silhouetted against the sky with an anchor light showing in the bow. The cargo laders had finished, the Island Trader gone. Asher and Harding sat in the cockpit sharing a bottle of rum. Samantha, the moment she stepped on deck, started in on Harding. "Weren't you supposed to go with the boat that brought our cargo?"

"No, I'm going with you guys. That was part of the deal."

She turned to Scheutz. "You didn't tell me that part."

"I didn't know. Nobody said anything about Harding going along."

Asher extended the rum bottle. "Want a sip?"

"Ugh. No." She stepped over his legs to reach the binnacle and flipped on the engine power switch. "Let's get the hell out of here. Get this thing over with." She pressed the ignition and the diesel turned over twice before starting.

Scheutz, ready for sleep, sagged from a long day. "You don't think we should wait till morning?"

"Nope. Asher and I will take the first watch. You and the dingdong can take the second. Let's go. Secure the dinghy; we'll tow it."

No one moved. Salsa music drifted across the water from somewhere near the shore and mixed with the low rumble of the engine below them. Asher and Scheutz exchanged looks in the dim light of the binnacle. Harding took a swift drink from the rum bottle.

Samantha turned her head from Scheutz to Asher and back.

"Clem, am I usurping your authority as captain here?"

"I don't see a problem."

"Then can we go? I don't know why we should wait till morning. We'll take first watch." She turned to Asher. "You okay for a few hours?"

"Yah. I can go all night. Don't mean nothing to me with Yemaya to guide me."

Harding capped the rum bottle. "Where do I sleep?"

Samantha stepped to the helm without turning her head to Harding. "Haul that anchor. Then you can go sleep in the dinghy."

Scheutz stood. "He can haul the anchor, but, come on, you can't tell him to sleep in the dinghy. Harding, you can sleep in my cabin. I'll bunk in with you, Samantha."

She gave him a long look, and then shook her head. "Okay. Anything. Let's just get this over with."

Within the hour, they were under way. Below, the entire main cabin had been filled with cartons leaving only a narrow aisle to walk through and a place to sit next to the ship's radio. Scheutz dropped into Samantha's berth, exhausted.

By the time the sun rose, during Scheutz's watch, they had cleared Punto Aguila on the southwestern tip of Puerto Rico, where they shifted direction to south-southwest to be sure to clear the southern tip of Hispaniola. The trip passed without incident. Samantha alternated shifts between Scheutz and Asher but refused to stand watch with Harding. Late the next night, sailing under millions of stars, a fair wind and a following current left Scheutz and Samantha with not much to do except make sure they maintained a course. They relaxed. He could feel it in them both, the way it had been years before when they were new at this. They talked, her at the helm, him sitting beside her, about anything coming up behind them on the wind, anything that had nothing to do with them personally, their past together, their potential future together, and certainly not their present together.

A boat owner had quoted to them a few years before, one night as they were all sitting around the cockpit at a mooring. The quote apparently came from Martha Gellhorn, one of Hemingway's wives, who said the ideal conditions for a relationship were if both people lived four blocks apart and each had a different career interest that did not include the other. If that were the case with him and Samantha they
would probably have no trouble being each other's best friend. When their watch ended, she let him he nestle with her in her cabin.

The wind picked up the following day. Asher and Scheutz set all four sails. Harding slept a lot, his absence on deck pleasing to Samantha. The weather channel announced that Hurricane Gabrielle in the Atlantic had turned north before making landfall, leaving behind some hefty winds and high surfs. But the cargo did not seem to add much weight and the boat responded lightly to her helm. There was nothing to do now but relax and enjoy the sail.

But he found he could relax only if he did not start thinking about where they were going. Migdala's warning against going to Cuba echoed in his head whenever he was not enjoying the sail, or chit-chatting with Samantha, or obsessing about something else. Samantha seemed to be enjoying herself as long as Harding stayed out of her sight. Asher, as usual, didn't care one way or the other, but he so obviously loved being at sea again. And Harding…there was no telling what that idiot would do next, especially if he was drunk, which he seemed to be pretty much all of his waking hours.

Lying awake in the sweaty enclosure of the bunk with Samantha asleep next to him, he realized that Migdala's warning against going to Cuba took second place to what really bothered him. Going back to Cuba for the third time loomed like an omen, like asking for trouble. What was the saying, twice burned, thrice shy? He argued with himself that he was just being superstitious. He shouldn't give in to it. But he had to admit, some of the worst things that ever happened to him had been in Cuba. The first time, thirty years ago, during the revolution, he had come as close to a nervous breakdown as he imagined a person could get without actually landing in the nut house. The second time, even worse, his brother Willi had gone with him and been killed. What was he thinking going back to a place that seemed designated by some vengeful God or cosmic joker as his own personal heartache pit? Or maybe it wasn't God; maybe Fidel was the problem. Those first two catastrophes in his life, his brother dying and, before that, his falling apart had both happened due to his encounters with Fidel's soldiers, the fidelistas.

And, like some kind of black aura, Fidel was still in power. From what little news from the north Scheutz bothered with, it looked like the coming breakup of the Soviet Union was beginning to have a serious effect on Cuba. Russia had already lowered its sugar subsidies, driving down the island economy. This could be good for Juaquin because people would be more anxious to get cheap smuggled merchandize. But it could be bad for the smugglers like himself because the government would be more diligent about going after import duties. Then again, those mini-computers did not seem like they were bound for sale to ordinary consumers. If they were microwave ovens he could see it, but their cargo was almost certainly for some government organization. Which would make sense if Russia was pulling back its support for Cuba. The whole thing made him superstitious.

Superstition. Rot. He had to stop thinking about this kind of stuff. Asher and all his Santeria sermons about the havoc the orishas visited on people were having an effect on his brain. Maybe he should go up to the bow of the boat and sacrifice a chicken or something. Does it count if the chicken has already been plucked and dressed and wrapped in plastic that says Garcia's Market on the side? And does the sacrifice still count if the chicken, instead of being burnt on a funeral pyre, is zapped in the microwave oven that Asher adapted to 12 volts so it could be used on the boat?

Scheutz sweated in the tiny space allowed for him on the bunk. The day had heated up already by the time the sun came up, and the tiny porthole didn't offer much breeze. Everything had been removed from the cabins to make room for the cargo, case upon case labeled as microwave ovens. Apparently, they didn't want their own people to know what was in the cartons. The table saw and the drill press and all of their shipwright tools had been offloaded, as well as the lumber they'd kept stored below decks. Tables and bench seats in the main cabin had been unbolted and stacked on their working dock back in Culebra with the tools, all protected from the sun by an old mizzen sail. And that was another worry, that something would be stolen in their absence. Juaquin had assured him that no islander would dare touch anything belonging to someone who worked for him; such was his reputation on there. But what about all those boats coming into Culebra seeking shelter from the coming hurricane, people who did not know about Juaquin?

They had stripped the *Panacea* down to what was barely needed to sail comfortably. What if an emergency happened? Anything. They had no tools on board to fix what might be needed. And beyond that there was no room to move. He could barely squeeze by the cargo cartons to get at the radio. Only one person could stand in the galley to cook at any one time. Fortunately, Asher was pretty skinny and could move around in there without banging his knees and elbows. God knew where he slept; someplace up forward in the anchor locker.

The space Scheutz and Samantha had to sleep in was barely wide enough for one of them to occupy alone. Last night they slept pressed together as tightly as they had done ten years earlier when they were first together and in love. In the September heat and stifling quarters they sweated so much their naked bodies slithered against each other. To the gentle lapping of the waves in the bay they made love with an intensity that had been lacking for years. Of course, the rum punch Asher had made for dinner the night before added an extra kick for both of them. But still, it felt to him as if they had fallen in love all over again and this trip to Cuba would be another beginning, a whole new start for them. They had fallen asleep kissing. And now he could finally feel himself falling asleep again, just remembering what last night had been like.

Scheutz set up alternate watches so that the first night he was on with Samantha, and the second with Harding. It would take them a week to reach the southern coast of Cuba from Ponce, six days if the weather held. The wind blew a pretty steady twenty knots and they would have no adverse currents until they hit the Jamaican Channel. Even that was not a worry this time of year. Unless, of course, Hurricane Gabrielle had caused an agitation that far in from the Atlantic. The scheduling of the overnight watch might get to be a problem as the trip went on because Samantha refused to sit up all night with just Harding, only with Scheutz or Asher. Asher and Harding was an okay combination because, even though Asher disliked Harding, he'd sit up by himself leaving Harding to sleep out the watch up on deck. Having Harding along was such a pain in the ass for so many reasons, the least of which was his constant drunkenness. Scheutz considered throwing his case of rum overboard, but Harding became even more obnoxious sober. At least, drunk or sober, the man was a decent sailor and could be a help pulling them out of a tough spot should one come up.

The wind and current held favorable. They kept the Haitian coast in sight on the starboard side and, having sighted Navassa Island, altered course again to point them roughly at Cabo Cruz on the southern coast of Cuba. Their goal was a point about fifteen miles east of Cabo Cruz called Punta Hicacos, which sheltered a marina at the small Cuban fishing village of Pilon.

Days and nights had become dreamy. He and Asher erected a bimini awning over the cockpit and they all lolled on deck in its shade, talking, sipping rum, snacking as it suited them. Even Harding became less of a pain. He told them stories of his childhood growing up in a lumbering town in northwestern Washington state, working as a child for his father and uncle who supplied food services for logging camps. He and Scheutz traded stories about the differences between cutting the huge Douglas fir trees on the west coast as opposed to the yellow and white pines in New England. Asher talked about growing up in the southern province of Brazil, called Bahia, of being abandoned as a street gamin in Sao Paolo and then shipping out at the age of eleven on a turtle boat, eventually leaving him on the island of Dominica.

And even Samantha, who normally did not talk about herself and where she came from, told stories about growing up in the small town of Acworth, New Hampshire. For the seven years she and Scheutz had been together she had always maintained that her life had not actually begun until she left the town at age twenty-two. But for these few days, her stories of high school adventures, some with Scheutz's own sons, took on a kind of ethereal glow, much like the stories the nuns in grade school told about the early lives of the saints, as mundane as they were, but seen anew in the light of later years. Listening to her, with the twilight sun setting off the port bow, all the tension they had experienced over the past two years faded away as if they had just run away to sea all over again.

And they could barely keep their hands off each other. They made love so much in their narrow berth that Scheutz's penis began to feel it was being rubbed raw. He developed a fantasy that their new-found love for each other spread to the other crew members, causing Asher, for the first time since he'd known him, to reveal to them who he really was. Even Harding's dark, foreboding undercast seemed to fade, giving him the feeling of belonging to the same human species as the rest of them.

Chapter 5

The first sighting of the coast of Cuba brought Scheutz a heavy lump in his chest. By the time they sighted Punto Hicacos on the afternoon of the sixth day out of Puerto Rico, the lump was complicated by a small sadness that the trip would soon be over. Their instructions from Juaquin were to sit three miles out on the night of the seventh day and flash a pre-arranged signal of light that would be picked up by the Cubans. Since they were a day and half early, they needed to kill some time. Samantha suggested they head east toward Santiago de Cuba and just do some sightseeing where the beautiful Sierra Maestra mountains ran to the water's edge along the coast.

The trip east toward Santiago de Cuba aggravated his anxiety. What if they were spotted by the Cuban Coastal Patrol? What if the United States Navy out of Guantanamo stopped them? How could they explain the boxes marked as microwave ovens? He didn't sleep much that night and the next day, returning to the point off the coast of Punto Hicacos, the tension in his chest became a sharp pain. They waited until close to ten o'clock at night, as Juaquin had suggested, moving slowly along the coast roughly three miles out, then dropped the sails and let the current drift them past the lights of Punto Hicacos. They had turned on no running lights, the only light the one Harding flashed as a signal toward the shore. With a faint quarter moon, the silhouette of mountains behind the town remained clearly visible. Snatches of music and voices drifted out across the water from the point. A deep sea fishing boat motored past them, running lights and cabin lights on full, and rounded the point into the little bay in front of the town. But no boat approached them.

When the shore lights of the point told them they had drifted too far, they raised the jib and the foresail and tacked eastward. They found that they were not moving forward enough against the current and the wind was inching them in toward the coast so they raised the main sail and worked their way back to a spot east of the point before drifting back down again. Once again no one came their way. On the third try, though, this time drifting almost midway down to Cabo Cruz, they spotted a cutter-sized boat rounding the cape and heading in their direction.

As the cutter bore down on them, Scheutz's muscles tensed up, ready to do something, he didn't know what. Beside him, Samantha muttered, "Coastal Patrol." The cutter had closed on them to the point where they could read the lettering on its hull.

"Oh, shit." Scheutz jumped into the cockpit and turned the ignition key, pressing the switch, waiting with his hand on the gearshift knob for the motor to catch. They did not stand much chance of out-running a coast guard cutter, but he would take whatever slight chance he had. Dammit, another round of bad luck from old Fidel.

"What the hell are you doing?" Harding shouted down at him from where he stood silhouetted on the cabin roof.

"I'm getting out of here. That's the Cuban Coastal Patrol bearing down on us."

"Whoa, whoa. Stop. That's who we're supposed to meet."

"We're supposed to meet the coastal patrol?" The engine caught, but Scheutz held the gearshift knob tight without moving it.

"Yeah. They're our contact. How the hell do you think we get this stuff ashore? That's them."

"Are you sure?"

"Believe me, I've been here before."

Harding was an idiot, but not that much of an idiot. It would have been nice, though, if he had told them ahead of time they were meeting the coast guard. Scheutz relaxed his grip on the gearshift knob and watched the cutter closing in on them. The idea of having the Cuban Coastal Patrol, or any coastal patrol, board his ship was not at all to his liking. He would never forgive himself for bringing his brother Willi here, and he would never forgive the entire country of Cuba for killing him.

He shut the engine off. As the cutter drew close he could make out a manned fifty-caliber machine gun mounted in the bow. The sight of the gun frightened him. Since the *Panacea* was already hove to there was nothing they needed to do but wait until the coast patrol cut their engine and let their boat drift in abeam of the schooner. One sailor tossed Asher a line, which he tied off. The cutter's deck lights illuminated the *Panacea*'s decks as well as its own. Another sailor hopped from the cutter to the schooner's deck, carrying a second line that he handed to Harding to tie off. The sailors looked to be very young, and handsome in their regulation t-shirts. The man who now stepped aboard, though, was not young, nor was he in uniform. He wore a plain gray shirt and gold-rimmed glasses just like Juaquin's, and looked about the same age as Scheutz. Had this man been in Castro's army thirty years ago? Had he been one the people who shot Willi to death?

The man said something quickly in Spanish, in that nasally Cuban accent, but Scheutz did not catch what he said. Asher answered the man. Both phrases were short but seemed to satisfy the man from the cutter and so he smiled and extended his hand for Asher to shake. Asher took his hand and then motioned to Scheutz, explaining that he was the captain and therefore the person the Cuban needed to talk to. The man took a step toward Scheutz and extended his hand. "Buenas noches."

"Good evening."

"Ah, I, ah, speak, ah un poco inglese. And you have a good trip?"

"Yes. A very good trip."

"Good." He grinned. "Y ahora. We do the business, no?"

"Yes."

"¿Tiene lo mio? Ah, um…you have my goods?"

"Yes." Scheutz smiled again. If for no other reason than the smile kept him from thinking how much he'd like to smack this guy. Smack him for no other reason than for being Cuban.

Harding's voice came from behind Scheutz. "Yeah, we got the goods. You got the money?" He sounded like a television tough guy.

"Money?"

"Money?" Scheutz turned to face Harding. "Nobody said anything about us collecting money for this stuff."

Harding nodded his head. "Yeah. We're supposed to get paid before we offload the cartons. Where do you think the money comes from for this stuff?"

"No." The Cuban stepped closer to Harding. "That is not our arrangement. We pay the money to Senor Juaquin."

"Well, that's all changed. Joaquin told us—me—to collect for this stuff. I guess they had a hard time getting paid last time."

The Cuban turned and gave Scheutz a questioning look. Scheutz shrugged. This was the first he had heard about collecting for the cargo. The Cuban turned back to Harding, shaking his head. "No. We will take the cargo and pay the money to Juaquin. Like usual."

"No you won't."

"Harding, why don't you just shut up?" Samantha's voice came from the cockpit.

The Cuban laughed. "Now we can begin to put the cartons on our boat, eh?"

"Not if I have anything to do with it." Harding turned to disappear down the gangway to below deck.

The Cuban said to Scheutz, "Now we can begin?"

Scheutz nodded. The quicker this was over, the better. Not only was Harding an idiot, but he was a dangerous idiot. Scheutz motioned for Asher to open the forward hatch. "Take one of the coast patrol guys with you to start handing up those boxes."

The older Cuban motioned to the crewmen still on his boat and two of them boarded the schooner. They followed Scheutz down the gangway to the main cabin. There they encountered Harding yelling into the radio for Juaquin to answer him. As Scheutz grabbed the nearest carton to hand to one of the sailors, Harding yelled at him. "You can't do this, Clem. We'll never get paid if you let them have this stuff without getting the money."

"That was not my deal. I'm just a shipper."

"We can't let them take this stuff then."

"We can't stop them. Every one of those sailors has a side arm, or didn't you notice?"

Harding shook his head, giving Scheutz a look like a belligerent child. "Look, don't you want to get paid for this?"

"At the moment, all I want is to get the hell out of here. I'll get my money from Juaquin. That was the deal. Now stop acting like a fool and give us a hand offloading this stuff."

"We'll see about this." Harding yelled into the radio's hand mike a few times more and then bolted for the gangway, pushing his way around Scheutz and one the sailors climbing the stairway with a carton.

On deck, Harding argued with the Cuban. The cutter had turned off its deck lights, casting the entire scene into semi-darkness with only a glow coming up through the forward hatch and one from the gangway into the cockpit. Scheutz handed the box he carried to the crewman on the cutter, and as he did he noticed Harding had stopped arguing and now pointed a spear gun at the Cuban with gold-rimmed glasses. The spear gun, cocked with heavy rubber bands, was the kind used by scuba divers to spear small fish. It could not do any real damage to a person unless pointed at some vulnerable spot like the heart, the neck or the eyes. The one in Harding's hands he had pointed directly at the Cuban's face. Scheutz moved toward the pair but before he was halfway there, Asher came like a shadow from around the mast and, with a quick, smooth motion, pulled the spear gun from Harding's hands. Harding reached for it but Asher pushed him back into the arms of the Cuban. In the struggle, another crewman grabbed Harding from behind and pulled him to the deck. He held him there while the Cuban with the gold-rimmed glasses pulled a pair of handcuffs from the coast guard crewman's belt and applied them to Harding's wrists.

Scheutz stood over Harding, resisting the desire to give him a swift kick in the ass. "See that machine gun on the deck over there? You want to get us all killed?"

Samantha came to stand next to him, looking down on the struggling Harding. "I'd settle down if I were you. You don't want to fall overboard with your hands like that." To the Cuban, she said, "Sorry about him. Can we get this stuff out of here really fast?"

The Cuban bowed his head. "Todo por usted, señorita."

It took them close to two hours to complete the transfer of boxes from the schooner to the coast guard vessel. The entire time Harding sat on the cabin superstructure like some grotesquely evil gargoyle muttering vile oaths. Asher had taken the spear gun below on his next trip down for another carton. When they were close to finished, Samantha asked the Cuban, loud enough for Harding to hear, if they could do her a favor and take Harding with them. The Cuban laughed, told her gallantly he would like to oblige her but could not. That bringing someone like Harding into Cuba would make trouble for all of them.

Harding jumped to his feet. "I'll make trouble for you when I get back to Juaquin."

Samantha shrugged. "Well, I guess we have no choice but to throw you overboard right here."

Harding danced on the roof of the cabin in what might look like a jig, but with the evil pouring from him, looked like someone whose feet were being burnt by fires from below. Scheutz backed away from him. "She's not kidding, Harding. You don't shut up and I will let Samantha have her way with you."

Once the cartons had all been stowed aboard the coast guard vessel, the crewman removed Harding's cuffs. Harding rubbed his wrists and approached the Cuban. "Where's my package?"

The Cuban raised a finger, which he shook in Harding's face. "I will not give it to you." He paused while Harding blustered. Then, as if teasing a child, he said, "I will only give it to your captain." He removed a small rectangular packet from his pocket and extended it in Scheutz's direction, smiling as he did so.

Scheutz did not move. Migdala had told him this would happen, and for him not to take the package. He shook his head and held his hand up, palm forward to indicate that he would not take it. Samantha stepped around him and took the package from the Cuban, who bowed and smiled at her.

"Hand it over." Harding extended his hand toward Samantha.

"Take a flying leap off the bow, buster. This is mine."

The Cuban let out a guffaw as he prepared to climb over the rail of the cutter. Harding made a move toward Samantha but Scheutz stood directly in his path.

Now that the coast guard vessel had moved away from the side of the schooner, they began to drift with the current again. "We must put up some sail," Asher said and moved forward to raise the jib. The Cuban boat had held them in position by running its engine against the current. Samantha walked away from Scheutz and Harding toward the cockpit. With nothing more to fear, she flicked on the running lights and took hold of the helm.

Harding started after her. "I want the package."

Scheutz grabbed his arm. "Just let it be. Help Asher with the sails. I don't give a shit what you want, Harding. And don't stand there staring at me. I didn't want to bring you along to begin with, so if you cause me any more trouble, I will throw you off this boat myself."

Harding stopped and held himself very still. He looked narrowly at Scheutz, the boat's stern light glinting in his eyes. "Juaquin's going to hear about this."

"Good. Because I'm not doing this for him anymore."

"Just give me the package."

"The package is safe. I don't know what's in it; I don't care. But just let it go till we're back in Culebra. Now get your ass forward and help Asher."

Asher and Harding raised first the jib and then the staysail and worked their way back to the foresail main and finally the main. Samantha at the helm held the bow into the wind until they had the mainsail up and line cleated off, and then put them on a south-southeastern course.

But heading home proved to be not the picnic sailing out had been. It was if Cuba had once again cast a pall over everything. From here on they would be sailing close-hauled, up against the wind. They would also be fighting the current the whole way. Six days out from Culebra to Cuba would mean nearly two weeks getting back. And if they got another hurricane warning there was no telling where they would need to hole up. Since they would surely need the engine's help, they had to plan the return from one refueling point to another. Fortunately, Juaquin had given Scheutz ample funds for diesel fuel. After much discussion, they decided to go with Asher's advice and take the northern route, tacking south-southeast to Jamaica, which would put them in position for a northeastern tack through the Windward Passage to the Turks Islands and approach Puerto Rico from the northwest.

Barely averaging four knots, even with the engine's extra push, they took two days to Port Antonio on the northeastern coast of Jamacia, where they refueled. Harding pouted the whole way, drinking heavily. Scheutz finally talked Samantha into giving him Harding's package which he tucked, without opening it, into a hidey-hole in the engine compartment only he knew about. He, Samantha, and Asher overlapped shifts with each other so each one could have four hours of uninterrupted sleep. The cabins and the galley, without the cargo now, seemed as spacious as a mansion. Harding kept to his cabin, and Scheutz considered locking him in just so they wouldn't have to listen to his ranting on about how he was the only one on the boat with any sense.

"I'm dying to know what's in that box," Samantha said late the second night as they both sat on watch in the cockpit.

"Leave it alone, will you? I didn't want to take it on board in the first place."

"So, you knew about it ahead of time?"

"Well, I was told by Juaquin's niece that we should not take any package from the Cubans to bring back with us. She warned me against doing any work for her uncle at all. I should have listened. After that little display back there with the Cubans it looks like there's a chance we might not get paid for this trip."

Samantha made a small adjustment to their point of sail and stood staring off into the darkness, the light from the binnacle casting moving shadows upwards on her face. "I'm getting really sick of all this, Clem. Being poor. Working on this boat. Drifting around with nothing to do and no particular place to go to. Do you ever ask yourself what's the point?"

"This is the point."

"Yeah, I know. For you this is it, isn't it?" She fell quiet. Then very quietly, so quietly he might not have heard her if he had been downwind of her, she said, "I can't do it anymore. I'm twenty-nine years old and I feel like I'm at the end of my life." Her voice broke and the binnacle light showed the tears that wet her face. He made a move to reach up and put his hand on hers but she pushed it away with her elbow. "Do you realize that we do nothing more than what people do who are retired. We could be living in Florida in one of those old folks' communities and probably have a more fun life playing shuffleboard or bridge all day."

"So, what are you saying?"

She put her head down for a moment on her hands that gripped the top of the helm, then raised up and turned to face him. "Just before we left, I called home. My father is pretty sick. I think I'm going to go visit them."

"Okay. We'll leave Asher to care for the boat and get on a plane as soon as we get back."

"No. I want to go alone. I want some time to think about all this. I'll be back. Just give me a little break, okay?"

From Port Antonio they sailed an easy broad reach on a northeastern course. A gulf had opened up between him and Samantha, the void between them creating a thickness of air that spread throughout the boat. Asher isolated himself by indulging in his own brand of silence, rarely moving from his perch on the foredeck except to go below to the galley or to wherever his bunk was. Harding ransacked the boat looking for the package the Cuban had handed to Samantha. He covered each spot below decks three times to make sure he didn't miss it. After seeing him look in the same place in the galley for the third time, Scheutz moved the package to a crevice in that place, thinking Harding would probably not look there again. And he was right.

Hugging the tip of Cape Haitien on the western end of Haiti as close as possible, they made good time, even without the engine. But the going was rough. Thunderstorms and heavy seas intermittently hindered their advance and removed any chance of repeating the relaxing sail they had had on the way west. They refueled again at Grand Turk Island and then tacked close to the wind and against the current to reach as close to the eastern end of Hispaniola as they could get.

Beating their way eastward, and refueling in the Dominican Republic and again in Arecibo on the northern coast of Puerto Rico, they finally worked their way to a point north of Culebra, putting them in easy reach of the mouth of the bay. For the last two days, weather alerts coming from the Roosevelt Roads warned of a mammoth hurricane, called Hugo, forming off the Canary Islands and moving westward. As they entered the bay in Culebra, the sight of so many boats moored there surprised them. Everyone was looking to hide themselves from the coming storm.

They dropped all sails and used the last of the diesel to maneuver the schooner slowly between the anchored boats.

Chapter 6

Samantha walked back toward him from the window with a ferry ticket in her hand. She smiled at him, her step a little too light. A little too glad to be leaving? Happy she was going home to visit her parents after all these years? Or happy to be leaving because it looked like the hurricane was coming? Or happy to be getting away from him?

Don't go. He told himself he should say those words to her. But there was the rub. He had to tell himself to say the words; they would not come naturally. If he really wanted her to stay, the words would come out by themselves. True, she planned on going only for a visit, because her father was ill, but it did not feel that way. She had accomplished her packing and ticket buying with the same casual air as the times she went to San Juan to buy supplies. On the ship-to-shore telephone connection to American Airlines, the day after they returned from Cuba, she sounded expectant, like a tourist looking forward to vacation. Or did he just imagine that? Being so close to someone for so many years, liking and disliking, approaching and dodging, wanting and avoiding the same things, the same ideas, the same experiences, made it difficult to tell subtle differences between who felt what when.

She stood before him at the edge of the crowd of roughly fifty passengers, ticket in one hand and small overnight bag in the other, as if waiting for him to say something. Don't go. He told himself again to say the words. She raised her eyebrows, maybe even telling herself to want him to say the words. The overnight bag, a small blue duffel, did not hold much, meaning she must be coming back soon. But then, she always traveled light. One of the things he loved about her; clothing did not count for much with her. She could wear the same thing for a month, working, lounging and swimming in the same shorts and halter. That small duffel could suffice for a week or for a year.

Behind the last truck, people began boarding the ferry, walking down the cement ramp and stepping onto the metal gangway that bobbed up and down with the gentle swell of the water. She leaned in and gave him a light, soft kiss on the lips. "Well, see ya."

"Bye. Call me." As she had turned to walk away he extended his left hand. After a step, she turned back and, seeing the hand, reached to take it. She squeezed hard, looked into his eyes and smiled. Was the pain he saw hers or his? Did her pain cut through her impulse to get away? Or was he just seeing his pain in her eyes? He waited at the top of the ramp until everyone was aboard, the gangway drawn up, lines cast off. As the rumbling engines pulled the boat away from the shore, he looked for her peaked cap among the passengers but could not find it.

He walked through the town, along the bay road, and into the barrio, to the El Tapon restaurant. Filled almost to capacity, the desayuno crowd drank their coffee against the background of an excited voice coming over the radio weather station. The hurricane came on, moving in its steady path across the Atlantic. It had left Guadalupe and turned northwest, had devastated the island of St. Croix and now headed straight for the eastern end of Puerto Rico. Culebra lay directly in its path. The bay, long famous as one of the safest hurricane hiding holes in the Caribbean, was due to get smacked down from its perch. The weatherman repeated his warnings, tracking the longitude, latitude, and wind strength of the storm minute by minute. One of Tapon's friends, Arturo, an on-again-off-again Christian Evangelical, railed against all the marital infidelity on the island that now brought the wrath of God down upon them like Sodom and Gemorrah. Scheutz, headed for where his apron hung behind the counter, once again trying to argue himself out of the suspicion that both Samantha's leaving and the hurricane coming were due to his tempting the fates by going back to Cuba.

He threw himself into clearing tables, washing dishes, making coffee. He needed no further guidance from Migdala, and as they worked around each other, nothing was said. Her daughter, in the blue and white school uniform, taller than Migdala, thin but sinewy, her face with high Indian cheek bones set in what seemed like a permanent sneer, passed through the restaurant with nothing more than a slapped palm on the counter to let her mother know she was on her way out the door. Scheutz's "Buenas dias" in her direction earned him nothing more than a sideways flick of her eyes. By nine o'clock, the last customers gone, except for Tapon and his friends, Scheutz finished up as fast as he could. He needed to get out to the boat, to get ready for the hurricane.

When he arrived at the boat an hour later, Asher had a good portion of the deck already cleared. As in the restaurant, Scheutz was thankful he did not have to enter into conversation; they both knew what needed to be done. Hopefully, he might never have to talk to anyone again, at least till Samantha returned. He and Asher carried tools and lumber stored on the working dock up to the deck of the schooner and then below to store them as compactly as they could in the main cabin. They unhitched the dock from the hull, towed it ashore with the dinghy, removed each of the flotation drums, hauled the wooden dock up onto the land, and secured it as best they could with heavy rocks. In the afternoon, they towed the schooner into deeper water of the bay and put down four anchors, two at the bow and two at the stern. After clearing the last of the materials from the main deck, they stripped the sails and stowed them in the forecastle.

The sun had dropped before they finished. Around them, throughout the day, other boat owners had spent their time going through the same routines of preparing for the coming winds. Scheutz and Asher took the dinghy in toward the inner shore of the bay, navigating between the crowd of boats, to the plank wharf extending from the mangrove, then tied up and walked to the restaurant. As Scheutz stepped inside the door, Migdala rushed from behind the counter to stand in front of him. "I am so happy you are here. You have to help me."

Her voice broke the bubble of silence he had found himself in during the day as he and Asher worked. "Okay. What?"

"I cannot find Blanca. I have looked everywhere."

"So what do you want me to do?"

"I'm just so upset. The hurricane is coming. I've asked everyone. No one has seen her. I have the police looking for her."

Asher moved to her side. "What can we do?"

"I don't know. Help me to think; where would she be?"

Scheutz shook his head. "I don't know Blanca. I don't know where she would go."

Migdala turned to Asher, who stood with his head tilted back and his eyes squinted as if trying to discern something just beyond sight. "I would say she's on a boat."

Migdala waved her hand sharply at him. "That's silly. She never goes on boats. Why would she be on a boat?"

Asher shrugged. Migdala looked back to Scheutz and then turned to look around the room. The restaurant was now empty of patrons. Even the old men were gone.

Scheutz tried to remember if he had seen Juaquin's van parked in its usual spot near the road. It had not been there. "Where is Juaquin?"

She shook her head. "He has not been here for three days. Maybe he has gone off to the main island."

Scheutz turned to Asher. "And he must have taken Harding with him. That's why we haven't been graced by a visit from him." Juaquin had not been there when they returned from Cuba. Harding had said he was going to find him and then he disappeared. Now it had been a few days. Before Samantha left they had opened the package the Cuban had given her. It contained emeralds, a lot of emeralds. Scheutz had no idea of the value of stones in general but Samantha guessed they were looking at a small fortune. No wonder Harding had wanted to get his hands on it so badly. Migdala had warned him that carrying the computers to Cuba was just a cover for what they would be asked to bring back. The whole thing didn't make any sense. Was Juaquin, with Harding's help, smuggling emeralds into the United States?

But the bigger question was, why had not Juaquin come to demand the package of emeralds? Scheutz had expected Harding to bring his boss back to the boat that first day. Wasn't the package of emeralds the real point of the Cuban trip? So why were they still in the hidey-hole aboard the schooner and not in Juaquin's possession? Samantha had refused to touch them, saying they probably carried some kind of bad karma. They frightened her, she said. Another good reason to get the hell out of this place, she added. Scheutz decided to give them to Harding when he came back, with or without Juaquin. Anything to get them off the boat. They probably carried the bad luck of Cuba with them.

Asher sniffed the air in the direction of the kitchen. "That smells good. What is it?"

Migdala walked past him, out the door, and stood looking in the direction of the town as if expecting her daughter to finally appear on the road. Scheutz went out and stood beside her. "You mind if Asher and I eat, quickly? Then we can hop in the Volvo and make a tour of the island, maybe catch sight of her someplace."

She turned to look first at his chest and then raised her eyes to his, her face softened from her usual take-care-of-business mold, now almost tearful. "Yes. Let's do that. Eat quick; whatever you want. I will start the car. I cannot stand around here doing nothing."

Scheutz and Asher filled their plates with rice and beans, pork and a few plantanos. Just as they finished, Migdala came in, slamming the door, some of the old harshness back in her face and her movements. "Instead of the car, can we take your small boat out to the far reach of Punta Aloe? And then we can go along the outside coastline of the island?"

Scheutz stood to carry his empty plate and silverware to the sink behind the counter. "I suppose. If that would make more sense."

She grabbed his plate. "Leave this. Come on." She set the plate on the table and, waving for Asher to follow, pulled Scheutz's arm to lead him out the door. Asher gobbled another quick mouthful and hurried after them.

Scheutz asked, "Don't you want to lock the door, let patrons know the restaurant is closed?"

"I never lock the door on this island. They know. "

Asher handled the outboard as they hugged the southern shore of the bay, Migdala sitting in the bow, scanning the road as if her daughter might just be strolling there with that way she had, as if there was no such thing as time, or hurricanes. When they reached beyond the road, Migdala signaled to keep going until the boat left the entrance to the bay and Asher maneuvered through the shallows between the coral reefs. It made no sense to look for the girl out there. What could they possibly see? When it finally became almost too dark to see anyone moving on the land, they turned back in through the channel and made their way along the north shore of the bay.

Suddenly, Asher cut the throttle on the outboard and nosed in toward the edge of the water. "Look up there." He pointed.

Migdala jerked her head around in the same birdlike movement it had made when he first met her. "What are you looking at?"

"Isn't that your uncle's van sitting up there?"

Scheutz peered through the failing light, trying to see what Asher pointed at. When the bow of the boat touched the shoreline, Migdala jumped onto the land and ran towards the van, visible now, parked at a slant and pointing uphill. The area had been the site of the old US Navy base until the early 1970s. A concrete ramp ran down to the water's edge and the paved road ran up the hill to where the water desalination plant had been built during the Navy's time. Scheutz followed Migdala ashore, leaving Asher to tend to the dinghy.

They walked around the van, which was empty and locked. Locking a car door was unusual on the island since no one ever worried about things being stolen. Stealing a car on the island was silly; where would you go? Maybe Juaquin, who spent most of his time in San Juan, locked his car door by habit.

Something was definitely not right. First, Juaquin and Harding did not show up to pick up the package of emeralds, and now Juaquin's van was parked in a place where it had no reason to be. Harding's boat lay anchored not far from the old Navy ramp leading into the water. "Well, my guess would be he's out on one of those boats. Somebody picked him up here." There was no dinghy tied to Harding's boat and no lights on.

"Why would Tio Juaquin be out on one of those boats. Those are all owned by gringos. And Tio Juaquin does not like gringos."

"He doesn't?"

"You could not tell that?"

"What about Harding?"

"You should hear what he says about Harding when he is not around. We should go. There is nothing here."

Back at the restaurant, Migdala called the island police station again to see if anyone had seen Blanca. The sound of the television came from their living quarters in the rear and she hurried through the door but came back a few minutes later to say that only Tapon was in there and he had not seen the girl. Migdala stood at the window staring out at the flamboyan tree that spread out over the fence at the edge of the yard and gave a red tint to the yellowish light of the street lamp. Every time a car passed on the road or someone appeared on the street at the bottom of the hill her head jerked in that direction.

Scheutz stood next to her. "Maybe she is with Juaquin."

"The thought of Blanca with Tio Juaquin always brings fear up from my stomach. I am so afraid he might just drive her onto the ferry in his van and take her back to San Juan. I told him—I shouted at him—if he ever tried that…" She shook her head, tears now in her eyes. "He worries about her all the time. He is always talking about Jesus to her. You should see him with her. It gives me the creeps. If he is just trying to bring her to Jesus, he tries too hard."

Out on the entrance to the bay two boats with running lights aglow motored in through the passage, one far behind the other. "You know… Asher and I ought to get back to our boat."

She turned from the window with a look that was almost pleading. "Okay." She nodded her head, but her unspoken appeal did not match her acceptance of them leaving.

Asher spoke from behind him. "Mister Clem, I can take the dinghy out to the boat and you help her. Everything almost done there, and the hurricane don't come to visit till tomorrow."

Migdala threw an expectant look from Asher to Scheutz. He couldn't really say no. "Okay, I'll stay for awhile."

Migdala smiled. "I'll give you a ride out there when we are done, if you want."

After Asher left, Migdala asked Scheutz to help her clean up the kitchen. "I have to keep moving." It occurred to Scheutz that the other person missing was Harding. Is it possible that Blanca might be with him? Or with him and Juaquin together? He didn't know Juaquin well enough to know what he might be doing with a fifteen-year-old girl, but he did know Harding well enough, and the image that popped into his mind made him shudder. He thought it best not to mention this idea to Migdala. That would really freak her out. Besides, if she was with Harding, on the one hand she would be safe from the hurricane, and on the other, they would have no chance of finding them tonight.

She prattled nervously as they worked. “I always like the way the sailboats look. They glide on the surface with no noise. Much better than boats with roaring engines, the ones that make a wake that slaps the little fishing boats against the dock. I have never been on a sailboat. Sometimes when I used to go out in the fishing boat with Tapon he would rig up his little sail, but that does not count.”

“Sure it does. It’s still sailing.”

“I would like sometime to go out on that big boat of yours. Could we do that?”

“Yeah. We’ll bring Blanca and Tapon, and sail over to Vieques for the day.”

She nodded, her lips in a tight line. Then she talked on as if to keep from thinking about where her daughter might be. She told him about riding in Tapon’s boat when she was a very tiny girl. She’d felt so grown up because she was able to control her fear of the water rushing by and sit up straight with her face to the wind. It was the same thrill, she said, she’d felt on her first flight to New York as the American Airlines airbus circled for a landing at Kennedy Airport and she’d watched the lights of New York City below her. She’d sat straighter in her seat and even reached her hand to comfort the middle-aged Puerto Rican woman next to her who was audibly praying to God for a safe landing. She stopped what she was doing and looked up in the direction of the bay as if she’s heard something. After a moment she shook her head. “Whenever Tio Juaquin starts that Jesus stuff, I want to give him a good slap.” He waited for her to continue but she went back to work.

Scheutz helped her close the wooden shutters on the front windows. They felt flimsy but should be able to hold the wind out. She turned out the lights and they left through the rear door into the apartment behind the restaurant. The living room, with a narrow hallway across from the entrance, was furnished like many houses Scheutz had seen in the islands, small but clean and comfortable. Besides the hall, a door opened to a tiny bedroom and another door opened to a bathroom. The walls were sparsely decorated with an unusual lack of Christian art. An array of photographs adorned a side bureau, showing a much younger Migdala and Tapon, Blanca’s grade school portrait, another very formal portrait of Juaquin and a woman who Scheutz took to be Migdala’s mother. Tapon sat on the vinyl-covered sofa watching the television, nursing a can of Medalia beer. A San Juan station weatherman showed the path of the hurricane, Hugo, moving north from St. Croix.

Tapon raised a beer can as if in salute and spoke to Scheutz. "This one es muy mal. The wind is one-hundred-eighty miles an hour."

"Where is Blanca?" Migdala threw at him. He shrugged without taking his eyes off the screen. She led Scheutz down the hall and out a rear door where she began banging window shutters louder than necessary to close them. "My grandfather." She shook her head. "He considers himself officially retired from business since I came back from New York. It just bothers me that he does not give me a hand once in a while. And he pays no attention to Blanca at all."

"He looks pretty old. What is he, at least eighty?"

"Hah. He is ninety. But he still has plenty of energy to help Sharkie with his old boat. And I have seen him dancing at the El Batey bar down on the coast road."

They finished the shutters and he helped her pile the outdoor benches together and tie them down with ropes she produced out of the back of the Volvo. "And I am so upset at Blanca. She is supposed to help at the restaurant, but nooo. She has to go every day and hang out with her friends. This is not the first time she does not come home."

Just as they were going back inside, the island's one police cruiser pulled into the driveway. The officer who Scheutz knew as Raul Otero stepped from the car. With its shiny belt and holster, he sported a tight, short-sleeved blue uniform shirt that showed off his muscular arms. "Ay, mamacita, como estas?" He grinned at her as he approached, his white teeth flashing in his dark, handsome face.

"Bien. ¿Y tu? Have you seen Blanca?"

"No." He gave a little laugh. "Every time I see you, you're looking for your daughter. You should let up a little. I'll keep her out of trouble. That's what I'm paid for, you know?"

"I can't help it. I worry. And there is a hurricane coming."

"I remember when you and I were that age. Dios mio, the trouble we did, eh? That's why you worry. Because you know." He flexed his knees with a little dance step and laughed, dropping his shoulders and wagging his head. A moment later, he straightened again, clearing his throat and looking authoritatively at Scheutz.

Her voice softened, talking to the policeman. "Blanca is not like we were. She is shy and she does not know how to keep herself out of trouble."

"Hah." Raul slid his eyes over at her, smiled and shook his head. "There is nothing shy about that girl." Migdala looked away from him, out toward the bay. Something unspoken existed between them; that much Scheutz could tell. Had they once been lovers; or were they now?

Otero walked back to his car. "Well, I got a lot to do. I just wanted to let you know that Blanca is not in the center of town. Besides, everyone is very busy closing up their houses and they would send her home if she was there." He got in the cruiser, waving to Migdala and ignoring Scheutz's presence.

Stepping back into the house, they heard a small noise coming from behind a closed door that led off the hallway. Migdala looked at Scheutz with her eyes wide. She opened the door to what was obviously the girl's bedroom, a small windowless room with clothes scattered everywhere. Blanca sat on the edge of the bed, staring at the floor. Migdala threw the door open wide and stepped into the room. "How long have you been here?" The girl did not look up or answer, but sat as if mesmerized by the bottom of the doorframe. "Blanca, answer me. Where have you been all day? How long have you been home?"

Blanca's body did not move other than to raise her eyes to meet Migdala's. Tears welled in her eyes and a sob convulsed her chest. Migdala went to sit on the bed next to her. "Blanca, carina, que te pasa? What's the matter? What's wrong?" Migdala hugged the girl to her breast. With her head on Migdala's shoulder, Blanca began to shake with sobs. Migdala held her, looking up at Scheutz with both relief and concern on her face. The girl stopped crying and then, with a groan, as if some new pain inflicted her, took up sobbing again. Migdala held her and let her cry, alternating between murmuring comfort and asking over and over what the matter could be. Blanca did not say a word, and did not look up again into Migdala's face. But she did allow herself to be held and rocked without squirming away. Scheutz left them and walked into the living room.

The old man on the sofa mumbled something Scheutz did not catch. His plastic glass smelled like rum. Scheutz realized the old man was drunk, his Spanish garbled, his hand wavering as it pointed at the weatherman on the television. Blanca's sobbing could still be heard from her room down the hall. Poor Migdala. She sure had a lot to contend with, a drunken grandfather, an apparently brokenhearted daughter, a crooked Jesus-freak uncle, running a restaurant alone. And a hurricane coming. Samantha had said she felt her life had no consequence, floating around the Caribbean on a big boat. Each of these women would probably trade places with the other.

Or maybe not. But the Puerto Rican woman seemed to be getting the best of the comparison. All the hassle in her life gave Migdala a feeling of substance and consequence that Samantha did not have. Then again, Samantha had never had the heaviness of consequence about her. That's what attracted him to her, the light, easy laugh, the playfulness, the willingness to run off and do whatever they felt like doing on the spur of the moment. Samantha was a perpetual vacation. Of course, as he'd heard someone point out years ago, if every day is a vacation, all that fun eventually turns into hard work.

Blanca's crying slowed to muffled sobs. Migdala eventually closed the door and came down the hall to the living room. "Something's wrong. I'm worried. I've never seen her like this."

"Mad crush on a boy?"

She wrinkled her nose and shook her head. "I don't think so. This is different. Something happened."

Tapon sat with his head tilted against the back of the sofa. He turned to hear what Migdala had to say and then, turned back to the television. The weatherman kept up his patter, drawing lines with a marker on the big map behind him. Hugo's wind speed had dropped a little but her course held steady toward Puerto Rico.

"She's not hurt physically, is she?"

"No. I checked her for bruises."

Tapon let out a loud snore. Migdala walked over and turned off the television set. "Can you help me get him into bed?" They lifted the old man by his armpits and drag-walked him into the bedroom across from Blanca's, where they lifted him onto his bed. Back in the living room, she thanked him for helping her as much as he had.

"Well, I really didn't do much. I mean other than help clean up the kitchen."

"You have no idea. It's just nice sometimes to have someone around who is sane." She stood in the middle of the hall, spread her hands toward the two bedroom doors and raised her eyebrows. "I don't get much of that around here."

"Well, I guess I better get back to the boat."

"I'm sorry but I don't think I can drive you. I'm afraid to leave her alone."

"I guess I could walk."

"I'm sorry. Or you could stay here."

"That depends on what you mean by 'stay here'."

Her face flushed. "I mean you could sleep here on the sofa."

They stood in the hallway, facing each other. Had it only been that morning since he'd seen Samantha off on the ferry? Depending on what time her flight to Boston took off, she might not have made it home to New Hampshire yet. "You know, sleeping on your sofa is actually not a bad idea."

Chapter 7

He woke to the sound of the television accompanying the thin dawn light and the sound of roosters filtering through the shuttered windows. The weatherman on the screen talked at a rapid pace. Hugo had a heading of 300 degrees and moved at about twenty knots toward St. Thomas and the eastern Puerto Rican islands. Tapon was standing in front of the television, shaking his head. "Es muy mal." Migdala came from Blanca's room, her face tight, but then relaxed into a smile as she went into the bathroom.

By the time Scheutz was finished in the bathroom, Migdala and Tapon had gone into the restaurant. He followed and took a seat across from the old man who pointed to a place just above Scheutz's head and nodded as if about to impart some piece of wisdom. "I have been through some hurricanes."

Migdala brought a tray with three cups of coffee and heated milk. She sat next to her grandfather. "I've never been through a hurricane out here, but I was inside my mother's apartment in Santurce during one. I remember watching it from the window of the apartment building. Trees and a bicycle and even a table went flying by. It was fascinating. I got filled with excitement."

Scheutz sipped his coffee. Asher should be okay on the boat. He certainly would not want to be anywhere else during a hurricane. And he would have everything he needed. "Do you have enough food, and water bottles here?" he asked Migdala.

Migdala paused and turned toward the kitchen, thought for a moment and turned back. "Yes."

"And matches?"

"And beer?" Tapon wanted to know.

"Yes. Yes. Don't worry, you can still get a drink in the middle of the hurricane." She smiled at her grandfather, poking his arm and making him almost spill his coffee. The tension in her face earlier had slipped and, now the worry over the whereabouts of her daughter was over, her mood had lightened. "I'm looking forward to the big blow."

Scheutz shook his head and sipped his coffee. "I'm not. I was in a hurricane once, between Bermuda and the Bahamas. Not fun, I'll tell you. Scared the hell out of me, bouncing around inside that hull, expecting any minute for the thing to break apart or go heading for the bottom."

Migdala laid a hand on his forearm. "I have an idea. Why don't you stay in the house with us? That way you don't have to be bouncing around in your boat out there. You can ask your first mate to come here, too, if he wants."

"Asher would rather be on the boat, I'm sure." But would she be all right here taking care of her daughter and her grandfather who did not look strong enough to get them out of a jam if they needed it? Maybe he should stay.

"I would feel safer if you were here. Especially, since Tio Juaquin deserted us."

Tapon nodded his head at Scheutz. "You stay. That son of mine is a bum sometimes."

"How is Blanca this morning?"

Migdala shrugged. "She is awake. But she will not come out of her room. She just lies in her bed, staring at the wall."

"At least you know where she is."

"But what could cause her to cry like that?"

He gave her a dopey teenager look. "Love."

Migdala shrugged again. "Maybe. I cried when I was in love. At her age it happened almost every week. I fall in love and he breaks my heart because he would rather shoot hoops with his friends. It doesn't change much." She sipped her coffee.

The front door opened and a man and woman walked in. Migdala turned to tell them she was closed till after the hurricane had passed. "I have enough to think about without cooking breakfast." The woman nodded and they turned and left.

Scheutz stepped outside to get a look at the bay, filled with boats. His own boat looked so calm sitting there at anchor, the dinghy still tied to the wooden boarding ladder that ran down the starboard side. The air gave a strange greenish-gold tint to the morning light, making it hard to believe that a ferocious storm advanced their way. The only clouds were thin wisps very high up. The wind on his face seemed normal enough, but the water in the bay, out near the passage, showed small white caps. The bay looked so crowded with boats that, from his vantage on the hill, there didn't seem to be room for any of them to keep from banging into each other.

He could make out Juaquin's van still sitting in the parking lot of the old naval base. It was odd enough that his van was out there, but that it had been left overnight was even odder. Nothing looked to be stirring on Harding's boat. Could they both have gone somewhere on someone else's boat?

By ten o'clock the wind had picked up to forty knots, according to Tapon who watched the weatherman on television. Tapon gave them a short essay on how the forty-knot winds were not part of the actual hurricane. Migdala stopped to listen to him. "The world's greatest expert on hurricanes in the Caribbean. I wish he was a little more of an expert on running a restaurant." Tapon continued on, telling them that the winds and the choppy seas were just smaller disturbances at the edge of the hurricane.

Raul Otero showed up again, rushing in, out of breath, wearing his uniform and a raincoat. He had been sent to bring the older people down to take shelter in the school building. Tapon shook his head and said he would be fine; he did not consider himself an older person and besides, he needed to help watch the restaurant.

Otero grinned at Migdala. "Why don't you come? We could go out to Flamenco beach for a picnic." She waved him away. "Ever have a picnic in the middle of a hurricane?" he said. "It's mondo cool." He wagged his head as he left. "We could have a comeda grande." She laughed and shooed him further out the door.

Scheutz helped Tapon tie down the Volvo and Tapon's small rowboat that lay upside down in the yard. The first wind would be coming from the direction of the bay, Tapon said, so they should open the windows and the door on the opposite side of the house. This was so the pressure didn't build up inside and collapse the walls. After the eye passes over, they had to remember to close those windows and open up the ones in the front. He had learned these things from experiencing so many hurricanes in his life.

Scheutz could feel a popping in his eardrums. Dogs all over the barrio had set up a yelping. Tapon pointed for them to listen to the dogs. "From change in the air pressure." Wind gusts came and went, but the water down in the bay kept up a steady pounding, bouncing the crowded boats like a party of drunken wingless ducks.

Scheutz's anxiety increased as the hurricane neared. It didn't seem to bother Tapon, though. And Migdala appeared too preoccupied with Blanca. He started obsessing about the schooner; would it be okay? Would Asher be okay? In his mind, he ran over everything they had done the day before to see if they had missed anything. He knew he could trust Asher to think of everything, and that he should not get too uptight about it, but that didn't stop him from going over the same things again and again. He tried to imagine himself and Samantha, as the policeman had joked, having a picnic out on Flamenco beach in the middle of a howling wind. Only it wasn't Samantha whose naked body he imagined wrapped around him. He imagined the woman who now sat across from him trying to get her daughter to eat something. Tapon concentrated on the television screen. And Migdala's attention did not leave her daughter's face.

Hugo smashed into the island of Culebra at noontime. It came with torrents of rain and lightening. The electricity on the island had gone out long before the transformers started to blow. First the electric transformer on the road along the bay blew with a loud bang from the air pressure. Then the transformer just outside the restaurant popped, making Migdala jump and let out a small squeaking scream like a cartoon damsel afraid of a mouse. She turned to give Scheutz an embarrassed chuckle just as Blanca screamed, the first real sound out of her all day. Migdala went to hug her, but the girl's body stiffened against her.

Tapon said it would be best to stay in the bathroom when the storm hit. The tiled walls and fixtures made it the sturdiest room in the house. Scheutz and Migdala carried in mattresses and a few pillows. Tapon lay down on one mattress in the tub. Migdala and Blanca sat on one end of a mattress on the floor and Scheutz on the other.

They waited, not talking much. Migdala pulled her daughter close to her side and stretched one hand into the bathtub to touch her grandfather's shoulder. "Where is Juaquin?"

The old man shrugged. "I think he has maybe gone on the ferry. He always goes to your mother's house in Santurce when the hurricane comes." As Tapon talked, the wind outside began to shriek. Blanca let out a moan and begin crying again, pulling away from her mother. Scheutz lit one of the votive candles Migdala had brought into the bathroom, and set it on the closed lid of the toilet. He sat with his back against the bathroom door. Now there was nothing to do but wait.

Scheutz lost track of time as the storm raged around them. The candle burnt down and Migdala lit another one. The house shook on its foundation like something bounced by a spiteful child, with creaking and tearing sounds but nothing being pulled away. Blanca lay on the mattress, silent but for an occasional sob. Tapon extracted two quarts of Bacardi rum from behind the bathtub, saying this sounded like it was going to be a two-quart storm. He tilted one of the bottles and drank, then handed it to Migdala. She took it. "What the hell, we could all be dead in the next hour."

The slug of rum Scheutz pulled from the bottle burned all the way down to his stomach. This was obviously not commercial rum, but island rum poured into used Bicardi bottles. The sugar cane cutters on the main island brewed this stuff for themselves. He and Migdala both coughed and he brought the bottom of his t-shirt up to rub his watering eyes. Tapon laughed. The wind howled.

Scheutz's gaze rested on Migdala sitting across the mattress from him holding onto her daughter. In the candlelight, her features were, as she watched her daughter, softer than he had ever seen them. Yes, there was the tint of worry there, but her concern for the girl seemed almost infectious. The rum in his belly changed from a burning to a mild warmth. Whether it was the rum or Migdala's concern, he found himself worrying about the girl. Or was he just getting concern for her mixed up with the feelings that had risen the night before while standing in the hallway with Migdala, feelings that only increased as he lay on the sofa trying to sleep. Was that the reason he had agreed to stay on at the house here instead of returning to the boat?

Now, with the storm raging outside, Scheutz relaxed as much as he could and tried again to let his thoughts drift. Migdala had told him that their bathroom was one of the very few on the island that had a bathtub. Most had shower stalls made from tin or some just a curtain ring in the corner. Her grandmother had insisted on putting the tub in a few years before she died, when she could no longer stand up in a shower. Tapon would carry her into the bathroom and undress her and place her in the tub, then sit on the toilet lid and tell her funny stories while she soaked.

Migdala watched her grandfather's face in the candlelight as he sipped the rum and lay back on the mattress. Scheutz thought about what it would be like to live with a woman for that many years, as the old man had done, and take care of her when she was as old as Tapon was now. That's what he had wanted with Gerry, his wife, the mother of his sons. Samantha, he had to admit, was a lark, a seven-year lark, but a lark nonetheless. Lark was a good word. Being with her was like hearing a lark singing in a meadow. But, like a lark's song, Samantha's very nature was so ethereal. She floated over the world like the song over a meadow. She was gone now and he was in no way sure she was ever coming back. And if she did…? When Tapon passed him the rum bottle again, he sipped and savored the taste in his mouth.

The afternoon wore on. The wind shrieked, making it hard to hear what the others were saying. The bathroom stayed fairly stable even though the structure around it, the rest of the house and restaurant, moved as if they were on a boat at sea. But at sea there was a rhythm to the waves that crashed against the hull. A wooden house in a strong wind moved erratically. A boat moved in unison with itself. A house, at least this house, felt as if it were being pulled apart at the foundation and the roof. The mattress Scheutz sat on leaned against the bathroom door and he could feel wisps of air leak in around it, bringing small pieces of floating grit. Tapon drank himself to sleep. Blanca alternated between whimpering in her mother's arms and sitting, staring at nothing. When she vomited into the toilet, Scheutz was surprised that it still flushed.

Migdala wiped the girl's mouth as if she were a small child. This seemed to be such unusual behavior for a fifteen-year-old, letting her mother treat her like a child. Scheutz wondered if this was usual for the girl, or if there was something else wrong, something besides the hurricane, something bigger than a teenage crush. He didn't fancy himself an expert on teenage behavior but he did have some experience with his own kids and all their friends—yes, including Samantha—who spent their high school years hanging around that house in New Hampshire. But what he was seeing in this girl, especially a girl as normally high-spirited and sassy as this one, almost looked like some trauma had happened that she was not talking about. If something bad happened within the last day or so, Otero, the cop would have said something when he stopped by. Then his mind jumped again to Juaquin and Harding and the van sitting out there new the desalination plant. Migdala had said something connecting Blanca with Harding. If that son of a bitch did something to this girl, he'd go after him himself.

As the wind peaked Migdala caught Scheutz's eye and held it with a look of abject terror in them. She reached her hand across the mattress and took his, holding it tightly and looking back to her daughter who cringed against her side. Scheutz took the hand and held it firmly in his own, feeling the strength it gave as well as what it took from his hand. The rum must have gone to his head because he began to feel that the bathroom had pulled loose from its mooring of cement foundation and water pipes and revolved slowly, ascending into the air as if attached to a weather balloon. He pulled his body close to the woman and the three of them crouched there holding on to one another while the wind tugged at the world outside them and the old man snored lightly in the bathtub.

Late in the afternoon, the wind stopped. Tapon startled from his sleep and exclaimed, "The eye is here." Scheutz moved his mattress to open the door.

Migdala untangled herself from her daughter's arms. She staggered slightly as she stood. "Ay, que Dios, I must be drunk on that rum." Together, she and Scheutz ran into the living room. He closed the back door and shutters on the windows while she opened the windows and the door on the opposite side. Scheutz rolled up the Volvo's passenger windows and rolled down the driver's side in the front and back. Inside, of course, the car was soaked, but it was better than having the windows blown out. He went back through the house and stepped out in front to see what the storm had done so far. Out over the bay, the boats anchored there, or those no longer anchored, looked to be in total confusion in the waning light. The Panacea appeared to have moved and listed far to starboard. He left off trying to see what shape she was in and walked around to inspect the edges of the restaurant's roof. The roof seemed okay so far, but the entire house itself had shifted about a foot off the foundation. A shiver ran up his spine. Except for his fantasy about the bathroom spinning in space, he had not felt the house shift when inside.

Tapon appeared beside him, laughing. "The wind from the backside of the hurricane will always be worse. Maybe it will push the house back in place." He staggered slightly as he went to check on his rowboat and then stepped back inside.

It was getting too dark to make out anything other than shapes in the bay. A sudden bolt of lightening lit the horrifying scene below. As if a huge tidal wave had come in, water covered the road and flooded houses along the shore. Boats lay scattered everywhere, on their sides, on top of houses, on top of each other. Only after another lightning bolt was he sure of what he had seen. In the third flash, he saw to his left the back of Blanca's pink blouse as the girl walked slowly and quietly toward the paved road.

Migdala shouted and ran, grabbing at her. Scheutz went to help. Migdala screamed at her daughter. "This is only the eye. You can't go out. The back wind is coming." She took hold of the girl's arm just as she reached the tarmac, but Blanca yanked away. When Migdala grabbed for her again, she turned and ran. Scheutz ran after her, caught her, with his arm around her waist, in the middle of the road. He and Migdala had just begun to pull the girl back to the house when the back wind of the hurricane hit pulling Migdala and Blanca away from him and onto the opposite side of the road against the chain link fence in front of their neighbor's yard.

Migdala dragged Blanca to the ground and covered her daughter's body with her own. The wind pinned them against the fence like flies on a screen door. Scheutz launched himself across the road to fall on top of them. Tiny particles of sand and dirt and salt water pelted their bodies. Larger pieces, leaves, twigs, splinters of wood smashed against them. The wind blew straight across the hillside as if whirling inside the bowl of the hills around the bay, coming from directly where they wanted to go, back to the house. Beneath them, Blanca seemed to have lost all her struggle and defiance. With Scheutz's head close to the girl's, he could hear Blanca's terrified gasps over the sound of the wind.

They could not stay where they were, they'd be killed. He had to get them out of the wind, back into the house. He nodded to Migdala to start pulling Blanca back to the edge of the road, but they could not move against the wind. Maybe they could find the gate to the fence and let themselves be blown toward the house behind it. But, from what he could make out of the shadows in the gathering darkness, the house behind the fence was no longer there. He could barely see the foundation, and the house itself was gone.

With the girl between them, her arms around her mother's waist, Migdala shouted in Blanca's ear to hold tight. Noticing the wind had a tendency to push up hill, Scheutz moved them as a unit along the surface of the road on their knees at an uphill angle to the house. In the middle of the road he forced himself to his feet and pulled the other two to the rear of the Volvo, then dragged them along the side of the car, holding onto the door handles, his face turned away from the debris carried on the wind. At the front of the car, he took hold of the back of both Migdala's and Blanca's blouses and pushed them before him in a run for the house. When he opened the screen door, the wind tore it from its hinges and blew it away toward the road. He pressed against the house, holding Migdala and Blanca against his lee side as Migdala pounded on the door.

Tapon opened it and said, "Sorry, no Jehovah Witness today."

"Pendejo." Migdala screamed at him, pushing the door against him and sending him stumbling backwards to fall onto the hall floor. The wind slammed into the house behind them, pushing Migdala and Blanca on top of Tapon. It screamed into the hallway, smashing lamps and wall hangings and a chair against the living room walls. Scheutz was forcing the door closed when a great ripping, tearing noise exposed them to the wind and rain coming. The roof moved, lifted on one end, wavered like a clamshell opening and shutting. Lightning flashed as the roof stood straight up in the air still attached. It hung there, or stood there, for a long moment before finally tearing away and tumbling backward toward the road. Migdala and Blanca both screamed. Tapon, half-upright, braced himself against the wind, holding his arm in front of his face to protect against flying debris. Scheutz heaved his body against the door till it closed and then herded the three others back into the bathroom. Migdala and Tapon forced the door closed. They pulled the mattress from the tub to arrange it above the sink and the edge of the tub to form a kind of shelter for them to crawl under. Rain poured in through the opening above their heads. Wind whipped at them but lost force in the small space of the room. Migdala squeezed Blanca into the middle between herself and Tapon and held up the soggy, sagging mattress for Scheutz to climb under.

They sat with their heads holding up the end of the mattress. It was stuffy under there and they were all drenched, but it seemed relatively safe, at least until something else happened. Tapon felt around outside the mattress and found the unopened bottle of rum. He drank and passed it to Migdala in the now pitch black cave they'd made for themselves. Migdala took a good-sized swig, Tapon chuckled and she took another, before passing it to Scheutz.

"We will be fine now," Tapon said.

The mattress weighed on their heads. Both Scheutz's knees were skinned bloody, as was the upper part of his right arm. The rum mixed with the taste of salt water that ran down his face and coated his lips. But Tapon was right—they were going to be all right now. They could wait out the rest of the storm right where they were. He drank again from the bottle and nudged Tapon's arm with it. The old man slurped a loud drink, belched and gave one of his deep, rumbling laughs. A small, frightened giggle escaped from Blanca, hidden under Migdala's armpit. Then Migdala laughed and Scheutz found himself laughing with them.

Chapter 8

The schooner lay at a thirty-degree angle on its port side. To reach it Scheutz took hold of a stanchion on the port side of another sailboat laying uphill from the schooner, and then hoisted himself off the ground onto the tangled life-line attached to the stanchion, then onto the slanted deck, up over the cabin to the starboard side, and from there jumped down onto the metal deck of the next boat, also a sailboat, lying next to the *Panacea*. The wooden hull of his schooner towered over the other two boats. It looked as if the schooner had pushed the other two boats, beam to beam, up onto the shore, stopping with its own hull in about six feet of water. Torn vegetation and man-made equipment, rigging cables, cushions, broken pieces of decking, tangled lines, and a shredded spinnaker littered the hillside, the shoreline and the boats themselves.

He climbed a pile of debris on the sloop's deck, its single mast crinkled and bent two-thirds of the way up, the shrouds sagging limp and broken. From the deck he stepped onto a makeshift wooden ladder someone, probably Asher, had placed there. Once on the schooner, he walked uphill on the slanting deck to the starboard rail, looking for what might be broken. Both masts appeared to be intact, their shrouds sagging with the exaggerated tilt of the deck. The bowsprit looked fine from what he could see. Same with the doghouse, binnacle, and taffrail.

The dinghy with the outboard motor in place floated placidly next to the schooner's hull, a painter line drooping from its bow up to the starboard rail of the larger boat. Asher must be aboard if the dinghy was here. He descended a rope ladder, which hung from the deck to the dinghy, stood in the dingy and hand-walked it along the line of the hull. The entire hull, both forward and aft looked to be in good shape, with nothing more than a few dings and scrapes in the wooden lapstrake.

Back up on deck, he relaxed against the rail. Great. His precious boat had weathered one of the worst storms it, would ever encounter. The day was beginning to warm, the sky as blue and cloudless as if denying that there had ever been such a thing as a hurricane, the water in the bay stretched like polished linoleum to the opposite shore, its surface broken in many places by the mast or upturned hull of some less lucky boat. Along the shore in both directions, and into the tangled mass of mangroves, boats of all descriptions were strewn as if thrown by a large child in a temper tantrum. Many had been pushed onto the shore itself, but most, like the *Panacea,* had gone no further than the water's edge.

He made his way slowly till he reached the hatch just forward of the main mast. It opened easily and he leaned down in, calling, "Asher."

"Yessuh." The voice came from the darkness just below him.

"What're doing down there?"

"Napping."

"What'd you do, sleep through the whole thing?"

Asher's dark, upturned face appeared, and Scheutz moved back away from the hatch as the man climbed to the deck. Asher rubbed his eyes and looked around. "Going to be a nice day."

"You okay?"

"Oh, yes."

"So, did you sleep through it all?" Scheutz teased.

Asher laughed. "I tried, but Yemaya kept waking me up. Had to bring the boat ashore to get away from her."

"You brought it ashore?"

Asher laughed again. "Well, no. Yemaya did. She get mad at me and push us out there." He pointed toward the entrance to the bay. "Then she still not happy and she push us back."

"But you're okay?"

"No, I am not okay. I drank no coffee yet today."

"And the boat is okay, yeah?"

Asher leveled a long look at him, then slowly shook his head.

"It looks all right to me," Scheutz said.

Asher waved his hand for Scheutz to follow him and then descended again through the open hatch. Pools of sunlight from the starboard portholes in the main cabin showed them a jumble of materials, lumber, sailing gear, the table saw, the drill press. They climbed over a scattered pile of lumber until they reached the bulkhead separating the main cabin from the two aft cabins. Asher waved his hand again, indicating a large hole in the hull, a splintered mess on the port side. A gray rock showed its ugly head through the mess of broken planks. One of the ship's massive ribs had been broken clear through and now-splintered timbers that had formed the bulkhead wall encased the head of the rock. At least two feet of mucky water lay along the entire inside of the port hull.

Scheutz stared at the rupture, numbed by it. Eventually, he backed up and sat on a pile of boards, looking from Asher to the hole in his boat and then back to Asher. A thought passed through his head quickly—why hadn't Asher protected the boat the way Scheutz inanely expected he might? Asher leaned against the lumber pile, his face impassive, waiting for Scheutz to say something. But he could not, could do nothing but gaze at the rock and the timber. What would the smashed hull mean? How could they possibly deal with fixing it, on no money? His mind could not wrap itself around this dilemma. One thing was sure; life would never be the same from here on. A pun raised its stupid head—I guess this is what they call a sea-change.

"Here's what we got to do," Asher said. He climbed down the angle of the deck to wade in the knee-deep water next to the protruding rock. "We got to winch the boat upright and then…"

Scheutz waved his hand for Asher to hush up. "I can't even think about it right now. Give me some time for it to sink in. Let's talk about it tomorrow." He put his head in his hands and stared at the boards beneath his feet, trying to calm himself. What would Samantha say about this? He couldn't even call her until the phone service was restored in town, which could be several days. Actually, he was afraid of what she would say. Even before they left St. Thomas she was complaining about how this boat had become an albatross for them. This hole in the hull just might push her over the edge, and she might never come back.

Well, whether she came back or not, he still had to make himself start thinking about what to do about the boat. But not today. Today he'd just let it sit on his mind. Tomorrow, he and Asher would start talking about their options. Maybe it was a good thing he couldn't reach Samantha; her solution would be to scrap the damned thing. And that was not an option. There was no insurance, and FEMA certainly did not help rebuild boats. Unless of course, he could say this was a business. What would he do, tell them he made a living smuggling computers into Cuba? Maybe he could sell the emeralds.

What about the emeralds? They would still be safe in their hidey-hole. Maybe he could "borrow" a few of them for a while and pay Juaquin back later. No, better to just leave them where they are and give them to Juaquin when he came back from wherever he was. Then again, he could always just say they had been lost during the hurricane; that would be a believable lie. No, he'd know that wasn't true and it would bother him. They were not his gems. He remembered something his father recited once—one the very few moral things he could ever accuse his father of—"That man may be drunk, it may be true, but that diamond pin don't belong to you. So let it alone son, let it alone."

"I can't sit here like this." He stood and lifted the table saw which leaned at a crazy angle, blocking passage to the stern companion way. "Let's take the dinghy and go into town. Or somewhere. See how much damage was done."

Asher nodded and pulled himself away from the broken planking. "We better go out through the forward hatch. We cannot get out this way." He led the way back through.

Just forward of the galley, an edge of sail had spilled from the sail locker. "I have an idea," Scheutz said as Asher made to climb to the deck. "Come help me get this mizzen sail into the dinghy."

"What for?"

"That restaurant in town had its roof blown off and I thought maybe we could loan them a sail to make a temporary roof."

Asher nodded and waggled his head. "Ya, ya. I know what you say. That sail probably bigger than the restaurant." He grinned at Scheutz. "And that woman sure is damned pretty."

"No, nothing like that. I wouldn't do that to Samantha."

"Ya, mon, but Samantha would do that to you."

"What do you mean?"

"Nothing. I didn't say nothing. Grab hold the sail over there. Help me pull."

They hauled the mizzen out of its cubby and wrestled it through the hatch to the upper deck. "You wrap it up better," Asher said. "And I'll put some coffee on."

"We can get coffee in town."

"Huh. They ain't no coffee in town. Where you going to go? This restaurant ain't got no roof. You think any of them other places going to have their electricity on?"

"I guess you're right," Scheutz said. He stretched out the sail as Asher went below. When he had finished folding it into as tight a roll as could be made, he sat on it and waited, catching the aroma of the coffee boiling on the gimbled propane stove. The smell of the coffee was the first sign since the day before when the hurricane moved in that the world he knew still existed. He tried to remove the image of the boulder below protruding through the hull of the schooner by looking out over the bay, but the devastation of that view was, if anything, even more depressing than the boulder.

He had to stop this kind of thinking. They would put the boat back together, he and Asher. Asher would stick with him. It was all the same to him—work, play, at sea, on land, all only minor differences to that man, who never seemed to want anything more than what he had at the moment. And what more did Scheutz want? Well, for openers, he wanted Samantha to come back. And then what? So, she came back and they patched up the *Panacea*, and…and then what? Could they go back to that life of drifting around the Caribbean picking up odd jobs for money to survive until the next odd job. There was a time when that felt like paradise, but—he had to admit Samantha was right—the last year or two, it had begun to really suck.

"Grab the cups." Asher's voice came up through the hatch. Scheutz reached down and took the two steaming mugs and carried them back to his perch on the rolled sail. Asher emerged on deck with a plate of half-burned toast and took a seat on the other end of the sail roll.

Scheutz sipped the hot coffee, reveling in its normality. He grabbed a piece of toast, folded it and dunked it into the cup. "So, tell me how this happened to the boat," he said to Asher.

Asher chewed his toast and then sipped from his cup. He turned and pointed to a line running from the main mast that Scheutz had not seen earlier. "Yemaya blow the boat out that way." He pointed to a spit of land that curved out from an inlet covered with broken mangrove where a large powerboat rested on its side. "She pull the anchors we have out and drag us over there. Then, when the eye come and Yemaya take a rest, I go down and tie the boat off to a tree on the land there. Sticker tree, got me stuck all on my arm." He pulled up the ragged sleeve of his faded blue shirt and showed Scheutz the punctures on the dark skin of his forearm.

"You mean an Acacia tree?"

"That what you call it? Well, it the only tree over there. Nothing there now. Then Yemaya come back the other way. I think she mad because she blow harder. Pull the damned tree out of the ground, slam into the other boats and push us back here. Bam, we push the other boat up on shore, and, bam, we hit the shore. Mon, I am bouncing all over inside there. You know when you play dice and you put the dice in the cup and shake it before you throw them. That dice is me, mon. And everything else down there that ain't tied off. I bang me head, I bang me knee. And then the boulder come inside the boat and yell at me. It go, 'Crunch, crunch, Yemaya send me for lunch.' I yell back at him, 'Hold the boat, mon.' And he do."

They drank coffee in silent contemplation of the boulder.

"And then what?' Scheutz said.

"And then it get dark."

"Were you scared?"

Asher thought about that and then shook his head. "No. We wasn't going nowhere. I go up forward, away from the boulder, crawl in my bunk. The bunk is dry. I let Yemaya do what she want to do. And I go to sleep."

"How could you sleep with all that?"

"The best thing, mon. When Yemaya being ignored, she go home. When I wake up, the sky is blue." He raised his hand with a half-eaten piece of toast in it and saluted the sky.

Scheutz looked from his outstretched hand to the line running from the mast and now noticed the tree that floated in the water ten yards out from the boat. "We should cut that tree off there."

"I don't touch that tree. Scratch me up like a cat do." Asher drank the last of his coffee. "I steer the dinghy, you cut the tree away." They carried the sail down the rope ladder into the dinghy and Asher started the outboard. "Going to need some line to tie her off with," Asher said as Scheutz climbed back up the ladder. He opened the main passage through the doghouse. Below, from the aft starboard cabin, he retrieved a large wooden toolbox that seemed to have weathered the storm intact. He lugged it to the deck rail and handed it down to Asher, then made his way to the forward hatch again, and down in search of line. With two tightly wrapped hanks of line, he perched himself in the bow of the dinghy as Asher steered them to the tree.

Scheutz cut the line attached to the Acacia and left it to dangle in the water until they returned from town. Asher turned the helm and they headed toward town, hugging the shore and trolling slowly, Scheutz in the bow keeping watch for floating debris or a submerged vessel that could entangle the outboard propeller. Moving between wrecked and some not-so-wrecked vessels, they worked their way to Harding's boat, which, strangely, floated peacefully at anchor, but still without its mast and rigging. Nothing had been repaired since they had towed it into the bay from St. Thomas. The broken bowsprit had been removed, Scheutz noticed. At Scheutz's signal, Asher came abreast of *Gaga's* transom. Scheutz yelled Harding's name but, receiving no answer, they continued on. On shore, exactly where it had been parked before the storm, Joaquin's white van sat next to the dirt road leading to the desalination plant, seemingly untouched by the hurricane winds, or by anything. Scheutz pointed out the van to Asher who nodded and made a "Go figure" gesture with his hands.

At the inlet closest to the restaurant, the planking of the little dock had blown away, only the posts protruded from the water. Asher cut the engine and Scheutz tied off to a post nearest the shore, while Asher stepped out into two feet of water to pull the stern of the dinghy up on land. Together they lifted the sail, each carrying a hank of line through the wind-mangled mangrove along a hard-packed and now debris-strewn path, coming out onto the road across from the small airport terminal.

The airport was devoid of aircraft, all the planes having been flown out before the hurricane hit. But loose pieces of building material, shrubbery, and an overturned jeep littered the runway. The wooden structure next to the terminal that housed a restaurant and bar seemed to have survived. Several men stood outside holding beer bottles and gesturing wildly to each other, much the way they did every Saturday night. Scheutz and Asher wove their way along the littered road, uphill, past the three cinderblock-built houses that appeared intact and the several wooden houses that had suffered varying degrees of insult. Some had doors and window shutters blown off, others were only half there, and even worse, other house sat totally crumpled into piles of large splinters. The house across the road from the restaurant had not only blown off its foundation, but had been pushed the entire length of the back yard so that it rested on its side against the chain link fence that still stood all the way around the property.

In the driveway at the back of the restaurant, Migdala sat in the Volvo trying to turn the engine over without much luck. The battery sounded as if it was just beginning to run down. When she saw Scheutz and Asher, she stepped out of the car.

"I brought a sail to cover the open roof." Scheutz lifted his end. "How's everything?"

Migdala nodded hello to Asher and then shrugged and shook her head. She waved her hand toward the house and gave a sigh. "I'm okay, but Blanca no es bien." She paused and looked at Scheutz and then at the rear of the house. "I don't know, the hurricane…Blanca just sits there staring at the wall and crying and then not crying and then crying." She shrugged again.

"She was doing that before the hurricane, wasn't she?"

"Yes, but I don't know, maybe she was afraid of it before it came?"

Scheutz shifted his weight from one foot to the other. There was nothing in the raising of his two sons that had any resemblance to what the woman was telling him about her daughter. There was nothing he could think of to say to her. Asher, holding up his end of the rolled sail, had nothing to add. He merely turned to look at the top of the roofless house. "If we going to drape the sail over the walls," he said. "We need to take off all those nails and pieces of broken wood so we do not rip the sailcloth."

Glad to have a problem he could do something about, Scheutz turned his attention away from Migdala to answer Asher. "If you go back and get the toolbox out of the boat, I'll find something we can stand on to get to the top of the walls."

Migdala led him inside the house. In the hallway, she opened the door to Blanca's room and leaned in. "Señor Scheutz is going to help us put a tent up, cariña, okay?" The girl sat on the edge of the bed, soaked though it was, just as she had sat the day before when they waited for the hurricane's arrival. The rest of the small room looked as if someone had taken a powerful fire hose to it; clothes, books, and furniture lay piled in soggy heaps, the floor holding puddles of water. The sun, though, filled the room with the brightness of a tanning booth. Blanca's eyes lifted to her mother's and dropped again to stare at the floor.

Migdala waited for her response and then said, "I'm going to leave the door open."

As she and Scheutz moved down the hallway toward the small living room, the door to Blanca's room closed very quietly.

The living room was empty except for the trashed, soggy furniture. Here too the sunlight poured in, as if mocking the dampness and the mess. The television had not moved at all but sat empty-screened, wet, and forlorn like the station wagon in the driveway.

"Where is your grandfather?" Scheutz asked.

"He's gone to look for Tio Joaquin. He's worried about him for some reason."

"I saw his van still sitting out there near the desalination plant where it was yesterday."

"I know. That's the problem. Tio Joaquin would never leave his van in a place like that. If he went to the main island, he would drive it onto the ferry because he would need it to go to San Juan." She shrugged. "I don't know, I'm not going to worry about Tio Joaquin. I have enough to worry about with that one in there." She waved toward Blanca's room.

"Well, let's see how we can get up to the top of the walls," Scheutz said. "I really doubt we can find a ladder anywhere.

"Come into the restaurant. We can take one of the tables and put a chair on it."

"Good thinking." They opened the door to front of the house. In the small restaurant they were greeted with a scene similar to the living room. Tables and chairs, artwork from the walls, all thrown about. But the drink cooler, not cool now, had resisted any attempts at moving it. Except for water everywhere, the kitchen seemed to be okay. Migdala had stored everything movable into cabinets and under the sink or inside the oven. There were a few palm fronds on the floor that must have blown in from the tree directly outside the kitchen, but other than that, the room appeared not much different than an army mess hall kitchen at the end the a day, everything scoured clean.

They tested each table to see which was the strongest and then carried one outside to place it against a wall. Migdala brought out a heavy wooden chair that Scheutz put on top of the table to stand on. "This'll work."

Migdala smiled up at him. "I am thankful that you can do this for us. Are you sure you don't need the sail for your boat?"

"We're not going anywhere for quite awhile." Over the top of the house he could see Asher walking into the driveway, the toolbox on his shoulder. "Tell Asher to bring the box around to the side here."

Migdala handed a hammer and crowbar up to Scheutz and then helped Asher set up a table and chair on the other side of the house. While the two men worked she set herself to clearing the mess inside the house. Scheutz worked his way along one wall, getting down to move the table as he finished each section. He pulled nails and levered off splintered wood. In places where the ceiling plate itself had splintered, he smoothed it roughly with a wood rasp. Asher worked at pretty much the same speed on the other side of the house.

Doing the outer wall around Blanca's room he could see her sitting there staring, reminding him of a small mouse traumatized by the big world. Migdala came into the room and asked Blanca to help her strip the wet sheets from the bed. The girl barely looked up at her mother, said nothing and made no move to even get out of the way, let alone help her. Both mother and daughter were dressed alike in shorts and white t-shirt. With the same colored hair, they could have been twins except that the girl's skin was paler. Migdala took her hands and pulled her daughter gently to her feet. The girl took two steps away from the bed to stand in the shade of the wall out of the glaring sunlight, her head lowered, shoulders drooped, and arms crossed in front of her, the most dejected thing Scheutz had ever seen.

He couldn't help making the comparison between Blanca and Samantha when she was that age. That was what—she was thirty-two now—sixteen years ago. And his son, Dan, was fifteen then as well. All those kids, just so filled with themselves. Marty was nine, obsessed with building car models the way Dan was obsessed with all the girls he'd just come to recognize as something other than alien beings. The memory of that house full of kids stopped him extracting a nail. As much work and worry as it had been taking care of those kids without their mother, he had to admit, it was the happiest time of his life. And looking down on this poor girl standing against the wall of her bedroom, he wished she had been one of the crowd of teenagers that gathered at his house then. She would have been very happy, no doubt about it.

Migdala finished stripping the bed and gathering piles of soggy clothes before Scheutz finished the top of the wall, and Blanca returned to the edge of the bed, staring at nothing.

When they were satisfied with the lack of roughness on the top of the outer and inner walls, Asher and Scheutz spread the tanbark-colored mizzen sail across the top, each one working the edge from the opposite side of the house. It covered almost fully but, because of its triangular shape, it did not cover the kitchen and a triangle section of the dining area of the restaurant. They looped a line through the grommets at the edges of the sail, zigzagging between the sail and wooden stakes made from large splinters they drove into the ground at the foot of each wall. When pulled tight, the sailcloth formed a flat tent roof, giving the interior an odd reddish light with the sun shining through the tanbark cloth.

The rest of the day was spent helping Migdala's neighbors clear debris from the road that ran from the bottom of the hill through the barrio to the top. The problem of the schooner festered in the back of his mind, breaking into his consciousness, the image of the boat breaking through like the rock that protruded through the hull.

In the late afternoon, Migdala succeeded in getting a cooking fire going in the side yard, using wood scraps dried by the sun. She warmed up already-cooked rice and beans that had been sitting in the refrigerator. It had only been a little over a day since the electricity had gone off and food was not yet spoiled. Asher passed around cans of warm Medalia beer and a Coca Cola for Blanca. Migdala brought Blanca out from her room to eat with them, but the girl touched nothing, her fork lax in her hand where it lay on the table. Scheutz tried to engage her in conversation; would she like to go with them down to the malecón after supper, if they could get the Volvo started? Blanca merely shrugged, glanced up once at her mother's face, then back to her plate.

After supper, Scheutz and Asher siphoned a little gas from the Volvo's tank to add directly to the carburetor. But the battery was too run down to turn the engine over. He and Asher pushed the car out into the road and faced it downhill. Scheutz drove while Asher gave the car a shove. It started as soon as he popped the clutch, but then died quickly. On the third try, halfway down the hill, the engine roared to life and then continued to idle as he pumped it, coasting with the clutch in the rest of the way down to the main road. He turned back up toward the house and, as he pulled into the driveway, the island's police jeep pulled in behind him.

Raul Otero got out, wearing jeans and t-shirt with his pistol belt buckled on. He nodded at Scheutz and Asher and went directly to the back door of the house, calling for Migdala to come out. She emerged with two more cans of Medalia, but stopped short when she saw the police officer. "Would you like a beer, too," she asked him.

He shook his head. "This is official business."

"What? Is Tapon all right?"

Otero held up his hand. "Your grandfather is fine." He shrugged. "Except that he just got some very bad news. That's what I came to tell you."

Migdala canted her head toward Blanca's room, then looked at Scheutz before focusing back on Otero's face. "Yes?"

"It's your uncle. They just found him. He's…um…he's dead."

Migdala's eyes widened and her mouth dropped open. "¿Tio Joaquin? ¿Esta muerto?"

Otero nodded solemnly and held out his hand to her as if to steady her if she needed it.

"¿Pero, porque? ¿Como?" she asked.

Otero paused, apparently choosing his words. "In a boat. They found the boat washed up on Cayo Norte. It was jammed between two trees with a bunch of wood and tree trunks and stuff."

"What kind of boat?" Scheutz asked.

Otero turned to him. "A rubber dinghy. I think it was an Avon. He was under the center seat. I guess it held his body from falling out. That's a good boat, you know. It did not get punctured during the whole storm."

"But why would he be in a dinghy? Whose dinghy was it?"

"It had the word "Gaga" painted on it."

"That's Harding's dinghy," Scheutz said. "But no Harding?"

"That dirty guy with the beard? No."

"I wonder what happened to Harding," Scheutz said.

"Mon coulda' got swept overboard," Asher said.

"Dios mio," Migdala said, shaking her head. "Tio Joaquin?"

"Si," Otero said. He paused. When Migdala did not go on he said, "We need you to come down to bring your grandfather home. He's not doing too good."

"I can't leave Blanca here alone," Migdala said.

"He won't leave with anyone but you."

She turned to Scheutz. "Can you drive me down? We can take Blanca along."

"I have to go," Otero said. "We got so much to do. I'm sorry about Joaquin."

Migdala nodded. "Thank you."

She led Blanca out to the station wagon and got in the back seat with her. Scheutz drove and Asher rode along in the front passenger seat. The road into town had been pretty much cleared of debris. Houses along the bay road had sustained various degrees of wreckage, the cinderblock and cement ones not so much, many of the wooden ones in states of collapse. Several boats had blown up onto the shore, some resting in yards of houses on the bay side of the road, several piled in a jumble at the small dock just before the road turned up into town. On the road leading to the malecón, they inched their way through the crowd of people outside Chuck's Bar and Pizza, all of them with beer in their hands, all gringo boat people with glum faces. At one edge of the crowd two people argued, shouting in each other's faces. On the far edge, an actual fistfight was in progress. A couple of people held up their hands in greeting to Scheutz as he passed.

He turned the corner onto the malecón. A red setting sun out over the water blinded him and he stopped the car to adjust the sun visor. A much larger crowd, mostly islanders, milled around the waterfront. In the middle of the malecon, it's prow hanging out over the water, the huge hull of the ferry reclined on its side, as if happy to be able to put its feet up after a hard life of traveling back and forth.

There was nowhere to park so Scheutz pulled the car over as near to the seawall as he could to get it out of the way. They left Asher to mind the car or move it if necessary. He had already engaged in conversation with people before getting out and walking around to the driver's side. Scheutz led the way through the crowd with Migdala tugging Blanca behind him. Near the liquor store next to the ferry dock, they found Tapon, sitting on a bench with Sharky and a few of his other old friends apparently trying to comfort him. Tears streamed down his face as he helped himself to another swig from Sharky's rum bottle.

When he caught sight of Migdala, the old man stood, swaying a little, and pushed his way through his knot of friends to rush toward her. She took him in her arms as he let out a high thin wail. "¿Quien hizo eso? ¿Quien mato mi hijo?" he cried. "Who kill my son?"

Blanca, standing behind Migdala so that she faced Tapon as he cried over her mother's shoulder, gaped wide-eyed at his face and let out a piercing scream. At the scream, Migdala let go of her grandfather and turned to her daughter. Blanca looked into her mother's face and screamed again, turning to push her way through the crowd behind her. Migdala called her name and ran after her.

Tapon startled and began to teeter as Migdala let go of him. Scheutz reached out and steadied the old man who glared at him. "Ay, tu. ¿Tu sabe…tu sabe quien mato mi hijo?"

Scheutz shook his head, holding the old man's arm to keep him from falling. "No. I'm sorry. The hurricane is to blame."

"No," Tapon said. "No. He is in a boat. My son is not in a boat in a hurricane."

"Come on," Scheutz said, leading him through the crowd. "Migdala wants to take you home.

Tapon let himself be led, sobbing again. "Juaquin. Mi hijo."

Back at the car, Migdala stood holding onto Blanca, and Asher leaned against the door talking softly to the girl in Spanish. As Scheutz approached with Tapon in tow, Blanca started and then tried to pull from her mother's grasp. When realizing she couldn't get away, she began to shudder and cry with her head down not looking at anyone. Asher and Scheutz helped the old man into the front passenger seat, and then Asher got in the back with Migdala and Blanca. Scheutz inched the station wagon into a three point turn and drove out of town. Asher continued to talk softly to Blanca the entire way back along the bayside road, up the hill and into the restaurant driveway.

Scheutz helped Tapon into the house as Migdala led her daughter into her room. She came back out to say goodnight to Scheutz and Asher. "Thank you," she said. "I don't know what I'm going to do with those two."

"Sorry about your uncle," Scheutz said. "That must be awful for you."

"To tell you the truth, I know I won't miss Tio Juaquin. I never really liked him, you know." He nodded, looking into the woman's eyes. She gave him a sad smile and then stepped forward to wrap her arms around his chest. "Thank you for helping me."

The hug surprised him. Mostly, because of how good it felt. "I'll help you more tomorrow if you like." He looked over at Asher who smirked at him with raised eyebrows. "I should say, we will come tomorrow and help you," he said, unsure what to do with his hands while he was being hugged. "I mean…that is…if you give us lunch."

Chapter 9

"Empujen."

"Push."

The crowd of men around the stern of the ferry boat pushed more or less in unison, leaned into the barnacled hull, straining with hands and shoulders, some grunting, some letting loose "aaghs" of frustration. The ferry loomed over them like a barnacled beached whale, resting on the edge of the sea wall where the hurricane had deposited it, prow extended over the water and stern across the road running along the malecón. Fifty yards offshore, as close as its draft allowed, a barge crane, attached with a steel cable to a sling amidship on the ferry, creaked and pulled, trying to lift it and haul it toward the water. And the men on land, nearly a hundred of the island's citizens and stranded boaters together, surrounded the ferry's hull and lent their muscle to help the crane.

"Otra vez."

They pushed in unison again on a signal from the little man shouting to them from above on the taffrail of the boat. The barge crane creaked, men groaned, and the ferry raised in its sling another couple of inches till the cable ran out and the hook of the sling jammed against the winch of the crane. The barge needed to be towed further out into the ocean to extend the cable, but the little man on the taffrail urged the men on. Scheutz, at the stern with Asher on one side and Arturo on the other, strained against the hull, scraping his hand on a barnacle enough to draw blood. The scrum of men struggled as a single force, as if each one alone and all together could counter the force of the hurricane that had flattened their island and ruined their boats just two days before. The metal hull inched forward, scraping the sea life off its bottom as it moved slowly over the timbers at the edge of the malecón.

"Se mueve." Behind them, on the street, and crowded up against buildings facing the water, practically everyone on the island cheered them on. Women, children, young men, old men, Puerto Ricans, gringos, FEMA workers, many with drinks in their hand—beers, sodas, water bottles—raised their arms and shouted each time the men pushed at the ferry hull. The band, which had been setting up at the end of the malecón for a party that evening, left off its preparations and began accompanying the crowd's cheers with a blaring calypso version of something that sounded vaguely to Scheutz like *Mataron ELena,* an old Puerto Rican Christmas song.

"Empujen." The cry came from the deck once again, and the crowd echoed the word as the men put their shoulders to the hull. Asher pushed in silence and Scheutz let out a low "uuugh" sound, which grew louder as the boat noticeably shifted its weight toward the sea. Ever so slowly, the stern began to rise, Scheutz letting go and Asher continuing to push with the crowd, gaining new handholds lower on the transom. Faster now, the stern higher in the air, the hull screaming, scraping on the edge of the sea wall, the band picking up the tempo, the supporters behind the men roaring and clapping in joy. The tug pulling the crane barge revved its engine, backing it away from the sea wall and pulling the ferry till it teetered on its midpoint for a long moment, and then dipped forward, the prow, with hardly a splash, touching the water which lapped lazily at the malecón, out of sync with the activity going on above it.

"Un poco mas." No longer able to reach the transom of the boat which now hung high in the air, Scheutz and Asher ran around to help push from the side, where men squeezed together as their hands found purchase on the beam of the hull. The bottom screamed again as it slid, scrapping across the edge until the stern itself went over the side to plop with a loud sploosh. The little man standing on the stern urging them on, began jumping up and down with excitement, lost his balance with the final splash, and tumbled over the stern into the water. The press of men, relieved of their struggle, applauded the man in the water, while cheering, whistling and shouting to congratulate themselves. Behind them, their well-wishers surged forward to line the edge of the malecón and raised their drinks to the newly launched ferry boat and to the man in the water who, taking advantage of his new notoriety, raised his clasped hands in a victory salute. "Haciamos. Haciamos."

Scheutz and Asher pounded each other on the back, laughing and accepting bottles of beer from women who passed them out to the pushers. True, yes, the barge crane had hauled the ferry off the malecón, but how wonderful it was, for a few minutes at least, to believe that the people of the island had pushed it off themselves, had pushed back against the power of the hurricane, putting the routine of their life back where they needed it to be, lifting the weight dropped upon them so it could float as it was meant to. They did it.

Scheutz and Asher found Tapon among the men who now backed away from the edge of the sea wall, clinking beer bottles. In contrast, the old man stared straight ahead of him, out to sea, in the mood the news of the death of his son had left him a few days before. Tapon's friend Arturo had told them the party tonight was in honor of Juaquin, but Tapon seemed to be the only one exhibiting any sadness over the death. Asher massaged the old man's shoulders, which did not seem to bring up his mood at all. Scheutz, feeling hedged in, moved backwards to stand at the edge of the crowd, sipping his beer, smiling and shaking hands with several of the other men who had participated in the big push. Tapon's friends Sharkie and Arturo pushed through the press of bodies to lead Tapon away to where their group had commandeered their usual spot near the liquor store. Asher, giving Scheutz a little wave of his fingers, drifted off to join a group he often spent time with outside Chuck's Pizza. Scheutz finished his bottle of beer and bent to set it with several others near the wall of a building. He inched along the wall toward the street corner. The band, in a blare of horns, blasted out a salsa rhythm and people began dancing in place with whoever was next to them. He could feel the rhythm pulsate in his own body but he caught himself and stiffened to avoid moving in time with the gyrating bodies around him. Pushing the ferryboat as part of a temporary work force was one thing, but dancing as part of a crowd felt foreign to him. He could dance with one person, maybe, but then only Samantha. Maybe he could dance with Migdala. He looked for her over the dancers' heads, but she was not there.

If Samantha were with him, he might have allowed himself to get into the music, allowed her to encapsulate him and bring him inside the group of people around them. She had done it before; he remembered a night in a pub on Virgin Gorda. But she wasn't with him. The rhythm leaked out of his body as if just thinking of her, dwelling on her not being there, loosened something, like pulling a drain plug on an engine's oil pan, emptying it of the lubricant that kept it going. He leaned his back against the wall and emptiness flooded into him to replace the rhythm. What had just happened? One moment he was with a large group of happy people and the next he felt as if he were standing out on a rock jutting over an expanse of sea into a dark sky.

He told himself he should just push himself away from the wall he leaned against and go dance, pretend the dancing was nothing more than pushing a boat out into the water. Do it. He edged sideways through the dancing bodies until he estimated himself to be in the exact middle, and then began dancing on his own. But it didn't work. His arms and legs felt mechanical, as if yanked about in a start and stop motion, like gears and pinions without oil to smooth grinding between them. He left off and squeezed again through the crowd to the tub of cold beer to the left of where the band danced in time to their own instruments. But even the beer had a metallic taste. Juaquin's memorial party was being put on by the FEMA people, and so there was all anyone needed to eat or drink. He stopped at the food table and nibbled on a few things, but had no appetite. Maybe he'd try to call Samantha. He filled a small plate with cuchifritos and made his way to the telephone booth where a line stretched from the booth along the dock and then along the malecón. As part of a FEMA arrangement, the only telephone now working on the island was made available for free to anyone who wanted to call their relatives, either on the main island of Puerto Rico, or in the states. Since that morning, people had been calling New York and Miami and San Juan to tell their loved ones they were okay even though their house had been knocked down by the hurricane. If Scheutz got in line now, he could probably get a chance to call Samantha in New Hampshire by around three o'clock in the morning. Forget it.

He walked around the crowd, looking for someone he could force himself to talk to. There were Paul and Joanne dancing and waving at him. Beyond them he could see von Fritzinger whooping it up with a chubby, middle-aged Puerto Rican woman he recognized from the barrio. Several people nodded hello, or smiled in his direction, but generally turned away as he approached. Well, he couldn't blame them, could he? The look he must have on his face would drive away even the happiest party-goer. Especially, the happiest party-goer. Three days after the hurricane ruined their island, the residents needed this break from cleaning up the place and putting their homes back together.

Raul Otero, the policeman friend of Migdala, gave him a curt nod, eying him in an unfriendly way. Did he suspect Scheutz of having anything to do with the death of Juaquin? Or was he just feeling paranoid? Otero did have a look about him that said, "I'm watching you." Surely, he associated Scheutz with Harding who everyone, including himself, suspected of having something to do with the man's death. Just that afternoon word had come back from Fajardo that Juaquin's death had not been from drowning in the storm, but from a stab wound, made apparently with a harpoon gun, the kind that scuba divers used when fishing along the reefs. That also pointed to Harding, who he knew had such a gun aboard the *Gaga*. And, of course, it was Scheutz who had brought Harding to this island, and who Harding had introduced to Juaquin's little smuggling business. Scheutz looked around the crowd again, this time to see if the other policeman watched him, too, maybe waiting for some signal from Otero to close in on him and carry him off to that smelly little jail cell inside the police station.

This really sucked. Not twenty minutes ago he'd been so elated by his participation in the grand community effort of getting the ferryboat off the sea wall where the hurricane had deposited it, and now look at him. Not only was he some pariah wandering on the lonely tundra, but he had attained the status of public enemy number one. He wove through the dancers again looking for Migdala, but finally gave up the idea. Near the wall he set his half-empty beer can down and then dropped the paper plate full of food in the trash. Off to one side, near Colwin's house, an elderly man in a dark suit, white shirt and tie, the preacher from the Iglesia Pentacostal church in the center of town, raised his hands and his voice, speaking against the community party. "The Devil walks the streets of Culebra," he ranted to a little clutch of women who also raised their hands in the air and intoned "Amen" in unison.

Working his way around the edge of the crowd, he avoided Otero and passed behind the band, then up the narrow street that led to the inner bay, past Chuck's Bar and Pizza, where Asher had joined the gringo boat owners whose own party spilled out into the street, the joy quieter, less rhythmic, and with a few faces as gloomy as his own. One young gringo boat-owner waved at him, and others nodded. But he certainly didn't want to talk to these guys, whose only subject was the devastation of their particular boat. They all definitely knew of his association with Harding and Juaquin. Not that they would care actually, but he scanned their faces to see if any of them might be whispering about it as he skirted the curb.

He walked through the ruined town and out onto the road that edged the bay, feeling slightly better alone, thinking he might just as well go back to his own boat and go to sleep. He was tired from the effort with the ferryboat this evening, after a long day of trying to make some order out of the mess on the *Panacea*. But it was better to walk, leave the dinghy tied at the dock behind Colwin's house for Asher to use to get back across the bay whenever the party died down, probably somewhere near dawn. It might do him good to walk all the way around the bay, make himself even more tired so he could fall asleep quickly and not fight the mosquitoes and then obsess over what a nasty blow the hurricane had dealt him. And, yes, he did get the pun he'd just made.

Electricity had not yet been restored to anywhere except in the center of town, the area near the malecón, and with only light from a slender moon, he found the road difficult to negotiate. Everyone on the island seemed to be in town, and only a few kerosene lamps could be seen on the hillside. Dark masses of wreckage or trash loomed here and there like some foreign landscape, and since the road had been cleared the day before, all he had to do was direct his footsteps into the middle of the blackness between the darker piles of debris. But each step felt like one more into a void where he could not be sure whether there would be ground enough to hold him. He stopped. Here again was the image he had earlier of a rocky promontory out over a dark sea? Admittedly, trying to maneuver his way along the road left him feeling less alone than trying to dance in the midst of a horde of soon-to-be-drunk revelers, but this was beginning to feel a little spooky.

Music from town started up again after what must have been the band's break, music so loud it could probably be heard all the way over on Vieques. And now, this far away, it was oddly comforting. It consoled him in a way to know that, even though he did not feel at ease in the middle of the world, it was still there, the way lights from another boat on the horizon gave him a certain reassurance sitting in his own cockpit far out at sea at night. In the middle of the dark road he made a little dance step, and then another one. Bumppa bum bum pah. He exaggerated the sway of his hips, turning in place on the two or three feet of road that he could be sure of for the moment.

He continued on, putting his feet down more lightly now, counting beats to the rhythm of the band behind him. This would be fine until he got to the place where he had to leave the paved road and make his way across the top of the ridge and then down to the water's edge where the *Panacea* lay. He'd just have to take his time; there was no hurry. And on the boat, he could get the ship-to-shore radio to connect him to a long-distance operator to call Samantha. He dreaded telling her about the hole in the side of the *Panacea.* Even though their radio worked just fine, he had been putting off calling her since the day after the storm. This might be the final nail for her. For months she had railed against the boat itself and then against them moving it to Culebra. It was she who had given him the image of being stuck out on a rock jutting from an expanse of sea into a dark sky. Now the smashed hull of their boat anchored them to this rock. He could see her lean, tanned body listing to port in imitation of the schooner's present position, shaking her fist at him as if he were the Devil that walked the streets of Culebra, accusing him of personally bringing in the hurricane to cement them to his precious little island, as far from her idea of paradise as a person could get without falling off the edge of the world.

Where the road curved around the north side of the bay, one yellowish light showed halfway up the road running off to the left, just about where the restaurant might be. Migdala must be at home. He stopped in the middle of the crossroad, debating whether to continue around the bend or knock at the back door of the restaurant. Maybe Migdala needed help with something; maybe she was ill, or maybe Blanca was ill. Or maybe Migdala might like to dance. How did that old song go? "If you can't dance with the one you love, dance with the one you're with." Something like that. What harm could it do? In all the time he and Samantha had been together, floating around the Caribbean, they had each, as far as he knew, never stepped outside their relationship to get it on with anyone else, unusual in this boat-bumming demi-monde dedicated to lazy, sun-drenched pleasure. But, if he did not need anyone but Samantha, why then was he even thinking about such a thing, standing in the dark looking up at the dim yellow light in the Puerto Rican woman's window? If he was merely thinking of a way to relieve the loneliness of Samantha's absence, why was he not back there at the ferry dock or the pizza bar yakking it up with anyone else besides this very pretty, petit, and compact restaurant-owner who threw out little signs of flirtation in his presence? Well, the fact was that he had been a little pissed-off at Samantha for taking off on him the way she did, and the fact was also that he would rather talk to this Migdala woman right now than talk with Samantha, which was why he really did not want to go back to the boat and call her tonight, anymore than he had wanted to call her since the hurricane. And if that constituted sulking, as she often accused him of doing, so be it; he sulked.

He knocked softly at the door.

"¿Quien es?" Her voice came quietly, as if she had been standing just inside the door waiting for his knock.

"It's me. Clement Scheutz."

"Who?"

"Scheutz."

"Oh. What do you want?"

"May I have this dance?"

"Que?"

"I said, 'Do you want to dance?'"

"Sssh. Blanca is asleep."

"Sorry."

The lock clicked and the door opened slightly, her head silhouetted in the light from the lamp behind her. "Are you drunk?"

"No. I don't get drunk."

"Then what is wrong with you? Why are you banging on my door in the middle of the night asking me to dance?"

"It's not the middle of the night. It's only about nine o'clock."

"It is eight-thirty." Her voice came out softly but like a snap at the end of whip. She made a small snorting laugh, and leaned against the doorjamb, still holding the door open only the width of her head. He waited. The music from the town took up again, this time a slow tune with what sounded like a muted trumpet. He could not see her face, only the shape of her head and neck against the lamplight. After a long pause, she straightened and moved back, letting the door swing open to allow him to enter.

"I saw your light," he said. "and…." She laid a quick finger on his lips and nodded toward the closed door to Blanca's room. Then she pointed in silence to the light at the other end of the hallway, and motioned him to follow her into the living room.

"I think she has finally gone to sleep." Migdala shook her head, the creases from frowning made deeper by the light of the kerosene lamp sitting on the table next to the blank television set. She looked away and then back at Scheutz, started to say something but did not.

"I wondered why you weren't at the party," he said.

She bent her head and shook it again. Then she looked up at him and took a deep breath. "I'm just worried sick about Blanca. I think she did not sleep at all last night. I did not sleep. I was up and then down and then up again. I try to talk to her, but she just shakes her head and cries. I am so tired."

"So, what's her problem?" He really did not want to be talking about a teenage girl's problems. He'd had a hard time dealing with his own kids' problem when they were Blanca's age, and they were boys. Girls, forget about it. He had known Samantha when she was this age but she never seemed to have problems, like she'd been blown full-grown from the head of Zeus or something. Or Athena, more like it. The way Blanca functioned totally flummoxed him. And besides, he had filled his quota of worrying about teenage *sturm und drang.*

"Yo no se. I took her today to see the counselor at the school." She shrugged and waved her palm in the air. "She can't help. She says to me, 'Blanca has always been a mystery to me. I don't ever know what to do with her.'" Migdala made a hissing sound and held her hands together as if squeezing a melon. "These people are supposed to be the experts. Huh. I tell her again that the hurricane has frightened Blanca. So she says she will have the counselors from FEMA talk to her. They are coming tomorrow. 'They can help for sure', she says. 'Those people are the experts. They talk to people about', what does she call it, 'post traumatic stress', she says."

Migdala had told him the day after the hurricane that her daughter had no memory of when she had walked out the door in the middle of it, that her memory only picked up again after Scheutz had brought her back inside. Shaking her head, she put a fingernail between her teeth as if to bite it, but did not. She turned and walked to the other side of the room, the way she always walked, with a purposeful stride, and then stopped, staring down the hallway toward Blanca's room. She stood, her back to Scheutz, saying nothing, just standing there as if the current that directed her movements had been abruptly shut off. He waited, the faint music from the town the only sound, and felt as if he were waiting for… what?...something to begin?… waiting for time to lapse? The music stopped and started again.

Finally, she turned. "Would you like some supper?"

"No." She must be waiting for him to go, asking if he was hungry just to be polite. "I guess you must be pretty tired. I'll let you get some sleep." He moved around her toward the hall but she stopped him with a hand on his arm.

"Stay. I cannot sleep. I just walk up and down and worry. Maybe if you stay I'll fall asleep."

"Thanks a lot. I've been told I'm kind of boring, but…"

"That is not what I meant. You take my mind off …" She threw her hand out toward Blanca's bedroom. "Are you sure you don't want some food?"

"They had plenty of food at the party, but I wasn't hungry."

"So, what can I do for you? Why have you come?"

He shrugged. "No reason. I just….I was on my way back to the boat and I saw the light in your window. Thought I'd drop in for a visit."

She stared at him, a look of mild irritation now on her face, a look he had gotten used to seeing down here in the islands, one that asked how he could lead such a frivolous life while others have it so difficult. The look betrayed an underlying tension that existed between people who lived and worked in places like Puerto Rico or Jamaica or Hispaniola and the mostly American, but also some European, half-assed ex-patriots who floated around the Caribbean in a perpetual state of lah-di-dah.

And then suddenly, the look was gone and she tilted her head, her face softening, her eyes lowering. "I am sorry but I am not good company right now."

"Well, I should go. I'm sorry to bother you so late."

"No. Please. Stay for a while. I am happy to see you. You have helped us so much." She made a gesture toward the canvas roof that covered them. Her voice and her movements seemed mechanical, more deliberate than usual, the way his had felt when he was trying to make himself dance in the middle of the crowd on the ferry dock. "Today we rolled the canvas back a little," she said. "So we could let the sun in and dry the rooms out."

The house smelled of damp wood and cloth, almost the way a wooden-hulled boat smelled below deck after a heavy storm. The lamp cast shadows in the room, which had been put back in order since the morning he had left, the day after the hurricane. What to do, stay or go? He surveyed the room and its contents. He scanned the canvas above as if taking a professional interest in its folds and wrinkles. "You must be very tired and want to go to bed," he said, finally.

"No, stay." It came out sounding like an order from a drill sergeant. "It is fine. Every little noise from her bedroom just sets me off. No, I am happy you stopped in. We can just sit and visit for a while. I can make coffee if you like. Or there are some sodas and beers in the cooler in the restaurant. Please."

She seemed sincere, insistent almost. "Okay." Maybe he was wrong, maybe she was not just being polite. They both had reason to seek company, quiet company, not the crowd in town. So, why not? All he needed really was to sit and talk to her for a while, and all she needed from him was the same. "I'll have whatever you are having."

She nodded and walked into the restaurant, returning in a few moments with two cans of Schaefer beer. "They are warm. We have no electricity." They each popped the lid and his spewed foam, which he caught by putting his mouth over the can opening. "Here." She motioned to two metal chairs with vinyl seats, taken from the restaurant. "The sofa is still damp."

Scheutz lounged on his chair, his feet extended before him, while Migdala sat upright on her chair, arranged at a right angle to his, both sipping their warm beer. A soft rustle came from the bedroom down the hall and Migdala started, listening, but when no further sound came relaxed again. They stared in silence at the kerosene lamp as if it were a hearth.

"Didn't you tell me that your wife has gone to her home for a visit?" Her voice sounded stiff with the tension of making small talk when she would rather be talking about something more meaningful. As usual, she spoke English in the formal manner she must have learned in grade school and high school, but even this tone was now even more clipped, as if to distinguish the sharper English tones from the softer tones of Spanish.

"Yes," he said. "She had to go to New Hampshire. Her father is ill." He did not want to talk about Samantha; he had come here as an alternative to sitting on the deck of that boat thinking about her.

She nodded, sitting upright, sipping her beer, the way some middle-aged matron might sip her cup of tea. "How long have you been together?"

"We've been living together for about seven years." He waved his own beer can at her, "But what about you? Where is your husband?"

She smiled and looked down, shaking her head. "I am not married. I knew Blanca's father a long time ago." She took a breath and continued. "We used to go to a lot of parties in San Juan. And concerts. And then I got pregnant and he disappeared. He was...how can I say it?...not grown up yet. Es un tipo. You know, muy machismo, pero no sesos. Stupid like." She made a face, shrugged and this time tipped the beer can up for a drink.

"And so you raised Blanca yourself?"

"No." She told him about her life, how she and her daughter had lived in Santurce with her mother, who took care of Blanca while Migdala went to work everyday in an office, and went to parties at night. She met another guy, Hernando, who talked her into going to New York with him when Blanca was in kindergarten. "I told my self that Blanca was fine with my mother and that I was in love with Hernando and off we went. Would you like another beer?"

"No. Thanks." As his body relaxed more, an aching from the tiredness set in. And he began to feel hungry. "What were you saying before about fixing something to eat?"

"I asked if you wanted supper. You want to eat or not?"

"Where is it? I'll help you." He stood. She picked up the lamp from the table and walked into the restaurant. He followed.

She set the kerosene lamp on a counter, then bent down to light a propane burner under a pot. "I am glad you stopped in. I wanted to go to the party in town, but I couldn't." She rubbed her eyes before lifting the pot lid to stir the soup.

He leaned in to the pot to smell the contents. Chicken soup with peppers. Delicious. No wonder her restaurant was such a favorite among the islanders. Straightening, he realized he was standing very close to her next to the stove, her hair within a few inches of his nose. He made a move to back away, but was held by the scent of her. The soup smell in her hair mixed with a faint odor of sweat and a deeper, richer, woman smell. It caught and held him. Next to her. Neither of them moved or spoke. The sound of the music drifted in on the night air from the town. The soup under the pot lid began to boil. Further up the hill behind them, a dog barked. Other than that, the world was silent.

They ate slowly, sitting across from each other. He slurped. She laughed at his slurping. "It's so good," he said. When he finished the bowl, he went to the stove and brought the pot to the table, refilling his own bowl and half of hers. She smiled at him. "I didn't know how hungry I was," he said. She smiled again, obviously happy that someone appreciated her cooking.

"Como un hombre. I used to say to Hernando—it was a quote I heard one time—Men are either horny or hungry. If he does not have an erection, feed him." She caught herself, frowned, and looked down immediately at her soup. It was hard to tell in the dim light from the lamp on the counter, but she seemed to blush.

"That's very funny. You think that's true?"

She shrugged without looking up. They ate without talking. He barely knew her but had no trouble sitting in silence with her, a peaceful silence, the kind that exists between two people who have been together for a very long time. She finished her bowl first and sat watching him eat. When he finished, he looked up into her eyes. "So what happened to Hernando?"

"I left him." She paused again as if her battery had been shut down, and then, as if pushing herself forward, said "Hernando…" Her eyes went up to the ceiling as if she was trying to think of the right thing to say. "…was good to me. He wanted to move out of New York and live in Connecticutt; he wanted to have children. His own children, not Blanca. Blanca was too much for him. But I could not stop thinking about my daughter." She told him how she and Hernando came down to Puerto Rico for every long weekend, Christmas, Easter, Fourth of July, Labor Day, and then she came down alone on her one-week vacation. Each time it was harder to go back. She wanted to bring her daughter to live in New York, but her mother on one side, and Hernando on the other, would not stand for having her in that tiny apartment in Spanish Harlem. And then finally, after one vacation, Migdala just never went back. "Blanca was having trouble in school. The counselors wanted to put her in a special class. My mother is just…you know…she just loves her, but she can't do a thing with her. My uncle, Juaquin, he tried to help out, but he is—was—such a creep."

"And Culebra?"

"They wanted to put her in a special school. They said she needed a special environment because she was…too much for the classes. They said she was hyperactive, you know? And my mother believes them. So, I just took her away in the middle of the night, and we came over here to my grandfather's house."

"You kidnapped her?"

"She is my daughter. How can you kidnap your own daughter? I told my mother, if she tries to take Blanca back, I will take her to New York. And I told Tio Juaquin that, too. I don't trust him. I never did. He's a liar. He's squeaky, you know what I mean, squeaky? Like a little mouse, running around chewing on everything. And if you don't watch him, he'll steal everything, even down to your underwear."

"Well, now you don't have to worry."

She watched him eat. "So, do you have children?"

"Yes. Two sons. But they're all grown up."

"And Samantha? She was a good mother?"

"She's not their mother. In fact, when they were in high school, she was my older son's girl friend for a while."

Migdala stared at him. "Excuse me, but she was your son's girl friend? I can't tell you how strange that is."

He laughed. "No. It's not as weird as it sounds. She was twenty-two years old when she and I got together. This was a long time after my son had grown up and left home."

"That is still muy raro. That would be like Tio Juaquin and my daughter Blanca going on a boat together. Or that vago friend of his, that Harding creep, taking her out on a boat ride."

"Well, no. First of all, she's only fifteen. Samantha was twenty-two. She was an adult woman. And second, I am not related to her, like your uncle was. And third, no matter what you or anyone else around here says, I am not like Harding. And he's not a friend of mine. And I had nothing to do with killing your uncle. And…."

"Whoa. Calmate. I didn't say you were like Harding. And I wasn't saying anything about my uncle. Is that what is bothering you?" She put her hand over his where it lay on the table, and looked into his eyes in the lamplight. "I could tell something was bothering you when you came in here tonight. Is that what it is? You keep looking around like you expect someone to jump out at you. Calm down." That also came out like an order from a drill sergeant.

She continued to look into his eyes, making him look back at her. He should not be sitting here like this with this woman. It was unfair to Samantha. But Samantha was not here. And he needed someone to tell him he was all right. Juaquin's death was not his fault. The hurricane was not his fault. He was not the Devil walking the streets of Culebra. Coming to Culebra was not his fault—well it was, but it was not the terrible thing Samantha made it out to be. The island was so much better a place than St. Thomas with all its glitzy tourism. Besides, Culebra was filled with people like…well, like Migdala. He turned his hand over so that her hand lay in his palm, and then he slowly closed his fingers around hers.

She smiled at him. "Would you like another a beer?"

"If I do I might get drunk. I'm already a little lightheaded."

"So maybe we will both get a little drunk. We missed the big party. I have not heard a sound from Blanca, so she must be sound asleep. And besides, tomorrow is the funeral for Tio Juaquin. Did you know that?" She walked to the warm cooler in the corner and took out two beer cans. Before sitting again, she raised one of the unopened cans, as if giving a toast, and cleared her throat. "Thank you all for coming here tonight to help celebrate the third day of being still alive after the Armageddon. As my Tio Juaquin would say, we are all sinners in the sight of God, so, in honor of my departed uncle, let us all take a break from doing his holy work and have a little sin."

"To the memory of Tio Juaqui. And to a little sin."

She sat and put the cans on the table. "He preached so much gospel, but he created the occasion for so much sin. When I was a little girl, I always asked myself if my uncle believed what he said and did not think what he did was a crime, or did he preach to cover up his crime."

"Maybe he didn't think crime was a sin."

She tilted her head down to one side and glanced up at him, then away. In a smaller voice she said, "And I want to thank all of you here for helping relieve the loneliness of an old woman."

"Old woman? You can't be that old. How old are you?"

"I turned thirty-five last June."

"Wow. You are old. That's six years older than Samantha. Maybe too old for me."

A loud laugh burst from her. She clamped her hand over her mouth and swiveled her head toward Blanca's room. When she turned back toward him, she took her hand away from her mouth and grinned at him.

He pictured himself pushing his ferryboat over the edge of the sea wall till he landed plop in the water. "If you get me drunk, I will not be able to walk back to my boat."

"The party in town will probably go on all night."

As tired as he was, he could sit here all night, watching her face in the light of the kerosene lamp.

Chapter 10

He came awake slowly, not knowing where he was, not feeling the gentle rocking of the boat under him, someplace strange in impenetrable darkness with no sound. Yes, there was a sound; the material he lay on crinkled as his body shifted, the crinkle made by the plastic covering on the couch in Migdala's living room, the last sound he heard before falling asleep. The couch smelled dank through the plastic but at least the wetness did not come through. They had sat in her restaurant, drinking beer, holding hands across the table while she talked about her uncle and her mother, then about Blanca. She talked about living in New York, in Spanish Harlem, the company she had worked for, the guy she had run off with, leaving Blanca behind for her mother to care for, the guilt she tortured herself with over leaving. "And now Blanca is my life," she said.

Over warm beer, he told her about his own children—the house in New Hampshire where he had raised them, how they had been his life, and then were gone—talking until his head drooped from fatigue and he could not finish his sentence. Her laugh brought him upright, mumbling something he could not remember, trying to grasp what it was he had been saying and fit it in with what had come to him in the few seconds his mind had gone into dream cadence. “Maybe I’d better go.” He gave her hand a last squeeze before letting it go.

She stood. “Thank you for helping me. Helping us.” She raised the newly freed hand to indicate again the sail canvas over their heads, and then waved it to take in the rest. He sagged, thinking of the walk back to the boat in the darkness, thinking maybe instead he would walk back into the center of town to pick up the dinghy and ride out to the boat, but it seemed like such a tremendous undertaking. Even standing upright seemed like such an ordeal. His eyes closed again.

“Why don’t you just go to sleep here?”

Lying here in the darkness now he had to laugh at himself. The first time he spent the night in her house, the night before the hurricane, when she had offered him her couch, he worried that she might be suggesting he sleep in her bed, and was relieved to find she meant the couch. This time he reached across the table for her hand again and looked into her eyes in the glow from the kerosene lamp. “I would love to sleep with you.”

She slapped his hand. “Not with me. On the couch in the living room.”

Last night Samantha seemed so far away, not just in miles, but also in time. It made no sense but it seemed as if she belonged to another reality, before Hugo. No, even before that, ever since they left St. Thomas. Ever since she began letting him know she intended to stay pissed off until she won their most recent battle over leaving a place that offered her at least some vestige of a social life and moving the boat to a place she referred as ‘this god-forsaken rock’, a place even the leatherback turtles abandoned as soon as they laid a few eggs on the beach.

It would have made no difference even if he had slept in the bed with Migdala since he did not even remember his head touching the arm of the couch. He certainly would not have remembered his head hitting a pillow on Migdala’s bed, he had been that tired. And she probably was too. These last few days since the hurricane no one on the island had gotten much rest. Where in God’s name did all those people get the energy for that party the night before?

His neck pained him as he moved. Dammit. He had a crick in it from lying at a weird angle on the arm of the couch. And all the rest of the muscles in his body ached as he moved and stretched on the damp, smelly couch in the damp, smelly room. He made a move to sit up but then lay back down. He let his mind drift again to the conversation he'd had with Migdala the night before, about his two children, and that house full of teenagers who always seemed to be around in those days; thinking about those days as he often did at sea at night, savoring little incidences, replaying them like reruns of old television sitcoms, laughing again at jokes, or else at the constant banter that bounced off their daily interactions like little white caps on the waves. The intensity in the voice of the woman he had sat with the night before, talking about her daughter and her dedication to raising the girl properly, gave him a pang of nostalgia for the years he had spent doing the same for his own children. That was the happiest time of his life, not this seven-year vacation he had been on with Samantha since. No wonder all these gringos floating around down here in the islands became drunks. And Samantha had fallen into the same pattern, whenever things got a little dull, go out and party again. He'd gotten so sick of that in St. Thomas, the image of Samantha laughing with a drink in her hand, her sun-bleached hair flicked by a sea breeze, flattened and froze like an ad on some billboard behind Migdala's dark, frowning, intense but animated features.

The crick in his neck clamored for attention and he sat up massaging it, then stood and winced at the pain moving through his muscles. Sleeping anywhere but on a boat could make anyone feel like an old man. He did not need to look for any clothes; he'd slept in them, even down to his Teva sandals. In the darkness he tried to orient himself toward the front door and then inched his way in that direction. The canvas roof above his head rippled slightly from the breeze blowing off the bay, giving him the heading he needed. The breeze always blew from the east toward the restaurant's front door.

Outside, a very subtle change of light showed over the eastern ridge of hills at the far end of the island. He stopped in the doorway and listened for any sound inside the house, but nothing came. From below in the bay came the sound of water lapping against the shore, the breeze ruffling leaves on the few bushes and trees still standing, and a bell tinkling somewhere on the rigging of a boat. Not an anchor light could be seen on anything still afloat. No one wasted energy on that kind of thing. He closed the door and walked toward where he knew her station wagon sat and then felt his way alongside the car to the road and slowly made his way down the hill. Around a bend he could see the glow of an electric light over where the center of town must be. At the bottom of the hill, rather than go out toward the boat, he turned toward the center where the walk got easier as he went with the glow from the town and the sound of the water lapping against the land to his left. The road followed the curve of the bay. The sky in the east had brightened perceptibly by the time he reached the school building lit by a dim electric light. The road turned off to the right and up a small rise. The town hall and the mayor's office also showed lights in several rooms.

Down along the seafront, not a single person moved about. The horizon of the Caribbean had become discernable against the sky in the west, the barge with its fifty-foot high crane rode silently at anchor, more brightly lit than any place on shore. The only people on the street running in front of the stores facing the sea, were the sleeping forms of two men on benches, one in the tiny park at the north end and the other nearer the ferry dock. Party debris lay scattered about, bottles and cans, paper plates, and a few articles of clothing.

A third of the way down the street, in front of the bodega, the telephone booth stood empty for the first time since the FEMA had come to town and connected that one line. Was it too early right now to call anyone? Samantha was almost sure to be out of bed, never having given up that old New Hampshire tradition of rising before the sun. He stepped into the booth and, without closing the accordion-folded door, lifted the receiver.

"Hello," the voice answered on the third ring.

"Hi. Is this Samantha?"

"No. This is her mother. Who is this?"

"Clement Scheutz."

"Oh." The 'oh' sounded the way someone might respond to being told their favorite TV show was being cancelled for the next season. Samantha's mother was never much for expressing an ardent opinion, good or bad, but she certainly let Scheutz and Samantha know every chance she got how much she disliked her daughter running off to sea with a man who was the father of a boy she used to date in high school. "What do you want?"

"I'd like to speak with her if I could."

"It's very early. I don't know if she's up."

"Could you tell her I'm on the phone please? I'm calling from Puerto Rico." In the long silence, he could see her in the renovated farm house, laying the phone down quietly—she would never bang it down no matter how much she disliked him—and walking up the stairs to Samantha's old bedroom to knock silently on the door.

Finally, Samantha's muffled voice. "Hullo?"

"Sleeping in, are we?"

"Oh, hey, Clem. No, I'm not sleeping in. Do you have any idea what time it is?"

"No. Don't you have a clock there?"

"Yeah. But my eyes aren't working this early. I was up late with my father. He's really sick."

"Sorry to hear that. I just called because I missed you. Wanted to ask how much longer you were staying up there." A long, silent pause on the other end. He finally broke the silence. "How long do you think you'll be up there?"

Another long pause. "I don't know." Pause. "As I said, my dad's really sick. I don't know where the hell my brother is. He doesn't answer his phone. Somebody has to take care of all this stuff around here."

"Stuff?"

"There's some chance my father won't make it this time. If that happens, Mom'll be totally lost. She doesn't know anything about their money, the insurance policies, the property, the trust fund, nothing. I've been having talks with their financial planner, with the banks. Everything is just a mess. My brother Joe is gone God knows where. So, there's only me. Even if dad does get better, it's all still a big mess."

"I'm so sorry to hear that about your father. Should I come up there and give you a hand?"

"No."

"I could leave Asher with the boat. It's also a mess, by the way. You'd have to wire me money for plane fare, but I could help out."

"I said no."

"Maybe you're right. Your parents wouldn't want me around. Besides, you should see the boat. That's what I called you about."

Another long pause on her end. "Don't you want to hear about what happened to the boat in the hurricane?"

"Um…yeah…well. So, what happened?"

"It was pulled off its anchors, all four anchors we had out. And it got pushed ashore. It hit a large rock at the edge of the water and there's a six foot hole smashed into the hull on the port side." Samantha kept her silence. He told her the story that Asher had told him about being aboard while the schooner was dragged off its anchors first in one direction and then, when the eye passed over, in the other, toward the shore.

"Is Asher okay?"

"Oh, yeah. That guy's indestructible. To hear him tell it, he slept through the whole damned thing."

"Well, I'm glad neither one of you got hurt."

"So, now the Panacea is lying at forty-five degrees, along the shoreline with the keel in about six feet of water." Another silence. He told her about the size of the hole in the hull and then outlined some of the things he and Asher had planned on doing to get the boat into the water. When she didn't say anything he asked, "You still with me?"

Silence.

"You don't have much to say about it."

"What do you want me to say, Clem?"

"Oh, I don't know, you could say something like 'holy shit, that's terrible' or 'my god, what are we going to do now?' or any number of things expressing shock and disappointment."

"Well." Pause. "Um...holy shit, what are you going to do now?"

"No. Holy shit what are we going to do now?"

"No. Holy shit, what are you going to do now? I know what I'm going to do now."

"I'm not sure I like what I'm hearing."

"Look, Clem. Maybe that boat getting busted up is all for the good. Maybe it's time to move on. You could sell what's left for salvage. Keep my share; I don't care. Or give it to Asher. A wooden schooner with a big hole in the side is probably not worth much anyhow."

"And then what?"

"I don't know. You'll have to figure something out."

"And you?" Another silence. That was the big question, wasn't it? The one that had hung in the air since the day they sailed from St. Thomas. Were they just having a difference of opinion or was this latest rift the one that finally tore the whole thing apart? He waited, leaning against the Plexiglas side of the booth. The island's one police jeep came slowly around the corner with its lights on. He could see from what light there was in the sky now that the driver was Raul Otero. Didn't that guy ever sleep? He was patrolling the party last night and now here he was again before the sun came up. "And you?" Scheutz asked again into the receiver.

"I'm here for now. I have to take care of my parents."

Anger rose like a tire's air pressure inside his chest. What the hell was she saying? His attention drifted away from her, from direct contact with her. In the almost full light of the morning, the police jeep crawled through the street to the end and parked near the ticket office for the ferry. Otero sat looking at something in his lap before looking up and spotting Scheutz in the phone booth. Scheutz did not bother to wave or nod. Otero's presence drove him back to the telephone receiver. "So you're saying you're not going to come back and help with the boat?"

"I'm saying that for now I have more important things to do."

She was right, but that was not what angered him, or maybe that was exactly what angered him. In her last years at home with her parents she could not even stand to be around them enough to stay home for Christmas Day, and in the years she and he had been floating around the Caribbean, she had not even bothered to send them a card saying where they had fetched up. Now all of a sudden she was the take-charge, responsible family member. Obviously, something else was going on. He hated to think of her as waiting for her father to die when she would inherit quite a bit of money, or else, trying to find a rationale to get away from Scheutz, get away from the boat she had accused of being an albatross around their necks.

"Listen, I've got to go," she said. "I've got a ton of stuff to do, and the home health nurse is coming this morning to change my father's IV pump. Clem, think about what I said about selling that boat." He did not answer. "Okay?"

"Okay." He waited for her to say something else. "I'll call again. This phone is free for now, courtesy of the FEMA folks." He waited for her to at least say she would like him to call again. He bit off the anger that threatened to spit from his mouth like a serpent's tongue. "I miss you," he said.

"Yeah."

Yeah? That was it?

"Don't call me so early next time."

The click of her phone in its cradle had a tone of finality about it. Next time? He held the receiver away from his ear, staring at Otero, and replaced it with a force that felt like banging on a large bell. What was that expression for hanging up the phone? To 'ring off'? That's what this felt like. He and Samantha had just rung off. Just like that. They had just disconnected, the way the telephone line had just disconnected. He stepped out of the booth and stood in the shadow of the building looking out at the sea. A large vessel moved southward on the horizon. A ray of sunlight showed at the side street between the restaurant on the corner and the town hall on the hill. Otero walked along the storefronts checking doorknobs. The ferryboat tugged lightly at its hawsers, and now a crewman emerged from the cabin to walk along the deck.

He could not say that this was his favorite place to be, but then he could not say it was not; the only thing he could say for sure was this is where he was right now. A numbness overtook him as he stepped away from the booth, realizing he knew for certain Samantha was not coming back, but not sure how he felt about it. Yes, he was pissed off, but he couldn't tell why. Except that he'd been pissed off for the past two years, pissed off at her for taking the tack she had about the schooner. He'd been controlling the anger till now and this phone call had somehow cut the leash.

He had been angry with his wife, his children's mother, because she left, but this was so different. Samantha's leaving released a long-time smolder. And the effect of those two different kinds of anger caused two different kinds of reactions in him. When Gerry left, even though she had moved to New York, he felt as if she had not left him. He kept her with him as part of who he was all those years until the kids graduated high school and left home, and only then did he let her go.

But this was different. Samantha was truly gone. Snap, just like that. Ringing off. And even if she did come back to help with the boat, it would be the opposite of what had happened with his wife. His wife had been physically gone but still with him. Samantha might be physically present, but no longer with him. Did that feel good or bad? He was too numb to tell.

"Buenos dias." Otero stood at his elbow.

"Oh, hi. Good morning. Looks like it was some party last night, huh? Did you know Migdala's Tio Juaquin?"

Otero smiled and nodded. "Everybody knew Juaquin. You left early, no?"

"I left early, yes. I was just so tired. I'm surprised everybody else wasn't completely wiped out."

The policeman's face lit into a wide, toothy grin. "Nobody in the whole world knows how to party better than the people of Culebra."

He caught Otero's eye and they shared the same grin. As wary as Scheutz was of this man, his grin was infectious enough to spread to his own face.

"But tell me, Señor Scheutz." Otero's grin dropped, leaving a look of business-like concentration. "Have you heard from your friend Harding? Why was he not at the party? He was a friend of Juaquin, no?"

"You asked me yesterday if I knew where Harding was."

"I will ask you every day. And one day maybe you will tell me yes. You know that we have found the spear gun on his boat. What you do not know yet is that an investigator is coming from San Juan today to go over the boat very carefully to see if there is any evidence showing that Juaquin was ever on board."

"Well, that won't tell you much. Harding and Joaquin had business dealings together, so he could have been there any time."

"Maybe so. Just as you had business dealings with Juaquin and Harding. Were you there at any time?"

Scheutz could only stare him, trying hard not to betray anxiety that would make him seem guilty in the policeman's eyes.

Otero shrugged. "But also there may be something on the boat that tells us where Senor Harding has gone."

Otero moved on past him to the next doorknob. Beyond him, in the little park at the north end of the street, the sun had become strong enough to rouse the man on the bench, who sat up, looked around and rubbed his eyes as if he could not believe another beautiful day had just dawned.

Scheutz couldn't think about Harding, didn't want to think about Harding. The man was not his friend no matter what Otero and the others thought, merely someone Scheutz always seemed to find himself helping out. And if he did shoot Migdala's uncle with that spear gun, he ought to be caught. But forget about him, Otero seemed to be suspicious that Scheutz himself might have had a hand in Juaquin's death. Obviously, he would like to think it had been done by a gringo and not by any one of the several islanders, many of whom might even have a better motive. Juaquin, the Christian evangelist, was always screwing somebody on this island. Otero walked back the length of the malecón to his jeep, nodding solemnly to Scheutz who had not yet moved. Scheutz couldn't seem to pull himself away from the phone booth, as if the booth were his last link to Samantha.

But maybe letting go of her was not so bad. All the tension that had existed between them over the past couple of years seemed suddenly to have lifted. A green Chevrolet, came around the corner and parked along the malecón facing out to sea. A man and a woman whom he recognized as the grocer and his wife got out and proceeded to the front door of the bodega close to where Scheutz stood. They nodded to him as they passed. The malecón slowly stirred to life. The sun now lit up the water beyond the sea wall.

He needed a shower and a cup of coffee. And then he'd find Asher so they could start doing something about the schooner. No, that's right; he couldn't do anything about the schooner today. Last night's party was partially about Juaquin because his funeral was today. Maybe he could get a shower at Migdala's place before she and Tapon and the girl were up. At the end of the street he turned the corner and faced into the glaring sun.

The funeral was scheduled for one o'clock in the afternoon. Migdala had closed the restaurant for the day in honor of the funeral, and hung a sign on the front door to that affect. Tapon moped around the apartment until Arturo and Sharkie came to see him. Blanca stayed in bed. After his shower and coffee, Scheutz borrowed the station wagon to drive out to where he could walk down to the boat. He and Asher talked for awhile, sloshing around in the water below decks and taking measurements of the busted rib. Around noon Scheutz put on clean shorts and t-shirt and drove back to the restaurant.

A service was to be held at the Evangelical church in town and then a procession mounted to drive through the town and out past the airport to the cemetery. Migdala asked Scheutz if he would drive the station wagon carrying her, Blanca, and Tapon. The old man was crying and in pretty rough shape. He stumbled as he reached the car. Blanca was also crying when Migdala led her out.

The girl ran to Tapon and threw her arms around his neck. "Lo siento, lo siento mucho. I am so so sorry." Tapon began sobbing harder, his whole body shaking with grief. Blanca stepped back from him and let out a small scream before shoving her fist into her mouth. Her eyes widened as she looked at her great grandfather in tears. "I didn't mean it," she said. "I am so sorry."

Migdala walked over and put her arms around Blanca. "Calma, calma, mi amor…"

Blanca's face froze in what looked like abject fear, turning from Tapon to her mother. She let out another, slightly louder scream and tore herself from her mother's arms, running back into the house. Migdala followed her.

Arturo and Sharkie stood by the car, each helping Tapon into the front seat, talking to him and patting his shoulder. They waited for Migdala and Blanca to return and finally Migdala came back out of the house and suggested they leave without them. Blanca was not budging from her room, and she could not just leave her there in the state she was in. She suggested that Arturo and Sharkie go instead and watch out for Tapon.

Juaquin's casket rode mounted in the back of a pick-up truck with the Evangelical minister in the passenger seat. Scheutz drove behind the truck and behind him came a white Mercedes with three people in it. As the funeral procession detoured through the town and then up into the barrio, other cars joined behind the police jeep with Otero and a man in a dark suit Scheutz had never seen before. The Mercedes had come from the main island on the ferry that morning and carried a round-faced mustachioed man and a middle-aged woman, plus the man who Scheutz had met before the Cuba trip, the man with the pipe who had been introduced as J.R. Dobbs, but who insisted they call him Bob.

At the graveyard a small crowd milled around between the variously ornamented tombs and statues, apparently waiting for them to show up. With the people from the cars, the size of the crowd of mourners seemed to belie what Migdala had said about Juaquin, that he had been generally disliked by everyone who knew him. Including herself. People, she said, had trouble reconciling his incessant bible-thumping with his apparent need to screw everyone around him. "The one person who did not feel that way," Migdala had said. "was Blanca. He treated her differently than everyone else."

Tapon, Sharkie, Arturo and Scheutz stood together on one side of the open grave as the young Evangelical preacher ranted on in Spanish, as best Scheutz could translate, something about a large wave that washed in from the sea carrying Jesus who scooped up Juaquin to sit at the right hand of the Lord. He talked about how much Juaquin had done in the Lord's name.

Bob, with his perennial pipe, and the other two from the Mercedes stood opposite them. When they had disembarked from the cars, Tapon had approached the woman, a not very tall, somewhat chubby middle-aged woman, to give her a hug. She wore a deep purple pantsuit and her hair had been dyed bright red and set in a tight perm. She allowed herself to be hugged but the look on her face did not soften from its severity. Arturo whispered to Scheutz that the woman was his daughter, Juaquin's sister.

"But not Migdala's mother, right?"

"O, si. Es su madre."

That was a little shocking. The woman had made no attempt to visit her daughter and granddaughter in the two hours since they arrived on the ferry. He gave Arturo a questioning look and received in return a shrug and face that said, "¿Quien sabe?"

The third man, the driver of the Mercedes, like Bob, wore a dark blue suit, looking like it had been designed specifically for funerals. His dark hair and thin dark mustache had recently been closely trimmed. He stepped daintily over the uneven ground of the graveyard in shiny wing-tip dress shoes. Once out of the car he gazed around much like a tourist who had never visited the island before. While the minister said a last few words over the gravesite, the man maintained an aura of disaffection, as if he were there only in some official capacity and had no personal interest in Juaquin. The three of them stood side by side, Bob a happy face, Tapon's granddaughter a severe countenance, and the round-faced driver idling in neutral. They reminded Scheutz a little of the three monkeys—hear no evil, see no evil, speak no evil. Or, more likely, enjoy the scene, act put upon, and don't give a damn.

Several workers attended to the necessary duties of the burial. A cement slab had been removed from the top of what looked like an upside down cement shed in the ground. Arturo told Scheutz that Juaquin's mother was already buried in the bottom of the tomb under a cement slab and Juaquin's coffin would be placed on top of it, covered by another cement slab. There would then be room for one more coffin on top of that one. Most graves on the island were family tombs, originally dug to hold three people, one on top of the other. Juaquin's coffin, which looked like some inexpensive metal made to look like silver, sat above the grave on two poles, one a digging tool and the other a rusted pipe.

Arturo and Sharkie propped up their friend Tapon who sagged between them, tears running down his weathered face. The cop and his suited friend at the end of the grave busied themselves glaring at all the attendees, especially Scheutz.

After the preacher stopped, another member of the church, a middle-aged woman, gave a short talk, gesticulating toward the coffin and then at the sky in what sounded like praise. Scheutz didn't bother to translate what she said. As she talked, one of the workmen filled the cement mixer that stood next to the grave, dumping in cement powder from bags and then pouring in buckets of water. Another man turned the mixer handle. When the woman finished her prayer, the metal bars the coffin sat on were removed and four men from the crowd lowered the coffin into the hole with the use of two lines slung underneath it, one a length of yellow rope and the other a strap that looked like a tie-down for the back of a truck. A sheet of plywood was placed in the hole on top of the coffin and then the cement was poured onto it using the five-gallon buckets the water had come in. As the cement was being poured, people in the crowd begin to clap. Eventually, everyone without a bucket in his hand was applauding. Scheutz gave Arturo a questioning look and the old man explained around his clapping hands that applauding for the deceased at a burial was an old Puerto Rican tradition.

After the ritual, Scheutz drove the three old guys down to their favorite drinking spot next to the ferry dock. Back at the restaurant, the white Mercedes had been parked in the Volvo's usual spot and he pulled in behind it. He opened the back door to the apartment to the sound of two women screaming at each other in a rapid Spanish that he was glad he could not understand. He closed the door and walked around to the front door of the restaurant. Inside, Bob and the round-faced man sat together having coffee. Asher was there, and asked him how the funeral went. Scheutz just shrugged. How do all funerals go? Good or bad; nothing detracts from the main event of putting someone away. Asher tilted his head toward the rear apartment and raised his eyebrows in comment about the argument emanating from there. He asked if Scheutz would also like a cup of coffee. He nodded. The sound of the two women was joined by a third. Blanca's youth probably gave her an edge over the competition when it came to yelling the loudest. He asked Asher what the women were yelling about and received another Hispanic shrug in return. Even if he had been able to understand Spanish spoken that rapidly, the over-babble would prohibit it.

Bob put his cup down and replaced the pipe in his mouth. "I'd like to introduce Senor Beltran," he said, extending his palm-up hand toward the round-faced man.

Beltran offered his hand. "You are Senor Harding?"

"No, no, no."

"I am looking for Señor Harding."

"So is everyone else. Are you with the police?"

"No. I am Juaquin's business partner. I was told that Senor Harding would be here."

"Who told you that?"

Beltran turned toward Bob, who gave a not-quite-Hispanic shrug. "I did not know Harding was hiding from the police."

Beltran leaned across the table and touched the back of Scheutz's hand. "We are looking for some of our product that Juaquin might have left with Harding."

"You mean the computers? We took them all to Cuba."

"No, I do not mean the computers." He lowered his head slightly and raised his eyes in what looked like a flirtatious smirk, causing Scheutz to immediately distrust him. He was on the one hand effeminate and seductive, and on the other made Scheutz want to rush to the sink to wash the hand that had been touched. He knew the product Beltran was talking about, but indulged himself in his own Hispanic shrug. Asher approached behind the man and gave Scheutz a pointedly conspiratorial look as he set a cup of hot coffee in front of him. The look told him to go with his instincts and not tell this Beltran about the emeralds. If it had been someone else besides Beltran he would have given the emeralds up in a flash. They were not his to keep, and he would have Harding out of his hair.

The door to the apartment opened and Migdala's mother, Marisol, slammed her way into the restaurant. "We are leaving." Bob puffed slowly, coolly, but Beltran seemed to shrink a little beside him. "Well?" she said. Bob removed his pipe and drank off the dregs of his coffee. Beltran tapped nervously on the table with the index finger of his left hand. Asher gave Scheutz the tiniest smirk that he interpreted as, "How lucky we would be to stay away from this family."

"Leave me alone. Just leave me alone." The sound of Blanca still ragging at her mother came from the apartment hallway.

For some reason Scheutz's mind slipped off to a particular moonlit night not long ago, far out at sea, all by himself at the helm with the schooner heeled gently over, making seven knots in an easterly wind.

Chapter 11

The captain of the crane barge, a short pudgy man with very dark skin and a dyed black mustache, shook his head, interrupting Asher again as he tried to explain what needed to be done. Scheutz, with his limited Spanish, could not follow the flow of conversation coming from the captain who spoke too fast and dropped his 's'es. They stood near the operator's seat of the crane on the deck of the barge, with its patina of rust underfoot. The crane barge had been towed around the island after pulling the ferry off the malecón and now sat inside the bay, just off the south shore. All morning the crane had been chugging along, dragging up sunken boats that had become marine obstacles and depositing them in the belly of the barge to be hauled out to deep water where they would grow to eventually become part of some new coral reef, rendered unrecognizable for the sea-life that grew on them. Asher, in a newly acquired red baseball hat, his dark arms protruding from a yellow oxford cloth shirt from which he had removed the sleeves, explained again to the barge captain that it would only take a very few minutes to attach the crane's cable to the main mast of the *Panacea* and then haul the boat upright in the water, holding it till they could prop the hull up from the back side.

The captain, bareheaded in the bright midday sun, shook his head again, turning toward his crane operator, a dark-skinned, lean, middle-aged man wearing cuffed work gloves, who manipulated the hydraulic handles to lift a half-sunk power launch from the water of the bay. The captain looked back, first at Asher and then at Scheutz, with his eyebrows raised as if to say, "What's the matter, you guys stupid or something?" He dropped his hand to his side and rubbed his thumb and forefinger together.

Oh, that was it, money on the side. "Ask him how much," Scheutz said to Asher.

Asher nodded and held his hand, palm up to the barge captain. "How much to do it. ¿Cuanto por eso?"

Keeping his gaze on the hulk coming up out of the water, the captain did not even bother to look in Asher's direction. "Mil dollares."

"A thousand dollars?" Scheutz said to Asher. "For fifteen minutes work? Is he crazy?"

Asher walked around the captain to stand in front of him, dropping his mouth open in mock surprise with his palms outspread.

The captain gave a little Caribbean shrug and tilted his head with his eyebrows raised as if to say, "Life is tough." He shouted something at the crane operator, again too fast for Scheutz to catch, and the crane operator shouted back at him, motioning with his hand and pointing to the upside-down boat at the end of the crane cable, water pouring from its cabin as it lifted from the water. From the look of the smashed-in hull, it had once been someone's very expensive sixty-foot cruising yacht, the kind that an owner would have a high-premium insurance policy on, the fiber glass and the bright work on the deck and the cabin still gleaming, none the worse for being under water, but the gaping hole in the hull just starboard of the keel leaving the craft a total loss.

The negotiations stopped while all three watched the crane lift the boat corpse clear and turn it 180 degrees to deposit it on top of two other wrecks piled in the bed of the barge. As the barge crew climbed over the hulk to unhook the cable, the captain turned back to Scheutz and Asher. "Ahora. Somos muy ocupado. Busy, busy, you know." He gave them an impatient, questioning look, rubbing his finger and thumb again. Scheutz wanted to slap him. Asher explained that they did not have that kind of money. The captain suggested they ask FEMA for the money, and Asher explained they could not get FEMA money because they were not residents of the island. The guy smiled. He knew that. Just like all rest of the gringo boat owners who had miscalculated how much protection they might get from the hurricane by sailing into this bay, there was no FEMA money. And for a lot of them, from what Scheutz had been hearing for the last few weeks at Chuck's Pizza Bar, no insurance money would come, leaving them with nothing but what they could salvage off their wrecked boats.

On an island like Culebra, the gringo boat owners were considered tourists. Even the "boat bums" who spent their lives sailing casually from one island to the next, and would not be caught dead doing touristy things were considered tourists by the islanders. But there was a big difference between sailors and travelers, or tourists. Sailors may wander the globe, but in truth, they never left home. Their boats were their homes. In the days of the old sailing ships, relatively few sailors even knew how to swim, and the thought of ever leaving their boat, leaving home, was so inconceivable to them.

Another quick exchange between Asher and the barge captain yielded for Scheutz only the word 'insurance'. Obviously, this was not getting them anywhere. The captain, like most other Puerto Ricans, or anyone else from a country other than the United States, naturally assumed that a gringo who owned such a large boat had plenty of money to waste. Scheutz touched Asher's arm and tilted his head for them to go. Screw this little con artist; he was being paid big bucks by FEMA for his company's work here, and the thousand dollars Scheutz might pay if he had that kind of money, he knew, would never be seen by anyone besides this pudgy little captain.

While Asher gave it one more try, Scheutz climbed over the side of the barge, down the iron ladder into their dinghy tied to the bow. What the hell were they going to do? There was no way they could work on the hull of the schooner as long as it lay on its side. If they could get it upright, the hole in the side would be out of the water and they could remove the smashed ribs and replace them. Having the crane lift the boat long enough to prop it there was such a simple solution, would take nothing more than towing the barge to the other side of the bay and attaching the crane to the schooner's main mast and pulling it upright. It could have been accomplished easily the week before when the barge was over in that area pulling out boats. But, no. They could not be talked into it then and they certainly were not doing anyone any favors now. The barge company was on a feeding frenzy in this bay since the hurricane; probably scarfing up more money than they'd normally make in five years. Scheutz had been a fool to even bring Asher over here to talk to the guy again, a move that came only out of his long-standing faith in the idea that his henchman could talk anyone out of anything, given enough time.

In a motor launch, two barge crew members transported the hook at the end of the crane cable out to a mast sticking eight to ten feet out of the water about thirty yards to port. Scheutz sat quietly, leaning his elbows on his knees in the stern of the dinghy, waiting, staring across the bay to where his own boat lay along the shore, by itself now since all the other boats around it had been cleared away. Up on the deck of the barge, Asher's and the captain's voices rose above the noise of the crane motor.

With the end of the crane cable attached to the mast, the crew in the motor launch backed off, and the crane began lifting the mast out of the water, bringing the sailboat attached to it clear of the surface and rising slowly into the air, spilling a cascade of water from a crushed bulkhead. Twenty feet above the surface, the boat disconnected from the mast with a loud ripping sound, and then hung there, swinging in the eastern breeze, still attached by its metal shroud lines, flapping crazily until one of its forward shrouds snapped and the bow of the boat plunged toward the water. Above, on the deck of the barge, the captain screamed at the crane operator as if the mast separating from the boat's deck had been his fault. The crane stopped moving while the operator took time to yell back at his boss, the two of them sounding as if they might come to blows at any moment. That might be fun to watch.

Eventually the crane began to move again, lifting and turning, the sailboat hanging limp like some dead sea creature hunted for sport and waiting to be photographed at the wharf next to a smiling middle-aged fisherman in Bermuda shorts and a sun hat. The mast had obviously been stepped on the deck, unlike the masts on his own schooner, which went through the main deck and were stepped on the keel below, so that if his own boat were lifted like that, the mast would never break off. But that gave him an idea. What if he were to attach a line to the mast, to both masts actually, and have someone then haul the lines horizontally until the boat came upright? That might work. To hell with the barge. He yelled up for Asher, who hung his head over the side. "Forget about him. Let's go."

"But I almost got him convinced."

"We can do it ourselves. Come on."

Asher shrugged, said something more to the captain, and clapping his shoulder in farewell, climbed down from the barge deck into the dinghy as Scheutz pulled the starter cord on the outboard motor. Asher cast off the bow line and Scheutz let the dinghy drift away from the hull of the barge before throwing the outboard into gear and steering out around the sailboat dangling at the end of the crane cable, airlifting it on its final voyage to the pile in the belly of the barge.

In the last few weeks, the bay had slowly been cleared of wreckage, though here and there along the shoreline, in against the mangroves, hulls and occasional masts could be seen projecting up from the water or the vegetation. Out around where the *Panacea* lay against the shore, everything had been cleared away except one boat entangled in the mangrove still further out toward the entrance to the bay. Scheutz had learned that all the land along the bay on that end of the island had once belonged to the United States Navy, and when the small naval base closed back in 1974, ownership of the land turned over to the island government as public access under the management of the Bureau of Natural Resources. It had been left to revert to its natural state, but still had a cracked and overgrown helicopter pad about thirty yards up the hill now strewn with torn vegetation and debris from the hurricane. Scheutz had talked with people at the land management office in town to ask them to let his boat remain where it was until he could get the hole in the side repaired enough to allow it to float. The schooner now lay as if someone had placed it peacefully and purposefully on its side, framed against a background of dark green vegetation running up to a ridge a hundred yards from the shoreline.

Further in towards the town, near the road that led to the water desalinaton plant, a few smaller sailboats, Harding's boat included, rode quietly at anchor, just off shore, near a clump of hurricane-damaged trees where Juaquin's white van still sat with yellow police tape around it warning people away. It looked like Harding's boat had also been draped with the yellow police tape.

He cut the outboard motor ten feet out from the work raft at the side of the schooner and let the momentum of the dinghy drift it in to where they could jump out. Asher tied the line to one of the wooden cleats they had fashioned along the edge. Scheutz led the way up the makeshift ladder attached to the side of the hull, describing to Asher how he intended to have a boat pull the schooner upright.

Asher added. "We don't need even a boat to haul it. We can put down two anchors and then use winches on the lines from the masts out to the anchors."

In the end they decided on three anchors. They could winch each one in turn, propping up the other side each time they raised the boat an inch or two higher. It could work. The hardest part would be finding braces to prop the hull as they winched.

The moment his feet touched the slanted main deck of the boat, Scheutz sensed something was wrong. He stopped near the gunwale and listened, but heard no sound other than Asher climbing aboard. "You hear something?" he asked Asher.

Asher stopped and listened, shook his head, but then stopped again, raising one finger and cocking his head, squinting his eyes at Scheutz. "Rats, maybe. They got plenty of place to get in the boat where she sits now." No further sound came from below.

"Well, why don't we get some lunch?" Scheutz said. "And then we can get started with these anchors."

Asher nodded and asked, "Can of soup?" They had picked up canned goods a few days earlier from the FEMA trailer parked near the ferry dock. "You like that stuff?"

"No, but it's easy. And free. That always makes it taste better." Scheutz moved across the slanted deck as Asher made his way forward toward the open hatch leading down into the galley. Whatever they were going to do about getting the boat into an upright position, there was certainly no rush. With no money, they were not going anywhere for a long time. Not that Scheutz had anywhere else to go even if he did have a boat under him. The twinge of something that felt like guilt nibbled at him again. Not guilt exactly since he had nothing to feel guilty about—he wasn't doing anything wrong, but he wasn't exactly doing anything right. He wasn't doing anything; that was the problem. Even getting the schooner repaired felt like lounging around in his pajamas, in a place made for lounging, except for people like Migdala. At least it was better for him here than in St. Thomas, a more expensive excuse for wasting time. He'd gone from wasting time to lounging, a subtle difference, but more palatable, as if lounging on Culebra was more like purposefully wasting time, where St. Thomas had been more like partying by default.

He would probably be better off if he did have something he needed to feel guilty about. At least then he could tell himself that this life in the Caribbean was an escape from the deep hidden secrets of his past. But he did not have any secrets, deep or otherwise, to hide from. Guilt over some awful thing he had done might be welcome, better than the feeling that nagged at him now, had been nagging at him for a while, that was so amorphous he could not even put a name to it. It felt like nothing, a whole lot of nothing.

Samantha and he had crewed on a boat a few years back owned by a physicist who had taken his family on vacation. At a mooring one night off Anagada, the physicist had gone into a long explanation, for

Scheutz and Samantha's benefit, on recent theories about the energy that existed in the vacuum between particles in outer space. It may be devoid of any matter but, as the theory goes, it is charged with energy. That was close to what Scheutz felt, an emptiness charged with some kind of un-namable energy, energy that ate at him.

From below came sloshing sounds again. Had to be rats. If he and Asher could get the boat upright, bring the hole in the hull up out of the water, they might be able to keep the rats out. He shook his head. What a sorry state to be in, when keeping rats out became the urgency that gave meaning to his life. Well, as soon as lunch was over, they would get on with it. He stopped at the entrance to the doghouse and tried to remember why he had walked this way instead of following Asher to the forward hatch. Nothing came. The hand spokes on the helm, like everything else in the place, reminded him again of Samantha. He imagined her standing behind the wheel wearing that long-billed cap she always wore to hold her hair in place, not saying anything, just smiling, looking up at the luft of the sails as she steered a course up into the wind.

"Soup, mon." Asher's call came from the forward hatch. Scheutz turned to walk up the slanted deck and then along the gunwale, using the handholds on the rigging to make his way forward, past the piles of lumber and roles of metal rigging and other marine parts they had scavenged in the few weeks after the hurricane. Asher handed up the bowl of hot soup for Scheutz, and then his own bowl before climbing up through the hatch himself. Scheutz settled himself sideways in the hammock slung between the foremast and a jib stay, his feet propped on the slanted deck rising before him, while Asher sat on the deck facing him with his back against the gunwale. The soup tasted not much different from the day before.

Asher raised a spoonful of soup. "Today our house special is come from the Cayman Islands." Every day it was some other island. Asher had been to them all and could detect subtle differences in the way the natives spiced their food, just the way he could detect subtle differences in the taste of the rum distilled on each Caribbean island. Scheutz did not possess the discerning palate Asher claimed to have; to him all this FEMA food tasted like variations on the same theme, not much different from the C-rations he'd been made to eat in the army.

He ate in silence. Between spoonfuls Asher entered into a long story about working a turtle boat out of the Caymans. Across the bay, the crane barge crew had apparently stopped for lunch. A midday quiet had settled over the basin between the hills of Culebra, nothing but the occasional call of a seagull and the very faint sound of an engine over near the town at the other end of the bay. The deep water of the bay lay as flat as glass and not even the wisp of a cloud marred the blue surface of the sky. A telltale, a foot-long string tied to a starboard shroud to show which direction the wind blew, hung limp. The sloshing sound came again from below, and then a rustle in the galley just beneath them. Something hairy came up from the forward hatch. The sight of a potential rat froze him and Asher, both with spoons half raised to their mouths. It showed itself to be a hand, which moved up again and then the bearded face of Harding popped up from the hatch only to quickly disappear again.

"What the hell are you doing here?" Scheutz flung his words at the hatch opening.

"I don't want anyone to see me." Harding's voice came barely above a whisper. Only the top of his frizzy hair showed above the deck level.

"I see you," Asher said in a high voice as if they were playing a children's game. Scheutz laughed. The hair disappeared. They waited and the hair came back. Scheutz took another spoonful of soup.

"Is anyone else around?" Harding asked.

"Nobody but us, mon," Asher said.

"You know they're looking for you," Scheutz said.

"I know."

"And you know we could get in trouble if they find you on this boat."

"You have to help me."

"Why do we got to help you?" Asher asked. "It seem like every time you show up we got to be helping you. And it seem like every time you show up—you like a jack-in-a-box, mon—you want us to do what they call 'criminal activity', you know that? If it ain't smuggling to Cuba, it is helping you out of a criminal jam. And you in one this time. Instead of asking us to help you out, you ought to be helping us out. I'm talking about helping us out by removing your evil ass off this boat and don't come around wanting us to aid and abet in your criminal activity."

"I'm not doing any criminal activity."

"But you doin' evil activity. If you hiding out from the police because they think you committed a criminal activity on that Juaquin tipo, then you are doing a criminal activity. And..."

"Can you get him to shut up?" Harding's hair-bound face appeared above the deck level as he directed his question at Scheutz.

"Don't tell me to shut up, mon. I will stuff you in the box where you belong and nail the lid shut. How stupid can you be? You pop your head up to ask us to help and then you tell me to shut up. That is almost as stupid as coming back here in the first place."

Harding laid his forehead on the sill of the hatch and then looked up at Scheutz. "Please?"

"Screw you. You get our asses in a sling by showing up on this boat. I am done helping you out. What the hell are you doing here, anyhow?"

"I have to get my boat out of here."

"Your boat? Your boat has no rigging. And the bowsprit is broken off. You can't sail it."

"Well...if you can get the gas tank filled, I can motor out of here at night."

"Tell me the truth," Scheutz said. "Did you kill Juaquin?"

Harding shook his head. "No, I didn't."

"You can tell us, you know. We won't snitch on you."

"We promise not to snitch on you if you go away and leave us alone," Asher said.

"No, I did not kill him."

"But you know who did," Scheutz said.

"It was your spear gun." Asher jabbed his spoonful of soup in Harding's direction. "They found it on your boat."

"They found the spear gun?"

"Yah, mon."

Scheutz leaned forward in the hammock. "Was that my spear gun? Samantha's spear gun, actually. The one you pointed at that guy over in Cuba?"

Harding put his head down on the hatch sill again.

"How the hell did it get over on your boat?"

"It's a long story, Clem. Yeah, Juaquin got killed by it, but I didn't kill him." He sounded like a whimpering child, an evil child, but nonetheless a helpless one.

"How do you know whether you killed the mon or not?" Asher waved the empty spoon in the air. "You don't know what you are doing most of the time. You could have killed the mon and said, 'Now let me see, I wonder where the spear gun is? It was right here. Oh yes, it is up on the deck. What do you think about that, Juaquin? Juaquin, are you asleep again? Now what did I do with that spear gun? Oh, here it is, but the spear is shot. I wonder where…"

Without raising his head, Harding said, "Clem, please make him shut up."

"I will shut you up." Asher slurped another spoonful of soup. "I will slap you on the side of your fuzzy head. What do you mean coming down here and bothering decent people? We got enough problem without you bring the Puerto Rican police all over us."

Harding looked up at Scheutz with tears in his eyes. "But I didn't do anything."

"Then let me finish my soup," Scheutz said. "And I'll take you in to town so you can tell them how Samantha's spear gun got on your boat, and how it got used to kill Juaquin and why you have not been around since Juaquin got himself killed. You can explain this whole thing to the police. Because they sure think you did something to Juaquin." Harding looked over the sill of the hatch toward the town without answering. He shook his head slowly and then stopped and looked from Scheutz to Asher and then back to Scheutz. Scheutz put his bowl on the slanted deck. "What the hell do you expect us to do? What're you doing coming onto the boat for anyhow?"

"I need to get that package the Cuban gave you."

"The emeralds?"

"Yeah. Juaquin's partners are looking for them."

"Is that what got Juaquin killed?"

"No. Well, come to think of it, maybe we could say it did. That would take the heat off all of us. Look, you give me the emeralds so I can get out of here, I'll get them to that Beltran fellow who works with

Juaquin and then I'll call the local cops and tell them Beltran killed Juaquin. Would that make you happy?"

"But it's a lie."

"So what?"

Asher had a disgusted look on his face. He wanted no part of all this. And neither did Scheutz. "The emeralds are not here. They're gone."

"What do you mean gone?"

"Samantha handed them over to some guy in San Juan before she got on the plane to the states." An absolute lie, but Scheutz saw no reason why he had to be in the middle of this whole thing, and he did not really care any longer whether Harding was in trouble or not. "So, I'd say the best thing for you to do is let me take you in to talk with the police."

Harding's eyes filled with tears. Scheutz tried to keep himself from feeling bad for the guy, he looked so lost. Yeah, he was a bum, and an evil, greedy one at that, had probably done a hundred things since coming down to the Caribbean that he ought to be sent to prison for. If he and Juaquin were ever caught for a third of the deals they had pulled off, they would both be sent up for the rest of their lives. But right at that moment he resembled nothing more than the little orphan he'd grown up as in whatever midwestern city he came from. If he was convicted of killing his boss, he probably wouldn't go to prison for any longer than he deserved anyhow. It'd be good for him. He'd have someone to take care of him for a while; god knows he couldn't take care of himself. But still.... From what Scheutz had heard of Puerto Rican jails, this poor schmuck wouldn't last a month.

Asher finished off the last of his soup. Scheutz had lost his appetite half-way though the bowl but made himself eat the rest of it. He needed to eat for energy if not for taste. Harding's head disappeared below deck. He could be heard sloshing around toward the rear of the boat. Asher took Scheutz's bowl and his own and climbed down through the hatch. Scheutz yelled down into the cabin below for Harding to come up and get in the dinghy. He called to Asher to ask if he wanted to go along to town and, when Asher said no, asked if there was anything he needed to pick up while he was there.

"Lot's of things," Asher said. " 'cept we don't have money for none of it."

"Well, I'll see what else I can mooch off the FEMA people." He stepped onto the ladder leading down to the work raft, yelling again for Harding to get a move on. He finally appeared and Scheutz preceded him down the ladder to the work raft. The guy really smelled bad, like he'd been hiding in somebody's bilge for the past month, and he looked as if he'd lost some weight. The cut-off jeans hung on his hips and the dirty t-shirt was made for someone much larger. His head with its wild hair plus his beard looked much too large for his scrawny body, a veritable Robinson Crusoe without the umbrella and funny hat.

Scheutz climbed into the stern of the dinghy, lowered the propeller of the outboard into the water and pulled the starter cord while Harding, still not saying a word, pushed off. Scheutz let the nose of the dinghy drift around till it pointed toward the bay and was just about to put the outboard in gear when Harding stood in the bow of the boat, turned toward the shore and without a word dove into the water. He swam the twelve feet or so to land, his head moving on the surface of the water like a poodle after a downed bird.

Goddammit. Getting Harding to go with him to the police was an idea too good to be true. He and Asher ought to tie up the son of a bitch and drag him into town. Scheutz put the outboard in gear and turned the dinghy to go around the stern of the schooner toward the shore, where Harding waded the last few feet to dry land. He jumped over a large boulder and began running up the hill to where Migdala and her daughter walked down the path from the ridge, just about to reach the weed-grown helipad. Scheutz nosed the dinghy into the shore, shoved the outboard gear into neutral and ran forward to jump onto land. Just as Harding came within a few feet them, Migdala dropped the shopping bag she had been carrying and moved to stand between her daughter and Harding, pointing her finger at arm's length and yelling at Harding to get away from them. Blanca struggled to move around her mother, but Migdala grabbed her wrist and pulled her to her side, throwing an arm around the girl's neck.

"Please." Harding held his hands out in a pleading motion, then turned to look at Scheutz just as he was about to reach them.

"Get away from them." Scheutz made a grab for him. Asher appeared from behind Scheutz, also trying to lay hands on Harding, who spun away before Asher could reach him, and continued running up the path to the top of the hill. Asher pursued him a short distance, but stopped and came back. Blanca squirmed, trying to pull away from her mother but Migdala tightened her arm around the girl's neck, holding her close. She cooed into the side of her daughter's hair, "Calmate, calmate. Esta bien ahora." The girl quieted down, gave up struggling and finally just stood next to her mother sobbing into her hands. Migdala looked up at Asher and then at Scheutz and reached for Scheutz's hand, clutching it. Blanca's body shook and she began to pull away, but then stopped again, sobbing loudly. Migdala gripped Scheutz's hand bringing it to her waist and so forcing him to stand close to her. He reached his other hand to Blanca's shoulder to comfort her, but the girl shrunk away from him.

Harding disappeared across the ridge of the hill. Asher picked up the shopping bag Migdala had dropped and now turned to lead the way back toward the boat. Scheutz took his hand away from Migdala's and let her walk in front of him on the path down to the deck of the schooner that lay at its crazy angle along the shore. Migdala directed Blanca to walk in front of her up the planks that angled from the ground to the deck and then up the slanted deck. The girl, still sobbing, turned back to scan the hill where Harding had disappeared. Instead of following the others up the plank Scheutz walked to the dinghy and pushed it off from shore, slipped the outboard into gear and drove it back around to tie up to the work raft. By the time he climbed on deck, Migdala and Blanca were seated together in the hammock.

Asher grinned at him as he made his way forward. "The bag is full of food for us." He held the shopping bag in front of him by its two handles and looked down into it. "We don't have to eat FEMA soup for days."

Migdala talked quietly to her daughter who sat with her body slumped and her face turned away in the direction Harding had taken. Scheutz sat facing them on the starboard gunwale while Asher carried the shopping bag to the forward hatch and went below with it.

"I'm sorry about that," Scheutz nodded toward the hill.

"Are you hiding him here?" Migdala asked, jerking her head around as if not believing that Harding had actually gone.

"No. He just showed up a half hour ago. I was going to take him into town to the police station because I know they're looking for him."

She gave him a look that said she did not believe him. "I hope they get him before my grandfather finds out he is back on the island. I do not want Tapon to go to jail for killing that creep."

"I don't think they'd send anyone to jail for killing Harding. But I'm sorry he ran off. I wanted to take him to the police. Your boy friend Otero already thinks I had something to do with Juaquin's dying. Once he finds out Harding has been out here on my boat, he'll be convinced of it. I thought if I took Harding in there and turned him in, Otero would let me alone about it."

"He's not my boy friend."

"So, what brings you all the way out here?"

Migdala pointed to the hatch where Asher had disappeared. "I brought you some lunch."

"Really? I wish you had been here an hour earlier. And to what do I owe this surprise bag of goodies?"

She smiled at him. "I want to ask you to help me build a new roof on our house."

Blanca tried to get up, and Migdala tightened her grip. "No," she said to the girl. "You stay here with me." Blanca turned her back to her mother. Migdala looked up at Scheutz, the sadness in her eyes alternating with flashes of anger and frustration.

"We're not getting much done out here. I guess Asher and I could come in and help out. Can you get building material yet?"

"Oh, yes. The hardware store has been buying all kinds of things from Fajardo. All I have to do is take the papers from the FEMA office and I can get what I want. The FEMA will pay someone to build the roof, and I thought you guys maybe could use the money."

"Well, we certainly appreciate it. Yes, we could use the money. When should we start?"

"You can start right now."

"Did you hear that, Asher?" Scheutz yelled into the hatch.

"Yah, mon. Yemaya is looking out for us."

"Migdala is looking out for us." He turned to her. "You are going to have the most beautiful roof on the whole island."

Chapter 12

Asher poked a stick into the wood where two walls met just over the foundation at the southeast corner of the restaurant building. Wood dust from termite munchings drained in a steady stream like sand in an hourglass. He, Migdala, and Scheutz leaned with hands on knees around the corner as if in a football huddle, studying the punky wood. This wall would never sustain a new roof; probably not even hold up a man climbing around on top of it.

Migdala grabbed the stick and poked into the wood further away from the corner, then, up a foot, two feet up from the foundation, swearing at the island termites that had eaten their way to the top. Scheutz threw back the sail canvas from the eave of the roof and grabbed a handful of wood the way he might a chunk of pound cake, crumpling it so that small bits rained down. "Can't do it. Not with this wall. "

Migdala smacked the building with the stick and then turned to throw it down the hill. "What am I going to do?"

"You need cement walls." Asher pointed to a house at the bottom of the hill, built of cement block and painted a bright Caribbean green.

Scheutz nodded. "He's right. I'd redo the whole building with cement block. At least the outside walls. Then, if you wanted, you could partition off the restaurant area from your apartment area with an indoor wall of wooden studs."

Migdala turned back toward him. "But the FEMA man said they would only give you the material to rebuild your house exactly the way it was before the hurricane."

Asher snorted. "Exactly like it was? They also give you a new family of termites?"

She gave him a snarly look. Her shoulders drooped and tears came to her eyes before she turned away again toward the bay. Scheutz picked at the top of the wall trying to find a place where it was not eaten away. The tropical termites on the island were notoriously destructive, had been known to take down the wall of a one-story house inside of six months. Most of the more recent wooden houses on the island were built with pressure-treated wood to combat the termites, but Tapon's restaurant had existed before the use of pressure-treated wood. It was amazing the thing still stood at all. The weakness in the wood probably accounted for why the roof had ripped off so easily in the hurricane.

"You'll have to renegotiate with the FEMA folks." Scheutz replaced the corner of the sail canvas over the edge of the wall. "They can't just give you materials for a falling-down house. Did Tapon have any insurance on the place?"

"Are you serious? Did you have insurance on your boat?"

"Well, no, but that's different."

"How is that different?"

"Well…" It was different because he and Samantha had been merely floating around the Caribbean. But Tapon, and now Migdala, had run a business in the house they lived in. Insurance was supposed to fit into a stable life like theirs, but not his, an existence composed of skimming the surface of life. Insurance was meant for trying to preserve something you owned, and what did he have to preserve except for what felt like a big wooden albatross, something he wanted at this point only because there was nothing else. "Well, this isn't getting us anywhere." He tied the line holding the sail canvas to the trunk of the small bush that had survived the hurricane intact. "Why don't we go down and talk with the FEMA folks."

"I can't do that right now." Migdala turned and walked away. "I have to take Blanca to see the counselor in a few minutes." She kicked at the porous chunks of wood on her way to the back door.

Asher moved along the length of the wall, kicking at the bottom of it every few feet. Scheutz followed Migdala into the house. "Is that counselor helping her?"

Migdala stopped in the hallway in front of the door to her room. "I don't know if it helps. She was in there only twice and she doesn't talk to them, so how does anyone know what is wrong?"

"If she doesn't talk to them, why do you take her there?" Talking about Migdala's daughter made his stomach a little queasy, but he couldn't just turn around and walk off the way Asher could, go kick a wall or something, think about getting a house rebuilt. How do you think about rebuilding a fifteen-year-old girl?

"I don't know." She went into her room, her voice coming back to him, peevish, impatient. "Maybe they will tell me what I can do. Today the counseling session is for me and her together."

"I'll tell you what. When you go to the counselor—where is it? In the school building?—Asher and I'll take the car and go to the hardware and lumber place. Maybe we can talk them into giving us cement blocks instead of the material for the roof."

She walked out into the hall wearing a knee-length kimono."I am going in to take a shower before we go. I'm covered with dust." She passed close to him on her way to the bathroom, stopped and laid a hand on his arm. "Thank you." She continued on and then turned. "I am happy I asked you to do the roof for me."

He smiled and shrugged. "What else do we have to do instead? Besides, I have to keep Asher busy or he gets un…" He had meant to make a joke about Asher getting unstrung if he didn't have enough to do, but he caught himself. You don't say things like that to a woman who has an unstrung daughter. What was it his father used to say? "Don't talk about ropes in the house of a man who's been hanged."

But there it was again, the feeling this woman was flirting with him, or maybe laying a hand on someone's arm was something Puerto Ricans did all the time without meaning anything by it, though he doubted it. The sweat from her hand mixed with the sweat and wood dust on his forearm. He could not meet her eyes and felt his own face flush.

He had laid his hand on Samantha's arm once like that and seen her face flush. That had been in New England in autumn; her face had colored like a leaf at the edge of the old logging road they walked on. That would have been right around the same time as it was now; the leaves would be just starting to turn in New Hampshire and they would have had their first frost. That day on the road through the woods was the day he first decided he loved her. Her swinging gait made him think all he had to do was just tag on and float with her through a red and green and yellow cinematic world of laughter and no pain.

Migdala left her smell behind in the hall. Her scent, all sweaty like that, was so like the way his wife, Gerry, had smelled, leaving it behind with the kids when she ran off to New York City. So much for following your nose. What if he followed his nose again here? He could end up waiting tables in a falling-down restaurant, taking care of the woman's unstrung daughter and her unpredictable old grandfather. This woman, just like Gerry, got a little touch of excitement in her voice whenever she talked about living in New York City. God, if he could only stop thinking about this kind of crap. He headed back outside.

In the bright sunlight, Asher handed him the end of a tape measure and motioned for him to walk to the corner of the building. Working silently, they calculated the square footage of the apartment and restaurant, an overall rectangle, thirty-two feet by sixty-one feet. The best way to do the project would be to build a cement block wall just outside the existing wooden wall, coat the outside with a thin layer of cement and then take the wooden wall down before coating the inside. That way Migdala could continue to operate the restaurant, still using the sail as a temporary roof. It was going to take a while to build this thing, especially if they had to find a way to scrounge materials, or buy a little at a time.

Cement block would be a difficult material to get from FEMA since houses made from it were not the kind that were damaged by hurricanes. About half the houses on the island were built from cement block, with the other half wood in the old Caribbean style. Building a substantial house was normally the first thing people did who had gone off to the states to work and either sent money back or came back with their own money. The newer houses were all built and painted in a Spanish style much like what could be found in places like New Mexico, but with cement block and cement roofs instead of adobe walls and tile roofs.

Scheutz and Asher left off measuring and waited by the Volvo till Migdala and Blanca came out. Blanca was a full inch taller than her mother and at fifteen had already lost any teenage awkwardness. Her disheveled black hair was straight, unlike Migdala's still-wet kinky wavelets, and was held back by a pink plastic band. Blanca's t-shirt and over-sized athletic shorts were smudged. Migdala wore a white blouse tucked into a cotton skirt with small pink and green flowers. Scheutz had never seen her in a skirt before, and it seemed a contrast to the quick movements of her lithe, sinewy body.

With the mother and daughter in the back seat and Asher in the front, Scheutz backed out onto the road and drove to town. On the bay road they passed quite a few people, walking, or in cars, and here and there, sitting outside their houses, or standing outside the little bar called El Batey. But the entire route these days had an air of casualness or even idleness, no longer the beehive of activity of trying to rebuild after a hurricane. Behind one house whose back yard faced the water, a twenty-eight or thirty foot sloop which had been blown up by the hurricane had now been righted and its owner sat on the deck reading a newspaper, waving to them as they went by.

Asher, waving to people he knew walking on the road, seemed to know everybody, his arm out the window cranking up and down. "They ought to invent a device that waves a mechanical arm," he said. "This could wear you out."

Scheutz stopped behind two other cars in front of the elementary school building. No students lingered or played in the yard. The school only went to the ninth grade, Blanca's grade, and after that the children from the island took the ferry to the main island, to Fajardo, for high school. Blanca had not been to school at all since the hurricane. The one time Migdala had taken her to school turned out to be a bust, with the girl refusing to go to her class, refusing to talk to anyone coaxing her into a classroom, and finally just walking out and back home, where Migdala found her in her room at supper time. Now Migdala opened the back door and tugged the girl from the car. She embraced her shoulders and steered her across the sidewalk and the schoolyard.

Scheutz waited until they had entered the school door before backing up to drive around the car parked in front, but before he could pull out, the police jeep with Raul Otero driving stopped next to him. He waited for the jeep to move but instead Otero and two other men got out and approached the Volvo, one of them another island policeman whom Scheutz recognized. The third man, short and stout with a trim mustache, in a dark blue suit and tie, inappropriate for the tropical heat was the man he had seen with Otero at Juaquin's burial. Otero leaned down to the driver side window while the other policeman walked around and stood next to the passenger side. The third man stood back and waited.

Otero said in his tone of phony politeness, crisp like his uniform, but mixed with a hint of insinuation. "I would ask you please to step from the car."

"Why, was I speeding?"

"Please." Otero opened the car door and stepped back with his right hand resting on the butt of the pistol on his belt. Scheutz shut off the engine, left the car in gear and stepped out. Asher got out on the other side and closed the door.

"So what's up?" Scheutz leaned against the car facing Otero.

"We would like you to come to the station and talk with us."

"Are we under arrest?"

"No, senor, you are not under arrest." The man in the suit moved around to face Scheutz.

"Well, we're kind of busy right now. Can we come over later?"

"No." The man in the suit leaned his jowly, slightly pop-eyed face up to scan Scheutz's. "If you do not wish to come with us now, we will have to put you under arrest."

"So, if I do come, I'm not under arrest, but if I don't want to come, I'm under arrest?"

The suit raised his eyebrows to indicate that was correct.

"So, technically, I'm under arrest."

"No. Not technically."

Across the top of the car, Scheutz gave Asher a look that asked, "What do you think of that?"

"You go on, boss. I will stay here and guard the car."

Otero placed his hand on the back of Scheutz's arm and nudged him with gentle pressure. "Please get into the jeep, Senor Scheutz."

Scheutz shook the arm off. "What the hell is going on? You think I stole your girlfriend's car? She's right there in the school building. Why don't you go and ask her?"

"This is not about the car." The suit tilted his head at Otero as if to tell him to get on with it. "Your friend can stay here with it until its owner comes back. Please get in the jeep."

Scheutz gave Asher a little wave and made to climb into the front seat of the jeep. Otero blocked his way. "Get in the back." When he did, Otero climbed in back with him, with the other policeman in the driver's seat and the suit on the passenger side.

They drove through the center of town, across the rusting metal bridge over the inlet to the bay, up the road on the south side of the bay, then up a steep driveway to the police station parking lot. Juaquin's white van sat at the far end of a line of cars.

Inside, in a blast of arctic air, a short hallway led to a large room containing four desks and metal lockers along one wall. A heavy-set, middle-aged woman with puffy cheeks and a permed hairdo, wearing a blue flowered dress, sat at one desk, typing on an electric typewriter. On one wall hung a map of the island of Culebra, on another a map of the main island of Puerto Rico, large enough to show all the smaller outlying islands. The room, with its telephones, desks, file cabinets, a small eight foot square holding cage, looked a little like the only other police station Scheutz had ever been in, the one in Georgia when he was fourteen-years-old. Police stations, like kitchens or auto mechanic garages probably all looked basically alike the world over. The unnatural coolness from the air conditioner affected everyone's mood. No one said hello to the secretary, who did not look up from key-tapping, no radio played salsa music which you were liable to hear in any restaurant, store, office, on the island or anywhere else in Puerto Rico. An occasional blurt in rapid Spanish from a police scanner cut into the tap of the typewriter and the steady drone of the air-conditioner.

Scheutz shivered in the artic gale from the air-conditioner. Otero motioned him to a chair next to a desk. The other policeman grabbed a folder and left the room. The middle-aged secretary, as if on cue, stopped typing, got up and walked to a corner of the room where she began heating milk and spooning coffee grounds into one of those long sock-type things that Puerto Ricans use for dipping into cups of hot water. Scheutz watched her and then amused himself looking at the map of Puerto Rico, picking out different port cities he had sailed into over the years—Fajardo, Ponce, Mayaguez, Arecibo, and of course, San Juan. The man in the suit, who looked very comfortable in this icy climate, busied himself at one of the desks reading material inside a manila folder.

Otero, not reacting to the air-conditioner, sat behind the desk. He leaned his elbows on the desk top, very still, staring at Scheutz, moving his eyes away for only a second when the secretary set a cup of coffee in front of him. If his purpose in staring was to make Scheutz nervous, he was doing a good job. The secretary placed a cup of coffee on the desk next to the man in the suit. Scheutz, just to break the tension, raised his hand to signal the secretary. "Any chance I could get one of those?" Otero shook his head slowly, giving Scheutz a punkish look he must have been practicing since he was thirteen. Scheutz wanted to slap him. This was obviously not going to be a friendly chat. The man in the suit closed his folder and got up to leave the room.

Scheutz tried again waving his hand at the secretary. "Mind if I make a cup of coffee for myself?"

She turned to him with a confused look, turned to Otero who ignored her, and then resumed typing. They waited. The typewriter keys clacked, the radio scanner spit out short bursts, the air-conditioner hummed, Otero stared and Scheutz shivered.

Scheutz stood. "I need to go to the bathroom."

Otero gave him a look as if he didn't understand.

"¿El baño?" He didn't have to go, he wanted to break the mood.

Otero shook his head slowly, picked up a pencil, and began tapping a slow rhythm on the desktop. The secretary made a mistake in her typing and swore just audibly as she applied white correct-type to the paper. Otero must be getting to her too. Scheutz predicted the error rate about to go up, and sure enough, in the next sentence, more correct-type. She stopped to light a cigarette, the air-conditioner fan blowing the smoke toward the hallway to the outside, but then Otero lit up, his smoke blowing directly at Scheutz, who turned away to study the map of Culebra on the wall next to a flag with the outline of the island in green inside a yellow stripe. Below the flag hung the seal of the municipality, which carried in its center the shield of the island's patron, Saint Ildefonso de Culebra, who had apparently been a bishop of Toledo in Spain. The island was seven miles long and four miles wide, mostly small hills, the highest six hundred and fifty feet. Twenty-one small islets lie scattered around the outside of the island. A legend at the bottom of the map stated the only town on the island had been called San Ildefonso until 1902 when it was renamed Dewey, the hero of the naval battles in the Philippine Islands who commanded the American troops in the Spanish American War. Next to the legend was a paragraph too small to read so Scheutz stood to walk closer to the wall.

Otero came quickly to his feet. "Sientate, por favor." He pointed to the chair Scheutz had just left.

Scheutz returned to his seat, not looking at Otero who returned to his seat. Then Scheutz stood again and turned to Otero, who jumped up. Scheutz met the policeman's eyes and drew his words out slowly. "I'm going to the bathroom."

"No." Otero stood.

"Am I under arrest?"

"No."

"Then I'm going to the bathroom."

"No." Otero almost ran to block the door to the hallway, stopped in front of him, glaring like a movie caricature of a Keystone Cop, until Scheutz turned his back on him and winked at the secretary who gaped at him, letting out an involuntary giggle.

Otero placed his hand in the middle of Scheutz's back and pushed. "Please sit down, Señor Scheutz."

Scheutz resisted the push and looked again at the secretary who closed up her face and returned to her typing. Otero pushed again, stronger. Scheutz resisted until the door opened behind Otero, hitting him in the back and pushing him into Scheutz's back. Scheutz lurched forward a step, smiling at the secretary who smiled to herself without turning her head.

"Oh. Perdon." The man in the suit stood behind them.

Otero drew himself upright. "Sit down, please, Señor Scheutz." He turned and said something in rapid Spanish to the suit.

Scheutz sat in the chair behind Otero's desk, and leaned as far back as the chair would allow, putting himself in a position to make it more difficult for Otero to intimidate him. Otero barked at him to "Please sit over here." Scheutz looked to the man in the suit to see what he had to say about it. The man shrugged, gave a little hand wave, and made a face as if to say, "Whatever."

"You are Señor Clement Scheutz, is that correct?" The man in the suit took a pace forward, holding the manila folder in one hand, looking for all the world like a trial lawyer in a television show.

Scheutz nodded. "And you are?"

"I am Raphael Collazo. I am with the CIC." He paused. "I am here from San Juan." He emphasized the words 'San Juan' as if they might be impressive in some way.

"Oh, really?" Scheutz grinned at him. "I went to a party there not too long ago. San Juan is kind of a fun place to hang out. You do a lot of partying there?"

"This is serious business." Otero leaned over the desk. "We are not playing here."

Collazo's face pinched slightly in the center, as if he were smelling something not quite right. Scheutz glanced at the secretary seated behind Collazo. She had stopped typing and wrote, or pretended to write, something in long hand on a form, obviously finding to the conversation taking place behind her more interesting than the report she worked on. He looked back to Collazo, deciding to ignore Otero all together, just for form's sake.

"I need to ask you some questions." Collazo opened the folder.

Scheutz raised his eyebrows at Otero to let him know he was odd man out in the new buddy-buddy relationship he and Collazo had just struck up, and then looked benignly on his new friend. "And what is the CIC when it is at home?"

"We investigate crimes that the local police cannot handle. I have been sent to investigate the murder of Juaquin Arraca." He took up his television trial lawyer pose again.

"Is that why I was asked to come in here?"

"Yes."

"You are our prime suspect." Otero sounded like the scanner.

Collazo closed his eyes, looking like he was almost at the end of his patience with the local police. The secretary turned her head to look at Scheutz, her eyes wide, obviously shocked that she might be in the same room as a bloodthirsty killer.

Scheutz waved a dismissive hand at Otero, giving Collazo a conspiratorial look to let him know he too was as the end of his patience. "Horseshit. Do you think I am a suspect?"

Collazo leveled his gaze at Scheutz and narrowed his bulging eyes. "We are considering all the facts."

The secretary looked back again and Scheutz made an ogre face at her, snarling and extending his hands like claws.

"I have to ask you, Señor Scheutz, to please treat this in a serious manner. It is not funny that there may be a murderer, or perhaps more than one murder collaborator, on this island."

Scheutz tipped the desk chair forward until the front legs hit the floor. "You say it isn't funny, but I think it's a joke that you and this muchacho think I might have had something to do with murdering someone." He turned his head from Collazo to Otero and back, putting on the best hard guy look he could manage. "And especially Juaquin. I barely had anything to do with him."

"You worked for him."

"I did one job for him; that was all. I talked to him twice. Everything was handled through someone else."

"And what was that job?"

"We transported some material."

"To where?"

"Does it matter?"

"Yes."

"To Cuba."

Collazo nodded his head as if weighing evidence, or else pausing for dramatic effect. "Were you aware you were breaking the law?"

"Well, Cuba's law. But that has nothing to do with us."

"You were breaking our law. We are part of the United States, and the United States has in place a trade embargo against doing business with Cuba as long as Fidel Castro is in office. I am sure you were aware of that when you went to Cuba with Juaquin Arraca's material."

"That embargo is stupid."

"That is not for you to say." He straightened and paused for dramatic effect again. "So…we have established that you were involved in criminal activity."

A tiny tingle of fear started up in the nape of his neck. This visit to the police station had just taken an icier tone. Much icier than the air-conditioning. This criminal investigator from San Juan was obviously in the process of building a case against him. And whatever Otero had to say to the CIC man would obviously slant that case further against him.

"Do you know a man named Harding?"

"Yes."

"Did this Harding come to Culebra with you?"

"Not exactly. I towed his boat over here from St. Thomas."

"And you and Harding both worked for Juaquin Arraca?"

"Harding worked for him. As I said, I did only that one job."

"But Harding went along on the trip to Cuba." Collazo's tone became more accusatory. Scheutz nodded. "And on the trip..." Collazo was sounding more like Perry Mason as they went along. "...did not you and Harding plan to do away with Juaquin Arraca and take over his business?"

"What? Where did you come up with that bullshit? You been smoking those funny cigarettes they all smoke in San Juan?"

"We are back to being funny again?"

"I don't even know what business Juaquin is in. And I didn't plot anything with Harding. In fact, I have as little to do with Harding as I can."

"Harding was seen coming from your boat yesterday," Otero blurted again.

"I was trying to talk him into coming down here and talking to you, but he ran off."

Otero laughed. "You were trying to talk him into coming here and talking to us?" He laughed again.

"Señor Scheutz, I ask you again to take this matter seriously," Collazo said. "Please tell us where Harding is."

Now he got it; they were trying to scare him into telling them where Harding was, and that's why they brought him here alone and not with Asher. This whole thing was a set up for him to give up Harding in confidence without anyone else knowing he did it. They could have merely asked him about it before bringing him in here and saved all this trouble, because, of course he would tell them where Harding was, if he knew. "I don't know where Harding is. Before yesterday, I hadn't seen him since before the hurricane. I knew you were looking for him so when he showed up on my boat, I asked him if he had killed Juaquin and he said no." He could tell by the look on Collazo's face that he wasn't buying any of this. "And I believed him, the way he said it. I told him that if he didn't do it, the best thing would be for him to come down here and talk to the police because, by hiding out, he was looking guilty to them. To you."

"And where is he now?"

"I have no idea. Juaquin's niece came down to the boat with her daughter, and Harding saw them and ran off."

Collazo pursed his lips like the television lawyer.

"He's lying," Otero said.

Collazo waved a hand to shush him. "Do not make light of this, Senor Scheutz. This does not look good for you. If you can tell us where Harding is hiding, and we can talk to him, we may not need to talk to you any further. Until then…just in case we need to talk to you, we will need you to stay here with us."

"You're going to keep me here? Where?"

Otero smiled and pointed to the eight-foot by eight-foot cage in the back corner of the room.

"You can't do that. I'm not under arrest."

Collazo shrugged. "That is up to the local police." His buddy-buddy mode disappeared as fast as it had come, leaving Scheutz, despite telling himself he should have known better, feeling betrayed. Collazo turned away toward Otero. "I must go to talk to some other people. You will take care of this?" He turned his back abruptly and walked away. The secretary rose and followed him to the door. Otero waved his hand for Scheutz to stand up and go to the cage.

"No. You can't put me in there."

"Yes, I can." He laid his right hand once again on the butt of the pistol on his belt.

"This is ridiculous. You don't have to keep me here. You know where my boat is, you can come and talk to me any time you want."

"This is more convenient."

"Screw you, Otero. You're not putting me in that cage." He stood, hitting the chair with his legs, causing it to fall backwards.

Faster than Scheutz could react, Otero rounded the desk, laid one hand on his neck and squeezed his adam's apple while turning him around and bending his arm behind his back. Taken by surprise, Scheutz tried to resist, but found the more he fought, the more Otero hurt his arm, twisting it up toward his shoulder. The policeman, though shorter, was much younger and stronger. He rushed Scheutz before him up against the bars. Painful to resist, Scheutz let himself be shoved into the cage.

The door clanged shut, and Otero stood in front of it with his fists on his hips, looking like some alpha male baboon who'd just bested his love triangle opponent. Maybe he had. Even though Migdala insisted there was nothing going on between her and her old school chum, Otero did not seem to feel the same way. Scheutz's right arm and shoulder hurt. He rubbed it and groaned aloud, exaggerating it just in case he might want to sue for police brutality some day. Otero grinned at him. On second thought, maybe giving the cop the satisfaction that he had hurt him wasn't such a good idea. He left off the rubbing and the groaning and stood just inside the bars, glowering at Otero. "I suppose this means I am under arrest, huh?"

"Claro," Otero said.

"Well, aren't you going to read me my Miranda rights?"

Otero paused, not moving his eyes. "Senor Miranda does not live in Culebra."

"What happens now?"

"Now you tell us where Harding is."

"But I don't know where he is. Honestly. I'm not lying."

Otero nodded, the punk look on his face again. "I hope you like rice and beans, Senor Scheutz. That is all we serve here." He turned to walk toward the door.

"Hey wait. I'm allowed to have one phone call, aren't I?"

"No." Otero did not even bother to turn around before he went out the door.

Chapter 13

The secretary opened the door and, without looking in Scheutz's direction, walked to her desk, sat with her back to him, fitted a sheet of paper into her electric typewriter, shuffled a small stack of papers which she laid next to the typewriter and began typing. The only sound in the room came from the clacking, interrupted by the intermittent whiss-bump of the carriage return. Scheutz sat leaning against the back wall, listening for some kind of sound coming in from outside. Nothing.

Not the normal sounds of boat motors in the bay or cars on the road, or even the wind across the water. Was it just his imagination? He listened for a possible low hum of the air conditioner or the tick of the clock on the wall, even a blip from the radio scanner. Nothing but the clack clack, whiss-bump of the typewriter. The world may end in a bang, or a whimper, but will probably end with the clacking of a typewriter, someone making a report on how the whole thing went down.

"Excuse me?" He stood and walked to the bars of his cage. "Con permiso." The rhythm of the keys broke for a moment and then continued. "Hello?" Pause. "Hola, Senora." She spoke English, he was sure, because she had responded with certain looks during the conversation between himself and Otero and the CIC man, had turned to look at him in horror when Collazo—was that his name?—had accused him of murder. "Excuse me, Senora. Can I ask you something?"

"No." Pause. Clack clack, whiss-bump.

What was it with these people and their *NO*. She and Otero both. Not, "No, I'm sorry I can't talk to you now because I'm busy" or "No, shut up and sit down" or "No, you are probably a murderer and you scare the shit out of me" but just "No." On that television show his kids used to watch called Get Smart, secret agents would have a Cone of Silence that descended over them when they told secrets to each other. This police station had a cone of silence over it, nothing allowed but clack clack, whiss-bump.

He leaned with his face and his chest against the bars and stared into the back of the secretary's head. If you stared—or was it glared?—at someone long enough, they would feel the vibes and turn around. Samantha used to do that to him, and he would turn around, not knowing why, but when he tried it, it never seemed to work, probably because he just hadn't done it long enough, or concentrated hard enough. What the hell, he didn't have anything else to do, so he stared at the secretary's head. He tried glaring, but glaring took too much out of him, so he went back to staring. Clack clack, whiss-bump. He stared harder. She shuffled papers from the stack on her desk and started another pile. He tried glaring again for a while and then went back to staring, but it felt ridiculous. Okay, so he didn't have the cosmic energy it took to make somebody turn around, but wouldn't it at least make her nervous, knowing he was behind her back not making any noise?

He went back to lounging on the bench, letting his mind drift off to Samantha again, her staring at him to make him turn around, laughing when he did. She would talk about cosmic energy late at night in the cockpit of a boat on a wine-dark sea, staring at him—not staring, just gazing at him—in the light from the binnacle, and his feeling the energy surging through him even while he lolled at rest, the energy brought on by the lovely tension in his hands between the pressure of the helm and the pull of the mainsail on a broad reach on a tropical night far beyond the bounds of what other people wanted him to do or not do. Staring at the back of the police secretary's head, whatever it was that Samantha was calling cosmic energy seemed now to be taking on a life of its own, bubbling its way up to the surface. He stood again, paced back and forth and then stopped to clench the bars with both hands, tap his forehead against the two bars that framed his face, and allowed a low growl with a life of its own to release itself from the bottom of his stomach. The typewriter stopped for a brief moment. Had she heard the growl? He gripped the bars and tried staring harder at the back of her head, just to have something to do with whatever was building up inside himself.

She did not turn around, but she took the latest sheet from the typewriter carriage, put it with the others, then stood, picked up the new pile and carried it from the room. Just in time because he was about to say something to her again, but glad she had snubbed him because whatever he said would have come out sounding as if he were very angry, which he was, and that would only convince her that he probably was a murderer. The radio scanner blipped once, cut off, and then silence, the little red light on the scanner racing across its bank of channels over and over again. He slouched on the bench, wrapping his arms around himself in defense against the room's polar conditions, too much for his t-shirt, shorts and Teva sandals. He looked around the room for something to divert him, a few "wanted" posters with names of people he had never heard of, the map of Culebra on the other side of the room. If he was Harding where would he hide? He could be anywhere; up on Mount Resaca? On one of the outlying islands? In somebody's house? Or below decks on one of the boats pushed up on shore during the hurricane?

The door opened, Otero entered, walked to his desk, opened a large lower drawer, and took out a three-ring binder.

"Hey," Scheutz tried to keep the animosity out of his voice. "Any chance I could get a sweat shirt or a jacket or something? I'm freezing in here."

"Where is Harding?"

"I swear to God, I don't know. I'd tell in a second if I did."

Otero shrugged and spread his hands in a what-can-I-do gesture. "I will trade you a sweater for a hint."

"I'll tell you what. Let me go with you to look for him."

"Do I look stupid to you, Meester Gringo?"

"I won't answer that."

Otero grinned. "Don't be cute with me. Let me tell you something. I used to work as a guard in the prison in Old San Juan, and when the prisoners started rioting, we blasted them down with fire hoses." He leaned in toward the cell and spread his hands again. "Of course, we don't do that here because we will get the desks all wet." He waved the binder at the room behind him. "But we have been known to splash rioting prisoners with a bucket of cold water."

"You'd never get away with that."

"Quizas si, quizas no. But nobody would blame me if I have to calm a prisoner who is rioting." Another big grin. "And we have nice cold water here."

Asshole. "So I have to stay in here till you find Harding?"

"Yes." He pointed the binder at Scheutz. "But if you tell me where he is I will bring you a sweater."

Scheutz shook his head in despair. "You won't find him. Even if I knew and could tell you, you probably wouldn't find him. You morons'd have trouble finding your own shoelaces."

"Morons?"

"Dumbasses."

"Be careful. You are coming closer to the water bucket."

Scheutz sat back against the wall again. They stared at each other. Insulting this asshole was not going to do him any good. He'd have to do something else, he could be in here a long time if it depended on them finding Harding. "You know, my friend Asher might have a better chance of finding Harding."

"We are watching him."

"Look, it doesn't make any sense to keep me in here. Where am I going to go? You know Harding is on this island. Where else could he be? Let me go back to my boat and then watch me as well as Asher if you don't believe me. Come on, what have you got to lose?"

Otero shrugged, with his spread hand. "I think you might know."

"You are talking about Migdala?"

Otero cocked his head to one side and said nothing, tapping the binder into his palm.

"That's ridiculous. The only connection I have with your girlfriend is helping her out fixing up the restaurant. And, yeah, okay, Asher and I wash dishes for a meal now and then. But you certainly do not have to be jealous of anything going on between Migdala and me."

"Not yet."

"Bullshit." Scheutz shook his head again. So here he was caged like an animal because Migdala might have done something or said something that made this bozo think she might be interested or attracted to him. He looked up and met Otero's eyes again. "That's just bullshit."

Otero pursed his lips and nodded. Then he waved the binder in a farewell gesture and turned to walk toward the door.

"Cabrón," Scheutz called after him. "Mamabicho."

Otero turned, grinned, pointed to the water cooler in the corner, and walked out the door. One-and-a-half minutes later, according to the clock on the wall, the jeep in the parking lot outside backed out and drove away. The air-conditioner started its hum. The scanner broke into conversation for twenty-five seconds and then fell quiet. Sometime later, from out of the interminable silence, a single-engine airplane took off from the little airport across the bay and droned loudly as it climbed and then turned almost directly over the police station.

A telephone rang and an answering machine instructed the caller, in Spanish and then in English, to leave their name and phone number. If it was an emergency, they were told to call another number. The caller, a man who sounded peeved, spoke in Spanish in a slow voice as if losing all patience with whoever was supposed to answer the phone, asking someone named Estrella where the hell was she and why wasn't she home where she was supposed to be? Was Estrella the name of the secretary, or had the call been a wrong number? It was entirely possible that until the police succeeded in picking up Harding he, Scheutz , was going to be left with brooding upon such momentous questions as the Estrella probabilities. He decided most probably Estrella was in fact the secretary and the caller her husband who expected her at noon to fix his lunch since he needed a break from the rigors of playing dominos all morning at the El Batey.

The phone rang again but the caller hung up as soon as the answer machine clicked on. Scheutz put his feet, one at a time, up onto the bench, took off each teva sandal in turn, brushed the sand off it, then the sand from the bottom of his foot and cleaned the toenails on each foot. That done, he tried lying down on the bench with his feet up on the side bars of the metal cage, but the bench hurt his back which didn't help his mood. The free-floating anxiety he'd felt since getting into Otero's jeep that morning now gained in intensity, knotting his stomach and rising up through his lungs and into his throat causing his mind to race—Harding, Asher, Samantha, Harding, Asher, Samantha. To make it stop he concentrated on Migdala, but as soon as he did so her daughter, Blanca, popped up, increasing the anxiety, but not before he dwelt on the connection between Harding and Blanca. What was that all about? He pictured the scene again on the little ridge just above the shore where the schooner sat. Why was Harding so anxious to get up there to confront Migdala and Blanca? He must have met Blanca because he worked for her Uncle Juaquin—her great uncle. Migdala had said something once about not wanting her daughter to talk to Harding because he seemed like such a creep with his wild hair and long beard. So, her reaction up on the ridge was consistent, but what was not consistent was Harding's being so anxious to talk to them, and Blanca's fighting against her mother's grasp to talk with Harding.

He had not known Harding for very long, but felt he knew him well enough to believe him when he said he had done no harm to Juaquin. But then again.... Harding's behavior on the boat the day they met the Cuban Coastal Patrol showed that when he got flustered he might be capable of doing any sort of silly thing, not maliciously but out of frustration, and, like a lot of people Scheutz had met who lost themselves in the Caribbean, Harding did not have too solid a grip on controlling himself. So, maybe he did let Juaquin have it. And the fact that it happened with a diver's spear gun just added to the probability that it was an accident. They could have argued about something, money, whatever, as Harding was getting ready to leave for a dive out on the reefs, getting his gear ready and the spear gun went off by accident because Harding was making some point, waving the thing around the same way he had waved that spear gun around the day they were unloading their cargo off the coast of Cuba, and shtcck, the thing goes off. But Harding said he didn't do it and Scheutz couldn't help but believe him. Well, even if it was the truth it was not going to help get Scheutz out of this stupid cage. Maybe the CIC guy had a brain, but from what Scheutz knew of Otero, the odds of them finding Harding soon were not good.

Damn, it was cold in this place. Worse than working in the woods in New Hampshire in the middle of winter, where at least you moved around to keep warm. Down here in the tropics, if it got down to sixty degrees it felt like arctic winds. He got up and paced the cell—three steps one way, three steps back. He still had to go to the bathroom, even worse now. So, the cell measured three paces wide by two paces deep. Six square paces, one bench, two paces wide by one pace deep, no toilet. So much for his physical world. Outside lurked the police station desks, maps, waste baskets, telephones, typewriter, file cabinets, papers everywhere, window looking out on the road that led across the bridge, and beyond that the town with the ridiculous name, the island, the Caribbean, the ocean, America with Samantha up north. He missed her. Actually, he missed the way she used to be. He couldn't say he missed the way she'd been for the last year or so.

Migdala took over his mind, then Otero, then Harding. He had to stop this. He had to make himself think about something else. Years ago, back in New Hampshire, his previous girlfriend, the one who gave yoga classes, had showed him how to meditate. He'd actually gotten pretty good at it, all those nights on watch in a sailboat far out at sea. He'd give it a shot. He sat very still on the bench and tried to focus his mind on.... Dammit, the only thing he could focus on was the goose bumps on his skin. How did those Eskimos get through long winter nights when the sun didn't come up at all? Well, for openers, they didn't have to piss so bad.

Here was a worse thought—what if they could not find Harding and decided to transfer him to the prison on the main island? Puerto Rico had some notoriously awful prisons. Even the jails where people were sent while waiting trial had the reputation of being places where you checked your humanity at the door. Well, that thought was guaranteed to make his stay here in this freezing cage with no toilet a much more unpleasant one, and speaking of checking one's humanity, if he did not get to a bathroom, he was on the verge of descending a few steps down the evolutionary ladder and pissing through the bars onto the office floor.

Against the back wall of the room, near a desk, sat a metal wastebasket that looked to be almost within reach. If he could…he knelt and stretched his arm through the bars pushing head and torso against them to gain another fraction of an inch. It was just a little too far. He took off one sandal to extend his reach. Now he could hit the sandal on the upper rim of the wastebasket. He tapped it, trying to tip the basket over in his direction, the way he had seen a chimp once do in a television show. The wastebasket finally tipped and hit the floor with the tinny sound of metal on linoleum. Papers spilled out and the basket rolled slightly to the left and then the right, coming up against the back wall. He now had to piss so bad he had started jiggling up and down like a pre-schooler. With the sandal he tapped the edge of the wastebasket to get it just into his grasp, and finally, touched the tips of his fingers onto the rim to scoot it forward. Once against the bars of the cage, he emptied the remaining papers out of the wastebasket, stood it in the corner of the wall and the cage and immediately stood to urinate into the basket. Aaaah. A momentary vision flashed of the secretary opening the door and catching him at it, screaming and running from the room. The sound of water on the bottom of the metal wastebasket was the most beautiful sound he had heard yet that day.

When he finished, he picked up the papers strewn around on the floor and put them back in the basket on top of the water, and using his sandal again, pushed the basket as far back into its original place against the desk and the back wall as he could. He then replaced the sandal, zipped his shorts and composed himself on the bench in the cage like the pre-schooler might, feigning angelic innocence, the only evidence of his naughtiness the few papers he had been unable to reach. And, of course, the smell.

Time dragged, he began to shiver, but the smell didn't bother him. The smell of one's own waste was never a problem; it was only other people's waste that was hard to take. Back in his days in the army, it seemed as if they lived with those smells all the time. You get that many men in one place and it's impossible to get rid of all that piss and shit fast enough. You get used to it, the way a farmer gets used to the smell of his stables. But here, in an air-conditioned office...Well, fuck 'em. Otero should have let him use the bano when he asked. He stretched out his feet, leaned back onto the rear wall and closed his eyes.

The only other time he had been in a jail cell was the time in Georgia, when he and his little brother, Willi, had run away from home when he was fourteen years old. Willi fantasized about going to Florida to live in a tree house on the beach and eat coconuts every day, and they made it hitchhiking as far as that dismal little town on the Slough River in southern Georgia where he had sat just like this in a damp cell in the police station watching Willi sleep on the bunk on the opposite wall. The police station and the cell were not much bigger than this place, and felt the same way. After being on the road for a week, and living—the cliché kept running through his head—as free as the birds of the air, they ended up caged and eventually sent back home. They had spent no more than a day and a night in that cell but that was enough to last him a lifetime. How did people do it? How do people adapt their minds to accommodate the idea of being hemmed in at someone else's whim? He sat back, hugged himself against the cold, and let his mind drift. Even if he tried he doubted he could imagine himself boxed up into anything pleasant. The only pleasant images that came to mind involved exactly the opposite of being cooped up in a box, hitchhiking in the early morning in the Smokey Mountains at age fourteen, jumping from a C-119 airplane in the army as a paratrooper, heeling over in a schooner in a 20-knot breeze on the Caribbean Ocean.

He had to stop this. Sitting in a cage thinking about running free would make him crazy. He'd only been here a few hours, what was so bad about that? Except for freezing to death. What really was the difference between sitting here looking at his toenails or sitting on the deck of his boat watching the sun advance across the sky? Even that was getting a little boring lately. Samantha was right, the contentment of the freedom they'd had over the past few years had become worn at the edges, a little less content, one day stretching into another, which was okay if you didn't think about it. But ever since she left, he found himself thinking about it. Which is what jail cells were good for, sitting and thinking about your life so you could see how you'd been wasting it. Even before Samantha left, she had already left in spirit—had tried to tell him that several times, tried to tell him how he was—they were—just wasting away, floating on the ocean like pieces of flotsam. The schooner they'd bought was really just a distraction, something to do for no other purpose than take up time. No wonder she went home to New Hampshire. Maybe he should go back there too, sell the schooner and go back north where he'd spent the happiest time of his life, raising his kids through high school. But he didn't have the kids any longer, so what else was there to go back for, to get some meaningless job, or go live in a cabin in the woods and become the crotchedy old man whose house none of the neighborhood kids would go near because it was so spooky?

If he kept up this train of thought he'd really depress himself. Maybe this was why a lot of prisoners hung themselves in their cells, why the jailers always took their belts away. Come to think of it though, why didn't Otero take his belt when he pushed him into this cell? Nor had he taken contents of his pockets. Weren't police supposed to do that when they locked you up? For all they knew, he could have a weapon in his pocket, could murder the pusillanimous secretary, or chuck a hand grenade to rearrange the police station décor. No, but seriously. Why hadn't Otero made him empty his pockets? There were only two answers, either Otero was more of a ditz than he appeared, or else he had no intention of leaving Scheutz in the cell in the first place.

While he contemplated this somewhat cheering thought the office door opened, bringing in the secretary who went immediately to her desk, ignoring his greeting of "Buenas tardes", to push the button on the telephone answering machine, listen to the calls and then delete them as they finished. The call to Estrella demanding that someone come home to fix lunch did not seem to concern her. That was interesting; maybe he'd try the same tactic since he was a little hungry. "Estrella," he called out, mimicking the tone of the man on the phone. "Why haven't you brought my lunch?"

She turned and wrinkled up her nose as if smelling something funny. "¿Que?" she said.

"Mi almuerzo," he said. "¿Donde esta?"

She shook her head, almost, it seemd to him, as if in defiance. "I do not have your lunch, senor."

He stood and walked to the cage door, and said in a demanding tone. "According to the law, you are supposed to bring your prisoners breakfast, lunch and supper. And a sweater if he is cold."

"I am not supposed to do that."

He raised his voice. "Oh, yes you are. And if you don't, I will tell the mayor, who is a friend of mine."

"Hmmp. He is also a friend of mine. He is my cousin."

"Well, then I will tell the Governor in San Juan. He is my very good friend."

"I don't think he is."

"The law says that you must feed your prisoners. Now you should go to Tapon's restuarant and tell Migdala to bring my lunch here. And do it soon because I have a sickness that, if I don't eat on time every day, I could die. And you will be charged with murder."

Estrella turned her back and picked up the phone. When the person she had dialed answered she began yelling into it in rapid Spanish. All Scheutz could pick up was that she complained to someone that he was yelling at her. She finally hung up the phone and turned to glare at him, as if to say "now you'll be sorry."

"Did you call the restuarant?"

"No." She wrinkled her nose again and turned back to her desk. But apparently Scheutz had made her so nervous that she did not seem to be able to do any of her work. She turned her chair sideways, looked around the room as if trying to find whatever it was that smelled so bad, and then gave up and sat glaring at him.

"I mean it.You're going to be in a lot of trouble if you don't get me some food and a sweater. You're all going to be in big trouble. I'm going straight to the President of the United States with this."

"Hmmp."

"And besides, what is that awful smell?" He wrinkled his nose in imitation of hers. "It smells like a kitty litter box in here. This is cruel and unusual punishment." He guessed that she could be intimidated the same way the voice on the answering machine was used to intimidating her, and extended his hand through the bars to shake a finger at her. "They will find my frozen, emaciated body clutching these bars, and the scandal will be brought up before the Supreme Court."

She wrinkled her nose and shook her head in disgust, simultaneously widening her eyes in fear of his wagging finger, as the office door pounded open and Migdala strode in with Otero right behind her.

"What are you doing in there?" She turned to Otero. "What is he doing in there?"

"We are holding him as a suspect. He might have killed your uncle."

"He did not do any such thing. Now let him out of there."

"I cannot do that. I am under orders from..."

"I said let him out of there. Where is that key? I will let him out." She opened the top drawer to Otero's desk.

"Give me that key." Otero extended his hand.

"Take him out of here," Estrella shouted. "I cannot do my work with him yelling at me like that."

"I will say when he goes out," Otero shouted back, reaching for the key in Migdala's hand.

Migdala balled the key and its ring in her fist and held it away from the policeman. "Stop being such a pendejo. This man had nothing to do with killing my uncle. I know it for sure."

"How do you know that?" Otero reached again.

"I will vouch for him. You can... what do they call it?...remand him to my company. If he runs away, you can put me in jail instead."

"I cannot run the police station that way." Otero wagged a finger of his own.

"If you want me for a friend, you better let him out of there."

"Stop this." Estrella put her fists on her hips like an irate school teacher. "Por favor. Everybody get out of here. And take him along. I have too much work to get done."

Migdala clicked the key in the cell door and pulled the door open allowing Scheutz to slip out as fast as he could. Otero started for him but Migdala stood in his way. Still wrinkling her nose, Estrella waved her hands, shooing them as Scheutz made a quick exit with Migdala right behind him, cursing in Spanish at Otero and placing her body in front of Scheutz as he lunged forward. The Volvo sat with its engine running just outside the police station with Blanca in the front seat and Asher lounging in the back. The argument between Migdala and Otero followed them out the door to the side of the station wagon and continued as she got into the driver's seat. Otero seemed to forget all his policely duties concerning Scheutz as he degenerated into a tirade at Migdala, alternating between pleading and furious accusation. Scheutz took his time, strolling around the car to get in the back with Asher, basking with exaggerated deep breaths and spread-wide arms, in his new-found freedom to enjoy the tropical afternoon sun.

Chapter 14

Scheutz stopped the Volvo in the yard, not in its usual place, but next to a haphazardly stacked pile of corrugated metal roofing. He and Asher had been round the island collecting building debris blown off in the hurricane that might be used for rebuilding the restaurant. Rain clouds had moved in before they could unload.

Inside, the restaurant felt stuffy and hot. Two fans blew from two different corners underscoring a hum of conversation and rain drumming a rhythmic tattoo on the canvas overhead. Water leaked down one of the outside walls. Scheutz grabbed two cans of Medalla beer from the glass-doored cooler in the corner and brought them to a table. Asher handed him a towel he had gotten from Migdala to dry his wet hair and face. Tapon and Arturo sat at the other end of the table with a lunch that Migdala was busy serving up at the counter to patrons in the half-filled restaurant. She called out as she set two plates of food on the counter and a woman got up to bring them to her table. Scheutz left his beer can on the table and walked to the counter.

Migdala barely glanced up from her work. "You're dripping all over the floor."

"I thought you'd be too busy to notice."

"I could use a little help back here."

"Where is your daughter?"

"She better be in school."

"Any chance we can get some lunch?"

"Any chance you could come back here and help me out?"

"Yeah, sure." He turned to look back at Asher in conversation with Tapon and Arturo. "Hey, Asher, what do you want for lunch?"

Asher looked down at what Tapon was eating. "He always knows what's good. Get me what Tapon has."

"You hear that?" he said to Migdala as he walked around the end of the counter.

"Yes. Get back here. Put some rice and beans on those plates."

They worked silently in tandem, he putting side dishes on warm plates just out of the dishwasher, her telling him what to give each one and then scooping fish or meat off the grille onto each plate, tossing them onto the counter and yelling out names. "Everybody comes in at once," she mumbled.

"Maybe you could find a way to have people come in at different times," he suggested. Moving past her or standing next to her in the tiny kitchen space, the smell of her mixed with all the different food smells, relaxed him and at the same time excited him. "Let's see, you could set up a system." He slid two more plates in front of her. "Everybody whose name starts with A to G, they can only come in from eleven-thirty to twelve; H to O, twelve to twelve-thirty. We call them the 'water people'."

"Huh?"

H to O; get it? Water?"

She shook her head. "Put some tostones on that one."

"And then P to T, from twelve-thirty to one."

"Will you please shut up?" She wiped her forehead with the back of her wrist, called out another name and tossed a plate on the counter.

"You want me to help you and you want me to shut up. That's asking a lot, lady."

She turned and grinned at him. "That's right. I want you to help me and I want you to stop talking bullshit." She scooped two long slices of fried plantanos off the grill.

He set the half-filled plate on the edge of the counter and turned to stare at her. "That's rude."

"Oh, don't be so sensitive." She nudged him with her elbow. "Give me that plate." He handed her the one he had been filling.

"When I say you are full of shit, I mean it in the best possible way. Put rice and beans on that next plate, too."

When the lunch traffic lightened he sat with Asher and the two plates he had prepared for them. Asher had moved to another table away from Tapon and Arturo and now leaned over his plate to talk in a low voice. "You want to hear what Arturo told me about where Harding is?"

"No."

"I don't know for sure, but he thinks he's been hiding somewhere up on top of Cerro Resaca."

Scheutz gave an answer that came out somewhere between an "ugh" and a "humph."

"And you want to know something else? I think Migdala knows something more about her uncle getting killed than she is letting on."

Otero and the CIC cop, Collazo, came in the door and took seats at a table recently vacated. Both stopped talking and looked over at Scheutz and Asher, then went back to the conversation they had been having when they came in. Migdala finished with the last lunch and came over to sit with Scheutz and Asher, causing Otero to turn away from Collazo to glare at her.

"I'm sorry for telling you to shut up before. It's just that you get so silly sometimes."

"Look…"

She waited for him to continue, her elbows on the table and her chin resting on her cupped hands. Her eyes were very large and very brown. They gazed directly at him without flickering off in all directions the way Samantha's eyes did whenever they talked quietly together. "Look, what?" she said. "What did you start to say?"

"Nothing. Forget it." He ate quietly and she watched him. "I mean…." What did he mean? He could not stop looking into her eyes.

"I mean, so what if what I say is silly. This whole life is silly. Hanging around in a place like this doing jack shit."

"What do you mean? You are not just hanging around. You are helping me build my restaurant."

"Big whoop. And then what?"

"And then you will find a way to fix your boat. And then you will go and have the life that you had before the hurricane."

He ate in silence. "You know, I hate to say it but, even before the hurricane smashed up my boat, the life I had before was kind of shitty."

"¿Que dices?" Her eyes widened in disbelief and her mouth dropped open in a cartoonish depiction of shock. "You sail around in your boat. You go where you want to go. Nobody tells you you have to go here or do that. Every day is a vacation. How can you say that such a life is mierda?"

"If every day is a vacation, it's not a vacation. It doesn't mean anything. That's why Samantha left."

"She's coming back, no?"

"She's not coming back, no. She's gone back to New Hampshire to live. I guess all that ice and snow in the wintertime is there to make people think their lives mean something. It's serious business trying to keep warm." He waved his fork in the air. "And then, of course, in the summer you have black flies and mosquitoes and mud…"

"We have mosquitoes."

"Well then, I guess there's hope for you yet."

She laughed. "I have to go and pick up my daughter from school. Are you two going to work on this house this afternoon?"

"Can't Blanca walk home?" He did not want her to leave.

She shook her head. "No, I still do not trust her to be alone by herself. She still cries all the time. I'm so worried." She touched her hand to the back of Scheutz's left hand where it lay on the table. He turned it palm up and took her hand in his. She lifted her hand, putting it next to her mouth to cover it from the eyes of the police men. "Can you come with me?" she said in a hoarse whisper.

He nodded and then motioned to his plate of food. She waved her hand as if to say, go ahead and finish. As he took another forkful she stood and walked behind the counter. He finished his meal and made a silent sign to Asher that he was going with Migdala. As he passed the table with Otero watching his every move, he said, "I heard a rumor that Harding is hiding somewhere up on Cerro Resaca." Collazo turned to look at him, his eyebrows raised in question as Scheutz walked on and then turned at the counter. "It's just a rumor. I have no idea if it's true."

"Who did you hear it from?" Otero asked.

"Tu madre," Scheutz said.

"Pendejo. I'm asking you a serious police question. Be careful I don't kick your ass right here."

Collazo waved his left hand at Otero to tell him to shut up. "Señor Scheutz, please. If you have any information at all about this man Harding, please tell us. Who did you hear the rumor from?"

"He heard it from me," Migdala said.

"And you heard it from who?"

"From whom."

"¿Que?"

"'From whom' is the correct English way to say it."

"Por favor."

"I heard it this morning at the produce truck," she said from behind the counter. "A bunch of women were talking about it. I don't know who said it."

Collazo drained his can of cola and motioned for Otero to hurry and finish eating. In two minutes they were out the door.

Scheutz laid his fingers on the back of her arm. "Thanks."

"Come on, school is letting out about now." She took off her apron and he followed her through the rear door and then the apartment and out the back to the Volvo, her motioning for him to drive. Coming down the hill toward the main road along the bay they could see the police jeep hurrying out the road that led eventually up the hill toward Resaca.

"I have to tell you something," Migdala said as Scheutz turned onto the main road. "You know..." She paused, worrying a thumbnail with her teeth. "Mi Tio Juaquin tenia mucho dinero."

"He had a lot of money. That makes sense given the business he was in. So?"

"You know he lived in the same house in Santurce where I lived with my mother and Blanca before I went to New York. He bought a house in Mayaguez a few years ago but he kept the one in Santurce to be near San Juan. I think he only came over here to Culebra when he had some scheme going on with Harding. My mother called me yesterday. She was cleaning out the house and she found a lot of money. He put it everywhere; in boxes, in his dirty clothes hamper, inside his jacket pockets in the closet, in his rolled-up socks, in his shoes."

"Why didn't he put it in the bank?"

"He must have put some of it in the bank. But I think he had some problems laundering the money."

"So he put it in his laundry." She gave him the you're-talking-silly look again. "Okay, okay, I'm sorry. I'll make an effort..."

"My mother said he would want the money to go for Blanca."

"Really?"

"He loved her very much, you know."

"No, I didn't know. He didn't seem like the kind of guy who gave a shit about anybody."

"He did. He loved his sister, my mother. And he loved Blanca. I think the other reason he came over here to Culebra was because I brought her here."

Students in their uniforms of dark blue pants or skirts and light blue shirts milled around on the street and sidewalk in front of the school entrance. The seventh, eighth and ninth grades let out before the lower ones so only the bigger kids could be seen, walking away in groups or standing and talking. Near the entrance, a male teacher seemed to be trying to break up an argument among a group of students. Several students formed a circle, watching two in the center.

"Ay, Dios mio!" Migdala opened the door even before the car came to a full stop. In the middle of the group of students the teacher had hold of Blanca, apparently trying to release her grip on the long hair of another girl.

He found a parking spot and pulled the Volvo out of the middle of the road. Standing outside next to the car he could see the argument in front of the school getting more heated. The male teacher held onto Blanca's right arm, Migdala pulled the girl's left. Everybody seemed to be pointing and yelling at once, in loud rapid Spanish. It reminded him of a few altercations his own kids had had during their high school years. Maybe he should go over there and help out? No, he wasn't much help back then and probably would not be much help now. Besides, he'd probably say something silly.

The heat of the argument finally dissipated and Migdala led Blanca by the hand to the car. He opened the door to let them both climb into the back seat, then, settling himself into the driver's seat, said in his best chauffer voice, "Where to, Madam?" Migdala paid no attention to him, but ran a monologue at Blanca, urging the girl to do something, in Spanish too rapid for him to pick up. Blanca rolled down the window, leaned her head out and shouted back at the teacher in the school yard. "Hijo de puta. Todos los maestros son patos."

Scheutz watched them in the rear view mirror as he moved slowly through traffic on the one-way street. The girl made him feel the way his own kids did in high school. But that was so different, his two sons were at least rational. Migdala's daughter seemed unreachable, all raw emotion. He watched Migdala's face as she murmured to her daughter, stroked her, tried to get her to calm down, all the while knowing there was nothing he could tell her that would help, that all he'd learned raising his own kids didn't apply here. But there must be something he could do.

Chapter 15

By the time breakfast was over on Saturday morning, he and Asher had almost completed the second tier of the cement block for the outer wall. They had twice circled the entire building just outside the existing, termite-ridden wooden wall. Suddenly, the entire wooden wall shook as Blanca stepped out and slammed the door. She then slammed it twice more. Each time the wall shuddered all the way to the corner, its top wavering with the attached sailcloth whip-snapping. She turned toward Scheutz and Asher where they had stopped their work, the anger in her face pushing though her tears.

Asher gave a short laugh. "The fiery wind of Shango. Goin'ta burn us all."

Blanca's glare turned to a burst of laughter to match Asher's. The laugh disintegrated immediately into tears. "I hate her. I hate her." Alternating between short laughs and long sobs, she back and forth between Asher and the recently slammed door.

Scheutz left off setting the cement block he held in his hands. The girl stood there in her white t-shirt and bright red shorts, her bare feet slightly pigeon-toed, sobbing as if wanting someone to comfort her. He did not want to imagine what was causing all these tears, could think of nothing more than putting the girl's head on his shoulder the way he had done so often with his own kids in the midst of some crisis so long ago.

She turned to face the road and then back to face them, then spun around again, her hands covering her face. She did another complete circle, stopping each time for a short moment to face the bay then the road then the door and back to where they stood watching her. Her hands dropped from her face and she beat her fist against the side of her thigh as she doubled over at the waist, tears dripping down her chin and nose, gritting her teeth.

Scheutz set the cement block down on the ground and started toward her but Asher, who had thrown the trowel into the mortar bucket, reached her first. He took her by the shoulders and straightened her to full height, placing his hand on her back and her head on his chest. A cross between a moan and a groan rose up from somewhere deep inside her, sounding as if it could have come from a man, a woman, or even a beast, and then subsided, leaving only a muffled sobbing. Scheutz walked behind her, facing Asher who looked up at him as if to say, "what now?" But Scheutz did not know what now. He'd seen his share of teenage angst with his own kids and their friends, felt some of it himself, but this was beyond anything he'd ever witnessed. Something horrible must have happened. Was it something with the hurricane? Her uncle's death? Did Harding do something to her? He reached out to touch her shoulder but she walked toward Asher who held his hand out to her. So, he went inside to see what had caused this latest outburst.

Migdala bent in front of the open refrigerator, cramming a plastic container of something into a space too small for it. He waited until she straightened and closed the door. "Your daughter is outside sobbing her heart out. What happened?'

"She hates me."

"Now what did you do?"

"Don't come in here teasing me. I'm having a very hard day."

"Okay. But she sounds like some catastrophe has ripped out her soul."

"It has."

He waited for her to say more but she picked up another plastic container filled with rice this time and walked over to the same overcrowded refrigerator. She held onto the container with one hand and shoved things around inside the refrigerator with the other. "You want to know what her big catastrophe is? She is in love."

"That's what all this is about?"

"No. What all this is about is that I will not allow her to go to her lover. Because I am a wicked mother."

"Why not?"

"None of your business."

"Oh. Okay. Excuuuse me."

"You want to help clean up in here? I can't get her to do it."

"We're right in the middle of laying block out there. Are my services as a dishwasher more important at this moment than getting that wall done?"

She shook her head and waved her hand for him to go. He stopped in the open doorway. Was that a sniffle he heard from her? "You okay?"

With her head down she nodded and a single tear fell onto the cutting board where her hands busied themselves piling dishes next to the sink. Outside, Asher had moved Blanca to sit on the tier of cement block they had recently put in place. He sat beside her, listening to her say something Scheutz could not hear. Well, they were not going to get much block laid right then so Scheutz might as well stay inside and help Migdala clean up. Besides, she could probably use someone to talk to. He closed the door and walked around the counter to stand next to her at the sink, touching the side of his arm against hers. She let go of the dishes, turned, threw her arms around the outside of his arms, and buried her head into his chest, sobbing not unlike her daughter outside on Asher's chest. What the hell was going on?

"What the hell is going on?"

"I can't tell you."

"What is so bad? Is she madly in love with El Diablo? Or one of his cousins?"

Sniff. "Cousin."

"She's fifteen; she's liable to be in love with any kid that sits next to her in home room. So, it's somebody in her class?"

"No."

"Look, this is no big deal. When I was fifteen I fell in love with some girl who sat in the first row just because I liked the way her hair fell onto her shoulders." It wasn't so bad standing here in the middle of a workday with his arms around his boss.

She stepped back. "This is a big deal, okay? You think I don't know, like I was never fifteen? This is not teenage tonteria, I'm talking about."

"Okay. So what are you talking about?"

"I'm talking about the worst scumbag that ever put his foot on this island." She reached for the napkin dispenser on the counter and blew her nose. Her face collapsed and she began crying again. He put his arms around her shoulders and pulled her to him. Her hands pressed into his back, her tears dampening the front of his t-shirt.

"You want to tell me who it is that is so bad?"

"No." Sniff. "You could not keep him away from her even if you did know."

"Well, what about your boyfriend, the cop, can't he keep him away from her."

She let go of him, stepped back and stamped her foot. "Will you please stop calling him my boyfriend? Raul Otero no es mi novio."

"That's not what he seems to think."

"Es un pendejo. If he was not so stupido he could catch that primo del demonio."

"From what I can tell he's too busy trying to catch Harding to… Wait a minute. Are we talking about Harding here? Is he…?"

She met his eyes. "Your friend, Harding…"

"Oooh, now I see what the problem is. This isn't just some tenth grade romance. What the hell is going on?"

"What's going on is that hijo de puta is hiding out somewhere on this island with the police looking for him and he is not leaving because he wants to take Blanca with him."

"Holy shit. Are you sure about this? That guy's twice her age."

"And he is your friend."

"He is not my friend, okay? Any more than Otero is your boyfriend. I don't know where he is, and if I did I would tell the CIC guy in a minute."

"So why was he on your boat?"

"You mean that day you and Blanca walked out there? He snuck on board and hid below deck. I was trying to take him to the police when you showed up."

She stared at him in silence.

"It's true. I don't even like Harding; he's a creep."

"See, I told you not to go to Cuba for my uncle. Harding made it turn out bad. And now my uncle is dead and my daughter wants to run away with a demon."

"Blanca is not why Harding is hanging around on this island."

"Oh no? Then you tell me why. Is he waiting for you to get your boat fixed so he can sail away with you?"

"Nope. The same reason he snuck onto my boat that day. He's looking for those emeralds we got in Cuba."

"Emeralds?"

"Yeah, don't you remember I told you about them? You were the one who told me not to take a package to bring back to your uncle. I thought I told you about it when we returned. We took it away from Harding and I hid it on my boat. And Harding is still looking for it."

She shook her head as if in disbelief. "Que Dios." She turned to look toward the open front door and then turned back. "I don't care about your goddamned emeralds. Give them to Harding so he can leave my daughter alone."

"I don't know where he is."

She bent again to the dishes.

"What're you going to do, keep her locked up here?"

Migdala shook her head without looking up. If only he could tell her what she should do. At least give her some advice or suggest a direction. But it was beyond him. He started to say something; he did not know what, anything just to be saying something. But nothing came. He let it go and went for the door.

Outside, Asher mixed a batch of new mortar, kneading the gray substance with a hoe while Blanca stood by holding a hose. What? What happened here? One minute the girl is sobbing her heart out and the next she's helping mix mortar.

Scheutz moved to stand next to Asher. "What's going on?"

"The other batch got all dried out. Get ready with some more block; we got to get this wall done sometime. Come on, girl, give me some water in the middle."

Blanca pressed the nozzle and the stream of water hit the mortar, splashing some up onto Asher. She let out one short laugh and then immediately went back to her dour look.

"Got-DAM, girl, watch what you doing."

She glanced up at Scheutz with the tiniest of grins at the corner of her mouth. Then she gave the nozzle handle a gentle squeeze producing a misty spray over the mortar. Asher nodded and then waved his hand to let her know to stop.

It was true that teenagers all went through very quick mood swings, but this was ridiculous. What the hell did Asher do, what did he say to her? He'd have to ask him about it tonight back at the boat. Not that the girl looked all that happy now, but at least she had perked up enough to stop sobbing, and enough to enjoy her little joke at Asher's expense.

Asher dropped the hoe next to the sheet of plywood holding the mortar. "We ready. Let's go. Mister Clement, grab the block. Blanca put that hose down and scoop the mortar in the bucket." He handed the girl a short handled shovel and pointed to the empty bucket. Blanca inched over to grab the bucket and then bent to scoop mortar into it.

Asher picked up his trowel and banged on a block on the tier already set in place. "Let us go. Let us move. We be here all day to get nothing done."

Blanca continued at the same pace. Scheutz walked over to pick up the cement block he had dropped when Blanca came out the door.

Asher bent to take mortar from the plywood and plopped it into place, buttering the block enough for Scheutz to place and position it.

They worked like that for the next hour, Asher moving along the wall with the bucket of mortar, Scheutz placing block, Blanca manning the hose and filling the mortar bucket when needed. Blanca worked in silence, responding to Asher's requests. Scheutz watched her as he worked, expecting any moment for her either to stomp off toward the road or just quit and sit down. But, other than letting them see her exaggerated sulk, she looked as if she were trying to keep pace with them. They moved completely around the entire building setting one tier of block and then another. At the four corners Scheutz broke blocks to maintain a rough vertical edge that would later be filled in by pouring the corner pillars. At the two doorframes, he used a four-foot level against the edges of the blocks vertically to assure they were roughly plumb.

The job probably could have moved along just as fast without Blanca's help, but it was nice to know where she was and what she was doing. Despite telling himself it was none of his business, Scheutz had found himself more and more thinking about the girl, not exactly worrying about her, but running little scenarios in his head about how to help her. Even though his lack of ability to be of help mostly stemmed from not knowing what the hell was wrong with her to begin with. Now that he knew about this connection between her and Harding, he would definitely find some way to step into the middle of it. At least do what he could to find Harding and make sure he got his ass off this island and stayed off. If that involved the police dragging him off in chains, so much the better. This Blanca thing was the last straw as far as Harding was concerned. He should have listened to Samantha way back in St. Thomas and just left the guy's boat stranded over there.

A little before noon, Tapon and Arturo showed up at the door to the restaurant. Tapon stopped and gave his great granddaughter an appraising look where she stood mixing mortar on the piece of plywood. He nodded and raised his eyebrows before turning to say something to Arturo. Arturo pointed at her and then raised his fist in salute. "Ay, chiquitta. Muy bien." She flicked a dab of mortar at him.

They finished a tier at the opening for the front door and Scheutz suggested they stop for lunch. The wall was waist high and they were practically out of the cement blocks Tapon had been able to secure with credit from FEMA. Hopefully, by tomorrow Gonzalez's hardware store could deliver another load of block and maybe the aluminum windows and doorframes would be on the ferry from the main island. Asher had Blanca wield the hose while they cleaned the tools and then rinsed the mortar and dirt off their hands and arms. Blanca rinsed off her legs and bare feet and the spots of gray mortar she had gotten in her hair. Her t-shirt and shorts were also flecked with gray and she brushed at them to get off the grit, which still left little spots behind. Scheutz wet his hands and lifted the girl's chin to rub off gray specks from her cheeks and nose. She gave him the same tiny grin as when she'd splashed Asher. He smiled. Today marked the first time she had given him anything but a casual sneer.

Inside, Blanca and Asher both sidled up to the table occupied by Tapon and Arturo. Blanca plopped herself with a sigh next to her great grandfather and Asher sat across from her next to Arturo. Migdala's eyes, from behind the counter, followed her daughter's movement from door to table. Blanca ignored her mother but gave Tapon a friendly punch on the arm. The old man wrapped his arm around her neck, pulling her to him to plant a kiss on top of her head.

Scheutz walked to the counter and, with his back to the table where Blanca sat, gave Migdala a look that said, "Go figure."

She looked around him at her daughter, then said in a low voice, "But if she thinks I am going to serve her lunch, she's nuts. And that goes for the rest of you."

"I'll take it over to them."

The restaurant had begun to fill with the usual lunch crowd. Migdala threw food onto plates and tossed the plates onto the counter, giving a name to each one. "Tapon. Arturo. You." He carried the first plates to the old men and then waited for her to fill the last two before carrying all three to the table. By the time he returned to the table, Asher had brought soft drinks and cans of beer from the cooler.

No one said anything while they all dug into their food. Blanca stopped eating to take a big gulp from her can of soda and let out a small belch in her great grandfather's direction. He winced and shook his head at her. She turned to Scheutz. "So, making progress, huh?"

He tried not to laugh. Her effort to sound like a construction worker was just so damned cute. "Yeah, we're getting there."

"Think we'll finish that wall today?"

"We're not going anywhere till we get more block."

She nodded, chewing. "So what do we do in the meantime?"

"We'll go out and work on the boat this afternoon."

She stopped chewing, looked over at her mother and then back to Scheutz. "Well, I'm sure I can help you out there, too."

"I don't know. What could you do?"

"I can do all kinds of stuff. What's wrong with the boat?"

"I thought you knew. It's got a big hole in the bottom."

"Oh. Well, we'll figure out something, right?"

Asher gave a little chuckle between bites. "Oh, yes. We figure out something."

Scheutz put down his ginger ale. "I'm not sure your mother will let you go out to the boat."

Blanca jumped up from the table. "I'll go tell her I'm going out." She went to lean over the counter to say something.

Migdala straightened like she'd been slapped. "No." Blanca leaned in again spewing words at her until Migdala slammed a plate of food onto the counter and shouted the name of the person who had ordered it. "I said, no. You want to go out there and find that Harding coño. No.You will not go unless I go with you. You finish your lunch and go to your room."

Blanca turned and stomped back to the table with tears in her eyes. She sat but did not eat. Instead, she mumbled just audibly, "Coño. Que cabróna." She looked up at Scheutz and then Asher, her eyes narrowed in anger. "I will be on the job this afternoon." She gave a decided nod of her head, lifted her soda can for a gulp, slammed it down on the table, stood and gave a loud belch in her mother's direction, then turned and walked from the room, leaving her half-finished plate of food. She slammed the door to the rear apartment, setting up a shudder in two of the outer walls. Migdala banged two plates onto the counter and called out a name. A woman came to pick them up without a word. Asher and Tapon looked at each other and laughed.

When they finished eating Scheutz carried the plates to the sink and ran hot water. "We'll clean these and head out to the boat."

She scraped the leavings off a plate and slipped it into the sudsy water. "What about the wall?"

"Ran out of material."

Migdala nodded, but Scheutz could not tell whether she meant the nod for him or for Senora Ochoa who, on the other side of the counter, had begun giving the order for her and her husband's lunch. Three people from another table set their dishes on the counter in front of Scheutz and went to stand by the cash register until Migdala had time to take their money. He scraped and washed dishes until she came back to stand next to him to scrape more dishes and slide them into the soapy water.

"Did you talk to Gonzalez about sending more block up here?" he asked her.

"Yes. The load was supposed to be here today."

"And when are the doors and windows supposed to come in?"

"¿Quien sabe? Tapon has to talk to him again about money."

"What about it?"

"We don't have any."

"I thought you told me your mother found all kinds of money that belonged to your uncle. What's up with that?"

"You don't know my mother."

"She wouldn't help Tapon get his restaurant back in shape?"

She laughed. "She thinks he is getting a whole bunch of money from FEMA for rebuilding the restaurant."

"He is, isn't he?"

"He's getting some, but not enough. And my mother is asking him for some of that."

"So what are you going to do?"

"Oh, we will get the material from Gonzalez. Tapon is an old friend of his father. They lived on this island since back before Columbus found it."

"Gonzalez must be making tons of money right now."

"Por montones. Oh, by the way, I just remembered something. Gonzalez told me he has one of those big iron jacks that you use to lift houses with."

"Really?"

With lunch over and the place cleaned up, Migdala drove Scheutz and Asher to the hardware store run by Gonzalez. She talked to the owner about sending more cement block while Scheutz and Asher went to look for the house jack. It turned out to be a big one, with a piston a good foot in diameter. It took both of them to carry it out to the station wagon. They dropped Asher off near the dock so he could bring the dinghy back out to the boat and Migdala and Scheutz drove the heavy jack out to the ridge above where the schooner still rested at a forty-five degree angle at the shoreline. Asher tied off the dinghy and climbed to the ridge to help drag the heavy jack down the hill.

Migdala followed them down to the boat. "I guess this means no more work on the wall today."

Scheutz was busy planning how they would set up the jack to start hoisting the boat upright. "Uh, yeah, I guess so."

She shook her head. "You guys look like two kids who just got a new toy for Christmas."

They positioned the jack under the gunwale about where it met the deck. Scheutz tilted it while Asher positioned a rock under it. Scheutz found a heavy block of wood to put between the jack piston and the side of the boat while Asher went aboard to find a large pry-bar to give them leverage turning the screw. Migdala stood aside with her head tilted, watching them. "I'm going to go," she said finally.

"Bye."

"By the way, I don't know what you said to Blanca, but thank you for letting her help this morning."

Scheutz stood next to Migdala, away from the jack to let Asher take the first turn. "She could come and help us here if she wants."

Migdala shook her head. "No, no. She would love to come out here. This is the last place she saw Harding, and she thinks if she is out here he will come back."

"Yes, and if she is out here, and it brings him back, we'll grab his ass and haul him down to visit Otero."

"You want to use her like a rabbit in a trap to catch a wolf?"

He shrugged. "Yeah. Something like that."

"No, no, senor. Not my daughter. If you want to get that man down here, why do you not use the packet of emeralds as a bait? That would get him."

That was going to happen anyhow. It was just a matter of time till Harding showed up again looking for the packet. And when he did, he would not be given a choice as to whether or not he wanted to go talk with the police.

Asher turned the screw on the jack a full turn and the timbers of the schooner's hull began screaming as the boat slowly shifted its position. He stopped and looked toward Scheutz, giving him a white-toothed grin. Scheutz ran to hop aboard the tilted deck to find loose boards to prop up that end of the hull. Migdala shouted that she was going to leave them, but they paid her no mind.

After propping the aft portion of the hull for the small progress already made, they moved the jack down ten feet and repeated the process. Moving forward on the hull in that way, by the middle of the afternoon they had raised it from a forty-five degree angle to maybe a forty-two degree angle. Going at it like this would take them close to a week to move the boat upright, but at least for the first time they could see some progress. A glimmer of hope that this boat may float again.

It was hard to actually see the difference in the angle, but when Scheutz climbed aboard to fetch a water bottle from the galley, he could feel the slight change in the slope of the deck. They found shade from the afternoon sun and took a break before beginning the next round of lifts along the hull. Scheutz handed the water bottle to Asher after a long pull. "You know, I'm curious how you managed to calm that girl down so fast and get her helping you. What did you do?"

Asher sipped and then shook his head. "I didn't do nothing."

"You must have done something."

"I just talk to the girl. You know, tell her 'it's okay' and 'yeah, I understand' and like that. She slobber all over my shirt and I just hold my arms around her till the right moment and then I say, 'You got to help me with the mortar.' And she nod her head and wipe her face on her t-shirt and we go to work."

"How do you know what's the right moment? Where did you learn to do that?"

"I always knew it. Born knowing it. Everybody is."

"Not everybody is."

"Yeah they are. Just like everybody born knowing how to suck on a tit. And you know how to talk to a person like that."

"I do?"

"Yah, mon. But you got to pay attention. And you got to be interested. You can't be thinking, 'Oh, I'm late for work' or 'Why is this girl bothering with this shit?' That girl want to help me with the mortar because she know I'm interested."

While Scheutz looked for more boards to prop the hull, Asher set up the jack for the next round of lifts. They worked their way back down the hull and then stopped for another break. They had just sat down when Blanca showed herself on the ridge above them, waving and shouting, "Estoy aqui."

They passed the water bottle between them and watched the girl descend the slope, dodging the thorny raya bushes. Dressed as she had been that morning except for pink rubber flip-flops on her feet, she stopped below where they sat at the low end of the deck and spread her hands wide as if to say "Ta da."

Scheutz put on his most stern face. "Does your mother know you're here?"

She grinned. "Do you know what the Fifth Amendment is?"

"Yes. Do you?"

"Well, no, not really. But I plead the Fifth, anyhow."

"What the hell're you doing here?"

She pointed to the water bottle. "Im very thirsty."

Asher tossed her the bottle her.

"Your mother does not want you out here," Scheutz said.

She brought the water bottle down and shrugged with her lip curled. "Why not?" She tossed the bottle back up to Asher.

"Because Harding might show up here."

Asher caught the water bottle. "Harding? What that mon got to do with it?"

Scheutz nodded toward the girl. "You're in love with him, right?"

Asher curled his lip at Blanca. "Girl, are you crazy? That mon going to do nothing but nibble on your goodies and toss you back in with the baby shrimps."

She leaned forward with her mouth open. "Huh? ¿Que dices?"

"I say, if you got yourself set on falling in love, you do better to pick a mon with a heart."

"Harry is not like that."

"Harry?"

Scheutz laughed. "Yeah, that's his name, Harry Harding."

"His parents did not do him a favor."

"They probably thought the name was very funny. Hardie har har Harry Harding."

Now Asher laughed. "Harry Hardie-Har-Har Harding, got him a hard-on, but got no heart."

Blanca stomped her foot. "Stop it. Stop making fun of him."

"The mon is a joke."

"You both act like those stupid boys in my class that are always making fun of everybody."

"Blanca, por favor." Scheutz patted the deck next to him. "Come up here and sit in the shade. We are not making fun of you. But let us tell you about Harding."

"My mother is always telling me about Harry. And it's not true. He did not kill Tio Juaquin."

"Come and sit down."

She walked to the ladder and climbed aboard, then moved to step over Scheutz and sit next to Asher in the shade. She pulled her knees up, laid her arms across them and then put her head down on her arms. "Harry loves me." She spoke down into the space between her legs, her body shaking as if she had begun crying again. "He is the nicest person I ever met. He talks to me. And he lets me talk to him. He is not bad like everyone says."

No, on the surface Harding was not a bad person. Yes, he was an idiot. Thankfully. If he had half a brain he could do a lot of harm, but he just always seemed so lost. If he did kill Juaquin, it was by accident; it was not in his own best interest. Even the time he pointed the spear gun at that Cuban Coastal Patrol official; he was more like a child having a temper tantrum than some kind of menace. But beneath all that dopiness, there was a true menace. He gave Scheutz a very subtle sense of malice, of evil masked by the idiocy. There are people who are drawn to that kind evilness, and he found himself hoping that was not the case with Blanca.

Asher patted her arm. "Maybe the mon is just an idiot."

She looked up sideways at him, then caught Scheutz's eye and let out a teenage giggle through her tears. "He is, isn't he?"

Chapter 16

Scheutz swept the dining area, taking his time, moving slowly around the few people still sitting after the breakfast hour was un-officially over. A steady breeze disturbed the yellow curtains closed against the morning sun on the window facing the bay, lifting them so they wafted like a dancer's hands. The summer winds had shifted finally to the northeast by east, bringing ever so slightly cooler air. Outside the window, the now shoulder-height cement block wall contained an even larger opening for the new window that would give a better view and even more breeze once the inner wooden walls were removed. Salsa music played on the radio inside the restaurant.

At the table nearest the door, old Seňora Gomez lingered over her third cup of coffee, staring into space. Her house, higher up the road in the barrio, had been all but ruined by the hurricane and no one had done anything yet to help repair it. She had no family left on the island and the FEMA people had not yet been successful in hiring anyone to do the work; everyone was so busy.

At his usual table in the rear, Tapon sat talking to Blanca and the J.R. Dobbs character who had not been back since the funeral. Blanca had her arm over Tapon's shoulder as he bent his head. She talked with him quietly, turning once in a while to Bob Dobbs to ask if he agreed. Bob would merely raise his eyebrows, take his pipe from his mouth and nod. Through lunch Tapon had not been able to eat. Something reminded him of his son, Juaquin and, without Arturo around to cheer him up, he slid quickly into a depressed funk, pushing his plate of food away and burying his face in his hands. That was when Blanca moved to his side of the table and draped her arm over his bony shoulders.

Tapon kept repeating that his son's death had been his fault, and shaking his head whenever Blanca insisted that it was not. Bob Dobbs had come through the door in the middle of the old man's lamentations and sat down to see if he could help. He listened to Tapon's blubbering reasons why his son's death had been his fault and then quietly assured the old man that he was nuts. That was exactly how he said it; "You're nuts." Tapon glowered at him and Blanca laughed. Since then the three had gone on as they were, Tapon whimpering, Blanca whispering insistently in his ear and looking to Bob Dobbs for support, and Bob throwing little comments out of the side of his mouth opposite his pipe. He only took his pipe out when he nodded.

Scheutz picked up pieces of the conversation as he was sweeping close to their table, asking the old man to lift his feet. "It was not ever your fault," Blanca hiss-whispered at him. "It was all my fault."

"Everybody blames themselves when a loved one dies." Bob tilted the non-pipe side of his head toward Tapon.

"No, it really is my fault." She leaned in front of Tapon and laid her hand on Bob's arm. She turned then to Scheutz, who at that moment was replacing chairs at the table opposite her. "Tell him. It's my fault, verdad?"

Bob and Scheutz caught each other's eye and smiled. Given the right circumstances, that girl could be a real sweetheart. Scheutz moved away to ask Señora Gomez to lift her feet.

Raul Otero, in uniform, came through the restaurant's rear door from the apartment behind. He nodded, smiling to Migdala behind the counter and stopped at the table in the dining area nearest where Scheutz swept. Waving a white envelope at Scheutz, he tossed it on the table.

"For me?"

Otero nodded and went to the counter. "A letter for you."

"From who?"

"Your wife."

"My wife? How'd you get it?"

"She sent it to the police station."

"Why the hell would she send it to the police station?"

"I don't know." Otero spread his hands and grinned. "Maybe she heard you were in jail."

Scheutz rested the broom against the table and picked up the letter. "It's open. Did you open it?"

"Yeah."

"That's against the law, isn't it? Opening other people's mail?"

Otero shrugged. "Maybe it's not. Maybe it came that time you spent the day with us."

"The cancelled date isn't until after that day. What the hell you doing opening my mail?"

"I don't know, maybe it has to do with police business."

"Does it?"

"Maybe. You never know."

"Maybe I'll report you."

"To who, the police?" He turned his back to Scheutz and leaned his elbows on the counter to talk in a low voice to Migdala.

The envelope was addressed to him, in care of the Culebra Police Department, and held an Acworth, New Hampshire return address with Samantha's name. Scheutz removed the letter and unfolded the two pages of lined paper, torn from a spiral notebook. Dated a week earlier, the letter had indeed been written by Samantha, in her wide-looped, even script.

Hey Clem,

Boy, are you hard to get hold of. I tried calling on your ship's radio but you don't answer. I'm sending this to the police station as they might be able to find you if you're still on the island. Anyhow, I wanted you to know my Dad died last week. We're just getting done with the funeral and burial. My brother Joe helped a lot, but Mom wasn't much help. She's a mess. They were married thirty-five years.

So, the big question now is, where do I go from here? Being back at home is driving me nuts. My Mom is driving me nuts. I know she's bereft and all but...Jesus.

A loud banging came from where Otero and Migdala talked together, as if a pot had been slammed onto the cutting board next to the stove. Migdala voice rose for one word, "No" and then lowered again, spoke in rapid, hissing Spanish to Otero, who leaned toward her over the counter, growling at her in return.

Scheutz went back to the letter.

As always, she hangs all over Joe for support, but gives me orders laced with major rations of shit. "If you had stayed home and taken care of your father, he'd still be with us." Can you believe that? She actually said that to me.

I gotta get out of here. My Dad's estate is in pretty good order. We worked on it in the last few months before he died. What a pant-load of money. I had no idea. We're all left pretty well off. Joe's going to sell the house here in Acworth and move Mom in with him and his wife. So, I can go anywhere I want. But where? I could show up in the Caribbean anytime. And I'll find you. The last time we talked, it ended on a downbeat. Let's pick up the conversation again.

Hope this letter finds you.

Sam

ps. I stopped by your old farmhouse and talked with Gerry. It was really nice to see her again. I gather Dan and Marty are doing fine. They're both coming up for Thanksgiving. Maybe I should stick around till then. It's not that far off.

He folded the paper and put it back in the envelope. Instead of taking up the broom again, he sat at the end of the long table and stared through the open window at the cloudless sky. It wasn't the letter itself that caused him such deep pangs of longing, it was the 'ps' at the end. His sons, Dan and Marty and that house full of teenagers when the kids were all in high school, that's what he missed more than anything. In some kind of way, through these last seven years with Samantha, she had kept him connected to all that. He'd seen Dan and Marty often enough over the years, but they didn't need him anymore like they had when they were kids. They were each pretty good at taking care of themselves now.

That first year after leaving New Hampshire and coming to the Caribbean he'd felt as if he were taking care of Samantha. But she changed and adapted, faster than he did, actually. It wasn't long before they both propped each other up, in the same way Gerry and he had done years earlier. But with Gerry it was hard, raising the kids, finding places to live, finding employment. With Samantha it was all about just enjoying themselves, sliding down some long tube into a warm comfortable bath of pleasure. Nothing to prop up really, more like a seven-year-long fuck, each one shifting position occasionally to enhance the piquancy.

Probably why they'd bought that old wooden schooner two years earlier; without realizing it, the pleasure just got to them and they needed some old wreck to take care of to help balance things out in a yin-yang kind of way. He had once driven down through the Blue Ridge Mountains where every turn in the road brought another scene of beauty, to the point where he longed to see a slum or at least an old run-down shanty just to break the monotony.

Was that why he felt such longing for those days with his kids? Someone had said to him once that raising teenagers was a little like getting onto a bucking horse. The only way to do it was to just go with whichever way they jumped. That was what it felt like with his own kids, up and down, up and down, all that hassle just part of the joy.

Asher entered the restaurant through the front screen door. He stood in front of the door, folded his arms and sent an elongated "Ahem" in Blanca's direction.

Blanca let go of her great grandfather's shoulder and stood. "Okay, okay. I'm coming." She picked up her oversized work gloves from the table and put them on. "No te sientas malo," she said to Tapon. "No es tu culpa." She patted the table in front of Bob with her gloved hand. "You take care of him, por favor."

Bob took his pipe from his mouth, nodded and smiled. "I will think of something pithy and truthful to say to him. I always do."

Otero and Migdala had advanced to the yelling stage of whatever disagreement they were having, both of them in rapid Spanish, too fast for Scheutz to catch, talking over each other, him pointing his finger in her face and her beating on the counter with a wooden spoon to make her point. Otero moved away from the counter, turned and pointed at Scheutz. "Esto es tu culpa. This is your fault."

Scheutz gave him a wide-eyed look. "My fault? What the hell you talking about?"

Otero jabbed his finger back toward Migdala. "Ella." He turned and headed toward the screen door just as Blanca reached it, grabbing the door from her hand. "Get out of my way." He slammed his way through the door.

Asher waited for Blanca to go out and followed her.

Scheutz stood and walked to the counter. "So, do I want to know what that is all about?"

Migdala stared at the wooden spoon in her hand and then tossed it into the sink, shaking her head. "No. It's just silly."

"He doesn't care much for Blanca, does he?"

She raised her eyebrows and shook her head again. Whatever fire had caused her latest outburst at Otero winkered and went out. She leaned her back against the cutting board next to the stove and raised a hand to her forehead. "He won't let it go."

"Won't let what go? Let you go?"

She shrugged. "He loves me. He wants me to marry him. He thinks you are the reason I don't want to."

"Me?"

"He's so jealous. He thinks I'm in love with you."

"Me? Hah."

"And he thinks you're in love with me."

"Oh, for Christ's sake. What would give him that idea?"

"He thinks that is why you moon around here sweeping floors and washing dishes."

"Not because I need the money? Or the food?"

"No. You don't understand. If you are a gringo, an Americano with a big boat, you must have money." She waved her hand at the dining area. "It makes no sense for you to be hanging around here, working for food."

"Is that what you think or is that what he thinks?"

She half nodded and half shook her head. "He thinks that."

"And do you?"

Again the half nod half shake, she looked up at him with her head bent. "Mmm."

He laughed. "So you think I'm just hanging around your restaurant here because I'm trying to get next to you? Or trying to get in your pants?"

"He read your letter from your wife."

"From my girl friend."

"Whatever. She is coming back down here with all her money. Why are you sweeping the floor in my restaurant?"

He opened his mouth to say something, but closed it again. This was such a stupid conversation. He was tempted to walk out and slam the screen door the way Otero did, and then grab Asher so the two of them could just go out and work on the boat. No, that would not do. No matter what these folks thought, he needed to keep doing what he was doing just to survive.

He folded the envelope with the letter and put it in the pocket of his shorts, grabbed the broom to finish up a little pile of dirt he had swept together, and then put the broom away in its place behind the counter.

On his way back around the counter, Migdala stopped him with a hand on his arm. "I have to tell you something. I don't care why you want to work in my restaurant. I am flattered that you do want to work here."

"Why? Just so you can break Otero's balls?"

"No. I would not marry Raul Otero if he went to court and ordered me to. And it has nothing to do with you."

"He doesn't like Blanca, does he?"

She pursed her lips and shook her head. "He wants Blanca to go back and live with my mother in Santurce. And then he and I can have the great island romance." She widened her eyes and waved her hands like a teenager at a rave. "Pero, Blanca es mi vida."

"And I take it Otero is not her father?"

"No. Raul and I went out together in high school. A long time before I moved to San Juan even."

"Well, anyhow, I do appreciate you helping us out."

She shrugged and waved her hand. "So far, it is good for me, you working here. And Asher." She pointed to the open window where Blanca and Asher could be heard laughing about something. "But I have to tell you something, Clem. I have watched you and Asher with her, and I say you two can work in my restaurant any time you want."

"She reminds me of my kids in a way. She's just full of…I don't know what you call it…you know, like a wobbly-legged foal, everything going off in all directions. I used to love watching my kids like that… couldn't tell what was coming next. They sure didn't know what was coming next. Just like she doesn't. Kinda cool. And kinda scary, huh?"

He looked back from the window to where Migdala stood, quiet, watching him. She nodded, not taking her eyes off his. He looked into her eyes for a long moment until she blinked. "Clement," she said. "Gracias."

"¿Porque?"

She made a face and shrugged. "Porque sí."

"I know." He did know. And he had to watch himself around this woman. Her admirer, Otero, was not totally wrong. There was an unmistakable invitation in Migdala's eyes. He found himself becoming so comfortable in her presence. That was what happened years ago with Samantha back in New Hampshire. She just always seemed to be there, in his house, doing things, little things that he overlooked or neglected, the kind of things women noticed, that softened the edges of life. He barely noticed, or took them for granted. All the kids in those days did weird things, the way teenagers will. Hers were of a domestic sort. But he came to expect them; they did make life a little more comfortable. She remembered people's birthdays and baked cakes, something he could never do. She hung curtains in the kitchen windows—not something he even noticed until the day she took them down to wash them, and then realized how much warmer they made the room feel.

By the time she was twenty-two, she was so much a part of his daily life, it felt weird if she was not there. Now the same thing seemed to be happening with Migdala. The daily routine of working in the restaurant, eating meals here, constructing a new building on top of the old one, was all beginning to feel like home. And Migdala and Blanca, like Samantha years ago, had begun to feel like family. That's what was so dangerous—the feeling of family coupled with the allure in Migdala's eyes had the potential of sealing his fate. And Blanca wasn't helping at all. Her recent transformation from sullen brat to funny construction crew acted like a grappling hook in both his and Asher's hides. Transient sailors of the Caribbean said that if someone's boat stayed anchored for too long in any one port, it was growing roots. He could picture the *Panacea*, already sitting half on shore, with long tentacles extending from its keel like mangrove roots down into the shallow water seeking nutrients from the ocean floor while branches sprouted from the main and mizzen masts, sprigging out into wide green leaves.

Samantha's letter would save him from that. He had thought when she told him she was not coming back that she would leave a cavernous hole in his life, but the opposite was true. He'd noticed a sense of relief with her gone, relief from when she was not wholly there even when she was there. She would have the money to put the schooner back together, but she didn't like the schooner. If she came back she'd probably propose they get rid of it.

He ought to get to work helping Asher and Blanca. Migdala had finished behind the counter and was now escorting Senora Gomez to the door. She waved at Tapon and Bob, motioning them out also. The old man was laughing now and Bob beamed his wide grin at him. When they were all gone, Migdala turned to Scheutz. "Are you going or staying?"

"I don't know."

Chapter 17

Chuck's Pizza Bar was showing a video of *Who Framed Roger Rabbit,* with Spanish subtitles, on Friday night. At supper in the restaurant, Blanca bounced with excitement, wanting to see it. She poked Tapon, prodding him to go with her. He grumbled that he did not want to spend an evening in the "gringo" bar watching a movie about some conejo stupido. Arturo made a joke about calling the movie "Who Framed El Conejo Harding?" which the police had started calling him since it looked like Harding had disappeared down some rabbit hole on the island.

Arturo's joke stopped Blanca in the middle of cajoling her great-grandfather and left her glum for the rest of the meal. To cheer her up, Asher said he would escort her to the pizza bar so she could see the movie.

Scheutz carried plates to the sink and Migdala put away perishable leftovers in the refrigerator. They worked together, cleaning the dishes. Scheutz mentioned to Migdala that Asher had planned to take her daughter to the gringo bar, just in case she might have some objections to her daughter frequenting a place like Chuck's.

To his surprise, Migdala's face lit up. "Oh, I want to go, too. Somebody told me it is a very funny movie."

"Well, you better hurry. According to Blanca, it's supposed to start pretty soon. I don't know how she knows that."

"Oh." Migdala stopped what she was doing and looked around the kitchen area. "Maybe we can just leave everything and come back after the movie to finish up."

"You go ahead. I'll close up for you."

"You don't want to see the movie?"

"Nah. Cartoons don't do much for me."

Almost like a teenage girl herself, she squeezed his arm and stood on tip-toe to give him a quick kiss on his cheek. Then, pulling her apron off, she yelled across the room. "Vamonos. Vamonos. We will take the car." Asher and Blanca followed her to the door. Before she went out, she turned and waved to Scheutz. "We will help you when we come back."

He waved her on. "I'm going out to the boat afterwards. Give Asher a ride out later."

He was tired after a long day in the sun, working on the boat in the morning and rebuilding the restaurant in the afternoon. The muscles in his shoulders ached and a cut on his finger stabbed with pain inside the industrial strength dish soap. He had never been too big on hanging out in bars after working all day, but trying to do that at age fifty was what they called "above and beyond the call of duty." How the hell did Asher do it? If he had the money, he'd be out every night, down at the Dinghy Dock or over on the malecon or sitting in El Batey. But then, Asher could just as well be thirty-years-old as he could be sixty; it was so hard to tell.

It wasn't just the tiredness and the achy shoulders that kept him from going with them to see the movie. No, there was something else that bugged him about it. He missed Samantha. Somehow she had made the mindless existence he led seem worthwhile. With her he could sit and watch a mindless movie, and not even feel it was an escape from an otherwise mindless life. You could lose your mind with all this mindlessness.

He finished soon after Tapon and Arturo left. Outside, the humid air seemed to have shifted a little more northeasterly, the breeze picking up slightly. It would be a nice night with not too many mosquitoes. The moon had not risen yet but there was enough starlight and various shore lights to help him pick his way through the mangrove to the small wooden dock where his dinghy was tied. Out on the water, he puttered his way through the boats moored in close and then opened the throttle and pointed the lifted prow in the direction of the schooner. The tiredness and pain in his shoulders melded together to create a persistent dull ache.

With the dinghy tied up to the work raft, he climbed aboard the schooner and felt his way along the starboard rail toward the hammock tied to the forward mast. Just past the main mast, a screaming, writhing animal landed on his back, pushing him face forward onto the rail. Whatever it was had his neck in tight grip, choking him and hissing in his right ear. He threw his body backwards slamming the animal into the side of the doghouse. It gave a human grunt as an arm tightened its grip. They slid writhing to the teak planking of the deck as Scheutz's mind raced to identify the smell—definitely human, rank, vaguely familiar…Harding.

Scheutz jabbed his elbow backwards into the man's gut, and was rewarded by another, stronger, grunt. The arm around his neck slackened just a bit allowing him to turn to the side and dig his shoulder into Harding chest. He reached to grab a handful of the man's hair, the thinning hair on the top of his head and began yanking in short pulls, feeling strands tearing away from the scalp. Harding screamed but held tighter. Whatever sense of superiority he had when he realized it was Harding on his back ebbed with the awareness of how strong the man actually was. No amount of struggle worked against the arm choking him. The heat of the body and the smell and the force applied against him felt like being grappled by some fiend of hell.

Short bursts of light went off behind his eyeballs and he could not breathe. He considered the possibility that he just might die tonight, right here on the deck of his boat. If the man had killed Juaquin what would stop him from killing again. "Wha…" he choked out. "What do you want?"

"Emeraldzzzz."

So he wasn't going to die. At least not until Harding had the emeralds. He could feel himself begin to lose consciousness and let go of the hank of hair. He let his body go slack, which caused Harding's arm to lessen its grip. Scheutz nodded. And nodded again so Harding would get the message. "Okay." Harding let go his grip even further, allowing Scheutz to turn in to him fully, bring his hands up to jamb his thumbs into the man's eyes. He used the eye sockets to press the man's face away from his and pushed his own body upwards from the deck. The moment he had the advantage of distance he lifted his knee into Harding's groin with all the force he could muster.

That kind of kick in the balls would cripple a normal person, but while Harding cringed in a ball-busted, fetal position, he did not let go. Scheutz pushed back against the superstructure, panting and shaking his head to clear it. Glaring into Scheutz's eyes, Harding finally let go of his throat. Scheutz moved away from him and waited for him to come at him again. A small tuft of yanked-out hair had fallen onto Harding's chest, giving Scheutz a momentary sense of satisfaction. If this animal wanted to keep it up, he'd make an old man of him. Did he honestly think choking him like that would make him want to tell where the stones were? It was entirely possible that an impulse like that on Harding's part had gotten Juaquin killed.

Scheutz got his breath back and stood, rubbing his sore neck, looking down at Harding's half-snarl-half-grimace. He wanted to kicked him. Now what? He would like to drag this asshole into town and turn him over to Otero, but he was no match for him. He shook his head again to clear it.

Harding stood and moved forward to slump into one of the lawn chairs near the main mast. Tiny rivulets of sweat ran through the caked dirt on his cheeks. Scheutz lowered himself into the hammock across from him. Harding grimaced and adjusted his testicles. Then, as if a new person, or at least a new mask took over, his face softened into the usual conejo stupido, he said, "I'm sorry."

"You got that right."

"I mean I'm sorry for jumping on you like that."

Scheutz waited for what would come next. Harding slumped in the chair, looking in the twilight like he might even cry. Scheutz pushed with his foot to swing the hammock slightly. His body had begun to relax and his shoulders went back to ache mode. But he felt better than he had earlier. Maybe he was onto something here; maybe there was some form of tantric yoga that involved fighting for your life and thus attaining satori. Or at least attaining a relaxed state of mind.

He spread the hammock out behind him enough to rest his head against the netting and studied Harding's form in the chair before him. His hair and beard had become wilder, if that was possible. And he had lost weight. He looked like the Ben Gunn character in the Treasure Island movie, bony knees sticking out from ragged shorts, the dirtiest t-shirt imaginable. An animal smell without the mixture of rot came off him. Maybe the rot was from bad teeth breathing so close to Scheutz's face, but it made him think of a rotted carcass. The man had never been very far from the line that separates humans from beasts, but the rotten smell put him in mind of the chupacabra, the zombie-like goatsucker that was part of the Puerto Rico folklore. If the cops do catch him, maybe he could contact the ASPCA to provide him with a lawyer.

"Those are my emeralds, you know." Harding raised his head but looked off toward the bow of the ship as if unable to bring himself to meet Scheutz's eyes.

"That wasn't my impression."

"Well, they are. Who's else would they be?"

"Juaquin's. Or his estate."

"His estate?" Harding let out a squeaky, hyena-like laugh. "What the hell does that mean?"

"The people who would inherit anything he owned when he died. His father, his sister maybe, Blanca's grandmother.

"Hnnh. They wouldn't know what to do with them."

"Blanca's mother could help them. She's pretty smart, can find her way around."

Harding turned to face him for the first time. "You didn't give them to her, did you?"

"No. I still have them. But if I did give them to her, you better stay away from her. And, if I were you, I'd stay away from her daughter."

Harding shook his head slowly. "Tell her to stay away from me. I wish I'd never met that girl. She's the reason I'm in this mess."

"What mess?"

"Duh." He spread his hands and dropped his jaw open. "I'm wanted for murder. I'm hiding in a hole in the ground. All because I made the mistake of letting that bimbo hang around."

"You saying she's the reason you killed Juaquin?"

"I didn't kill Juaquin."

"So, who did?"

Harding started to say something and then stopped himself by putting his palms over his face. He rubbed his fingers across his forehead and cheeks and then rubbed his forefingers into his eyes. When he finally dropped his hands into his lap, the mixture of dirt and tears on the small portion of his face not taken up with beard and head hair looked like a primitive mask. He opened his eyes wide, as well as his mouth, and, his tongue vibrating outward. "Aagh." He glared at Scheutz. "Look, I don't know who killed him, okay?."

"Bullshit."

"If I could get those emeralds I could get out of here; leave everybody alone."

Good point. So why didn't he want to give them to him? If for no other reason than the fact that Harding worked for Juaquin, they belonged to him more than to Scheutz. If he gave him the packet of stones there was some likelihood they'd never see him again. Harding would abandon his boat, which was not seaworthy anyhow right now with its broken bowsprit. That would be the end of Migdala's worry about her daughter hanging around with him. And it would be the end of the police thinking he was hiding Harding from them.

So why not give him the emeralds? Something dragged at him, kept him from getting up out of the hammock and going below to find the packet and bring up to give it to Harding. Did he want to keep them for himself? He had to admit he did not know how to fence them, or whatever they call it, to get a decent value for them. No, that was not it. Somehow, even though it made no sense, he felt they belonged to Migdala. "I'll tell you what, I'll give you two of them and you leave Culebra. You can trade those two in wherever you do that kind of thing and tell the fence, or whatever you call him that you have more. Then you can have ten percent of whatever the rest of the stones bring."

"And you get the rest?"

"No. I'll take ten percent. Juaquin's father gets the rest."

Harding folded his hands and held them between his knees. He looked up at Scheutz and, for the first time looked him in the eye. "Tell me where they are.."

"What are they worth?"

"I don't know, really." He shrugged and looked away.

"Hundreds? Thousands?"

"Thousands if you get to the right person."

"And you can do that?"

"I've done it. I've been with Juaquin when he did it. The emeralds come from Colombia. I don't know how they get to Cuba. Same way everything else does, I guess, smuggling."

"That much I figured. Where do you take them?"

"There's a guy in Mayaguez, over on the other side of the main island. He works for an American company over there. Digital Equipment Corporation. He flies back and forth to Massachusetts about once a month and peddles all kinds of stuff up there."

"Would his name be Beltran by any chance?"

"How do you know that?"

"And I would bet he's the one makes all kinds of deals to have stuff removed from the Digital plant in Mayaguez for Juaquin to smuggle into Cuba, yeah?"

"Business is business."

"So how do we do business?"

Something subtle shifted in Harding's demeanor. He sat a little straighter and his face changed again from loser to demon. "You give me the emeralds, I'll get the money, and send you a cashier's check for everything over my ten percent."

"Well, that sounds a lot like, I give you the emeralds, you go get the money and I never hear from you again."

Harding grinned. "How about if I sign the title of my boat over to you. I'll never use that again."

Scheutz shook his head. "That boat has been confiscated by the police. For evidence."

"Well, what do you suggest?"

"I don't know." Scheutz stared out over the darkened bay to the lights twinkling in the town. "How about this: I'll give you the two stones. You go to your dealer in Mayaguez, and get what you can. Then you have someone get in contact with me and I'll bring over the rest. You take me to the dealer and then you get your ten percent."

"Make it four stones."

"Three stones."

Harding nodded slowly. "Migdala's mother lives in Mayaguez. I will get her to contact her daughter at the restaurant when I'm done."

"Then what?"

"Then I get away from here for good. But if I don't get my ten percent I come back. I take the girl and sink your boat."

Scheutz nodded. "I will bring the three stones to the ferry dock two minutes before the ferry sails with you on it."

"I am gone. I am a ghost on this island. See you in the morning." He crossed the deck and made very little noise climbing down the port-side ladder and moving through the darkness up to the ridge.

Chapter 18

The moment Scheutz stepped inside the door, Migdala came from behind the counter and rushed up to him. "Blanca is gone." She stopped with her hand flat against his chest, her face distorted with near panic.

Behind her Otero leaned a little too nonchalantly with his elbow on the counter. Tapon and Arturo sat at their usual table with coffee in front of them, but no breakfast. Three other regular breakfast customers all sat with coffee but no food. Except for Otero, Migdala's state of agitation seemed to affect everyone in the room. They all sat watching her, some absent-mindedly sipping their coffee.

"She did not come home from school yesterday." Migdala's turned to extend her hand toward Otero. "I talked to the police and they said I should not worry. She was probably just out with other kids having a party." Otero tilted his head and raised his eyebrows. She turned back to Scheutz, her eyes filling with tears. "But she did not come home all night." She looked at Scheutz's face and then at Asher who stood just behind and to the left of him; questioning them, her face collapsed into tears when she did not see the answer she hoped for, that her daughter had spent the night on their boat.

She wept into her hands. Scheutz stepped forward and put his arms around her, pulling her in so her head pressed into his chest. He held her there, her sobs filling the room, everyone, including Otero, frozen in place, watching her. Asher's voice infiltrated the silence. "We'll find her." His tone reflected Scheutz's own thought that, of course they'd find her, there was nothing to worry about.

Otero straightened himself at the counter. "And you think you can do a better job than the police in finding this girl?"

Asher took on a teasing tone. "We know you guys are good at finding people. That's why you still have not found Harding, right?"

Otero walked toward them and stopped, looking down at Migdala's forehead now resting on Scheutz's chest, his face set in anger. He motioned for them to move out of his path. At the door he turned. "Do not worry, Migdala. We will find her."

Migdala pushed herself away from Scheutz's chest, wiping her eyes on her apron. "Por favor."

Scheutz nodded. "We'll find her. The difference is, we want to find her, but I don't get the feeling your boyfriend does."

"She is with that Harding, I just feel it."

"Could be. But for right now, let's get breakfast on for these folks." He turned to Asher. "We'll forget about working on the building today and go look for Blanca."

Migdala took off her apron and walked toward the door to their apartment. "I can't do this. You cook; I'm going to look for her." She tossed the apron on a nearby table before opening the door.

Asher followed her. "I'll go with you. You go to the school and drop me off downtown."

"No." Scheutz stopped him with a hand on his arm. "I'll go with her. You cook. If I cook, none of these people will ever come back here." He followed her through the apartment and out the back door to the Volvo. She already had the car in gear as he jumped into the passenger seat.

The sun was just putting in an appearance out over the Caribbean as they headed down the road toward the bay. Migdala squinted and pulled down the sun visor. Scheutz pulled his sunglasses from the pocket of his shorts and put them on. Nothing moved on the flat surface of the water except a fishing boat with two men in it, its prow raised and its outboard engine making a lone muffled comment against the low hills surrounding the bay. On the road, a couple walked toward the town and only one vehicle, the Fish and Game Department truck, passed in the other direction.

Scheutz broke into Migdala's intense silence. "I didn't tell you, but I talked with Harding."

She jerked head around. "When?"

"Last night. While you were at Chuck's watching that Roger Rabbit movie. He wanted the emeralds that belonged to your uncle. I gave him three and figured that might be the last we'd ever see of him. That was the only thing keeping him here on Culebra."

Migdala slammed on the brakes, stopping in the middle of the road. "Now he is leaving with his emeralds and taking her with him."

"I don't think so. He told me himself he doesn't like having her around, and that he is trying to get rid of her."

"And you believe him?" She started the engine, which had stalled when she put on the brakes. They continued along the bay road and turned up toward town. She parked near the school, saying she was going in to talk with the teachers who must be there already. Then she would wait for the students to show up and see if they knew anything. Scheutz said he would go down to the dock to make sure she was not on the ferry.

The seven o'clock ferry was just beginning to load. Two cars and a one-ton truck waited in line on the ramp while another car drove up onto the ferry itself. Passengers milled around waiting for the vehicles to load before walking aboard. Most of the passengers Scheutz recognized as regular commuters who went to work every morning on the main island. Two gringos, boat people he had seen in Chuck's on various occasions, stood aside, each holding a small duffle bag. Another group of three men and one woman stood together talking, very possibly FEMA workers, since they did not look or dress like locals, tourists, or boat people. Another FEMA type stood a few feet behind them, with the group but not with the group.

Otero leaned with his back against his jeep, his arms folded in front of him, watching the loading. On the street facing the water, all the shops, including the tiny gas station, the restaurant and the liquor store, had not opened yet for the day's business. The sun had risen just enough to create a shadow line of the buildings out on the water just beyond the bow of the ferry.

Scheutz drifted through the waiting crowd, looking for a young, skinny girl who might be waiting with them, keeping herself behind another larger passenger. At the ticket window on the side of the ferry dock building, he asked the woman behind the plexiglass if she might have seen Blanca. She knew exactly who he was referring to because she was a sometime patron of the restaurant. She had not seen the girl but said she'd keep an eye out for her.

Only the truck remained on the metal connecting ramp from the ferry to the cement incline leading down to the water. The sun had moved to the front half of the ferry, which bobbed with the weight of the vehicles moving onto it. Otero had not moved from his station next to his jeep, but he had been joined by the CID man, Collazo, who had brought him a coffee.

Moving through the crowd again, Scheutz passed the small group of FEMA officials. The man who had been standing behind them, but not exactly with them, moved away to stand further to the side of the group. Scheutz looked at him now; something was not quite right about him. He wore sunglasses much too large for his face, the kind of sunglasses that you might expect to see on the cover of some women's fashion magazine. And the man was dressed in slacks, winged-tip shoes, light blue oxford cloth shirt and dark red and blue-striped tie. He carried a beige linen sport coat draped over his arm. His dark brown hair appeared recently styled and neatly combed. But there was something else odd about the man. His nose, protruding from under the sunglasses was deeply tanned and yet the face below the sunglasses, his cheeks and jaw, were as a pale as a winter city-dweller.

Scheutz moved around the group to get a better look but the man turned his back and moved further away, showing only the back of his head where the nape of the neck was also pale. What was there about the man that seemed so strange, yet so familiar? His stance was stiff, as if he were on parade, or posing before a camera. Without the face in front of him, Scheutz pictured it. The nose he recognized; it looked like...Harding.

It was as if an apparition had appeared before him. That was Harding standing there, only a few feet away from him. It was Harding without his body odor. And Scheutz did not recognize him. What's more, the man was parading himself in front of Otero whose main purpose in life these days seemed be focused on finding him. But, of course, Otero would miss him in this disguise. He would be looking for wild hair and beard and ragged clothing. Plus, to someone like Otero, most gringos, las caraquesas, all looked alike. This was Harding's escape from the island.

Scheutz walked away. He went through the crowd again, looking closer at all the passengers, who were now beginning to move toward the loading ramp since the last vehicle was aboard. He stood next to the seaman taking their tickets as they passed, scrutinizing everyone in case he should find Blanca in some other elaborate disguise. But he remained convinced she was not there. Harding was traveling alone.

As the FEMA people approached the ticket-taker, Harding sidled away from the line. Scheutz, moving slowly so as not to call Otero's attention to what he was doing, put himself directly in Harding's path. Harding stopped, holding his head up stiffly, confronting Scheutz with his ridiculous, opaque sunglasses. When he moved to the left to go around, Scheutz put his hand on the man's arm. "Where's Blanca?"

"I'm sure I don't know what you're talking about."

"You want me to tell those two cops over there who you are?"

"Let me go, Clem. I've got to get out of here."

"Tell me where the girl is or you will not get out of here."

"Do you have my emeralds?"

"Where's the girl?"

"Honest to God, I don't know."

"Have you seen her?"

"Yesterday. She came up to find me after school. She was the one who cut my hair." He cringed slightly away from the sudden movement of Scheutz's hand. But Scheutz did not touch him. Harding adjusted the sunglasses that had moved when he jerked his head back. "She left to go home. I swear, Clem. She left and said she was going home. Said she was going to her real home, whatever the hell that meant."

"Vamonos." The ticket-taker with the large belly motioned them aboard. The ferry let out a whistle and revved its engine. Everyone else had boarded and was walking forward around the vehicles parked on the deck. The ticket-taker waved his arm as if ushering small children onto the metal ramp.

Harding walked forward, holding his ticket out like some kind of peace offering. "Give me the stones, Clem. I have to go."

What could he do? He had to let the man go. Maybe it was enough that the girl was not with him. Maybe it was better that he was going. That might be the end of the nutty attraction Blanca had to this guy. He nodded and moved to Harding's side away from sight of the policemen, then, without moving another part of his body, put the folded envelope containing the three emeralds into the man's hand where it hung by his side. Up on the malecón, Otero and Collazo sipped their coffee and talked.

Scheutz watched the ferry until, its ramp up, the boat chugged away from the shore out into full sunlight. Harding stood stiffly near the back of the parked truck and waved at him, smiling. Scheutz turned and walked up the ramp, exchanging a nod of recognition with Collazo and ignoring Otero.

In front of the school building, Migdala talked with two girls, both in school uniform, who looked about Blanca's age. Scheutz stood next to the Volvo and waited for her. When the bell rang and the milling students filed into the front door, she came to stand beside him.

"They say she was in school yesterday, but she left early." She shook her head and let out a long sigh. "I don't know what I am going to do with that girl."

He waited to see if she had more to say, but she merely looked away from him, her eyes filling with tears. He spoke as gently as he could. "I'm afraid I have some more bad news for you. I saw Harding this morning." He told about his encounter with Harding, his makeover, that he had seen Blanca last night when she cut his hair. "I'm sure he's headed for Mayaguez."

Migdala moved suddenly to place herself directly in front of him, pointing her finger at him. "He said he would tell my mother to contact us when he had his money from his connection in Mayaguez." Why is he going to talk with my mother?"

"Because, I guess, she knows him from when he was doing business with your uncle."

"And if he was going to meet Blanca someplace, the best place for them to meet would be at her house."

"That makes sense. You know, he told me something she said, that I never thought anything of. When she left him yesterday, she said she was going home to her 'real home'. Any chance that might mean her grandmother's house?"

Migdala nodded her head slowly. "She always considers that house her real home. She never really liked it here on Culebra. She liked hanging around on the streets in the city. I'll bet that is where she has gone."

"She could have left on the ferry last night."

"And Harding is going to meet her there. Come on." She ran around to the driver's side of the car. Once again he barely got himself into the passenger seat before she screeched out into the street, cutting off a car coming up behind them.

At the waterfront, the bodega and the gas station were now open. Otero and Collazo had left and the ticket window in the ferry building had closed. Migdala stopped the car next to the telephone booth and jumped out. The phone lines still had not been restored to the barrio where El Tapon's restaurant stood. Through the booth's plexiglass he could see her gesturing and shouting into the phone, then slamming it down before stomping back to the car.

She let out a semi-strangled growl and hit the steering wheel. "Perra!" She paused with her hands together and eyes closed. "I know it is wrong to curse your mother, but that woman makes me so angry." They sat in silence looking out at the street and the water beyond the seawall. Migdala's breathing slowed. She placed her hands on the steering wheel. "She would not admit, but that is exactly where Blanca is, at my mother's house. I'm sure of it."

She started the car and made a wide U-turn. They rode in silence the entire way out of town, along the bay road, up into the barrio and into her driveway behind the restaurant. As he made to get out of the car, she finally spoke. "We have to get ourselves on the eleven o'clock ferry."

"We? Why do you want me to go along?"

She wrapped her fingers around his left wrist. "I need you to help me." She looked into his eyes, half pleading, half demanding.

How could he say no? Besides, what did he have to do so special it could not wait? He looked away from her eyes, too intense for him.

What was the big deal, really? The girl was safe with her grandmother. Harding had said he was trying to avoid her. But the Harding he saw this morning at the ferry dock could not be trusted with anything he said. "Okay. I'll go with you."

Asher said he would take over the cooking for the restaurant until they returned, hopefully, the next day. Arturo agreed to help him as long as he did not have to actually cook. Migdala and Asher would spend the morning making several different meals in advance while Scheutz took the dinghy out to the boat to pack a change of clothes into a small sea bag and retrieve the other half of the emeralds. By ten-thirty she parked the car on the malecón. Asher would take the car back to the restaurant, even though he had no driver's license. Migdala made a comment that, never in her memory had anyone been asked to show their driver's license on that island. A boat license maybe, but a not a car license. She didn't even think the mayor's wife had one, and that woman drove all over the place. Badly.

As the ferry pulled away, Scheutz gave a little wave to Otero who stood next to his jeep on the shore glaring at them. Once they were away from land, Migdala relaxed a little. They sat on a bench on the upper deck, under an awning stretched like an over-sized bimini to shade the benches set in rows like a waiting room. Sea gulls and boobies flew in arcs around the decks, waiting for food tidbits thrown by passengers. The birds floated on a strong eastern breeze that blew into the faces of the passengers as they sat facing the stern, watching the island recede in the distance.

Without looking at him, Migdala inserted her hand inside his where it lay on the sea bag in his lap. "Gracias. Thank you."

He turned to look at her, cupping his hand over her smaller one. She did not take her eyes from the island, which was fast becoming no more than a hazy blue jagged strip on the surface of the choppy water. "No es nada." How many years had it been since he'd used that expression? When he was what, twenty years old, in the army. Enrique and he used to say it to each other. They all said it. When things got rough, the little mantra was one way of helping them maintain. They'd say, "It don't mean shit." And for a short time, it didn't. Not the mud or the bugs or the cold or the punishing strain on the Darby tower at Fort

Benning during ranger training. Not even each hour of sheer boredom for every two minutes of stark terror.

And then later, after the army, he and Enrique in Cuba, when they gave each other the Spanish version. "No es nada." When the whole effort actually did mean nothing. That was his undoing. Fighting for Castro and then later fighting against Castro, either way it didn't mean shit. But it got his brother killed. And Enrique. So it must have meant something.

Not until his children came along did it change. Then, no matter how difficult it got, it always meant something. But after that, after they grew up and went away, he'd spent the last seven years with Samantha, lost in a world where again nothing meant anything. Not because they repeated the little mantra to themselves when things got rough, but quite the opposite, because life was all too easy. Nothing mattered. Nothing but leaning on a starboard tack in a healthy breeze on a white-capped sea, going nowhere in particular. Wouldn't that be a big problem with going to heaven when you die? Then what? All that bliss, it don't mean shit.

But watching Migdala's face, tense with worry over her daughter, he could not tell her "It don't mean shit." And he could not tell himself that either. Because it did mean something; the same as it did during all those years he took care of his own children. So, here's what it was all about, on a breezy sunny day in paradise, two things actually did mean something—keep yourself alive and take care of your kids. All the rest don't mean shit.

Chapter 19

The ferry turned slowly and then backed up to the cement ramp in Fajardo. Scheutz and Migdala waited in the midst of the passengers until the three cars and one truck disembarked. He tried keeping up with her quick pace as she moved through the milling crowd on the dock. On a narrow side street a block away from the water a row of publicos, passenger vans resembling a cross between taxi and mini bus, lined half of the street. She led him to one with a cardboard sign announcing it was heading for the San Juan area.

They were the first passengers into the vehicle but it filled quickly. In the hour and a half it took to reach the outskirts of San Juan they did not talk. The van had no muffler and three of the other passengers carried on a conversation so loud it was difficult for he and Migdala to hear what the other was saying. Migdala stared nervously out the window, chewing her lower lip. Scheutz watched the countryside, the fields, the small stores on the side of the highway, the closed sugar cane refinery. Off to the south as they passed the town of Rio Grande, the island's highest summit, El Yunque, rose out of the rain forest to meet low-lying clouds.

They passed the sign announcing the turn-off to the international airport, which for some reason made him think of Samantha. This would have been the way she came when she left the island to return home to New Hampshire. Was that only just a few months ago? The hurricane was in September and she left before that. Now it was close to Thanksgiving. It seemed like a lifetime. He waited for the expected sense of missing her to float into his consciousness, but it did not come. Weird. Missing Samantha had become an almost daily companion since she left, a strange comfort and bed partner. For a moment he missed missing her, then let out a snort of a laugh. It was almost like a small child missing the pacifier that substituted for the tit.

Migdala turned to look at him in response to his snort, raising her eyebrows in question. He merely shook his head and she went back to biting her lip. There was something oddly comforting in the closeness of her body next to his on the seat of the van, her upper arm touching his. But more than that, the intensity of her focus on finding her daughter made his missing Samantha pale in comparison. The more he thought about it, going to find this girl seemed more important than anything he'd done in the last few years.

The publico let them off on a busy corner of Calle Loiza in Santurce, one of the municipalities abutting San Juan. It had been a few years since Scheutz had been on a street filled with pedestrians and automobile traffic. Storefronts lined the sidewalks and second floor apartment windows reflected sunlight on one side of the street, shadow on the other. Migdala took off down the street at a walking pace to match the others around her.

Two blocks down, they turned in through an ornate wrought-iron gate into a cement courtyard and white stucco two-story house set back only five yards from the street. Migdala pushed the doorbell beside a grilled wrought-iron gate. After several tries, she reached through the grille to knock loudly on the wooden door, and then the glass panel. Nothing. Scheutz walked back out to the sidewalk and tried the gate to the carport at the side of the house, but it was locked.

"So what do we do now?"

"My mother's old friend lives next door and keeps a key for her." She walked around to a similar structure where an elderly woman answered her knock. "Hola, Señora Alvarez. Soy Migdala. Como estas?"

The woman peered at Migdala's mother's house, then at Scheutz. She shook her head, shrugged, and then said in English. "Hola, Migdala. I have not seen you in a long time. How are you?"

"I'm fine."

"Would you like to come in for coffee?"

Migdala smiled and shook her head. "No, gracias. I lost the key to the house. We have to pick something for mi mamma. Do you still have a key to her house?"

The old lady took the question as a clue to deliver a long speech in a tone too low for Scheutz to hear. Occasionally, she glanced over at him and held her hand up to her mouth on his side so he could not see her lips. Migdala gravely nodded her head and tried to interrupt several times but the woman leaned forward each time, tapping her finger on Migdala's chest. Migdala twisted her hand back and forth as if opening a lock. Senora Alvarez held up her hand for Migdala to wait and disappeared inside the house for the key. Migdala thanked her and then returned to her mother's front door.

"I hope Tio Juaquin did not change the lock."

"What was she going on about?"

Migdala let them into her mother's front door. "Oh, just how sad it was about Tio Juaquin. And how she thinks it was the gringos that killed him. Just like they killed President Kennedy. And then she had to tell me how sorry she was that she could not come to Culebra for his funeral."

The door swung open. "Oh, Dios mio, look at this house." The front room of the house had been totally trashed. Furniture pushed into a jumble, a chair and the television overturned. A religious statue of Jesus smashed on the floor, pictures taken off the walls and dropped on the floor. "Oh. Oh." Migdala hurried into the next room and from there into the kitchen, with Scheutz behind. The same chaos. Drawers turned out, refrigerator and freezer emptied, oven and broiler drawer open, cabinets open with dishes and pots strewn about.

She let out a groan before running up the stairs. The large bedroom, three smaller ones and the bathroom showed the same turmoil; clothes, boxes, pillows, linens everywhere, shoes, cosmetics, medicine bottles littering the floors. Scheutz looked under the beds and in the closets. The same mess. It felt as if the entire house had been injected with some evil energy, as if the perpetrator was still lurking out of sight. He scoured each room again, careful not to miss any corner, any closet where someone might be hiding. He expected at every turn to see Harding, hunched over, clutching a bag of loot.

Scheutz and Migdala met back downstairs in the kitchen. "Who could have done this? What do you think this might be about?" he asked her.

"I know what it's about. My uncle dealt with some very nasty people. And I told you about all the money he had stashed away in here, right? Knowing him, he probably had all kinds of other things hidden in this house."

"Like emeralds?"

"Quien sabe? I know my mother was in here after he died, but she would not leave the place like this. This was her home. Someone else broke in here."

"If someone broke in and left this mess, why would they bother to lock up again when they left?"

She looked around, raising her eyebrows and shrugging. "It doesn't make sense, does it?"

They walked through the house again, room by room. In the kitchen, behind an overturned chair, Scheutz found Blanca's school bag. Migdala snatched it from his hand. "Hah! So she did come here." She opened the bag and dug around in it, tossing books, notebooks and cosmetics onto the table.

"She wouldn't have done this, would she?" he asked.

Migdala stopped moving and stood quietly, looking around at the kitchen. She shook her head slowly. "No. I don't know what Blanca will do half of the time, but I know she would not do this."

"Maybe she helped Harding do it?"

"No. She could not do this to her old home, or to her grandmother's and Tio Juaquin's home. She loves her grandmother. To do this she would have to be crazy. And she is only teenager crazy."

"Well, she must be crazy in love. What the hell does she see in that guy anyway?"

"The same thing she always saw in Tio Juaquin."

"What do you mean by that?"

"I'll tell you later. Right now we have to clean up this mess and figure out what happened."

"If her bag is here, maybe she came here before going to where her grandmother is. I know Harding left Culebra because I saw him get on the ferry. So, let's say he came here, looking for money or jewels. No one was home so he broke in and trashed the place."

"There are no signs of someone breaking in."

"Harding must have had your uncle's key. I don't know why he would lock up afterward; no telling what Harding would do. He's the one that's a little crazy."

Scheutz opened one of Blanca's notebooks, flipping through the pages. Maybe he could find a clue, something she'd written that would give away what was going through her mind when she left.

Migdala shook her head, looking around again at the mess. "Ooh, I'm going to give that girl such hell." She stamped her foot. "Maybe I should go to the police."

He closed the notebook. "Probably not a good idea. Whatever your uncle had in here was most likely illegal."

She nodded and she sat down on a chair that she had set upright. Scheutz set another aright and sat with her across the table. "Now what?"

"We are going to wait. This schoolbag is like her purse. She is coming back here."

"What if she's not coming back? Waiting would waste time."

"What other choice do we have?" She jumped up and started across the room to the kitchen sink. "I'm going to clean this place up. You don't have to help if you don't want."

"Hey, give me lunch and a cup of coffee and I'm at your service." He straightened the furniture in the kitchen while she made coffee. The coffee grounds had been dumped out on the counter. He scooped uncooked rice back into its bag. She put water on to boil for rice and found a can of beans to go with it.

After lunch, they divided up the rooms, her taking the second floor and him the first. Putting the house back in order felt a little like a microcosm of putting the island back together after Hurricane Hugo. He tried the television set, which worked well enough. Two lamps needed bulbs and the blender in the kitchen needed a new receptacle even though the motor worked okay. Supper time came and went and still no Blanca. Migdala had a glass of rum before supper and another afterwards. Throughout the evening, Migdala paced, going to the window every time a car slowed down in the street outside. She had another rum, and then another. She sat in front of the television for a few minutes and then jumped up again. She went through Blanca's school bag one more time, thoroughly, studying every page of her notebooks and searching between the pages of each textbook.

Scheutz tried to relax. She made him tense with her fidgeting. Darkness fell and the streetlights came on outside. They decided not to turn on any lights and to just wait in the dark for Blanca and whoever else to return. The streetlight directly in front of the house gave them enough light to move around. She had yet another rum and brought him one. He didn't want it, but took it and sipped just to keep her company.

She stood in the middle of the room and took a sip from her rum glass. "Maybe I could call someone."

"I thought the phone was dead."

"I could go down to the bar on the corner and call from there." She took another sip. "Mamma has a cousin in Hato Rey." She paused. "No, she doesn't like her, though." She tapped her front teeth with her index finger, paced the floor and then, suddenly, seemed to just give up. Scheutz could feel his eyelids getting heavy and his head start to droop. He normally went to sleep by nine o'clock, and he had been up since before dawn that morning. The three rum drinks were not helping any. Migdala's body had sagged, the last of her rum untouched.

He stretched his foot and probed her with his toe. "Where can I go to sleep?"

She studied him for a moment, her eyelids at half-mast. "Come on, I'll show you."

He followed her up the stairs. She wobbled slightly. He was a little light-headed himself. Wasn't this strange, the two of them going upstairs to a bedroom like an old married couple. Something he had remembered missing after Gerry left so many years ago. A moment so normal and yet so strange to him, filled with both warmth and comfort and at the same time so deliciously exciting.

He watched Migdala's back and then her behind as she walked ahead of him. She had never appealed to him physically, even that time he met her several years ago when they had sailed into Culebra and he had danced with her that one night. He had never found dark, Spanish-type women to be especially attractive, being drawn more to the tall, Germanic. But there was something about her that fascinated him, some essence of solid female energy. It did not take a sexual form, like it had with Gerry and then with Samantha, but was no less attractive. Maybe it was the same thing, but without the sexual energy because he was so much older. At fifty, he was no longer the slave to his gonads as he had been at seventeen.

At the top of the stairs, he asked, "Which was your bedroom when you lived here?" She showed him one of the smaller ones, her room, she said, when she was in high school. A double bed with a high, carved headboard took up most of the room. The streetlight that lit the downstairs living room shone almost directly into this room. "I'd like to sleep here with you," he said. The words came out before he thought them, and it surprised and frightened him that he said them.

She stood directly in front of him, tilted her head to one side and looked into his eyes with her half-closed, half-drunken gaze. Her eyelids opened full, the eyes themselves narrowing into either assessment or disapproval. He was about to apologize for what he had just said, and intended to turn away when her face suddenly softened into a very small but decidedly undrunken smile. She wrapped her fingers around the wrist of his left hand and stood there smiling at him. But the smile faded as soon as it had begun. The look of pained concern came over her face and she shook her head slowly, sorrowfully. She dropped his wrist and moved into his chest allowing him to hold her.

Her breathing deepened and she began to relax in his arms, but she quickly pulled away and motioned with her head for him take the far side of the bed. After he lay down she sat on the other side looking toward the bedroom door as if unsure what to do next. He lay on his side facing her and willed himself to relax. They remained like that for a long time, until she suddenly sagged and let herself lie on the bed as far from him as possible, facing the door.

In the street, a car slowed to a stop in front of the house. Migdala pulled herself to a sitting position, poised to jump from the bed. But no, the car continued on. She lay down again, on her back, her small breasts and her chin highlighted by the glow of the street lamp. Slowly and then faster, the alertness drained from her body and her breathing smoothed. He could feel himself sinking as he lay there watching her. He wanted to lean over and kiss her, or at least to reach over and touch her, lay his hand on her stomach, or even her upper arm, anything.

When he came to she was gone from the bed. She stood before the front window, silhouetted this time against the daylight that streamed in around her. "Is she home?" he asked her back.

She shook her head, still looking through the window at the street below. "I don't know what to do."

"How long have you been awake?"

"Most of the night. Every time I heard a noise I jumped up."

"Lie back down. Let's figure out what we can do."

She came back to the bed and lay down as she had before, staring at the ceiling with one hand by her side and the other behind her head. He touched the hand lying next to her on the bedspread.

"I can hear your heart," she said.

"You want it, take it."

She cut her eyes sideways to his and closed her hand over his fingers. "Yes, I want it."

He could only smile. That old feeling of the married couple heading upstairs to bed came over him again. It had been such a long time since he had felt like that. But it was so familiar, like going back to an old neighborhood that had been gentrified under a massive urban planning effort. He could recognize little corners here and there, but it still felt like a whole new world. They lay like that without moving. She was becoming a different person than the woman who had befriended him since the hurricane. Not just the softness of her facial features but a change in the feel of her. She was different than the person he had known just the day before.

She lay quiet for a long time, but then her body began slowly to regain its tension and anxiety. Her eyelids fluttered and her entire torso seemed drawn in on itself. "We have to go to Rincon," she said.

"Rincon. I never heard of it."

"Remember that guy named Beltran who came to Juaquin's funeral? The one who was looking for Harding?"

"Yeah."

"If Harding left Culebra, he would go to see Beltran."

"Do you have his address?"

"No. But Rincon is a very small town. If we ask enough people we will find him."

"How do we get there?"

"We can rent a car."

"Won't that be expensive? Tourist season is just starting."

"I don't care. I want to find Blanca. If she ran away with Harding, I will kill him." She let go his hand and sat up, flinging her legs to the side so that her feet landed on the floor. "Vamonos."

He sat up and swung his feet to the side of the bed. She started to leave and then turned to him as he walked around the foot of the bed, staring hard into his eyes. "We are together, right?"

What did she mean by that? Were they together in the effort to find Blanca, or were they together together? Whatever. He pulled her close to him, inhaling the heavy, sweaty animal smell of her body.

Chapter 20

Migdala stopped the car next to the curb just outside the central plaza of Rincon. They each took their bags from the back seat and she locked the car doors. To anyone watching, the Ford Escort was obviously a rental car, meaning they would be pegged by idle onlookers as tourists. She wore blue shorts and a flowered blouse with floppy straw hat and he, a gringo, taller than the average puertoriqueno, dressed in shorts and t-shirt and Teva sandals, looked like any other tourist. On most Caribbean islands, idle youths did a brisk business every year in stolen rental cars. It was not unusual to see the burnt-out husk of a late model sedan alongside a back road in these islands, the car stripped of all its useful parts.

After a two-hour drive from San Juan they had arrived in the small town on the west coast of Puerto Rico's main island a little after midday. Even at its busiest, the town filled with Spanish-style stucco buildings could boast of no more than about a dozen people on the streets. Women shopped, four men lounged in the central plaza, two shopkeepers sat in chairs out front of their stores, two pairs of school children in their uniforms made their way to their escuela, probably coming back from lunch for their afternoon session. A young couple, obviously gringos, came out of a store and climbed into a Jeep with two surf boards strapped to the top.

He seemed to be seeing pairs of people everywhere. Could that be because, since last night in Santurce, he began to see himself as possibly part of a pair? He studied the woman walking next to him, one step ahead of him, as he once again tried to keep pace with her. She had pulled her hair into a severe ponytail giving him a view of her ear, jaw line, and prominent cheekbone. Her features were more sharply defined than when her dark hair framed her face. From this view and from trying to keep up with her, feeling like one half of a pair with her seemed a little far-fetched, but when her face turned toward him for a beat and softened into a fleeting smile, it felt possible.

On the drive along the northern coast of the island, past Arecibo and down the western coast past Aguadilla, they talked non-stop, one of those things people did after they first became intimate with each other. They had not been intimate, but somehow it felt like it. The floppy straw hat shaded her face from the sun and she slouched in the car's air-conditioning, rambling on about herself. "When I was in high school in Santurce, all I could think about was getting away from that place. Well, and all the boys in that place."

"How old were you when Blanca was born?"

"Sixteen. I was pregnant when I was old as Blanca is now."

He told her a little more about himself, about his two sons. For a short time she had been able to put aside her anxiety and let herself relax in his company. She had not slept well the night before and she looked it. For him, relaxing in a woman's company was something that had not happened in awhile. Over the last year his relationship with Samantha had been so strained; actually more than a year, now that he thought about it. The purchase of that schooner had come out of a strain, an attempt to relieve it, but all the schooner did was create its own brand of strain, a case of the cure being worse than the ailment.

This little car trip down the coast was the first time he had seen her without her brow creased in worry over something that needed taking care of. From what he'd experienced of her over the last few months he didn't think she was capable of much ease. But now that he had caught a glimpse of her relaxed, maybe he could help her keep it for a longer period.

He suggested they grab some lunch at a place called El Gaucho Pizzeria, on a narrow side street just off the plaza. The pizza turned out to be much better than anything put out by Chuck's joint on Culebra. Migdala engaged in a conversation with the woman behind the counter who spoke in an accented Spanish Scheutz had never heard before. Migdala told him the woman's accent was from Argentina where, apparently, due to the large Italian population in that country, making pizza was considered to be a higher art than in most Hispanic countries.

Migdala picked up the finished pizza and brought it to their table near the front door. They had not had anything decent to eat since before they left Culebra. Scheutz crammed his mouth with a delicious-smelling slice and washed it down with a slug of Dr. Pepper.

Migdala ate slower but with obviously just as much relish. She talked between bites. "That woman says she does a pretty good business here this time of year."

"Oh, yeah?"

"This is the big surf season here, you know."

"Mmph. No, I didn't know."

"Si. Right here on the west coast is one of the big surf spots of the world."

"Really?"

"Si. Did you ever see that movie, *The Endless Summer?* Well, the surfers go from one place in the world to another. Hawaii, Australia. And one of those places is right here at the right season. Which just ended. If we came here a week ago, this pizza parlor would be overrun with surfers."

"Oh, really?"

"You don't care about the surfers, do you?"

"No. Do you?"

"No. Not really." She shrugged and lifted another slice. "When I was young my friends and I used to come out here on the weekends and over Thanksgiving vacation. We had a lot of good times here."

"You surf?"

"No, no. We partied. Nada mas. Pero, ay, those pretty brown boys. Dios mio. I think one of them might be Blanca's father." She looked into his eyes and suddenly blushed and looked away. "Maybe I should ask the woman behind the counter if she knows that man Beltran." She put down her slice and jumped up to walk back to the counter, where she again pulled the counterwoman into conversation. While they talked the woman handed Migdala a thin telephone directory which they looked into. As she walked thoughtfully back down to the table, Migdala shook her head. "Nada. And he's not listed in the phone book."

"He'd have an unlisted number. Makes sense in his business."

"We should start asking the shop owners in town."

"Oh, by the way, yesterday, when we were talking about what

Blanca could possibly see in Harding, you said something about how she felt about your uncle. You said you'd explain later."

She nodded and finished chewing the last bit, then sipping her Coca Cola. "Si, pero es muy complicado. I am not sure but I think she likes this Harding pendejo because he is like a little Juaquin."

"But he's an idiot. Whatever else Juaquin might have been, he certainly wasn't an idiot."

"I think Harding is not an idiot like he looks."

"I've always wondered. But that little stunt he pulled over in Cuba was the work of a true dingdong."

"Whatever. You know Blanca grew up with my uncle and my mother in that house in Santurce. And I was not around for a few years when I was in New York. Tio Juaquin was always very protective of her when she was a little girl. That is one of the reasons I don't like him. I think he was too protective, if you know what I mean."

"What, you think he might have molested her?"

"No, I don't think he did that. I am pretty sure about that. Tio Juaquin did not like women, if you know what I mean. In fact, I think this Beltran hombre we are looking for was his boyfriend."

"Maricones?"

She raised her eyebrows and nodded. "In fact, I am sure Beltran es un pato. Just from the way he walks."

"Pato?"

"It's Puerto Rican slang for a homosexual."

"That's funny. I wonder how that came to be.

"Tapon told me that when he was un nino, they called them "puto" which means a male prostitute. And then it just turned into pato, which is a duck, because it was funnier."

"So what does that have to do with Blanca?"

"Blanca always loved Tio Juaquin. She did not have a father and he was very nice to her. He bought everything for her, and took her to school in the morning, and, you know, everything." She waved her hand, taking in the whole world.

"And Harding?"

"Blanca always likes to flirt with men, but last year she became like a…que?…como una…abeja." She put her thumb and forefinger together and moved them quickly through the air. "Like a honeybee.

All the time. Tio Juaquin was going crazy trying to keep her off of the muchachos. But then this summer, Harding comes along."

"And you knew about her interest in Harding?"

"No. I see it but I don't see it. I am trying to run the restaurant and take care of my grandfather and keep an eye on her and make her go to school. And then the hurricane comes."

"Sorry I didn't know. Maybe I could have helped in some way. At least helped with Harding."

She waved her slice of pizza, pointing her finger in his face. "I told you not to do business with my uncle, didn't I?"

"Well, at least I got Harding away from the island for a few weeks." She nodded again, her cheeks filled with pizza. "Samantha wanted to leave him in Cuba, he was such a pain in the ass. She also wanted to leave him in St. Thomas and not tow his boat over to Culebra. Would have been better for everyone to leave him someplace, but no, I had to take pity on the moron."

"Yeah, what is it with you and this pity thing you have? Is that why you came with me, because you pity me?"

He laughed. "Don't be silly. If I took pity on you I wouldn't let you get mixed up with a guy like me."

She smiled at him. "No, I don't think you take pity. I think you are with me because you like free pizza. That is why you keep coming to my restaurant, for the free food." She poked his arm. "Am I right?"

"Well, I will admit I'm a little bit of a lunch whore. But don't I always work for the food I get?"

She set her Coke can down. "And you will work for this pizza, mi amigo."

Before leaving the pizzeria, they asked two other customers if they knew a man named Beltran. Migdala described him and said she knew he lived in Rincon. Nothing. Outside in the hot afternoon sun, they walked from store to store asking the same questions, but no one knew of such a person. He obviously did not do his shopping in the center of town. And he must not have been originally from Rincon because in small Puerto Rican towns like this everyone knew or was related to everyone else.

But they kept at it. In the middle of the afternoon, on a road heading in the direction of the ocean, they stopped to talk with a middle-aged man and woman sitting outside a furniture store under an awning. The man spoke no English. As Migdala spoke to him, he remained paralyzed in a lounging position, only his eyes moving to look first at Migdala and then at Scheutz. Finally, he turned his head toward the woman sitting on the other side of the front entrance. "Te conoces este hombre?"

She stared straight ahead but nodded slightly, as if not wanting to outdo her husband in the movement department. "Yo conozco este hombre. El vive en Punta Higuera." Migdala made quick little movements with her hands, describing the man to make sure they had the right one. The woman, watching her hands, nodded slightly again. Migdala began bouncing on her toes as if unable to contain herself. She asked if the woman had an address or a phone number, but the woman said that Beltran came to the store only occasionally for a piece of furniture. She assumed he must live in a big house because he had a lot of furniture. Scheutz asked for directions to Punta Higuera and the woman raised her left hand and flicked her fingers toward the northwest.

Migdala thanked the woman and took Scheutz's arm to urge him toward the car. "I know where Punta Higuera is."

The feeling of doing something right rose up in him again, hunting down some quarry that could solve the problem of finding Migdala's daughter. Looking for this guy, looking for Blanca thrilled him in a way, but the rightness of it was something more than that. Their quest was a worthwhile thing to do. How many years had it been that he had been doing nothing worthwhile, nothing more than drifting across the face of the planet. It was no wonder most sailboat bums around the world ended up as drunken bums. What starts out as the great fantasy, the ideal prolonged vacation or retirement, without some sense of obligation to something, anything, will always end in a wish to destroy yourself, to throw yourself in some tropical gutter for people to piss on. Taking on an obligation to Migdala and her daughter may not be saving mankind from the forces of evil but it was worthwhile and, yes, he did feel a great pleasure in helping them.

Fifteen minutes later he steered the Ford down a steep incline on an unpaved road to another sandy road running north along the shore, waves of the Caribbean crashing to the left of them. Migdala pointed to the blunted point of land jutting out into the water. "That is Punta Higuera, the most western tip of Puerto Rico." Low waves rolled in and parted north and south just beyond the rounded tip of the point. A few surfers, he counted six, sat their boards beyond, waiting for a good wave. "A week ago, this place would look like a bird reserve with all the boys and the surf boards and the Jeeps, all of them painted bright colors and gathering like flocks on the beach and out beyond the breakers. Es muy fantastico." Her eyes lit up remembering, and she looked at him and laughed and winked.

Just before the road turned to go back up the hill, he pulled into a grove with an open-air bar and several crude picnic tables under the palm trees. As good a place as any to start asking around. A radio behind the bar played salsa music to a single bartender and no patrons. There were no stools at the rectangular shaped bar. Migdala and Scheutz stood facing the water and the steady breeze blowing through the palms. They each ordered a Medalla beer, which Migdala finished in three large gulps, and Scheutz taking his time with four. The bartender spoke English but had no idea who Beltran was. He suggested they ask at a colmado on the parallel road halfway up the slope of the hill. They thanked him and left.

One hundred yards up the hill, the road turned off to the right and ten yards down a small store with an easy-to-miss sign faced the water. The tiny, dark-skinned woman behind the counter knew Senor Beltran very well. He came in often for small items that he had neglected to buy at the large supermarket in Mayaguez. She did an imitation of how his belly fat jiggled when he laughed and how he lisped when pronouncing words like "ciudad," saying "thiudad" instead. But, other than that, his accent sounded like he came from rural Puerto Rico. In fact, he had told her once he grew up in a town called Guzman Abajo, just down the road from Guzman Ariba, in the hills near El Yunque. The woman took them out to the road and pointed to Beltran's house halfway down the hill near the road they had come in on.

The barrio of Punta Higuera consisted mostly of wooden, two-room houses with an occasional cinderblock house built away from the road. Beltran's house must have been built within the last few years and gave the impression of a landowner's hacienda in the middle of peon hovels. The only two-story structure in the area, it had been built up the slope of the hill with the bottom floor only one room wide under a sweeping veranda that overlooked the Caribbean. The uphill story, several rooms wide, looked more like a two-family home would look anywhere else on the island. Gleaming white stucco and vivid pink Miami shutters gave it a dollhouse appearance, like something Señorita Barbie might live in.

The long paved driveway in from the unpaved road ended at a parking area containing two late model vehicles, one a white Mercedes 280 SEL, the other a black Dodge RAM pickup truck. Lush vegetation spilled over the edges of the paved parking area except where it abutted the house. Only a wrought-iron gate covered the entrance to the house, which allowed a view through the interior to the veranda on the other side and the ocean in the distance.

There did not seem to be any doorbell or place to knock, so Migdala shouted "Hola. ¿Hay alguien en casa?" through the wrought iron gate into the house.

Footsteps brought a young woman in a red and black dress that looked like a Spanish flamenco dancer's outfit. "Can I help you?"

"We are looking for Señor Beltran."

A fleeting look of fear passed over the woman's face, rich with mascara, deep red lipstick and rouge. "He is busy right now. Who is asking for him, please?"

"Tell him I am Juaquin Arraca's niece."

The fear flitted again through the woman's features and then returned to a mannequin-like mask. The head turned slightly, then back and nodded. Her tall, thin body made a quick retreating movement but then stopped and returned to the static posture of a flamenco dancer poised and waiting for the guitars to begin.

Scheutz resisted the urge to begin clapping a three-fourths rhythm. "Tell Señor Beltran it is very important we talk to him."

"Are you the policia?"

"No. I am the man with the emeralds."

The woman turned and clicked back down the hallway in her high heels. Migdala turned her back to the doorway to face him. "You have the emeralds on you?"

"No. But I gave Harding three of them so he could go find a dealer."

The flamenco woman clicked down the hall again. "Señor Beltran will talk to you." She put a key into the lock on the inside of the gate and stepped back for them to enter.

The end of the hallway led to a room that ran the full width of the house with glass doors open to the veranda. The sun had advanced far enough in the day to cast the entire west-facing room into bright light, but the steady breeze off the Caribbean kept the room from getting too hot. Two separate clusters of sofa and chairs dominated the floor space with a short diagonal bar in one corner and various-sized oil paintings, all of Caribbean scenes in vivid colors, adorning the walls.

The flamenco woman left them standing in the middle of the room and disappeared. Scheutz walked to the open doors but turned at the sound of soft shoes shushing on the tiled floor. Beltran hustled into the room and made straight for Migdala. Scheutz started forward to intercept him, thinking he meant harm, but Beltran threw his arms around her, sobbing, "Oh, Migdala, I am so sorry about Juaquin." She stood rigid, her lip slightly curled. The voice repeated into her shoulder, "Lo siento. Lo siento mucho." With a light but noticeable lisp on the 's'. "Pobre. Pobre Juaquincito."

Migdala backed away from the blubbering. Beltran's eyes brimmed with tears gave him the look of a pudgy child dressed like an adult in light green guyabera and tan slacks, appointed with gold necklace, gold watch, and gold rings on two fingers of each hand. Scheutz noted again how much he did look like Oliver Hardy, shorter and with darker skin, but with the same pudgy cheeks and piggy little eyes. Beltran took a handkerchief from the lower left pocket of the guyabera and wiped his eyes. "Juaquin was my good friend, you know. For many years." He wiped his eyes again and, ignoring them, stared out toward the ocean.

Migdala interrupted his reverie. "Do you remember my friend, Clement Scheutz."

Beltran turned, wiped his eyes one more time and looked Scheutz up and down, then extended his hand. "Mucho gusto. Como te llama otra vez?"

Scheutz shook his hand. "Clement Scheutz."

"Shoots?"

"Call me Clem."

"Ah. Clemente. The peaceful one." He turned to Migdala. "¿Muy guapo, eh?"

Migdala's smile bordered on a smirk. "Yes, he's very handsome."

Beltran smiling at Scheutz, changed from a tearful child to a hopeful one. "You can call me Emilio. Were you a friend of Juaquin also?"

"Not really. I knew him. In fact, I did a job recently for him. That is partly what we need to talk with you about."

Beltran's face changed again, this time to that of a businessman. "Yes. The emeralds that you mentioned to my secretary, that…"

Migdala waved her fingers in front Beltran's face. "Before we talk about emeralds, we need to talk about my daughter, Blanca."

Beltran held up his hand to touch her waving one. "Before we talk about anything, I need to tell you that my secretary and I are just on our way out. We are late and must be in Mayaguez by five o'clock."

"Have you seen Blanca?"

Beltran' s eyes moved from Migdala's face to Scheutz's and back to Migdala. His fleshy lips pursed beneath the little mustache. "No."

"But Juaquin's assistant, Harding, did bring some of the emeralds we obtained in Cuba, didn't he?" Scheutz asked.

"Yes. And he said you had the rest and that I should contact you for them."

Migdala waved a hand in front of both Scheutz and Beltran. "Wait, wait. I don't want to talk about these emeralds. We must talk about my daughter. I know she is with Harding. If you have seen him, you must have seen her."

Beltran raised his eyebrows and shook his head. "He came in a blue Toyota and I did not see who else was in the car."

"Was my mother in the car?"

He spread his hands and shook his head.

"When did they leave? Where did they go?"

Beltran shook his head slowly, then looked at Scheutz and started to say something.

Scheutz said, "We will need to find Harding before we can talk about emeralds."

"Suit yourself. Now, if you will excuse me, I have to leave for Mayaguez." He gestured toward the door.

Migdala did not move. "Doesn't it bother you that Harding was the one who killed Tio Juaquin?"

"No. Because I know that Harding did not kill Juaquin."

"Everything the police have found so far points to it. The spear gun, the..."

"No. I am sorry, but no. I know better." His eyes teared up again. "It is a horrible tragedy, and it must be for whoever killed him. But I would prefer if it stopped now."

"But I need to talk with Harding. Where is he? Where he did he go?"

Beltran shook his head and walked down the hall to stand at the doorway leading to the parking space at the rear of the house. "Por favor." Scheutz led her down the hall and out through the gate. On their way out, Beltran said, "Por la mañana. We will talk in the morning about the emeralds."

In the Escort, Scheutz took the wheel. Migdala slumped in her seat, tears filling her eyes. She slowly shook her head. "I don't believe him, do you?"

He shrugged. It was hard to tell whether Beltran lied about Harding. He started the car and, on leaving Beltran's driveway, turned left up the hill. On the transverse road he stopped and got out. A few yards down, an opening in the vegetation allowed him to see the back of Beltran's house. Migdala came to stand next to him. They watched as Beltran came out of the house with the flamenco lady and both got in the Mercedes. The white car turned right out of the driveway and down the hill, then left, going south toward Mayaguez.

Chapter 21

Now what? The next best thing to do was head for Migdala's mother's house in Mayaguez. She had never been there. Her mother had kept the house in Santurce for Juaquin to use and acquired the one in Mayaguez only two years before. Or maybe it was the other way around, her mother used the house in Santurce and Juaquin used the one in Mayaguez. Migdala knew the address but did not know the area very well. Since it looked like Beltran was headed in that direction, why not just follow him?

So far he'd spent more time riding in an automobile on this day than he had in the last seven years altogether. Most people, he imagined, thought nothing of spending lengthy periods of time crammed into a moving vehicle like this, but he would never choose it. Traveling even great distances across large bodies of water in a small boat was heaven compared to this. In the same way, spending day after day in the middle of a deep New Hampshire forest made him feel alive. But this, sitting and maneuvering a mechanical device inside a designated lane, this was mind-numbing.

The road ran straight when it passed fields of pineapple or sugar cane, and then curved when it ran through copses of trees and undergrowth. He kept a distance from the Mercedes, allowing other cars to get between it and them. The inside of the rented car had not yet lost its new-car smell. Migdala fiddled with the air-conditioner, turning it down because she was getting goose bumps on her arms. Finally he asked her to turn it off, and they rolled down the windows to let in the thick warm heady odor of vegetation and sea air.

The open window blew Migdala's floppy hat off and into the back seat. She turned and knelt to lean over and retrieve it, giving him a delicious glimpse of the blue fabric of her shorts stretched tight across her ass. The force field of energy she had exuded in this entire day still had not abated a nickel's worth. Her nervous tension seemed to alternate between anxiety over finding her daughter and what felt to him like some kind of sensuous hunger. Whatever it was, the effect it had on him was very sexy. His thoughts kept returning to the night before, lying on that bed with her in the small dark room. As platonic as it was, he couldn't get it out of his mind.

And this entire day, during this whole little jaunt, she had emited a just-under-the-surface air of steamy passion. The anxiety she gave off about finding her daughter felt laced with a warmth that reached out to him. The smell of her body, mixed with that of the vegetation and ocean breeze, was the essence of Puerto Rico, different from any place, even any place in the Caribbean, he had ever been. And different from any woman he had even known.

The car in front of theirs suddenly turned off to the right, leaving nothing between them and the Mercedes, which had stopped at the juncture to Route 2. He applied the brakes to keep from bearing down on them. Beltran was taking his time at the stop sign, but the Mercedes took off before they came up to its rear bumper.

Something about this trip to Mayaguez, following the white car, felt so unreal. Driving an almost new car with less than three thousand miles on the odometer, following a man in a fancy car with his Spanish Barbie secretary in her ruffled flamenco dress, going to a city he'd never been to before, and going there for very specious reasons. The man they were following was an international gem smuggler, exactly the kind of person Scheutz had scrupulously avoided all his life. The guy had ties to a company with a branch in Mayaguez, Digital Equipment Corporation, which he knew made the mini computers they had carried to Cuba. The world of computers and industry and commerce and the smell of this car he was driving were all unreal to him, a world he had tried to avoid all his life.

Meanwhile, the woman sitting beside him stirred some very strange sensations in him. He had not felt like this since he had come home to his sons' mother thirty years earlier. Samantha, on the other hand, as much as he loved and enjoyed her, had always been like a playmate. Yes, now that he thought about it, even in the Playboy magazine sense of the word. She was pretty and sexy and young and funny and full of life—any old fart's dream. But she had never been part of him. Losing her was like losing a very close friend. But this woman in the next seat, in her floppy hat, seemed to be crawling inside his skin.

He waited at the stop sign until the Mercedes passed beyond a group of trees on the right side of the road and then he edged onto Route 2. He needed to orient himself, not on the road, but in his sense of reality. What was this like? He must have done something in his past that made him feel like this, something causing him to have to re-orient himself. This was a job that needed being done. He cared about what happened to this woman's daughter, so, whatever his little problem was with the unreal world around him, he'd just have to get over it. Here he was tooling down Route 2, following the white Mercedes the way Alice followed the white rabbit down a hole. Migdala, next to him fidgeted, adjusting the hat, biting her lip. She watched the car like a raptor tracking its prey, making involuntary hand movements for Scheutz to change lanes and pass the car the Mercedes had just passed. He tried not to let her nervousness and her instinct to tell him how to drive bother him, but it was getting harder as they progressed.

From Punta Higuera, they had by-passed the center of Rincon and turned onto Route 115 south until it met with Route 2, then south into the city limits of Mayaguez. He followed Beltran with only a hunch and lack of a better idea, and assumed that Beltran would not recognize the car behind him.

Migdala was having second thoughts. "Maybe we should just go back to Santurce and look for Blanca there. Or wait another day for her to come back."

"Since we're here, why not at least go to your mother's house. It's worth a chance."

The Mercedes turned right off Route 2 onto a one-way street named Calle Cristobal Colon. "This is my mother's street. Turn here."

"Yes, dear."

"Sorry."

"Yes, dear."

"Stop that."

The street narrowed as it ran toward the coast, through a residential neighborhood of small, then medium and eventually large houses as it grew closer to the water. The sun sat low on the horizon, shining directly at their windshield. A block from the water the Mercedes stopped at the curb. Scheutz pulled in behind a parked car a block away. Beltran and his secretary stepped out of the car and walked through a patio to a two-story house even larger than Beltran's in Punta Higeura. A male hand and arm opened the front door and the two stepped inside.

"Yes, that is my mother's address. Now what do we do?"

"I don't know." He studied the house, its windows and entrances. Another door on their side of the house led in from a carport. "From the looks of it, they're not the only ones in there." He motioned to the several other cars parked on both sides of the block in front of them. "It's probably because this has nothing to do with us. It's just some ..."

"Wait,. wait…." She took hold of his wrist.

"What?"

"The Toyota. See, the blue car in the carport in front of the gray one. That is my mother's car." She opened the door, hopped onto the sidewalk and ran into the driveway of the house next to the one Beltran and his secretary had entered, leaning over a waist-high wall dividing the two properties and scrutinizing the blue Toyota. When he reached her she pushed him back with her until they stood behind a coconut palm at the edge of the driveway, all the while hissing into his face. "That is her car. I know the license plate. And she has that statue of the Holy Virgin on the dashboard."

"So, she's home, so what?"

"So, let's go see if Blanca is here." She led the way back toward the street.

Another white car pulled into the curb behind the Mercedes. The driver, a tiny man, stepped from it and waved to them. Scheutz waved back. The man wore a flowery shirt with large blossoms on a beige background, a shirt that looked like it was the smallest he could find in an adult size, and still a size too large for him. They met in the patio and, seeing they were all headed toward the same front door, Migdala extending her hand to the man. "Buenos dias. ¿Como te llama?"

"Luis." He looked up at her, then past her to Scheutz, then took her hand. "And you?"

"Migdala. And this is Clement."

Scheutz came forward to shake the man's hand, which felt like a child's. "Are you a friend of Señor Beltran?"

"O, si. I am friend to all of them. We work together at DEC."

"What do you do there?'

"I am a programmer." Luis turned to walk toward the house.

Scheutz fell in beside him. "What do you program?"

"I am a computer programmer."

"Sorry. I guess I don't know what that is."

"It is the future."

"You don't say."

"And you? What do you do?"

"I'm the past."

Luis let out a laugh. "I thought you looked like a cowboy."

"I'm a sailor."

Luis turned to Migdala who walked on the other side of him. "¿Y tu, señora? Are you a sailor, too?"

"No, I have a restaurant on Culebra."

"Ah, Culebra. My good friend, Juaquin, he died in the hurricane there. Muy triste."

Migdala opened her mouth to say something, but looked at Scheutz and let it go. They had come to the front door. Luis pressed the bell and almost immediately a fair-skinned gringo wearing a straw hat like Migdala's opened the door. The hat had a rigid brim and was obviously too big for his head. It rested on his ears and sat just above his eyebrows. He wore a gray t-shirt and shorts, his freckled skin the reddish color of someone not used to the sun. He glared at Luis, then jabbed his finger toward his nose. "You are late again."

"I am sorry, I overslept."

"You know how angry she gets when anyone is late. I don't know how she puts up with you." He looked Scheutz up and down and then did the same to Migdala. "And who is this?"

"I thought you knew," Luis said. "I met them outside."

Migdala stepped inside and took off her sunglasses. The doorkeeper peered closely at her. "I know you. Where do I know you from?"

Migdala raised her eyebrows. "I don't know. Did you ever live in New York?"

"No. Wait a minute, I know. It was in San Juan, a long time ago. Did you go to school at Collegio San Augustine in Santurce?"

"Yes. Till the eighth grade."

"That's it. You were in my class."

She studied his face. "O, sí. I'm trying to remember your name. It's…it's…let me think."

"It's Larry. Larry Simons."

"Larry. That's right. We used to call you Colora because of your red hair. You still have red hair?'

Larry lifted his over-sized hat to show off his kinky orange curls and pulled the hat down again.

Migdala laughed. "Oh, yes. I remember you. You came there in the seventh grade. You were so cute."

He batted his eyelashes. "Well, I don't know about that, but I sure had a crush on you. You're Migdala, right? You were…wait a minute…

weren't you Juaquin's…?" He put his hand over his open mouth as if he'd just seen the light. "Well, then this must be your mother's house."

Luis snapped his head around, his mouth agape. "O, Dios mio. You're…you're Juaquin's niece. Oh, I am so sorry, I didn't know. Lo siento mucho. You should have said something."

"Well, let's not stand in the doorway." Larry stepped back and waved them in. "The mosquitoes start to wake up this time of day."

Scheutz stepped into the house and took off his sunglasses. They moved out of the foyer with Luis in the lead. The wide entrance led into a spacious living room, with what looked like a dining room at the far end. Beltran and his secretary were taking seats next to the J.R. Dobbs character at a dining table where about twenty other people sat. The table had been set for a dinner party. In the background what could only be called Caribbean elevator music, if there was such a thing, played a dream-like calypso rhythm. Several people turned to look at the newcomers.

Beltran stood when he saw them and came to stand in front of them. "What are you doing here? Were you invited?"

"Migdala moved away from Scheutz's side. "My mother is here?"

"This is her party, after all. And she's always upset if people arrive late for these things."

"What else is new? Everything upsets that woman. I've seen her get upset if her period is late."

Beltran raised his eyebrows and tilted his head. "You and your mother don't get along too well, do you?"

"Oh, we get along. We just don't get along together."

"Well, she and I get along fine."

"So, what is this party? It sounds like you do this regularly."

"Once a month. It was always Juaquin's party. But Marisol has kept it going since Juaquin…since Juaquin…a fallecido." Beltran looked like he might start crying again but he caught himself and gave her a weak grin. "Perdóname." He turned and walked away from them back to the dining table.

"Do you know where my mother is?"

The red-haired man pointed to a door at the right of the room. "She's probably in the kitchen.

Before Migdala could reach the door, it swung open and Marisol, with brilliant orange hair, stepped through. She clapped her hands while shouting "Atencion…" but stopped when she spied Migdala. She stared at Migdala, then opened her mouth but nothing came out. She was the same height as Migdala, an older version, in a bright red dress and an overload of jewelry, two necklaces, pendant earrings, bracelets on each arm, and rings on several fingers.

"¿Donde esta Blanca?" Both women asked where Blanca was at the same time. They stood six feet apart, glaring at each other, Migdala leaned forward from the waist and her mother tilted slightly back. Marisol brought the upper half of her body forward and the two women went nose to nose at each other in a rapid Spanish, the meaning of which Scheutz had not a chance of catching. Not that he needed to; the tone said it all. Even if he did understand the words, they would probably have made as much sense as the jabs of two long-time sparring partners well-acquainted with each other's vulnerable spots.

The hum of conversation at the dining table fell silent. The only noise accompanying the hissing duet was a soft bounce of calypso music. Behind Marisol the door opened again and a hawk-nosed man carrying a huge silver tureen called out, "Soup's on." He stopped short behind her, the tureen almost bumping into her back, then veered around the two women toward the head of the table. Beltran stood and made a timorous attempt at stepping between the two women, waving his hands with palms downward, begging them to calm down.

Migdala pushed him aside but Larry, the red-headed man, and two other men and one of the women stood and came between Migdala and her mother. Scheutz had difficulty suppressing a laugh. Strange as it seemed, nobody had gotten hit yet. The dinner guests crowded Migdala slowly backwards into the living room and her mother back to the door where she had come in.

Luis appeared at Scheutz's elbow. "Do they always do this?"

Chapter 22

Scheutz followed Migdala out the front door. Her mother remained near the dinner table with several of the guests trying to placate her. Once outside, he called for Migdala to wait but she kept on.

He felt a hand on his arm and heard Beltran's voice behind him. "Don't go. We have business to talk about."

Scheutz brushed the hand off. "Yes, we have business. But right now the only interest is the girl. Where is she? Or where is Harding?"

"Harding showed me the emeralds. They are good. Not the best, but still worth something."

"Listen, I've an idea." If this Beltran was a sleazy as he seemed, he might very well go for what Scheutz had to offer. "Why do we need Harding in the middle of this?"

Beltran looked away toward Migdala and then back. "What are you suggesting?"

"I'm suggesting that we split Harding's ten percent commission between us."

Beltran pursed his lips and then shrugged. "We could do that. Or I could keep all of the commission myself."

Scheutz nodded. "But then I definitely need the girl."

Beltran nodded. He pursed his lips and looked across the street, apparently considering. Finally, he said, "They are probably back at my house. Marisol's car is not here, so…" He spread his hands with palms up as if to say, "You understand." The blue Toyota that had been sitting next to the house was now gone.

Scheutz hurried to catch Migdala before she reached the car. "Were you going to run off without me?"

She stopped and turned to face him, tears streaming down her cheeks. She looked up at him for a moment and then covered her face with her hands and sobbed into them, her shoulders heaving.

"We'd better get moving." He opened the car door for her.

It was dark by the time they returned to Rincon. In Punto Higeura, he parked the car on the little parallel road above Beltran's house. Down the road, the little colmado still showed a light coming through the front doorway. Other lights in houses flickered across the hillside, including Beltran's house below them. Out on the Caribbean, the lights from a ship moved across the horizon. A mosquito whined just outside the car window Scheutz had left open for a little breeze. Small noises came up the hill, a coquil, seagulls cawing, the movement of the waves against the shore, people stirring outside their houses. The blue Toyota sat next to the pick-up truck behind Beltran's house.

Scheutz listened closely. Someone closed a door. They left the car and walked in the dark down to the paved driveway and then to the lower side of the house, the side toward the ocean. The walk reminded Scheutz of—how long ago was that?—thirty years ago when he was twenty, of being on night patrol in the cordillera of western Cuba. The same time of year, the same time of early evening, the same smells of the tropics and salt air coming off the water. Something awful happened that night. He could remember what if he took his mind off what he and Migdala were doing at present and concentrated on it. That would be silly. But the same sense of premonition visited him now as it did then. If something bad was going to happen here in this house, all the more reason to focus on what they were doing now.

The first sound to cut through the night noises was the sound of Blanca's voice as they stepped onto a patio below the second floor terrace. “”I don't care, I don't care, I don't care,” the girl shouted. Migdala gripped his arm, her face in the glow from a lower window, energized with excitement. Blanca's voice frightened Scheutz.

“Well, I care, so I don't care if you don't care.” Harding's voice. What an idiot. What the hell did the girl see in that guy anyhow?

Migdala grabbed the handle of a door leading from the patio into the house and found it locked. She began swearing in Spanish, but he shushed her, pointing to the terrace above. He led her back around the corner of the house and up through the low vegetation at the side. The handle of the door leading in from the rear parking area turned easily and noiselessly. He stepped into the hallway with Migdala crowding him from behind. In the living room, Blanca indulged herself in one of her rants in rapid Spanish while Harding, who had obviously no idea what she was saying, tried to calm her. Her voice sounded uncannily like her mother's and grandmother's.

Migdala pushed Scheutz aside and plunged into the room. Blanca stood far to the right next to the little bar while Harding stood near the glass door halfway across the room. The girl wore no clothes except for tiny bikini pants, her gangly, small-breasted torso leaning backwards like a town drunk against the bar. Harding, dressed in baggy swim shorts, turned at the sound of Migdala rushing at him.

"Mama…" the girl screamed and ran from the room.

Migdala took no heed of her but rather pounced upon Harding the way a lion leaps on an eland. The thought to stop her crossed Scheutz's mind but he decided to let her go. If she started to get the worst of that battle he'd step in, but otherwise, he might enjoy seeing Harding get his ass soundly whipped. Having tussled with Harding on a couple of occasions, he doubted the man had whatever it would take to counter that woman's fury. He thought about going after Blanca but instead shouted for her to get some clothes on and get back out there.

Harding defended himself very well. His bear hug had her arms pinned to her side and he successfully avoided her attempts to bite him. Scheutz moved to Harding's rear and put a chokehold on him to cut off his wind. "Go see about your daughter" he said to Migdala. Harding let go and Migdala stood stunned for a moment until Scheutz nodded toward the doorway at the other side of the room. She took off running and he tightened his hold on Harding's neck, enjoying the gagging sound coming from the man's throat. This exactly what Harding had done to him just a few days before.

He eased up a little and Harding gasped, "I'll be good. I'll be good." The moment he let him go Harding's elbow caught him on the side of head. Scheutz grabbed his t-shirt and twisted it up around his neck, tightening it like a noose. When the frenetic energy went out of Harding he sat him onto a chair against the wall, putting his weight into his spine and pushing his face into the stucco plaster. Harding coughed and held his hands to his throat. He finally got his breath. "Keep that woman off me, will you?"

"I don't know if I can do that. What are you doing with that girl?"

"You tell me. Her grandmother wanted me to bring her here."

"You're telling me her grandmother wanted her to hang around naked with a bum like you?"

"No, that was Blanca's idea."

"Which of course you took good advantage of."

"No, I didn't."

"Bullshit."

Harding's body sagged further and he rested the side of his face against the stucco. "You still got those emeralds?"

"Yes."

"Those guys are going to hurt me if I don't come up with the rest of those stones. Can I get them?"

"Depends."

"Listen, I need them. I'm afraid of those guys."

"You should also be afraid of Migdala. She is not going to let this thing drop. She's going to have you arrested for kidnapping and statutory rape."

"Didn't you just talk with Beltran a little while ago?"

"How'd you know that?"

"He called me. Told me you might come back here and to keep you here if you did. He's on his way up with a couple of people who work for Juaquin's smuggling cartel. You do not want to be here when they get here."

"I don't believe you. If you knew we were coming why didn't you get the girl out of here?"

"I'm sorry I ever had anything to do with that girl. Get her away from me."

Scheutz turned to shout toward the doorway on the other side of the room. "Migdala, get up here."

Her voice came from down the hall. "What is wrong?"

"Get up here right away. Bring Blanca. We have to go."

Migdala appeared, dragging the girl beside her. Blanca, dressed now in t-shirt and shorts, her hair a wild mat all over her face and head, looked as if she had been drugged into submission.

"What's the matter with her?"

Migdala waved her hand in front of her face. "Esta muy borracha. Como una callejeara."

"What?" Harding wanted to know.

"She's drunk," Migdala shouted at him. "You asshole."

"Come on, we have to go." To Harding, he said. "Stay here. Tell Beltran we're heading back down to Mayaguez to find him."

"Why?"

"My business."

Migdala tried leading Blanca toward the door and the girl struggled against her. Finally, Scheutz picked up the girl in his arms and led them to the lower door, standing aside while Migdala turned the latch. Before leaving, he turned back to Harding. "Be sure to tell Beltran I'm coming to find him."

Up behind the house in the parking area, he shifted the girl's squirming weight to his shoulder and motioned to Migdala to follow him up through the field to where the Escort was parked. "We need to hurry," he said to her.

"Why are we going to find Beltran?"

"We're not. I told him that so Beltran will be looking for us in a different direction."

Migdala led him through the dark, feeling her way through underbrush and around trees. The girl was so skinny she barely weighed on Scheutz's shoulder. They made good time, with only a few detours. When headlights pulled into the parking area of the house behind them they stopped and squatted close to the ground. With the lights still on, two men got out and went into the house.

"What are you doing to me? Put me down." Blanca's teenage voice slobbered in the night air. Migdala reached up and clamped her hand over her daughter's mouth. The girl resisted, wriggling but quickly gave up, laying her head next to his, drooling onto his neck.

Migdala pulled his arm and they moved behind a large shrub where they waited, watching the house, and then continued at a more rapid pace up the incline. Once in the car, Migdala took Blanca into the back with her where they lay down on the seat. Scheutz sped away, back through Rincon onto Route 2 and then north toward Aguadilla.

Once past Arecibo, almost halfway to San Juan, Migdala left the back seat, climbing over into the passenger seat. "She is passed out. Aye, Dios mio, that Harding. I could kill him."

Scheutz nodded, watching the road for possible police cruisers, careful not to attract attention by speeding. "So now what? Probably not a good idea to go back to Santurce." They decided to take the rental car back, then pay for a taxi to Fajardo, get a motel room for the night and catch the early morning ferry to Culebra.

In Santurce, Migdala put Blanca next to her in the back seat of the taxi and they waited while Scheutz paid for the rental car. Heading east on Expreso Loiza, Blanca began murmuring, her head on Migdala's shoulder. "Mama, te quiero mucho."

"Yes, I love you too, mi cariño."

"Y lo siento. Lo siento mucho. I am so sorry."

"Yo se. Yo se. But you must stay away from Harding."

"Mama…"

"¿Que?"

"Harding no es un bad man."

"Mmph. He got you drunk."

"No."

"He killed Tio Juaquin.

"No."

"No? Then who did kill him."

" I did."

Chapter 23

Migdala kept her daughter's head on her shoulder while the girl slipped into a drunken sleep. Migdala held Scheutz's gaze, a look of horror on her face. She placed her hand on the side of Blanca's head, caressed her and turned toward the front of the cab, shaking shook her head slowly, as if unable to absorb what she had just heard.

Scheutz took her shoulder and pulled both her and the girl to him. "It can't be. Don't believe her, she's drunk. Probably just trying to protect Harding."

Migdala turned back to him, tears in her eyes. "You're right. She loved Tio Juaquin."

In the town of Loquillo, about fifteen minutes from the ferry dock in Fajardo, she instructed the taxi driver to leave them at a cement-walled motel that had sustained little damage from the hurricane. Scheutz carried the sleeping Blanca from the taxi into a small room with efficiency kitchen. Wide double glass doors faced the ocean and let in the constant sound of the pounding surf. Blanca made "mmpf" noises as he deposited her on the sofa, but she did not waken. He took a light blanket from the bottom of the bed and draped it over her. The air-conditioner was too cold so he turned it off and slid open the glass door facing the ocean. A breeze cooled them enough for sleeping.

Migdala sat on the edge of the bed, staring at her daughter, her face drained of emotion. Scheutz felt drained himself; it had been a long, hard day. He sat next to her, wrapped his arm around her shoulder as he had done in the taxi. She slumped into his chest without taking her eyes off Blanca. "Come on," he whispered into her hair. "We've got to sleep." When she made no move, he gently pushed her back so she rested on the bed. He lay on the opposite side of the bed the way they had slept the previous night in Santurce.

He must have fallen into a deep sleep; the next thing he knew bright sun poured in through the open door at an angle to their bed. Migdala slumbered beside him. Blanca, snoring lightly, with the sheet thrown off everything but her feet, lay sprawled half on and half off the sofa on the other side of the room. He resisted the urge to reach across and touch the curve of Migdala's hip. Instead, he sat up and leaned against the headboard. He tried to imagine the horrible circumstances that would come about if what the girl had said last night turned out to be true. What would happen to that poor girl should not happen to anyone. She'd be locked up in some Puerto Rican juvenile detention center from which she would eventually come out a beaten-down adult with lots of criminal friends and a many-year hunger for the company of men. He could picture her lined up among the fat, ugly whores along Calle Tetuan in Old San Juan, the street near the port they called Calle de las Putas.

He wiped his hand over his eyes and looked away to drive the image from his mind. If what she said was true, it certainly had something to do with Harding. That son-of-a-bitch. Everyone, at least the police, thought Harding had done it. That was a good thing. The solution to the problem, obviously, was to make sure he did not come back to Culebra and to let the police keep thinking he had killed Juaquin. But the only way to make sure he'd stay gone would be to kill him. There was a scary thought. The ease of that solution scared him even more.

He had never contemplated killing anyone before. Dammit, he had to stop thinking like this. The girl was drunk, didn't know what she was saying. And if she did know what she was saying, she probably said it to protect Harding. That son-of-a-bitch. He rolled out of the bed and headed for the shower. A good dose of hot water would wash away his thoughts.

When he came back into the room, Migdala was in the midst of banging cabinet doors. "There's no coffee." She wore the clothes she had slept in, her hair sticking out at all angles and a crease across her face from lying on the edge of her pillow. My god, she was gorgeous.

He stood next to her to catch the pre-shower aroma of her hair. "We can get some breakfast in Fajardo. Can you get Blanca up?"

" 'Ey, no problema. As long as it is noon already."

"Well, we can't leave her here while we go get breakfast. But I am really hungry."

She tapped his chest. "You go out and get something and bring it back. And I'll see what I can do about getting Senorita Borracha back into the human race."

He made his way to the central plaza of Loquillo, careful to take in the faces of everyone he saw on the way. There was little to no chance of Beltran's amigos following them here, but he would rather err on the side of caution. By tomorrow they would be back in Culebra, but what then? Did they need to be looking over their shoulders for these guys to show up? But then, there was really no reason for those thugs to come after them. Beltran could come himself.

By the time he returned to the motel room, Migdala had had her shower, her wet hair still plastered to her neck. Blanca sprawled half upright on the sofa, her head tilted on the backrest, mouth open breathing out the foul stench of the previously drunk. Migdala met him at the door and took one of the Styrofoam coffee cups back to the sofa. She sat next to her daughter and pulled her head upright, holding the now lidless cup under Blanca's nose. "Bebes." She moved the cup back and forth under Blanca's nose. "Mmm. Que delicioso." Blanca wrinkled her nose and pulled back her head. Migdala reached for the back of the girl's head, but then thought better of it, smelled the coffee, and took a sip.

She let go of the girl and came to the counter in the small kitchenette where he had set the other coffee and muffins. They stood in silence, drinking coffee and eating muffins. He watched her face, waiting for her to say something. She finished her coffee, drinking the last in large gulps, and then leaned back against the counter, staring at her daughter, who had fallen asleep again, her mouth wide open. Tears welled up in Migdala's eyes. He set his coffee cup on the counter and took her in his arms where her tears once again soaked his t-shirt.

"Hey, take it easy," he said into her hair. "You're getting too upset over this. I'm sure it's nothing. Let's just wait till we talk to her. Wait till she's awake."

"No. Not now. Let us just get her home. We can talk with her at home." He put his arm around her shoulder again and she leaned into the side of him. This was getting to be a sort of natural habit between the two of them, his arm around her and her leaning toward him. Blanca had begun snoring again, this time louder.

"We should probably get going," he said. We missed the morning ferry, and if we don't get ourselves down there, we'll miss the afternoon one."

She made no move to leave his side. He held onto her shoulder gently, relaxing his hand. Eventually, she stirred. "Help me get her in the shower."

He left Migdala in the bathroom to undress her daughter and soak her down while he gathered their things, stuffing them into their two duffle bags. He drank the third coffee rather than let it go to waste. Periodic shouting came through the bathroom door, Blanca's as inarticulate as a teenager's can be, and Migdala's as tough as she'd shown
herself to be ever since he'd met her. When they finally emerged, Blanca came out with a towel on her head, in the same t-shirt and shorts.

Migdala came out behind her, carrying her toilet kit. Blanca threw herself on the bed and pulled the sheet up over her head. Migdala took the coffee cup from Scheutz's hand and finished it off. "If you carry her, I'll carry the bags." She slipped on her flip-flops, picked up the two duffles and then grabbed Blanca's flip-flops as she headed out the door. He had no choice but to gather up the girl and follow. She startled awake, made a meager protest, but then settled back again, curling herself into a fetal position in his arms.

With an hour to spare before the ferry left, Blanca came awake enough to have lunch with them at a little café around the corner from the embarcadero. Two cups of coffee and a swig of mouthwash turned her back into an acceptable human being, as acceptable as a sulky adolescent can be. When her mother brought up the subject of what the hell she thought she was doing running off with Harding, she had no answer except to get up and ask for another cup of coffee at the counter. "Harding is a very bad man," Migdala said as Blanca sat back down.

"And I'm a very bad girl."

Migdala's shook her head and made a face as if disgusted. Scheutz tried to come up with something to say that could alleviate the aura of anger and pain enclosing these two women. Anything he could say would certainly come in from left field. There was no way to lighten this, and deepening it right now would be like dropping sand into the wound. It was best he just shut up.

At boarding time Blanca walked between them after the last pick-up truck had inched over the ramp. He led, climbing the stairs to the seats on the upper deck under the awning. And there they sat, for the entire two-hour crossing, three zombies watching the horizon, just in case something mildly interesting should arrive out there to take their respective minds off what they did not want to look at in close.

Scheutz turned from watching the horizon to looking back on the main island of Puerto Rico. So that was civilization. It had been a long time, it seemed, since he had made a foray into what was considered the modern world. They had just been visiting, like some rube tourists, a world of commerce and money and technology and living in cities. It had been a while for him. Places like Charlotte Amalie on St. Thomas or Spanish Town on Virgin Gorda didn't count, even though they were technically cities. He tried to count up the cities—other than merely small island capitals—he'd been to in the last five years—Caracas, Kingston, Santo Domingo. Even in those cities, he had really done nothing more than sail into port, do what needed to be done and gotten the hell out. This trip to San Juan and Mayaguez had been the first visit to a city that did something besides support tourism and boat traffic since he and Samantha had shipped out of Boston years ago.

And from what he'd seen in the last forty-eight hours, they could keep it. He had to admit that what they had just gone through was not typical for most people who lived in that world and, like anything else, it would not be too hard to adjust to a way of life that would conform to city living. If he was twenty-two, he might even look forward to it, but at age fifty, and having adjusted to paradise, he could not imagine anything that might entice him to live in a city again.

Migdala stared hard at the horizon, her jaw muscles working as if she carried on some rant in her head. Blanca turned to give him a sheepish look but dropped her eyes to her hands in her lap when he smiled at her. She looked so defeated, but at age fifteen, she didn't know what defeat was yet.

At the ferry dock on Culebra, Asher stood waiting beside the Volvo. Migdala and Blanca walked together ahead of Scheutz up the concrete ramp, Blanca slouched as if she had been beaten into servitude, and from her occasional groans she was obviously oppressed by a hangover in the hot afternoon sun.

Asher held the back door open for Blanca and then as Migdala threw her bag onto the seat of the station wagon, he asked in a low voice, "¿Que pasa con ella?"

Migdala sighed and bent her head to enter the car. "She is in love with the devil."

Scheutz drove the car, inching slowly behind a short line heading away from the malecón. It didn't take much to cause a traffic jam in this little town; four cars at most.

"Did you have to close the restaurant for two days?" Migdala asked Asher.

"No, we did fine. Tapon helped me. He is very slow but he knows how to do it all. And the regular customers helped out. The tourist season is just starting, but it was okay."

"Not as many people this year because of the hurricane, I bet." Scheutz pulled out onto the road along the bay.

Back at El Tapon, Migdala led the girl inside, holding her by her upper arm. Scheutz carried the two duffle bags and Blanca's flip flops inside and set them in the living room. The door from the hall to

Blanca's bedroom stood open and Migdala sat on the bed talking softly to Blanca who looked like she had either fallen asleep or was indulging in a sulk. "You are grounded to your room till tomorrow, chica." She pushed the door closed and all Scheutz could hear from the hallway was Migdala's insistent voice punctuated by occasional mumbles from Blanca that grew louder until the girl screamed, "No. Stop it. Leave me alone."

Then Migdala's scream. "I will not leave you alone. Did you tell me in the taxi last night that you killed Tio Juaquin?"

"No, I never said that. Are you crazy?"

"You never said it?"

"No. Leave me alone."

"You did not kill him?"

"No. Stop it. Why do you care? You didn't even like him."

"I don't care about him. I care about you."

"If you really cared about me you would leave me alone. I have a terrible headache and you're torturing me."

The voices dropped again to a normal level. Scheutz stood against the wall across from the girl's door. There must be something he could do about this but he couldn't think what. The door opened and Migdala came out, then stopped and turned to her daughter. "You go to bed. Tomorrow we are going to have a long talk."

She glanced at Scheutz, her eyes filled with fury, then turned and walked down the hall. He followed her into the restaurant, which was closed until the supper hour. She walked behind the counter and immediately began slamming things onto the stove. "I'd better start getting ready for supper."

"Want me to help?"

She stopped at the cutting board and dropped her head, her body rigid and her hands clutching and unclutching. He moved forward to put his arm around her again but she held him away. Finally, she let her shoulders relax and raised her head. "Why don't you ask Asher to come in and help me. He knows where everything is from yesterday."

He went out through the front door to where Asher had joined Tapon, Sharkie, and Arturo on the bench overlooking the bay. Sharkie's dog scampered back and forth across the little front lawn, teasing his master by bringing the old man's hat almost to where he sat and then rushing away with it whenever he or Arturo reached for it. Scheutz found himself a seat and joined the others in the almost daily ritual of not doing much. The bay was quiet in the late afternoon sun, the only thing moving was the German's sloop heading out to the opening. Probably going for Vieques again, as he often did, to see his girl friend over there.

He nudged Asher. "Can you go in and help Migdala get ready? You put everything away in there."

Asher stood. "Okay." He stepped over the dog. "Oh, I should tell... no, it will be a surprise."

"What?"

"No, no. You will be so surprised."

"Come on, what?"

Asher turned toward the bay, first to the right toward the Dinghy Dock and then gestured with his thumb in the direction of where the schooner lay, out near the inlet. "You'll see." He gave Scheutz a wide grin and disappeared inside.

Supper hour went smoothly, mostly regulars and a few touristas. Scheutz helped out, as usual, with dishes and wiping off tables. Every time he prodded Asher about the surprise he'd mentioned, the man would only grin and wave a forefinger at him.

Blanca did not show her face. At one point, Scheutz made up a plate of food and took it in to her. Her radio played salsa music, and she sat against the wall at the end of her bed, her knees up and her arms wrapped across her stomach. She gave him an expressionless look, barely acknowledging the plate of food he set on the bed next to her. He made a comical grimace but she merely looked away. He offered the can of Coke; she refused to reach for it, so he set it on the corner of her bureau, within reach.

Darkness fell before they closed for the evening. Tapon and his buddies left, heading as usual for their favorite bar on the bay road. Asher helped Scheutz clean up while Migdala dealt with leftovers and made a list of what was needed the following day. She packed a serving dish of rice and beans and fish that would not keep for Scheutz and Asher to take out to the schooner.

Scheutz led her into the hallway to the apartment as Asher finished sweeping the dining room floor. "I can stay here tonight if you like instead of going out to the boat."

She gave him a quick smile before her face clenched. "We will be okay. I just want to talk with Blanca tonight."

"I wouldn't worry too much about it."

"You would not worry about it because she is not your daughter. What if one of your sons had said something like that? Huh?"

"She was drunk."

"Even if your son was drunk? Huh?"

"Yeah, I suppose you're right."

"Besides, if you sleep over again, people will start talking."

"You still worried about your boyfriend, Otero?"

She hit the side of her fist against his chest. "He is not my boyfriend. Will you stop that?"

He laughed. "Well, if Officer Otero finds out I stayed overnight here, he might toss me in his little jail cell again."

She looked at him and laughed. "Ese maldito. I am so sick of him drooling around me." She tilted her head back like a heroine in some romance novel. "I need you to save me from his clutches."

He laughed again. "You're pretty good at that."

She became serious. "But maybe sometime soon you can stay here again with me."

"Are you saying what I think you might be saying?"

"I…I don't know what I am saying."

Asher's voice sounded through the door behind him, "Hey, boss, I'm finished. You want to head out to the boat?"

"Hold on a minute."

She pushed him lightly. "Go. Okay? I have to talk with Blanca tonight. And it is better if I do it alone. I am so scared about her. I know I will not sleep tonight."

"I know. Should I call you later on my ship-to-shore radio."

"Yes, call me."

Asher waited for him out in front of the restaurant with the leftover food to take to the boat. He pointed to the top of the wall they had been building a few days before. "Only two more tiers to go." Asher spread his arms as if to signify the grandeur of it all. "I think it is going to be una construcion muy hermosa. It will be a beacon for the ships coming into the bay, the first restaurant they see as they sail in and drop anchor. 'El Tapon' the big sign will read, 'Comida Fina y Cervesa Fria'."

"You are a man of vision, Asher."

In the dinghy, Asher sat in the bow with the food. "Oh, by the way," Scheutz asked him. "What was that surprise you said I was in for?"

"You'll see."

"Come on, man. I hate people being coy about as much as I hate surprises."

"You'll see."

Scheutz manned the outboard, taking his time maneuvering among the various anchor lights on boats moored in close before heading out to where the *Panacea* lay. Approaching the schooner, it looked as if the boat sat more erect in her position at the edge of the shore. That's probably what the surprise was; Asher had succeeded in the last two days, while he was gone to the main island, in getting the boat jacked up to a perpendicular position. Great, now they could begin repairing that hole. Good old Asher; what a hot shit the guy was.

He had obviously left a light on below decks. Unlike him. And a radio played on deck, calypso music, the kind one heard on St. Croix. The light and the radio were running off the battery, so they'd have to start the small Yan Mar engine to recharge before going to sleep tonight. They tied up at the work raft and by the time he reached the deck of the schooner, Asher had already disappeared below with the food and bag of ice. Even though he had not done much in the way physical exercise today, he felt drained. He slouched in a lawn chair with his feet propped on the gunwale and let his gaze drift down toward the restaurant picturing Migdala with her daughter. In spite of himself, he felt a chill in his spine.

Something caught the corner of his eye as a shadow emerged from the aft gangway, backlit by the dim light coming up from below. Thinking it must be Asher, he turned away again. But he could still hear Asher clanking around in the galley below him.

"Here's your beer," a female voice said, and he could now make the form of a woman amidship, walking toward him.

Samantha.

Chapter 24

"Clem?"

"Samantha. Hi."

She wore a t-shirt and shorts but no hat, her hair pulled back in her usual ponytail. Her smell was different, though, not the salt air he had been used to on her. She stood next to the chair and handed him the can of warm beer, then opened her arms for him to give her a hug. He let her stand there, awkwardly, holding her arms out. "Come on, don't be that way." She waggled her fingers in a lifting motion. "Get up off your ass."

He stood and embraced her, still holding the beer can. Their embrace was light and he let go before she did. She backed away and they stood looking at each other in the light coming up from the hatch. A mosquito landed on his ear and he smacked it. He must have missed that spot with the repellant. The wind had died bringing the mosquitoes up from the brackish water along the shore. He could not look at her, and turned away toward the water crashing over the reefs out near the entrance to the bay.

"Asher showed me the hole in the hull."

"When did you get here?"

"I flew in yesterday; wanted to get away from the ice and snow." She moved toward the hammock and sat sideways in it, facing him and pushing it backwards to swing a little.

They sat silent for a while. He sipped the beer, his face toward the reef, but occasionally shifting his eyes in the dark to look at her. Nothing changed much, her hair a little longer. But what did he expect, it had only been, what, three months? It felt like thirty years. He looked away and then back again. Did he miss her? Maybe. Now that she was sitting in front of him again. He had put her out of his mind, made himself stop missing her. It surprised him, actually. It wasn't anything like when his wife Gerry left. That was an ache that just wouldn't go away, an ache that had led him to make her up in his own mind and have conversations with the image he had made up. No, with Samantha it was more like not seeing his brother Hank anymore. He loved Hank, he loved Samantha, but being away from them was more like not having a good friend around, whereas, with Gerry he had felt like that Salvador Dali painting of the structure with a large hole in the middle of it.

Sitting with her on the dark deck of a moored boat with the Atlantic breeze keeping the mosquitoes away was a pleasure he had gotten so used to over the years. She had taken that away with her. And now the breeze had died and she was back and the mosquitoes were back. But any minute the breeze from the ocean could pick up again and the mosquitoes would be gone, and she would be gone.

"You look different," she said.

"How so?"

"I can't put my finger on it. Not look, seem. Just different."

And if the breeze did pick up, it would always be nice for the mosquitoes to go away. But he honestly could not be sure whether it would be better for Samantha to go away. Migdala hung there just beside him, trying to help him figure it out, watching Samantha, giving him her—naturally—biased opinion of his beautiful ex-girlfriend who was, at this moment, not so "ex."

"I'm sorry." Her voice came quietly from the hammock. The apology hung there in the air. Asher had gone silent below deck, a small bell tinkled on a moored boat in toward the town, and the ocean broke over a reef out toward the open sea. The work platform bumped the side of the hull just lightly, a lapping of water tapping wood on wood.

He ought to tell her he was sorry also, sorry it had ended, sorry for the way it had been between them for the last year or so before she left. He ought to say it to her, but he couldn't. He reached under the chair for the mosquito repellent that was always kept there, dripped some onto his fingers and daubed both his ears.

He sipped his warm beer. She stopped the swinging hammock and sat very still in the dim softness of the kerosene light coming up from the forward hatch. Behind her the dark crest of the hill across the bay showed as a silhouette against the slightly less dark sky. No more tinkling bell, only the persistent spatter of the surf on the reef. The moment felt heavy, momentous in some way, important. His response to her apology could lead them off in either of two directions. It could be a path toward their reconciliation, or it could allow them to drift further in different directions. A stream of water flowing out of a bay as the tide ebbed could be separated by a rock in the middle, and then either gather together again in a pool on the other side, or flow into two different channels.

And still he said nothing. This felt like a continuation of the year before she left. Then he had turned off to her in some unspoken way that he could barely recognize. He was angry with her, for what he couldn't fathom. Even now, he could feel his anger rising inside him. He did not want to answer her. He did not want to give her the satisfaction even that he accepted her apology. And even while he was doing it he knew what a sulky brat he was being. He sipped the beer in silence as she waited.

"Did you hear what I just said?"

"I heard what you just said."

"Well?"

"Well, I'm tired from a long day, and I'd like to go to bed."

"Clem…"

Sip.

"Give me something, Clem. I'm sitting here with my heart hanging out."

"Want the rest of this beer?"

She sniffed, and he realized she must be crying, quietly.

"Right now I don't have anything to give you, Samantha. Maybe you could find your friend Colwin."

"I've never known you to be petty."

"I'm tired. And I'm angry. A lawyer I knew once told me you should never try a case when you're tired or angry."

"Is that what you're doing, trying my case?"

He sighed. "Yeah, that's what it feels like."

The hammock swung lightly again. No one spoke for a long while. Finally she said, "I suppose that's only fair."

"Well, I'm going to hit the sack. Did you get a place to sleep in town?"

"Asher brought me over here early today and I have no way of getting back. Unless you want to wake him."

"No don't wake him; I'll take you back."

"I could sleep here if you're too tired."

"Your old cabin was flooded and has never been cleaned up." He waited while she said nothing, hoping she would not suggest she sleep in his cabin.

"If you wouldn't mind taking me back."

He set the beer can under the chair next to the mosquito repellent, then stood and walked aft to the ladder and down to the work platform. After letting go the stern line he stepped into the dinghy and tilted the outboard to perpendicular. She let go the bowline and stepped aboard as he started the engine. Without a word, he turned the bow out into the bay and then hard to starboard to put it in line with the lights in the center of the town.

She faced him, sitting in the bow. He did not look directly at her, but kept an eye out for what might be in the water in front of them. He did not feel as tired as he had felt sitting on the deck of the schooner. He watched her out of the side of his eyes, where night vision was more acute, the image of her, small lights from boats they passed bouncing off her shoulders, making him angrier the further they proceeded across the bay.

At the little dock behind Colwin's guesthouse he cut the engine and let the dinghy drift in next to Sharkie's. She stood and jumped from the bow to the dock, holding the bowline in her hand. When she did not move to toss the line aboard he said, "Well, I gotta get back."

"You want to come up and have a cold one?"

"No."

She stood, perfectly balanced with one foot on the dock and one on the bow of the dinghy, keeping the boat away from bumping the side of the wooden dock. He had always loved to see her in poses like this, taut, showing off for him, ready for anything that came along. She stared at him for a long time while he kept his eyes just to port of her shoulders, her thin, athletic torso infuriating him not quite as much as the inviting gaze of her eyes. But he had to smile at her clenched right hand signifying that, knowing her as well as he did, she would love to sock him one. Something he had always loved about her was the contrast of her two sides, that you would never get to know them unless you knew her really well. On the one side she would love to hold you close and cuddle you while the on other she longed to punch you out. Or maybe that was just the way she responded to him.

She tilted her head as if trying to catch his gaze. "What are you grinning at?"

"I'm not grinning. Just happy to see you."

"You don't act like it."

"Like I said, I'm really tired and I'd like to go to sleep."

"You could sleep here."

"In my own little trundle."

"Well, screw you then." She took her foot off the bow of the dinghy and put it onto the dock. "Geez, you try to be nice and what do you get?"

That caused him to laugh. And she laughed with him. He put the outboard in reverse and goosed the throttle till the dinghy cleared the other boats tied up at the dock. "See ya."

"Night."

Once in his bunk, he could not sleep. Three months earlier he lay in this same spot retracing all the events that seemed to lead to Samantha's leaving. Now he retraced the same events to find the reason for her return. Outside a breeze must have picked up because the work platform began a regular two-four beat against the hull. He reached up and opened the porthole to let the breeze in and blow away the stuffiness of the cabin. Nice breeze; maybe now he could sleep.

No such luck. Before he was uncomfortable and awake. Now he was comfortable and even more awake. Why had she come back to Culebra? She probably had some money now from her father's will. Was it for him or for the boat? Maybe she still had some idea of sailing to the South Pacific; claim her half of the *Panacea.* The thought that she might still love him brought tears to his eyes. And then the anger rose again to cut them off. Her running off was not capricious; her father was sick and she was obligated to go. She stayed away too long. If she had come back last week even, it would have been a different story. Now there was Migdala.

His eyes were gritty with trying to hold them closed, the muscles in his arms and legs beginning to ache from his effort to relax them. The two women took their own forms, little cartoon characters sitting on his chest, Samantha to port and Migdala to starboard. They both talked at once, Samantha about how beautiful and serene life would be on the island of Bora Bora, Migdala about how she needed him to finish building the restaurant and to help take care of her daughter. Samantha wore the yellow bikini and peaked cap she favored while standing at the helm of a ship, her tanned body glowing in the sunlight. Migdala sported the smudged apron. The South Pacific would be more like the boat-bumming he had been doing in the Caribbean for years, Culebra would be more like what he had done in New Hampshire with his kids in school.

Blanca was not his kid but she was a pretty neat person once you got around the pressing need she seemed to have to bug the shit out of everyone near her. And if she had done what she hinted she'd done in the middle of her drunken slobber, she didn't have much of a future ahead of her. So, was that an argument for helping out or for staying out if it? He couldn't say. Either way, Samantha or Migdala, his choices here both involved putting himself almost entirely in the hands of some woman. So, what was the other alternative? What did he want to do? There was the schooner, and making this boat seaworthy again could take a while, even with Asher's help. Then what? Charter the boat for tourist cruises? That could work. It was a pretty cool old wooden-hulled schooner that many of those subscribers to Sail magazine would enjoy a week's vacation on. And he could get good money for it. He'd be his own boss, and not be led around by his dick.

The image of some beautiful woman leading him around by his dick seemed to relax him and the next thing he knew bright rays of sunlight shone through the porthole near his head, and he could hear Asher banging around up forward in the galley. Asher always banged around especially loud in the morning as a way of letting Scheutz know he ought to be out of bed. He rose and, not bothering to put on clothes, opened the cabin door to the wonderful aroma of coffee. He made it up the aft gangway, across the deck, down the side of the hull, across the work platform and into the water of the bay before he was fully awake. After a brief swim and a piss, he climbed back onto the platform and used the soap set aside there in a coffee can to lather himself before diving back into the water.

Several minutes later, dressed in clean shorts and t-shirt, he made his way to the galley. Asher had eaten some of the leftovers they'd brought from the restaurant the night before, and had left enough in the cast iron skillet for Scheutz. With that and a mug of coffee, he climbed up through the forward hatch to his lawn chair. Asher relaxed with his own coffee, swinging in the hammock the same way Samantha had done the night before.

"You like your surprise, boss?"

"Umph."

Asher let out one of his truncated guffaws.

"I wish you'd told me," Scheutz said.

"Better this way. More fun for me."

"You were listening?"

"Small boat."

"She wants to go to the South Pacific."

"I know. And she want you to go, too. She told me."

Scheutz concentrated on his refried leftovers.

"Yesterday, when you and the restaurant lady were gone, Samantha come into the restaurant looking for you. She probably be there this morning, too." Asher held his coffee cup up to his face, looking over it to catch Scheutz's eye, and then gave another of his big-toothed guffaws. "Heh, heh. De bossman, him got him de womans trouble."

"Shut up."

"We better get going. The restaurant be open already and Migdala expecting us to help out." He handed his empty cup to Scheutz for him to take below with his own cup and dish. "I cannot wait to see the fun."

When they pulled away from work platform Scheutz sat in the bow of the dinghy while Asher worked the outboard. They passed close to Harding's boat with its yellow police tape draped along both gunwales. Since Harding dared not show his face on Culebra, what would become of that boat?

At the restaurant, the moment he opened the door he sensed the tension in the air. Samantha sat at a table against the back wall facing the door. Tapon and his usual compadres, Arturo and Sharkie, sat at their table, not saying anything for a change. Five other people sat scattered about, either eating or sipping coffee, waiting for their food. Blanca, of all people, scurried back and forth in an apron that threatened to engulf her, carrying plates of food. Behind the counter, at the grill,

Migdala carried on her usual morning hustle, giving as always the sense that she was not quite keeping up with it all.

Scheutz walked straight to the corner by the refrigerator to retrieve his own apron. Blanca passed him and gave him a shot to his shoulder with her fist. “Buenas dias, viejo.”

As he approached the counter, Migdala, without so much as a glance in his direction, banged a plate of eggs and tostados onto the counter with such a force he thought the plate might break. Oh, boy. This was going to be a long day. He looked toward Samantha who sat with her head tilted and a questioning look on her face, probably confused as to why he did not immediately come over and sit with her. Asher grabbed a cup of coffee and sat down across from her. Scheutz waved and made his way behind Migdala to where a pile of dirty dishes waited in the sink for him to get to work.

It was bad enough having these women on the same island, without having them in the same restaurant. He burnt his fingers on the scalding water in the sink full of dishes. Now what? Migdala was obviously spooked just seeing Samantha show up here unannounced. If he did not go talk with Samantha, Migdala would be even more suspicious of what he might be trying to hide. He leaned in close to her. “Well, look who showed up. What a surprise, huh?”

Migdala glopped a spoonful of beans on an already full plate and slammed the plate on the counter. Turning back toward the grill she gave him a passing look of pure vitriol. Blanca appeared and picked up the plate. He turned back to the sink. After washing a minimal number of plates and cups, he said, “I had better go talk with her.” Migdala made no sign she had even heard him.

He sat down next to Asher facing Samantha at the end of the long table. Asher was in the middle of describing the aftermath of the hurricane to her. She glanced up at Scheutz as he sat down, still wearing his apron. His scalded fingers still hurt and he shook his right hand lightly.

“What’s that mean?” She imitated his finger shake.

“Burnt ‘em.” She gave him a look that had “bullshit” written all over it. “Well, if you insist,” he said, making the same gesture again. “This hand movement is actually a signal to the goddess of the sea asking her to stop fucking with me.”

Asher laughed, obviously enjoying his ringside seat. He turned to Samantha. "He got the sea goddess and the food goddess, both of them to arm-wrestling for his soul."

"Huh?"

"Don't mind him," Scheutz said. How the hell does he know this stuff?

She waved her hand dismissing the whole thing and asked Asher to go back to describing the aftermath of the hurricane. He eventually came around to what he and Scheutz were doing here at the restaurant, how they were building a new wall of cinderblock and concrete outside the old wooden walls.

"So that includes washing dishes?"

"No. For the dishes we get free leftover food." Asher patted the table in front of him. "And I tell you, I never eat so good in my life. That woman can cook her ass off. We going to sign her up on our world cruise when we fix the hole in the Panacea."

"You're going on a world cruise? When was that decided? That boat is half mine, you know."

Scheutz shook his burnt fingers at her again. "Relax. We're not going on any world cruise. As usual, Asher's full of shit." He shook the fingers at Asher. "Why don't you shut up a little bit?"

Asher's guffaw came out not so truncated. He was obviously enjoying the hell out of himself.

Samantha focused her blue eyes deep into Scheutz's. "So, you are rebuilding this restaurant? For FEMA money, I suppose. And then you're using that money to rebuild the Panacea? And how long do you think this is all going to take?"

Scheutz shrugged. "You know how it goes down here. It could take a long time. You know, the mañana complex.

"Well, I have a say in what happens to that boat."

Blanca brought a plate of eggs and ham for Samantha, who thanked her. The girl motioned to Scheutz and Asher. "You guys want anything, you can get it yourselves." As she turned to go, she pointed at Scheutz. "And you better get back to work. My mom is really pissed."

Samantha shoved a hunk of eggs and toast into her mouth. "Is that her mom behind the counter? How can you stand working for her? I came in this morning, smiled at her while I ordered my breakfast and she almost bit my head off. What a nasty bitch."

This brought another guffaw from Asher.

Samantha laughed as a reflex to Asher. "What's so funny?"

Asher, barely containing himself, waggled his thumb in Scheutz's direction.

Samantha, grinning expectantly around a mouthful of food, raised her eyebrows in question at Scheutz.

Scheutz, who did not see the humor in any of this, shook his head and looked away from them toward where Migdala struggled on behind the counter. Two more customers had come in while he sat there and two more were coming in the door. "I'd better get back to work." He stood to go.

"What time do you get off?" Samantha asked him.

"After breakfast we're working on the walls. And then I'm back in here for lunch. And then when that is over, we're back on the walls for a few hours and then, hopefully, Asher and I can get some work done out there on the Panacea."

"So, I'll see you this afternoon. I'll put my work clothes on, give you a hand out there."

Back at the counter, he asked Blanca why she wasn't in school.

"Because it's the weekend."

Oh. It had taken him awhile when he first came to the Caribbean to adjust to the fact that for him there was no difference between one day and another. It had only been lately, in the last few weeks, while trying to help Migdala deal with her daughter, that he had begun to take note of the fact that people did lead more structured lives, that there was a difference between weekday and weekend, and an adherence to time other than merely getting light, light, getting dark, and dark. And, of course, here in Puerto Rico, the tide was barely measurable, maybe a couple of inches, so you couldn't tell time by that. He imagined being in the South Pacific would be the same as the Caribbean, no time, no tide. The guy who said, "Time and tide wait for no man" surely was from the north. If he was from the tropics, he would have said, "Time and tide exist for no man."

Bang. Another plate slammed onto the counter. "The dishes are piling up."

"What did you do before I came along," he asked.

"I was not so aggravated, so I could get more done."

When Samantha finished eating, she lay her money on the counter in front of Migdala and the two women looked hard at each other for a moment, Migdala glaring and Samantha giving her a look of "Well, fuck you, too" before walking out the door.

When Samantha left, Asher sat down to have a few words with Tapon and then came to the counter to tell Scheutz he was going to work on the walls. Before leaving, he stopped and said, "You two should cheer up, you are ruining everybody's breakfast."

Scheutz flipped a handful of soapy water at Asher as he went out the door. Migdala flipped eggs on the grill making it look like she hated eggs.

"What are you so mad about?" he asked.

"I'm not mad."

"Did you and Samantha have an argument?"

"No, we did not have an argument and I'm not mad at anybody. Especially you."

"Oh." Well, that was nice. Especially not him. She was jealous of Samantha. He stopped washing the dishes, placed an arm against the counter and leaned sidewise grinning at her until she allowed herself to snarl in his direction and give him the finger. What was there about a jealous rage that made people so sexy?

Chapter 25

Samantha did not show up for lunch, thankfully. Her presence would have been like poking a stick into an open sore. Migdala's rage had subsided into a seethe, but she still banged things around. Scheutz couldn't decide if he enjoyed it or not. One minute yes, another no. He almost couldn't take his eyes off her to get his dishes done. Standing near her behind the counter made him tingle. She must be really turned on to him to be that jealous. And that turned him on. Watching her stirring the boiling rice gave him an erection so that he had to back away from the side of the sink. He kept himself bent a little from the waist so that the apron hung loose in front of him and did not show the bulge.

When it got too bad he tried thinking of Samantha. Not the way they had been the last couple of years, but before that, her squirming languidly in the V-birth of a boat moored in the gently rocking waters of some bay. What the hell was wrong with him? How could he switch from one woman to another like that, in a matter of minutes? He had to admit, though, it was what he did not know about Migdala's body that turned him, whereas it worked the other way with Samantha, what he did know about her in the middle of her passion. He rinsed several clean plates and stacked them on end in the rack next to the sink. Here's where it starts to get weird, he realized. He could only picture Migdala being quietly angry in bed, the way Samantha had been the last two years. He began to wonder if he wasn't some kind of sicko, if he only got turned on to women who were pissed off at him. He thought back. Yeah, Gerry had been pissed off a lot. And they had great sex. The lesbian yoga instructor? Not really. At least not while they were in the middle of their truly hot Tantric rituals. But then, she carried what felt to him like a couple of burning rocks in a few of her chakras.

Well, okay, he'd try some tantric dishwashing here. He'd concentrate on the dishes, wiping any and all images from his mind and see what filtered in. He blocked out the woman standing near him at the grill. His hands took up a gentle rhythm of scour, wash, rinse, pile, scour, wash, rinse, pile. Slowly, as if like a vapor rising from the suds, Migdala came to him, her eyes half closed, her breathing deep and arhythmic, her warmth enveloping him, her smile inviting him. That was it; that was what he wanted. He wanted to lose himself in her softness. See?, he taunted himself. You're not such a sicko after all.

By the time he finished cleaning up and had the floor swept she still had not said a word to him. He wanted to get out of there, to go work on the boat. The top tier of the new outer walls of the restaurant had been completed that morning, meaning they could now concentrate on the boat for a bit. But before he left, he wanted to suggest that they make some decision about where to go from there on the building.

As he talked with her about it, she continued with the preparation of some vegetables. She finally looked up. "We should have a meeting and all of us decide what to do from here. Come back early this afternoon and bring Asher."

"In that case can I borrow your car? I want to get some work done and still be able to get back here."

"That depends on who is going to ride in my car."

"Oh, Jesus." He put his hand over his heart. "I promise I won't give a ride to the wrong people…to the wrong person. Okay? She can swim back."

"Or she can just stay there."

When she turned away from him he put his arms around her from behind and pressed his nose into her hair. She jabbed backwards with first one elbow than the next but he evaded both, laughing and pressing his pelvis into her rear. She did a half turn and slammed him with her hip. That cut his laughter and allowed her to turn fully facing him, still in his arms. But instead of her daily scowl, she smiled at him. "Careful who you mess with, boy."

He kissed her. She stiffened and then softened for a long moment before breaking away. They stood staring at each other in the empty restaurant. His immediate erection must have seemed obvious to her but she did not respond to it one way or the other. Before breaking away, she said again, "Be very careful who you mess with."

"I am. I will." It occurred to him that they were the only two people in the building. Blanca was at school. Tapon had left right after lunch. As if both on the same cue, they turned toward the door to the apartment. She walked ahead of him to her room where she pulled him toward the bed. He found himself inside her before he realized that they had each taken off their clothes. And before he was fully aware of what was happening she was grasping his head, pulling it toward hers, coming even before he did, if that was possible.

When he lay next to her, still breathing heavily, it occurred to him that there had been no foreplay to their lovemaking, and it was the foreplay he always enjoying even more than the sex. But, what the hell, hadn't the last two months been a kind of foreplay? She moved toward him and, extending an arm over his chest, draped one half of her body along his right side. Her breathing matched his, both of them slowly abating to normal.

Now what? Something big had changed. It felt like the little tumblers in a lock had suddenly slipped into place. But was the lock opening or closing? Oddly, it felt like both. It was possible he was now locked in to her, but it felt as if he had just been released from something, too.

He stared at the ceiling for a long time, his arm wrapped around her shoulders. Her breathing told him she'd fallen asleep, and he felt himself drifting in that direction. He awoke to her kissing him. Her hand held his cock, which had started to come to life again. That was weird. He was fifty years old, lucky to have an erection every other day, let alone twice in one afternoon. How often over the last couple of months had he imagined this. And then she was on top of him, lowering herself onto his cock, the tip of her breasts touching his chest, her face hovering close to his. He gazed into her eyes in the afternoon sunlight coming through the room's only window. She began to move her pelvis as he watched her eyes. He may have had two erections in one afternoon but it was doubtful he'd have two orgasms in one afternoon. So, she was in for a long haul. As she moved, he watched an entire range of moods and emotions play through her eyes. She was as lovely as he had imagined her to be. The soft side and the rough side played against each other, moved in tandem with each other, pushing and pulling, accepting and giving. When her orgasm finally came, her chest constricted in spasms of passion.

She lay on top of him for a long time, his own un-orgasmed cock slowly shrinking inside her until it fell out on its own. And still she lay there, the sweat on her chest mingling with his own, her face nuzzled into his neck with her hair covering the left side of his face and tickling his nose. He moved his hand to remove the few strands of hair from his nose and the side of his mouth. She reached up and took the hand in her own and held it against his other cheek. She wanted him not to move, to stay rock solid under her. They stayed that way for a long while.

He gave up the idea of going out to work on the boat, but after an hour or so she suggested they get up. Blanca was due home from school soon. She wanted to take a shower, but he asked her not to; the lingering scent of sex on her was an even more delicious aroma than the smell of her cooking. She called him a pig and bounced off into the shower. So, he followed her.

She gave him the keys to the Volvo and he set out first to find Tapon and maybe pick up Blanca if he saw her outside the school. Tapon sat with Arturo and Sharkie playing dominos in the patio just outside El Batey. They all piled into the station wagon when Scheutz told them about the proposed meeting. After dropping them off at the restaurant he drove out to get Asher, parked on the old helipad and walked down the hill to where the schooner lay.

He found both Asher and Samantha below decks scraping the two broken ribs in preparation for sistering the new wood. They both looked as if they had been wandering in a hailstorm of mud, soot, and sawdust. Asher, barefoot, wore only dirty khakis cut off at the knees. Samantha had on jeans, cut off very short, and a soot-smeared halter. She'd tied her hair up in a yellow bandana but loose strands hung out and stuck in the sweaty grime of her neck.

"We appreciate all your help," she said. "Where you been?"

"I got tied up."

"We are almost ready for the new ribs," Asher said. "Maybe we can finish today."

"Well, I came to get you. We have to have a meeting about how to proceed on the restaurant. Migdala wanted to hear what you had to say about it. So she sent me out to bring you in."

"What about me?" Samantha asked.

He studied a piece of broken hull planking that lay half in the bilge water. "Um. Probably not. It's just all the people who are working on the building."

"Your new girlfriend?"

"What do you mean?'

"You don't want me there because the cook might be there."

"Well, she kind of owns the place. She's not just the cook."

Asher sloshed through the bilge heading forward to the galley. "I be gointa get clean."

Samantha moved to the starboard side of the cabin, tossing the sander she had been using onto the table there. She wiped her hands across her eyes and then her face, brushing off grains of sawdust. "So, is this what it is, Clem? I go away for a few months and you right away find yourself another tootsie roll?" She didn't sound angry or bitter the way he had gotten used to her before she left for New Hampshire. Her voice held a kind of sadness he had never heard from her before.

"No."

"Yes."

"Samantha, listen…"

"No, you listen. I thought a lot about us while I was home with my folks. My dad's death really caused me to think about you and me a lot. About what we've been doing for the last few years. I know it was tough before I left, and yeah, I really wanted to get away from you. But, I wanted to come back. Not just to get the boat and go to Tahiti, but back to you. We are good together. We were. We used to be happy, right? We can be again."

It was so nice to hear her speaking in a voice that was not filled with resentment. And, God, the dirt and grime made her so sexy looking, her hair pinned back like that under the bandana, her face streaked where her hands had tried to clear the sawdust away. What the hell was wrong with him? Here he came, fresh from having all but fallen in love with one woman to find her covered with grime in this dirty, sodden hole and he could not take his eyes off her. He thought of Ulysses tying himself to the mast of his ship to keep him from the temptations of the sirens. And she was still at it. Look at her eyes.

"Hey, Mister Clem, ready to go." Asher's voice came down the companionway.

"I've…I've got to go to this meeting." He wagged his thumb in the direction of the barrio.

"Don't go," she said.

"I have to. I've got Migdala's car and I've got to take Asher down there and I've got to help plan what we are going to do next on that building and I've got to…" He knew he had to do something else but he couldn't think what it was. He had to get away from Samantha right now, is what he had to do. He had to fight the urge to take her up into his arms, dirt and all, and hold her to him. What was he going to do? "We'll come back after the meeting."

She did not move.

"Or I could drop you in town on the way." He had promised

Migdala he would not give Samantha a ride in her car, but he could not stand the look on Samantha's face.

She looked away. "I'll wait here."

When he and Asher walked into the restaurant, everyone was already seated at one of the long tables. Blanca had apparently made it home from school on her own. Asher poured coffee for himself and Scheutz before sitting down and they jumped into the middle of the ongoing conversation. The big question was what day to close the restaurant. The outside walls were finished and it was time now to pour the roof. Arturo, who had spent his young lifetime in this kind of house building, drew the plan for constructing the form for the roof and the two interior pillars. They estimated that with a little help, they could pour the concrete roof slab in a single day. And they certainly could not do that with the restaurant open below them. But what was the best day?

Migdala, Tapon, Asher, Arturo, Sharkie, Blanca and Scheutz, everyone threw in their opinion. Sharkie's dog, who was not allowed in the restaurant when it was open for business, ran freely around the room, ecstatic, sniffing every corner and table leg for traces of food. Tapon argued for Sunday and Blanca argued for a weekday. There was no early breakfast on Sunday but people came in after church for late breakfast or brunch. Early breakfast during the week was necessary, argued Blanca, before people went off to work, and besides, she got to sleep in on Sunday.

It was finally decided that the target day would be the following Sunday. And everyone would help. Migdala would be up on the roof with Scheutz and Asher, pushing cement, Blanca would be mixing. She would bring one of her classmates from the ninth grade, a shy boy named Eusebio, to help her. Arturo volunteered for duty up on the roof. He didn't know how long he'd last till he pooped out but, since he had once been so good at pushing cement around, he figured he'd still outdo all the others. Tapon and Sharkie offered to at least keep everybody well supplied with cold drinks. "No beer till we are done," Migdala told them. "Only water and soda and lemonade."

Tapon folded his arms and nodded at Sharkie. "Lemonade."

The Sunday date left a lot to be accomplished before then. Supplies had to be brought up, plywood, rebar, two-by-fours, and cement.

Arturo estimated how many fifty-pound bags of cement would be needed, how much rebar. They could remove the sailcloth used for a roof and build the forms in the afternoons when the restaurant was closed. It would be an interruption and an annoyance, but only for the next three days until Sunday.

Scheutz and Asher would not be able to work on the schooner until the following week. They had gotten so far as to cutting out the broken boards on the hull and sanded the sides of the two broken ribs. The hull pushed in by the rock resembled a dented eggshell. By the time they cut away all the broken boards, they had a hole big enough to drive a Volkswagon through. Scheutz was anxious to get started on fashioning the new ribs for the ship's frame, but it would have to wait until the roof of the restaurant was complete.

So, everything was settled and it was time to start getting ready for the supper hour. The winter tourist season had started now that the Thanksgiving holiday was over and the supper crowd especially had swelled as it did every year at this time. Not being able to work on the schooner was offset by the satisfaction he anticipated being part of this little group, working together to finally push the old family home into some semblance of the twentieth century. This was the closest thing to family he had experienced in many years. He had not ever had that feeling with Samantha. All those years together and he had never gotten beyond the feeling of them being on some kind of extended date.

The original house that later became the restaurant and the apartment behind it had been built around the same time as the schooner, sometime in the 1920s, both of them in their respective traditional style. The wooden structure on shore was originally been built when Tapon was a boy, a two-room island home like most others on Caribbean islands, the kind of cabin that dated back to the 18th century. And the style of the schooner probably dated to around the same time, even though that same construction was still used in England many years later. The 671 diesel engine had been added to the schooner in the 1940s around the same time the restaurant had been added to the house on shore.

The restaurant had been the dream of Tapon's daughter and son-in-law, Migdala's parents. But the son-in-law died and Marisol gave up the restaurant and moved to San Juan. Migdala's grandmother ran the restaurant successfully while Tapon and Sharkie continued their daily fishing trips into the waters of the Caribbean, bringing in a profit from the catch and fresh fish to the restaurant. When his wife died, Tapon kept the restaurant going with minimal success for a few years until he was able to convince Migdala, on one of her vacation trips to the island, to leave New York and come down for a "permanent vacation" as he put it, to run the restaurant.

And now, after sixty years of keeping up the old wooden structure against the weather and the termites, the building was coming down. "Que viva el progresso," Tapon had cheered during the family meeting, rapping his knuckles on the tabletop. Everyone else applauded, while Blanca gave Asher a high-five.

That was fine for the restaurant, but not the schooner. Samantha certainly had felt that way—get rid of the old thing and move on to a new and better life. But that all changed now she had money to fix it up, to not only repair the hole in the hull but make other changes she had always wanted.

Migdala gave him a look and waggled her fingers saying he ought to get off his ass and get behind the counter. He heaved himself up and headed for his apron. The idea of spending day after endless day lounging on the deck of the *Panacea*, reading a good book and sipping rum over ice as the boat all but drifted through the placid waters of the Pacific had a certain appeal. Since the hurricane, it seemed he had done nothing but scut work in the kitchen, and on the wall of the restaurant, and in the bilge of the schooner. What else was there? Well, there was an afternoon with the loveliest woman he knew.

Samantha came in for supper again, all clean and chipper. When she finished she stopped at the cash register to pay the tab. She handed the money to Blanca at the register and yelled past Migdala down to Scheutz at the sink, asking if he'd like to go dancing later after he finished cleaning up. He thought she might have yelled just a little too loud, making sure Migdala heard her. He merely waved to her and went back to his dirty dishes. This was a problem he'd never encountered before. Going back as far as high school when he first went out with Gerry who later became his wife, there had never been more than one woman for him at one time. After Gerry, there was the yoga teacher for a while and then only Samantha. And now here he was with two women on a small island, both wanting him for herself.

The problem ate at him. By the time he finished with the dishes and wiping down the counters and the tables and mopping the floor in the kitchen area and the dining area he slid into an old familiar rotten mood. Why did he always end up getting involved with women who needed to tell him what to do. This was his own fault. He asked for it the same way a lot of guys seem to always attract a fistfight wherever they went. By the time he slammed the mop and the bucket into their place in the back hall he was ready for his own fistfight. The next attractive woman who smiled at him or asked him to dance he was ready to defend himself against her with his fists. Hell, he'd probably lose.

At least he and Asher were getting paid well for rebuilding the restaurant. Good thing Asher was along or he'd probably end up doing the whole thing for a roll in the hay. No such thing as a free lunch or a free piece of ass. But the money for the construction was going to go a long way toward paying his half of the money needed to buy material for repairing the schooner. The one thing he did not want at this point was to be indebted to Samantha.

Migdala worked around him during the after-supper clean up, stepping out of his way without looking at him and not saying a word to him. To make matters worse, between waiting on tables, Blanca had taken to sitting and jawing with Samantha, the two of them hunched over, whispering and laughing like a couple of teenagers. Scheutz wondered whether Samantha was cozying up to Blanca just to bug Migdala, but still, it was nice to see Blanca in such a light mood. She was the last customer to leave and after Blanca and Asher were gone, which left Scheutz and Migdala alone, he stopped next to her and said, "Can we talk?"

"No." She moved away from him. This was not a 'no' that sounded like she wanted him to ask again, but a flat, resigned 'no' that said to leave her alone. Okay, fine. But, he hadn't done anything to deserve it. It was not his fault that Samantha had come sailing back into his life. And, in fact, he had given her no positive hints that she could just pick up where they had left off. Then again, he had also given her no overt hints that she should leave him alone. So, yes, maybe he was at fault.

Either way, it wasn't going to help matters if he and Migdala couldn't even talk about this.

Outside, the last rays of the setting sun lingered on the tips of a few masts of boats moored in the bay. Out on the north side of the bay, the dark wood of the schooner's stern absorbed the rays and turned a reddish color in deference, as if blushing in shame for its forlorn appearance.

He ached with tiredness as he walked down the hill and through the mangrove to where the dinghy awaited him. He untied the painter and sat in the stern letting the boat drift on its own, looking back at what they had accomplished that day. Not a bad day, though he ought not feel as tired as he did. This problem between Samantha and Migdala was sucking the life out of him. With no current and no tide, the dinghy refused to drift anywhere except further into the mangrove. He roused himself and pulled the starter for the outboard, then steered out into the bay.

It really was too early to just go back to the schooner and crash for the night. And he certainly did not feel like going down to the malecón where the dancing that Samantha mentioned would be in progress. Calypso music drifted in over the rooftops from the other side of town. He turned the boat toward the old dinghy dock where a little restaurant called "The Dingy Dock" had opened. Apparently, the new owners didn't get that they had spelled the name wrong. He felt a little dingy himself at the moment. It would be nice to just sit in a civilized café for a few moments, sip a beer and think about his double-woman vision.

He cut the engine and drifted in to the newly replaced wooden walkway at the water side of the café, tied up and walked the few steps to where empty tables on the cement patio ran along an iron railing looking out over the bay. He ordered a Medalla beer and sat facing the water, his feet stretched out to rest on the lower rail. The music from town had changed to a salsa beat. The rest of the café's usual patrons must have been over at the dancing because only one other person, a gringo like himself, sat at the tables. Scheutz slumped at the railing where he could see Migdala's restaurant and, in the last rays of light, the masts of the *Panacea*. Just what he needed, a new perspective

But nothing new came. Samantha, Migdala, the schooner, he envisioned putting all three on one of those game show wheels and spinning it. "I'd like to buy a vowel, Alex." He envisioned that lady with the over-sized head turning over different letters to come up with different answers, answers that made no sense other than inane sayings like 'Life is just a chair of bollies' or 'He who laughs lasts' or 'A mind is a terrible thing' or 'Absence makes the fond heart wander'. Round and round the wheel spun. Each one of those places, the restaurant, the South Pacific, were both places he could imagine being happy.

Behind him, coming down the cement steps from the street, came the click of a woman's high-heeled shoes. What the hell was someone doing on this island wearing high heels? The heels clicked across the cement floor to a table at the far end of the railing where a woman in a red blouse sat down. She looked familiar, but he couldn't place where he'd seen her before. The movements of her head and long thin fingers as she talked with the waitress were exaggeratingly feminine, with an affected daintiness. Scheutz froze and snapped his head in the other direction so the woman would not recognize him. This was the woman he had seen in Beltran's house in Rincon, the woman who had accompanied Beltran to the party in Mayaguez.

He could not recall the woman's name, if he ever knew it, but remembered the bright red flamenco style dress she wore to the party. Red must have been a favorite color because now she wore a bright red blouse tucked into a tight beige skirt, an outfit that, with the stiletto heels, made her look totally out of place in this casual vacation and sailboat environment. What could she be doing here? Obviously, she was not alone; the waitress set the table for three. So, she must be with Beltran and someone else, possibly the mamaluca Scheutz had seen with Beltran returning to the house in Rincon as he and Migdala carried Blanca away from there. That was a frightening thought. He had best get his ass out of there before the others arrived.

He waited until she was absorbed in a menu, then slid up and away from his table, leaving two single bills for the beer. Keeping his face averted he descended the steps and untied the boat, letting the bow drift away from the lights of the café before starting the engine.

He retraced his path back to the restaurant, and around to the rear door to the apartment. Blanca came to the door and when he said he needed to talk to her mother, she wagged her finger at him. "I don't think she wants to talk to you. You're a bad boy."

"Come on, cut the shit. This is important."

The girl shouted down the hall. "Mamá, tu novio esta aqui."

"Yo no tengo novio."

Scheutz pushed past the girl and headed for the open door to the living room. Behind him, Blanca laughed. "You're going to get it."

In the living room, Migdala slouched on the sofa watching the television with a beer in her hand. He stopped directly in front of her, blocking the TV screen. "Beltran is on the island. I don't know who is with him, but I am willing to bet it's not your mother."

She set the bottle down on the floor next to the sofa and stared up at him, turning to look at where Blanca stood in the doorway and then back to Scheutz. After a long silence, she said softly, "What do you think he wants?"

"Well, I'm sure he's not here for a vacation."

"You saw him?"

"No. I saw his lady friend over at the Dingy Dock. I don't think she recognized me. And, yeah, I'm just assuming that if she's here, Beltran will be here with her."

"This is all your fault, you know?"

"How is it my fault?"

Migdala leaned forward and extended two fingers as if giving a victory sign. "Two reasons. They are after those emeralds that you brought back from Cuba—after I warned you not to go there. And they want my daughter." She pointed at Blanca. "And you were the one who brought that awful Harding to this island. He is like some evil spirit, some chupacabra."

"Mama, that is not true," Blanca yelled across the room.

Migdala pointed at Scheutz again. "Are you going to run off with your girlfriend on your boat and leave me here to deal with these people?"

He knelt on the floor in front of her and put his arms around her bent back. "I'm not going anywhere."

Chapter 26

Asher dropped two canvas bags filled with extra tools into the dinghy with a double thunk that caused the boat to bounce against the work raft, which in turn bounced against the hull of the schooner. Scheutz paused at the rail to give a last minute thought to anything else they might need for the long day ahead of them. Over the prow of the schooner, out toward the inlet, the sky showed its first glimmer of gray light. The breeze, in anticipation of the coming sun, held its breath. Even the gulls ceased their eternal screeing in homage to the rising sun. It seemed that the only light, movement, and sound in the world came from Asher and himself. He extinguished the kerosene lamp on the rigging and descended the side of the boat.

Scheutz steered in a wide arc to the middle of the bay and then in toward the town. In closer to the shore there were still sunken boats with masts or an occasional hull showing above the water line, boats that had not yet been removed after the hurricane. Asher made a grunt and pointed to where Samantha could be seen walking on the road running along the far side of the bay. Scheutz slowed the outboard and watched her, keeping pace with her. She saw them and waved, causing him an unexpected pang of sadness. Another wreck floating above the waterline. Asher let out one of his little sniggers.

Having someone like Asher around, who got where you were coming from could be a comfort, but could also be a little spooky. Especially if he knew things about you that you were not too willing to admit to yourself. He wished he could read Asher as well as Asher read him. Here was a case in point; he was unable to ascertain whether Asher had a preference for Samantha over Migdala, or vice versa. It all seemed the same to him, as if Scheutz's problem picking between these two women was just some playground folly mortals got themselves all in a twist over. Well, the hell with him; this was certainly not something he planned on discussing with the man. Even if he did suspect that Asher might lay some tiny bit of wisdom on him that could help him, it was none of his damned business.

Before they reached shore two different high-prowed fishing boat passed them heading out to sea. He nosed the bow into the dock at the end of the mangrove and they carried the tools up the road to the restaurant. The only sounds to be heard in the barrio were the three or four roosters crowing in their pre-dawn back yards. Tables and chairs had been piled outside the restaurant the night before. Inside, the empty room seemed strangely smaller with all the furniture removed. Migdala, in a short bathrobe, and the policeman Otero, stood at the counter drinking coffee.

Otero put his cup down. "Ah, the criminal element."

Asher gave him a big grin. "Si. As Columbus said when he invaded our lands, 'Lafayette, we are here.'"

"Lafayette?" Otero frowned at him. Migdala laughed.

"It is not important. Where is the coffee?"

Scheutz looked from Otero to Migdala and back. What the hell was the cop doing here? Did he spend the night here? Migdala would not meet his gaze, and she looked as if she had just had a rough night. The muscles in the back of his neck tightened and he could see himself smacking Otero who wore a smug little grin. Migdala pushed herself away from the counter and walked to the stove where she set two cups out and began pouring coffee grounds into the long sock.

Scheutz stretched his back in an effort to relieve the tightness in his neck muscles. He needed to cool it. "You going to help us with the roof today?" He leveled the question at the policeman in what sounded, even to himself, like a challenge.

"No, I been on duty all night. I'm going home to bed." He smiled, looked over at Migdala and then turned back to Scheutz. "It has been a rough night."

Migdala set two cups of coffee down on the counter.

Otero picked up his own coffee cup again. "I understand your friend Harding might be back on Culebra. Are you hiding him again?"

"No. And he's not my friend."

"Maybe he is and maybe he is not your friend. I have heard about your trip to Rincon. Why did you not call the police when you had Harding there?"

"Because we were too busy getting my daughter out of there," Migdala said.

Otero shrugged, took a last sip from his coffee and turned to go. "Good luck on your roof," he said to Migdala. To Scheutz, with a snarky little grin, he said. "Don't work too hard."

As he left, Migdala turned to the door leading to the apartment. "I'm going to take a shower."

"Getting light," Asher said. The decision had been not to try to tackle the entire roof in one day, but to close the restaurant for two days, finishing only that part over the restaurant area and then, the second day to finish the roof over the apartment behind. They had tried, even Tapon had tried, to find other people to help with the roof to get it done in one day, but with all the rebuilding from the hurricane, no one was available.

Scheutz and Asher set to work, pulling the sail cloth from its temporary use as a roof since the hurricane, now leaving the entire restaurant area open to the ever-lightening sky. Using the old wooden walls as props, they dragged the wooden forms up and connected them to vertical four-by-fours in the center of the room. Just as the sun came up, Migdala brought out their breakfast of huevos y jamon con patatas fritas. She sat with them while they ate, but avoided looking at Scheutz. When they finished, Asher put her to work helping to haul in the precut four-by-fours and holding them erect while the forms were fastened from above.

Around nine o'clock, a skinny young man showed up, announcing that he was Blanca's friend Eusebio and that he was ready to work. Blanca, meanwhile, was still asleep, unbelievable in the midst of all the banging they were doing. Eusebio told them he was in Blanca's class in school. He wore a blue baseball hat, t-shirt, jeans and sneakers and looked to be as thin as Blanca but a few inches shorter. When Migdala asked him to go in and wake Blanca his face lit up like a kid about to get on an amusement park ride. Several minutes later, over the din they were making in the restaurant, they could hear Blanca yelling at him to get the hell out of her room. He showed up back in the restaurant looking a little embarrassed, but pleased with himself.

Scheutz showed Eusebio what he wanted him to do, to bring in the rebar, to lay out a grid pattern and tie each bar crossing with short pieces of wire to hold them in that position. The kid seemed pretty bright and quickly picked up on what was expected.

And so the morning went. Asher and Migdala setting up four-by-four braces and attaching wooden forms above, Eusebio setting up the rebar grid on top of each new form, Scheutz building forms for the four vertical cement columns running down the length of the restaurant that would support the roof, and Blanca sound asleep in her bed.

Tapon, Sharkie and Arturo all showed up around ten o'clock. Tapon had decided to sleep over at Sharkie's house until the roof was finished. The three old men occupied themselves with handing around coffee cups and Pepsi to Eusebio who now had his t-shirt wrapped around his head like a turban, his bony chest heaving with exertion in the already hot morning sun. When they were not handing out drinks, the viejos sat outside at one of the restaurant tables regaling themselves and everyone else with stories of past heroism in the service of erecting various houses around the island, including some no longer in existence, thanks to age, termites, and the recent hurricane.

By noon they were almost ready to start pouring cement. Eusebio and Asher had begun hauling bags of dry cement up to the roof area where they had set up the hand-cranked mixer in one corner on top of the wooden forms. It would have gone so much easier if they had been able to get the island's only cement-mixing truck to deliver the mix, but the truck was booked for days in advance. Scheutz continued nailing up the forms for the columns underneath, and Migdala moved between the four-by-four uprights pulling food out of the refrigerator to prepare lunch. They could have been merely two construction workers on different crews. When the food was ready they all, including the old men, moved into the apartment living room to eat and escape the hot sun.

They had all just begun to eat when Blanca slammed her way out of her bedroom, her hair in a disheveled mess, complaining That no one had bothered to wake her earlier. Everyone except Eusebio burst into laughter. From the startled look on Eusebio's face it was apparent the boy was gravely smitten with this girl. He almost choked on his mouthful of food, his dark-skinned face turning a deep red. Blanca ignored him and slammed her way into the bathroom.

The afternoon went on it seemed forever, the work hard, hot, and tedious. The wet cement was poured first into the columns, one on each corner of the restaurant area and then into each of the center columns, and then, tying the vertical rebar in with the roof grid, onto the roof forms. They traded off, mixing, carrying and spreading the cement over the forms. Blanca atoned for her morning in bed by being everywhere and helping everyone, a bundle of energy. And quietly, without attracting attention to what he was doing, Eusebio seemed always to be in her wake, adding water to the cement powder as she turned the handle on the mixer, helping push wet cement through the sluice trough, working next to her as she maneuvered a long-handled hoe or rake to spread the cement over the grid of rebar. Migdala showed a level of stamina Scheutz had never seen in her. Even if her level of energy was being fueled by her wanting to let him know how irritated she was, he had to admire it. Even the old guys, between fetching beer up and down the ladder, pitched in with a hoe or a rake, or with turning the handle on the mixer. They tried to approximate a continuous pour of cement to keep one section of cement from drying faster in the afternoon sun than the section next to it, thus creating a seam. Only one person at a time took a break.

Somewhere in the middle of the afternoon, Scheutz heard someone shouting, "Hey, Clem" from below. He handed his rake to Arturo and walked to the edge of the roof on the side facing the road where Samantha stood in her shorts and bikini top, her hand across her eyebrows, shading her eyes from the sun.

"Yeah. What's up?"

"What're you doing up there?"

"Making a roof. What do you need?"

"Want to know if you want to do a sunset cruise in an hour or so. I'm going out with some people on their ketch."

He shook his head. "No. Can't. No idea when this'll be done. Thanks anyhow."

She paused, watching him, then took her hand down from her brow and squinted at the furniture and debris piled up outside the restaurant. She pursed her lips in disapproval and looked back up at him with her hand back at her brow. "Well, let me know when you get done there." She turned and started down the road toward the bay.

"See ya." He watched her walk, the casual way her tanned body moved and the way her blond hair swayed against her back. "You want to come up and help?" he yelled before she got too far away. "We'll get done quicker."

She did not stop or turn, but merely raised her right hand and wiggled her fingers at him.

"Thanks anyhow." Migdala's voice came from just behind him. "You want to come up and help?" He turned to look at the disgusted glare painted on her face. "You want to go sit on your boat with her, then go. We don't need you." She went back to hoeing.

He teased her. "I'd rather be on a roof with you and than on a boat with her."

"Bullshit."

He reached down to pull up on the rebar grid to allow some of the wet cement to flow under it. Migdala's irritation at his talking to Samantha made him smile in spite of himself. She really did care enough to be jealous. It was a whole lot better than the stony silence she'd been throwing his way the past few days. Eusebio moved the sluice trough to the area where he had just been talking with Samantha
and he moved away from Migdala to help push the mix out onto the grid.

His back hurt. Sweat poured onto the wet cement. His legs and feet kicked up a fuss with the ache of tiredness. The sun had begun to dip into the western sky. They had better move faster if they were to finish this section of the roof before nightfall. If he were on that sunset cruise with Samantha, they would be out beyond the reef by now and he would be sitting facing aft with his feet resting on the cockpit seat cushions with a very cold rum and coke in his hand, watching the sun slowly turn bright red in its descent. Samantha would probably be in her usual stance at the helm, her feet wide apart, her bikini halter barely covering her nipples, her hair billowing out behind her in the eastern breeze.

Wasn't that always the way of it? If he was sitting on that boat watching the sun go down, he would most certainly be thinking of this roof he stood on. Too much yang and you yearn for yin. In the hot sun you long for nightfall and in the early morning fog you cast your glances eastward looking for the sun. Tapon, Sharkie and Arturo left the roof together under the guise of bringing up more beer and Pepsi. Only Sharkie made it back up the ladder, depositing the cans on the last section of wooden forms that had yet to receive wet cement. Blanca immediately went for her break, grabbing a can of Medalla beer instead of her usual can of Coke. Migdala didn't seem to notice, and when Scheutz gave her a look meant as parental disapproval, Blanca showed him the tip of her tongue. Eusebio laughed and then all but cringed when Scheutz turned to glower at him.

Tired as he was, Scheutz would not stop for a break now. Both Asher and Migdala, if anything, seemed to be pushing faster, outpacing him. He expected such energy of Asher, but the woman continued to surprise him. Around the straps of her tank top, the working of the muscles in her shoulders, arms and back were erotic. It had never occurred to him before how sexy a woman's muscles could be. But now that he thought about it, one of the biggest turn-offs in pictures of swimsuit models was their bony shoulders. As if they had never done a lick of work in their life. How could someone find that attractive?

Migdala pushed cement coming out of the sluice trough onto his foot and waved the back of her hand at him. "Vamos, vamos. Stop daydreaming; we need to get done here."

"I was thinking of you, mi amor."

"No, you were not. You were thinking about that boat trip you wanted to go on."

Why do women have such a great need to tell you what you are thinking? His wife used to do that. And Samantha was no slouch in that department. If she didn't like what he might be telling her, she would let him know what was actually on his mind. Usually an extension of what happened in her mind; usually something negative. If he let himself—god knows he was tired enough—he could work himself into a pout over the way Migdala had treated him all day. That would be a good enough excuse to climb down off the roof and rest his weary bones. Screw her; if she wanted him to be thinking about being on the boat, he would think about it. But it was too late. He could see a ketch, probably the one with Samantha on it, motoring out toward the inlet. He had missed the boat. He would stay here and finish; and he would just ignore the great clairvoyant working next to him.

Asher and Eusebio lifted the mixer onto planks laid kitty-corner on the top of the concrete block walls. Blanca applied water from the hose to the last batch while Scheutz and Migdala worked a rake and a hoe to spread the last of the wet cement into the final corner of the roof form. Each exited the roof by different ladders, bringing down everything but the mixer itself, which Asher secured to the planks with a length of line. After the cement dried they would add another layer of concrete block on top of the walls to form a low parapet, leaving a drainage hole on either end for rainwater run-off, and topping the parapet with a layer of red clay tiles.

God, it felt good to be off that roof. And the sun was still up. In the parking area behind the apartment Blanca hosed down the tools and sprayed everyone else. And that felt good. Eusebio, drenched now more from water than from sweat, took off his t-shirt turban and held it up for her to spray. Then he threw the sopping shirt at her, which she caught and threw back in his face. He laughed and applauded. Sharkie brought more drinks while his little dog ran through their legs dragging Eusebio's t-shirt through the dirt. Tapon and Arturo came out with their own cans of beer and they all stood in a circle, some leaning against Migdala's Volvo, toasting themselves and the roof. Scheutz clinked his beer can with everyone except Migdala. When Eusebio clinked his Pepsi can against Blanca's, she wrapped her other arm around his neck, pulled him to her and smacked a big kiss into his ear. Eusebio looked as if he might faint from ecstasy.

Otero's jeep pulled into the driveway and he walked toward them, wearing his civilian clothes. My god, why doesn't he go away? No one, not even Migdala, moved, or even made any sign of saying hello. They all just stared at him in their exhaustion. He stopped at the edge of their circle with feet spread and hands in the back pocket of his jeans, nodding his head.

"You're timing is perfect," Scheutz said to him.

"I just met your friends," Otero said.

"Who is it this time?"

"They are staying out at Punta Aloe. Some hombre named Beltran. And his sexy girlfriend."

"Hah!" Blanca let out a laugh. "The one with the red dress? That's not his girlfriend; that's a man."

Otero's face contorted first in confusion, then embarrassment, and then indignation. "No way that is a man."

"Oh, yeah." She gave several exaggerated nods of her head with her mouth wide open. "His name is George. He's a real flamer. And he's not even a puertoricano; he puts all kinds of cream on his skin to make it look dark."

Well, that was a shocker. But it made sense, given Beltran's obvious proclivities. He didn't want to think about those people. Like Otero, they were nothing more than an intrusion. But even worse than Otero, who at least helped maintain the tranquility of this island, these friends of Juaquin's tracked in the muck of that dirty business they were involved in. "Beltran's the guy you should be talking to about who killed Juaquin," Scheutz said to Otero. "He's his ex-business partner."

"Is that true?" Otero asked Migdala.

She nodded without looking at him. "He is also a friend of Harding. Is there anyone else out there with them?"

"Yes. A fat man with a round face. He kept smiling."

Migdala gave an involuntary shudder. "That is the man you probably should ask about Tio Juaquin."

Otero nodded his head slowly, his brow furrowed and his eyes narrowed in thought, looking for all the world like some movie detective solving the crime of the decade.

"I know that man," Tapon said. "He is called El Gato. He is very stupid, but he was also a friend of my son. You will watch them, Raul, right?"

"Yes. I will be on duty tonight at eleven o'clock."

"But I'm telling you to watch them now." He turned to Migdala. "And what about supper?"

"I'm too tired to cook. Somebody else do it."

Everyone else in the group, even Asher, seemed to find something interesting happening on either their feet or the ground next to them. Finally, Tapon walked across the circle to place his hand on Otero's shoulder. "My friend, remember when I helped get you this job on the police force?"

"Yes. And I always appreciate it. That was a long time ago."

"Well then, while you are watching these people, how about getting us some pizza?"

Blanca looked up from her shoes and applauded. "Yaay!"

"I will pay for it," Migdala volunteered. It was the first time today Scheutz had seen her smile. She pushed herself away from the car and walked into the building.

Arturo crossed over to stand on the other side of Otero. "Pizza. Buen muchacho."

Otero looked from one face to another around the circle, as if someone had just pulled a not-very-funny joke on him. Scheutz would have loved to point out to him that he was after all a civil servant, but that would have pushing him too far. As it was, he found himself enjoying the caged look on the cop's face. Asher threw him a look and then turned back to grin at Otero.

Migdala's voice came from inside the door to the apartment. "Clement, will you come in here for a moment to help me?"

What was this all about now? Had she finally decided to let him have all that hostility she'd been harboring all day? He hesitated, thinking maybe he'd just go back to the boat; he was too tired to listen to any of it right then. But, he had to go in. Inside the back hallway, she motioned from her bedroom door for him to step in. Inside the room he leaned his back against the wall, ready to ward off what she had to throw at him. She closed the door quietly and, without saying a word, stood close to him. She bent her head, giving him only the top to look at, and then press herself into his chest.

"I don't want you to go to the boat tonight."

He realized he'd been holding his breath, and let his body relax. He put his arms around her and held her to him.

"I'm afraid to stay here alone with Blanca with El Gato here," she said.

Chapter 27

It would be nice to strangle all those damned roosters. He was pulled once again out of a deep dreamless sleep by the arrogant crowing of that out-of-sync and out-of-tune chorus of otherwise idling macho chickens. It took him a while to figure out where he was. Pitch black outside, no idea what time it was. He listened for the slap of rigging in the wind and the lap of water against the hull, but no sound reached him. What did reach him was the scent of Migdala lying with her back to him, her own peculiar aroma—not soap or perfume or shampoo that always seemed a part of Samantha's olfactory repertoire—of something deeply female, mixed with cooking spices, cumin and saffron.

Besides the noise of roosters, there came the light trickling sound of rain on the metal slats of the open Miami shutters near the bed. He listened for anything else and heard nothing but the even breathing of the woman next to him. He lay very still in the blackness, not wanting her to move. Her breath and the smell of her body were enough. She was there, and that's all he needed her to be, just there with him.

This was something new, wasn't it? He could not remember ever admitting to himself that he needed anything from anyone, especially a woman. Of course, he must have spent a lifetime of needing things from people, especially women, now that he thought about it. But what he needed had always taken a form not a whole lot different from thin king about what kind of tool he needed from the hardware store. Until now it had never occurred to him that he might need something more.

So why did he need to drive himself nuts trying to decide between staying here on Culebra with Migdala or sailing off to the South Pacific with Samantha. The decision was right in front of him, but it seemed he was afraid to make it. Making decisions was not exactly his forte. In fact, when had he ever? Everything he'd done in his life, it seemed, had been nothing more than a reaction to whatever was going on at the time. When he and his little brother ran off to Florida when he was fourteen years old, it had taken no thought. Willi wanted to live in a tree house by the beach and they just took off hitch-hiking south. Going to Cuba was Enrique's idea.

Hooking up with his children's mother seemed to be all her doing. And when she took the kids off to New York and he puffed himself up enough to drive down there to try to get them back, she easily, it seemed, talked him out of it. When the kids did come back to live with him, it had more to do with his accepting their decision to come home.

He even ran off to the Caribbean with Samantha because she wanted to. And if he sailed off to the South Pacific now it would be because she wanted to. It was amazing, now that he could see the pattern, how anyone could reach the age of fifty without at least making one big decision about their life. True, in each of those cases before, there was not much holding him to wherever he was doing at the time. But this was all different. Going with Samantha to Bora Bora was a fantasy. Migdala, her restaurant, and her barely controllable teen-aged daughter were boots-on-the-ground reality.

He drifted back to sleep when the roosters started in again. His mind began to race, as if the roosters were chasing it around the yard. He tried thinking about Migdala, next to him, again, but all that did was send him off to thinking about the restaurant. They were in a push now to get the place finished. What had started out to be a one-day, then two-day closing for renovations had turned into several days. The plan for that day was for Migdala, with help from Blanca, Eusebio, and the old guys, to give the interior walls of the restaurant a skim coat of stucco plaster. Once that was done, they could, hopefully, set up the restaurant again and maybe get the place opened in a few days.

As usually happened when his mind raced like this, he went over each little detail of what they planned for the day. Asher had decided to take the day off, since it was Sunday, and go work on the boat. The two busted ribs had been sistered with the embouje and the two-inch planking patched with new wood. Now came the caulking.

Then his mind hopped to Blanca. The girl had become a default mode for his brain when it wasn't necessarily occupied with something else; and sometimes, like now, when he was thinking about something, she intruded. He tried once again to picture what might have happened the day Juaquin was killed. The strange relationship between Juaquin, Blanca, and Harding turned around and around. What exactly did go on between Juaquin and Blanca? Was it all fatherly as Migdala seemed to think, or were there some other possibly negative implications there? From whatever Scheutz could tell about the guy, he seemed like a total sleaze. Even his Christian proselytizing had had a slimy feel to it. That didn't mean he had any predatory designs on the girl, though. In fact, after meeting his partner Beltran and Beltran's supposed boyfriend, George, it seemed more likely old Tio Juaquin filled more the role of

Tia Juaquin. But you never know. What was that old saying Harding told them once about the folks who all lived in some valley in eastern Kentucky where he grew up, "The family that lays together stays together."

And speaking of Harding, he seemed like such a chameleon there was no telling what his relationship was to Juaquin and his colleagues. Or to Blanca. There was no question about the fact that he had been doing nasty deeds upon Blanca's body, but did that mean he'd actually killed Juaquin because of it; because maybe Juaquin found out about it and tried to stop him? That's what made the most sense. And, of course, since everyone including himself suspected Harding of only the worst things any human being could do, they all wanted to believe he killed Juaquin. In fact, even if he didn't, it would still give everyone who knew him a great sense of satisfaction to have him punished for it. Except for the person who actually did kill him. On second thought, that wasn't true; the real killer would enjoy getting away with it.

It would be convenient to just say Harding did it and move on. But he didn't. Scheutz knew in his gut Harding didn't do it. He wanted to believe Harding did it because he wanted to believe Blanca did not do it. Even by accident. What she had said in the taxi that night in the middle of passing out still bothered him. Couple that with how upset she was during and after the hurricane. .

Migdala moved, turning slightly and pressing her back against him. He turned onto his side and put his arm over her, cupping her breast in his hand. She let out a low "Mmmpf" and then settled back into her even breathing. He tilted his head back slightly on the pillow to keep her hair out of his nose and closed his eyes. When he opened them again he could discern faint rays of light coming in between the slats of the Miami shutters.

Well, if Blanca did not shoot Juaquin with the spear gun, as he hoped, and Harding did not, then who did? The first person to come to mind was El Gato, Beltran's friend. The only reason why his name popped up was that all he had heard about the man was that he was a scary dude. And, of course, that he would be acquainted with Juaquin through Beltran, maybe even with Juaquin directly. The memory of his grinning face at that party in Mayaguez reminded Scheutz of the Cheshire Cat from Alice in Wonderland. Maybe that was how he got his nickname. He was certainly memorable enough that Scheutz would have noticed him if he had seen him here on Culebra before. And somehow it did not seem likely that he would have any use for a scuba diver's spear gun.

So, what then? Who else could have been connected with that unholy pair, Juaquin and Harding, here on the island? He tried to remember anyone else he'd seen with Migdala's uncle. His father, Tapon; but that made no sense. There was no way that guileless old man could have had anything to do with the death of his son. And that ruled out Tapon's two friends, Arturo and Sharkie.

So, who did that leave? According to Migdala, Juaquin had a huge network of people he dealt with, from Columbia to Cuba to Massachusetts and anywhere in between. And, what about the one other person in the background of that network, Migdala's mother, Marisol? She was certainly in the thick of it, could have had a falling out with her brother, or could have had much to gain from his removal. What he had seen of her in Mayaguez, she seemed like the kind of person who could hack someone down while looking them in the eye.

Here was his mind racing again. The light from the shutters was more pronounced now. Migdala moved again snuggling closer in against him, then stirred and turned to face him, murmuring softly and taking his erection between her thighs. Thank God. It was so nice to climb down out of his head. She stirred herself awake, slid her body on top of his and put him inside her, all without a word. Ever since she had asked him to stay with her at night because she was afraid of El Gato, he had taken to referring to their love-making as "putting out the cat." And she had taken to purring as she felt her orgasm coming on. He suspected her telling him she was afraid of El Gato was merely an excuse to get him to stay with her. By the time she stopped purring, her body spasming in smooth little jerks, her mop of hair pushing its way into his nose and mouth, and her toes beating a tattoo against his legs, he had worked up his own zen-like version of orgasm that didn't require him to move at all. Then she kissed him lightly on the lips, pulled her hair away from his face, tucked her own face into the corner of his neck and shoulder, and lay quietly on top of him.

A light breeze from the rain blew across their bodies, cooling their commingled sweat. He lay entranced, watching the light from the window strengthen and bring the contour of her body into view. It was amazing, really, how sometimes you don't have to do anything more than just be there, like going to some kid's birthday party where the parents give all other kids a gift for just coming. Like Woody Allen's famous phrase that ninety percent of life was just showing up.

He dozed off again and was awakened by the buzzing of the first flight of the daily five-seater airplane taking off from the airstrip at the bottom of the hill. Migdala was gone and the rain had stopped. He never slept this late. After a quick shower he got himself into the kitchen in the restaurant area where Migdala and Tapon were already hard at work, he mixing the plaster and she applying it on the far wall. Her hair, tied high on the back of head, had attracted a few globs of plaster, as had her face and right arm. As he helped himself to coffee, Eusebio came in the front door. Migdala and he exchanged knowing glances and she motioned toward Blanca's bedroom. Eusebio and Blanca had gone to school during the past week but did help some afterward. On Saturday, the boy attempted to wake her again as he had done before and received a ration of abuse for his effort. Now he braced himself, as if girding his loins for battle and headed for the door to the apartment. Scheutz grabbed two cold fried plantanos and with his coffee headed out the door before the yelling started.

Half way down the hill he remembered Asher had taken the dinghy out to the boat the night before so he had no way getting there except to walk. Instead, he walked back up and stuck his head in the door to ask Migdala if he could take the Volvo. At least that way he could drive out past the water desalination plant. It was only short walk from there. He came in the front door just as Eusebio scooted out into the restaurant area, laughing with glee at the sounds coming from Blanca's bedroom.

"Yes," Migdala told him. "But bring the car back by two o'clock so I can meet the produce truck when it gets off the ferry."

"What do you need with produce? The restaurant's closed."

"Oh, that's right, I keep forgetting. We have to get this place open, it's screwing me all up closed like this."

He drove out past the airport and the cemetery and up the dirt road that led to the desalination plant, then further across the ridge to park on the old cement helicopter pad left there by the US Navy when they moved out back in 1974. From there he walked further on the ridge and then down the hill covered with raya bushes to where the schooner lay at the water's edge.

Asher was already at work, squatting precariously on the curved hull with a caulking hammer and a wide-bladed caulking iron. The previous weekend, before nailing on the last of the boards, they had winched the boat over to a forty-five degree angle, the opposite of the way it had been left months before by the hurricane. Asher had climbed the main mast with a line he had run through the hefty starboard winch and then to an anchor they had placed twenty yards out in twelve feet of water. The deck now tilted at such a degree it was difficult to walk on, but the area in need of repair was completely out of the mud and water.

Scheutz climbed the ladder from the ground to hull, then walked up the curve of the hull to where Asher had set a canvass bag containing the other caulking tools. Asher looked up from his work and, without saying even "good morning" nodded his head toward another bag containing the oakum caulk they had brought over from Tortolla a month earlier. The stuff was hard to find because it wasn't used much any longer, since boat hulls were now manufactured with fiberglass and very rarely did a boatyard have a call for repairing a wooden-planked hull. But the oakum and the pine pitch that went into the spaces between the planks were inexpensive. In what came as no surprise, Asher knew the people who ran the boatyard in the West End of Tortolla. The two men not only knew Asher but treated him as if he were some long lost relative, the three of them linking arms in a circle and dancing around like children at a picnic.

He set to work on the opposite end of the repaired area, watching the way Asher wedged the oakum strand into the crevasse between the planks, tapping it into place with the wooden hammer on the caulking iron. The going was slow, two inches at a time. By midday, with the sun doing its daily job of beating down on them, they were not nearly half finished. Fortunately, a steady north northeast breeze cooled their bare skin and drove the mosquitoes away to wherever one wished they would always stay.

"Hey." Samantha's voice came from above them. She sat on the gunwale at the top of the hull. They had not heard her come up, had not even heard her outboard when she pulled into their work raft on the other side of the boat.

"Hey, yourself." Asher stopped his rhythm with the hammer and looked up to where she sat.

Scheutz put his tools down, bracing them against the roll of oakum to keep them from sliding off into the mud below. He couldn't tell whether he was glad to see her as an excuse to break from this tedious chore or whether he was just glad to see her. She perched there like some artist model, her long tan legs crossed at the ankles and her hair blowing out to the side in the breeze. He walked up the slanted hull and turned to sit next to her. Asher finished two more inches of oakum and then joined them.

"Every time I see you guys you're working your asses off. Don't you ever take a break?"

Asher scratched his chin. "Let's see. I took a day off last year 'bout this time."

"No, seriously. What's the rush?"

She had a point. This was not New York City. For a small island in the Caribbean, imbued with the manana complex, they did seem to be out of step. "Well, we've got to get the restaurant finished so that Migdala can get it opened again."

"And what does that have to do with this broken old boat?"

"Well…I don't know…we only get to work on it on Sunday."

"So she's paying you to work on that restaurant?"

"Yeah. Well, her grandfather is actually. It's technically his restaurant and he gets money from FEMA because of the hurricane."

"And we get paid pretty good," Asher said.

She nodded slowly, uncrossing her ankles and bringing her knees up to lean her elbows on them. "And you probably spend it all on this old pile of wood."

"Well." Scheutz spread his hands to take in the glorious sight of old wooden planks, the new planks patching the hole, the mud and lightly lapping water at the shoreline still strewn with debris deposited there by the hurricane and never yet cleaned up. "Where better to spend a balmy Sunday in the park."

She bent her head and looked over at Asher. "You really like this boat, don't you? I'll tell you what; if you like I'll sell you my half."

"I don't have that much money."

"You're getting plenty from working on the resta

Asher shrugged and nodded.

"So?"

"It's not that much."

She turned to Scheutz. "What about you? You could loan h
of what you're making. And I wouldn't want very much to sell him my share."

Scheutz and Asher held each other's gaze for a long moment. Finally, Scheutz asked, "Why would you do that?"

"Because, first of all, I don't know if the boat is worth much with that hole in the side..."

"Which we are fixing up as good as new."

She smiled as if she didn't believe him. "Eh...maybe."

"What? Look at the patch. A fine piece of shipwrighting."

"Even if it is. The hull has been seriously compromised by the hit it took on that rock. You won't know till you get it back into deep water whether something may have shifted slightly along the keel."

"Good point. But we'll just fix it."

She nodded her head again, looking up at him as if to say, "Yeah, right."

"You don't have any confidence in me at all, do you?"

"That's not the point, Clem. I do have confidence in you, but I think you might have your head in the clouds over this one. Are you guys sure this patch will make the boat sea-worthy?"

"So, you want to just give up the whole thing and go buy some new boat to sail to South Seas."

She looked up sideways at him, smiling lightly. "Yeah, I guess so. Just like we did with your old farmhouse in New Hampshire. Sell it and move on. New life, new ocean." She waved her left hand in the air. "We will go and dwell east of Eden in the land of Nod."

"That's west."

"Whatever."

They sat for a long time watching Asher who moved back to his workspot, poking the oakum strand into the crack between two hull planks and tap tapping with the wooden mallet. He looked intent on what he was doing, but Scheutz was sure he was closely concentrated what he and Samantha were saying. Hell, he stood a chance of becoming the proud owner of his own boat.

"I'm not at all sure about going to the South Pacific, Sam, " Scheutz said.

She did not respond, merely laid her chin on her forearm on her knee, her eyes still resting on Asher. Scheutz was not sure she heard him. He said it loud enough, though he could not keep a little quaver out of his voice. He didn't trust himself to say anything more and stood to walk down the hull to pick up his caulking tools again. Samantha sat perfectly still, not looking at him. Then she stood and brushed her hands against the back of her shorts. He knelt on the curve of the hull, leaning with the caulking mallet as if it were a cane. He wanted to say something more to her, but what else was there to say?

"Are you saying you don't think we could try again?" she said.

"I don't know; it didn't seem to work out all that good the last time, did it?"

"It did in the beginning. How about a new beginning?"

He stood up off his knees. He wasn't the one begging here. But on the slope of the hull like this he could not stand facing her so he walked back up to where she stood on the edge of gunwale. "I'm getting too old for beginnings, I think."

"So you're telling me that's it. After all this time, you can just chuck it aside?"

"Isn't that what you did a while back?"

"But I was wrong." Her eyes filled with tears. "There, you happy? I said it. Is that what you want from me? Can we go on now?"

He wanted to reach out and touch her arm but kept his hand at his side. He could count on one hand the number of times he'd seen her cry over the last few years. And the times before had never had anything to do with him. He felt like crying himself, but his resolve against her would not let him.

She looked down at Asher and then looked away toward the inlet from the ocean, then back toward him, tears streaming down her face, drying in the hot sun before they could leave her chin. "Is this it, Clem? Forever?"

He didn't trust himself to speak. Or to keep from moving his hands up to put them around her. He put his head down and thrust his hands into the pockets of his shorts.

She waited, looking at him without touching her tears. She looked once more toward Asher, then turned her back as fast as the clumsy footing allowed. She climbed over the gunwale and inched her way down over the steeply sloped deck to the opposite rail, and from there over and down onto the work raft. She did not look back as she started the outboard on the dinghy she had obviously borrowed, and turned the bow away from shore.

He watched her until the dinghy became small in the sunlight and disappeared between the moored boats in the closed end of the bay.

Chapter 28

It would have been so easy to put the schooner back in deep water using the salvage crane, but the salvage crane had left weeks ago. Hauling the boat off the shoreline was now more a problem of synchronization than anything else. Scheutz had enlisted the Naegle's dinghy plus the fishing dories of both Tapon and Sharkie besides his own. Before the others showed up, which he expected wouldn't be well after dawn, he and Asher unmoored the work raft, floated it out of the way, and tied it off fore and aft to Harding's sloop. Asher climbed the schooner's main mast and foremast to attach lines three quarters of the way up. These lines they would tie off to the stern of the two dinghies with the fishing dories attached to the bowsprit on one end and the taffrail on the other. The trick would be to get all three motor boats pulling in unison to drag the schooner's hull through the mud far enough out for it to float upright.

As the sun peeked over the islands to the east, all four dinghies were ready; Tapon's showed up with Migdala in the bow, Sharkie's with Eusebio at the tiller, and Samantha with the young couple who owned the dinghy. Finally, Naegle came looking like he'd just rolled out of Chuck's Pizza Bar. Scheutz tossed him the line attached to where the bowsprit extended from the deck. Asher gathered the two lines drooping from the two masts and tossed one each to Migdala and Sharkie. While the three boats attached their lines and prepared to pull, Scheutz and Asher climbed into their own dinghy, taking with them the line attached to the stern.

At a signal, the four people at the engines of their boats gunned their outboards and pointed their tillers directly away from shore. Slowly, the masts lowered toward the small boats and the deck of the schooner leaned even more toward the bay. But the boat itself did not move.

"That's not going to work," Samantha shouted over the sound of the outboard engines. "You're trying to pull a few tons of lead keel through thick mud."

Tapon shouted for them to try to pull the boat in the direction the prow was already pointing, describing a curved motion with his hand along the shoreline and then outward at a forty-five degree angle into deeper water.

"He's right," Samantha shouted. "Besides, if you keep pulling on those masts like that, you're going to do some damage down below where they're stepped on the keel. Don't pull against the mud, pull the keel through the mud trough."

Scheutz nodded. "Let's do it."

Asher went aboard to retie the lines, two on the port side of the deck at prow and two on the starboard. At the signal, the four outboard engines revved and strained against the mud. Scheutz turned to see if the schooner whose starboard gunwale was just barely above the waterline had moved. His mouth opened in surprise as he saw Blanca's head appear through the schooner's forward hatch. The girl pulled herself onto the deck and, balanced near the bowsprit, began punching her fists into the air like a cheerleader, shouting what looked like "Go, go, go." but could not be heard above the noise of the motors.

In Tapon's dory next to his dinghy, Migdala stood facing the schooner and screamed in indecipherable anger at her daughter on the deck of the schooner. It was dangerous for the girl to be on the boat; no telling what could happen as it was being dislodged from its months-long bed in the mud. But, Scheutz had to admit, her antics were pretty funny.

And slowly the schooner began to move. The bow lifted slightly, as if out of the trough it had settled into, and then, a little faster, the hull moved along the shoreline. At a midpoint the bow lifted higher still as the stern remained in the trough, and the weight shifted forward as the bow splashed down into the water and the stern raised. Now Samantha waved franticaly for the four boats to turn to starboard, pulling the bow in a long curve toward the open bay. The bow of the schooner turned with them and suddenly plunged into deeper water until the entire length of the schooner floated free of the mud.

As the schooner righted itself in a great heave in the water, Blanca lost her cheerleading perch. The overcompensation of the hull to the port side nearly threw her over the gunwale but she hung on to a line with both hands. The line swung her outside the deck and her high-pitched squeals penetrated even the sound of the motors. As she swung back over the deck she dropped and disappeared behind the capstan. But before the boat stopped rocking she was up, jumping up and down, punching the air and shouting. The outboard motors had all slowed once the schooner was afloat and a cheer to match Blanca's cheer went up among those in the small boats.

Scheutz and Asher motored to the side of the schooner so they could climb aboard. On the schooner's deck, Asher headed below to start the diesel engine while Scheutz took the helm. The boat drifted gently in the direction it had been towed out of the mud. Blanca stood out on the bowsprit now holding onto a jib line and carrying on a bantering discussion with the people in the small boats below. Migdala continued scolding her for climbing aboard the schooner without anyone's knowledge. The diesel coughed twice and quit, coughed again and quit, coughed a third time and caught, setting off the familiar rumble of the schooner's deck. It seemed like such a long time since Scheutz had heard that sound coming up from below. What was it now, over three months since the hurricane had blown her onto the shore's edge?

He put the propeller in gear and motored slowly away from the shore, turning the helm so the bow faced the inlet. Asher had come on deck and now made his way forward to where Blanca crouched on the bowsprit talking to Eusebio. When Asher reached her she stood and made her way back onto the deck and stood at the capstan as he unlashed the anchor and dropped it into the water. At his direction she guided the capstan winch to let out the anchor chain. Scheutz took the propeller out of gear and let the light drift of the water in the bay carry the schooner sternward to let out enough length of anchor chain.

Once the anchor was set Scheutz shut the engine down and went below. In such a short time afloat there was already an inch of water in the bilge. The new boards they had used to repair the hole in the hull would allow seepage until they had swelled with water to seal the caulked seams. He started the small auxiliary engine to run the bilge pump. They would have to let that run for a few days until the wood in the hull swelled.

Back on deck, he found Samantha standing next to Blanca, both waving to those in the small boats. Samantha's two young friends headed back toward the town in their dinghy. Tapon, with Migdala in the bow of his boat, followed Sharkie's boat, and Naegle brought up the rear. As the small boats left, they created enough of a wake to rock the schooner where it lay. Scheutz had to hold onto the jamb of the gangway to keep his balance. It was so nice to have a rocking boat under him again. Asher stood in the bow of the schooner untying and coiling the lines that had been attached to the small boats. Scheutz went to stand next to Blanca. "Where's everybody going?"

"My mother has to go to get ready for the party."

"Party?"

"We are having the big opening today."

"Why aren't you helping?"

Blanca let out what sounded like an exasperated snort. She shook her head slowly. "I hate that place."

Samantha let out a short laugh. "I don't blame you."

Asher shouted from up forward. "Anybody want coffee?"

Both Blanca and Samantha shouted "yes" in unison and then looked at each other and laughed again. They turned and walked forward as Asher disappeared down the forward hatch. Scheutz climbed down the stern ladder to make sure the dinghy was tied up properly. They had been in such a hurry to get aboard once the boat was afloat. Coming back on deck and walking forward, he found Blanca and Samantha sitting sideways together in the hammock in the middle of what sounded like two schoolgirls in Blanca's grade giggling over some topic that suddenly became a behind-the-hand secret as Scheutz approached. Blanca looked up at Scheutz. "Is she really your wife?"

"What?"

Samantha flashed him a grin and turned to Blanca. "No, no. I didn't say I was his wife."

Blanca looked back and forth between Samantha and Scheutz. "¿Es tu novia?"

"She was my girlfriend, but not anymore." He sat in the lawn chair facing the hammock. From below, Asher shouted for them to come and grab coffee cups.

Blanca squinted her eyes at Scheutz and then at Samantha. "You know he's been doing my mother, don't you?"

Samantha looked up at Scheutz and then back to Blanca. "I wondered about that."

Scheutz moved to the hatch, reaching down in for two cups that Asher held up to him. He handed the cups to the two women. "I don't think that's a proper subject to discuss with young girls."

The women let out a hoot, Samantha almost spilling her coffee. "This is the guy who had no problem talking about such things when his own kids were your age."

He reached down for two more cups, his and Asher's, and went back to the lawn chair as Asher climbed on deck. Asher took his cup and pulled up another lawn chair. He raised his coffee in the air. "We should have a toast to the new launching of the Panacea." They all raised their cups, and then sipped the hot coffee. "Now we can make plans to go to Bora Bora."

Samantha raised her cup again. "Not until we find out if this thing will actually float."

"I want to go, too," Blanca said.

"You can't, you're in school," Scheutz said.

"I'll ask my mother if I can go. She'll let me; I'll just tell her Harding is after me again."

Scheutz shook his head and sipped his coffee. It was ridiculous to think of Migdala letting the girl go, Harding or no Harding. It was surprising though how well she and Samantha got along. The friendship seemed to have pulled the girl out of funk she had been in since the hurricane. And Blanca seemed to have pulled Samantha back into that age, the age he first remembered her, back in New Hampshire with all those kids hanging around the house with his own sons. She had been the same kind of playful teenager as Blanca. And her mother, as little as he remembered her, was a lot like Migdala, all serious and responsible.

The two women and Asher fell into a conversation about how long it would take to sail to the Panama Canal, get though it, then sail to the Galapagos and from there to Papeete. Scheutz backed off from the conversation. Something about it bothered him. This had been a dream of all of theirs for some time now. They had talked about this back in St. Thomas. Even before that; back in Bermuda when they first bought the boat two years ago. Why did it bother him now? Was it the idea of the girl wanting to go along? He watched them over the rim of his coffee cup. She seemed so excited, but not in her usual hyper way. She sounded sensible in the things she said, actually a lot like Samantha, who had been, for all her playfulness, very sensible at that age.

No, it was something else that bothered him. It was the whole idea of the thing; it didn't make any sense. What was there in Tahiti that did not exist here? A tropical island, people spoke French and Tahitian instead of English and Spanish. Other than that, what? Both had tourists, ocean breezes and a lot of salt water. He could see himself lounging on the deck of a boat, probably this same boat, drinking coffee in the middle of the day with no great expectation of doing anything more than that the next day.

Maybe it was he who had the problem. He had already decided he did not want to go to the South Pacific, had decided on the alternative, staying here on Culebra with Migdala, helping her establish her restaurant. Was he nuts? Would he really prefer washing greasy pots and pans to floating around viewing marine life in a glass-bottomed boat on some lagoon on Bora Bora?

A movement off the stern caught his eye. He wasn't sure what he'd seen, but when he looked again he saw something move in the cockpit of Harding's boat. Someone was out there. The yellow police tape was still in place warning people to stay off the deck. The water was calm, especially on this side of the bay, out of the way of what little movement the wind caused coming through the inlet. He watched the boat closely. Yes, there was someone definitely aboard that boat. He nudged Asher's leg with his foot and tilted his head in the direction of the sloop when Asher looked his way. Blanca caught them looking and stopped in the middle of a sentence. She stood and walked aft. Then Asher stood and Scheutz behind him.

Samantha called after them, "Hey, what's going on?"

Scheutz waved his finger in front of his mouth for her to be quiet. She followed them to the stern of the schooner, where they all four stood with their coffee cups watching the sloop moored behind and a little closer to the shore than the schooner. A shadow moved by the forward porthole.

"What are we looking at?" Samantha asked.

"Someone's on that boat."

"Isn't that the one we towed over here from St. Thomas? Harding's boat?"

"Yes."

Blanca turned to Samantha. "You know Harding?"

"Oh, yes. If I had had my way we would never have towed that thing. Especially with him in it."

"Why not?"

"He's such a creep. Is he still around Culebra?"

"He's not a creep." Blanca sounded insulted.

"Yes, he is," Scheutz said.

"So you finally agree with me." Samantha gave him a wry grin. "What do you say, Asher?"

"No comment."

"Can we go over to see if it's him?" Blanca asked.

"No." Scheutz and Asher answered at the same time. "Stay away from him, Blanca." Scheutz's statement felt more like an appeal than a command.

"You're not the boss of me. I don't care if you are screwing my mom."

Samantha gave him a long look, and then turned to the girl. "I agree with him; that guy is bad news. Didn't I hear something about him killing your Uncle Juaquin?'

Blanca touched Asher's arm. He sipped his coffee, glanced at her and then looked back toward the sloop. "Tell them, Asher."

"Tell us what?" Samantha asked.

'Tell them who killed Juaquin."

"Shut up, Blanca," Scheutz said.

"You guys know something about all that that nobody else knows?" Samantha asked.

Asher set his coffee on the deck near the taffrail and walked to where the ladder descended to the dinghy. "I think we should go over and look at who's in the boat."

"Yes." Blanca set her cup down and turned to follow him.

"Not you," Asher said as he descended.

Scheutz said, "You stay here with Samantha. Please."

Samantha put her arm around the girl's shoulders as Scheutz followed Asher to the dinghy. They turned out and away from the schooner and twenty yards from the sloop, cut the engine and drifted in to its side. Scheutz held the dinghy off with his hand to keep it from bumping the hull. It might be better to surprise whoever was aboard. He hand-walked the dinghy around to the stern so they could look into the cockpit and the cabin. The cockpit was empty and the passage door to the cabin was closed. Scheutz called, "Hallo aboard the Gaga."

Silence. The boat stopped moving.

"Hallo. Coming aboard." Asher stood and held onto the lifeline as Scheutz climbed aboard. At the passageway to the cabin he slid the hatch cover back and looked down into the cabin below. Seeing no movement, he lifted the top board and then the bottom, laid them on top of the cabin and stepped slowly down into the cabin itself. Sunlight showed in through the starboard portholes, lighting the cabin, which appeared to be empty. The door to the forward berth stood open but was not latched back against the bulkhead so it moved lightly as he moved. Just aft of the forward berth, the door to the head remained closed. He walked quickly but silently to the head door and listened. Nothing. But he knocked anyhow, and placed his body against the door. "Come out, come out wherever you are." A sudden thump against the door from inside told him he was right.

He braced his feet against the cabinet opposite the door to the head and the thump behind him came again, stronger. But the door was not moving. Whoever was in there did not have much room to maneuver in the tiny space.

"Now, now, be nice," Scheutz taunted. "Who are you and what are you doing on this boat?"

"Cabrón. Dejame salir. Go away.."

That certainly wasn't Harding. He tried to place the voice. Maybe it was just some vandal trying to rip off what he could find.

"¿Que pasa?" Asher had descended the steps into the cabin.

"I think I trapped a burglar."

Asher laughed. "Let him out. We'll throw him overboard and he can swim to shore."

Scheutz eased up on the door and the next thump brought the man out of the head, crashing into the cabinets across the aisle. Asher reacted with surprise on seeing the man. "Gato. What are you doing here?"

"Hijo de puta." Gato rushed at Asher, crashing his weight into him and bringing both of them to the narrow cabin sole.

Scheutz stepped forward and got a forearm around El Gato's neck to choke him. He pulled him back and up away from Asher who did everything he could to block the man's hands and feet from striking him. Scheutz kept a choke-hold on El Gato's neck until he settled down, his breath gurgling in his throat. "Stop it," he yelled into El Gato's ear. "Calma, calma."

Asher got to his feet, continuing to push El Gato's hands a way from him. Scheutz finally let El Gato loose, turning him so he sat on the side bunk. "Don't move. What the hell are you doing in here?"

El Gato put his hands to his throat, coughing and gasping for breath. He glanced up at Scheutz and then turned to glare at Asher. "Pendejo." Cough, cough. "We will get you."

"What the hell is this all about?" Scheutz asked Asher.

"They think I have their emeralds."

"We know you have them." Cough, cough. "Assasino." He turned to Scheutz, pointing at Asher. "This man kill Juaquin; you know that?"

Scheutz started to laugh at the absurdity of Asher harming anyone; but he stopped when he saw the look on Asher's face, a look like nothing Scheutz had ever seen on him. But how could that be? As long as he had known Asher, he could not imagine him doing anything he needed to hide from anyone, let alone hide from Scheutz, as close as the two had been for the last couple of years.

He and Asher held each other's gaze for a long moment. Without a word between them, Scheutz knew two things: Asher felt totally justified in what he had done, and at the same time apologized to Scheutz for his finding out in this way.

"I will get up now," El Gato said. "I will do you no more harm now. Let me go back to shore."

"You'll have to swim," Scheutz told him.

"Can you give me a ride in your boat?"

Asher shook his head, so Scheutz shrugged and said, "I guess not. How did you get here?"

"Senor Beltran drop me off."

"Well, there's nothing here. I can tell you for sure that the emeralds are not on this boat." Scheutz put his hand on El Gato's shoulder and motioned with his head for Asher to go topside.

Once Asher retreated up the ladder to the deck, El Gato stood and turned to Scheutz. "We are not after you, Senor Scheutz." A grin spread over his face. "And we have no interest in involving the police in the death of Senor Juaquin." He walked toward the ladder and then turned. "But I tell you this; we will not stop until we have the emeralds. And we will not stop until we have avenged the death of Señor Juaquin."

"How do you know it was Asher who killed him?"

"We know. Senor Harding was there. And that young girl."

"Blanca?"

"Si."

Chapter 29

Tapon and Scheutz sat in the idled dory and gazed at the schooner as it headed toward the inlet under diesel power. Aboard the schooner Asher raised each sail in turn, the jib, the staysail, the foresail, the main, while they faced directly into the wind. Samantha stood at the helm and Blanca waved to them from the stern. As the schooner reached the inlet, Tapon put their own motor in gear and slowly turned in the other direction, toward the town. He faced toward the restaurant at the end of the bay while Scheutz, in the prow, continued to face the sun rising in the east, unable to take his eyes off the schooner as it cleared the inlet and turned to starboard after skirting the coral reef. The tan bark-colored sails filled with the eastern breeze and the schooner heeled over in a reach. She really was a beautiful ship under sail.

Scheutz longed to be aboard in this her maiden voyage after the months stranded along shore, and after the repair of the hull. This was only a test run, out for the day to see how she performed after all she'd been through. Scheutz had had to choose between taking her out himself and helping Migdala get the restaurant ready for the day. Tapon eased the throttle up and soon the schooner disappeared from view, on past Punta Aloe.

The restaurant had had its big opening the day before, a Saturday. The place had filled early with islanders and tourists alike. He and Migdala had worked the counter and the stove while Asher and Blanca waited tables. Coffee and desserts were free for the opening day and the four of them barely kept up with the flow. During both peaks of lunch and supper they fell behind and had people hanging around outside the door waiting their turn to be seated. Today might be just as bad, but Migdala had doubted it. She argued against letting Asher and Blanca help Samantha take the schooner out when there was so much work to do. Asher and Samantha finally decided to go out for the day, but Scheutz discovered just now that Blanca had snuck on board to go with them. Migdala was going to be furious. But Scheutz just knew Samantha would be tickled at the idea of undermining Migdala's efforts.

It was nice and a bit of a surprise how well Blanca and Samantha got along. Since Samantha had been back in Culebra the two of them were like old high school chums, even to giggling behind their hands, most likely whispering about the folks around them. Samantha seemed to have lost the sour weight she had carried with her for the year before she escaped back to New Hampshire. She reminded him of how she had been all those years ago when she was not that much older than Blanca now. And for her own part, she seemed to be a subtle but settling influence on Blanca. The girl had changed from her roller coaster mood swings these past few months. Maybe that was all it took, just having somebody to giggle with.

Tapon steered the boat in toward the little dock in the mangrove, waited until Scheutz hopped ashore and then reversed the outboard and backed out into the bay again. Scheutz made his way through the mangrove and up the hill to the restaurant. The place was already packed with Sunday after-church fast-breakers. Migdala gave him her exasperated, where-the-hell-have-you-been glare and slammed a plate of huevas y patatas frittatas onto the counter. At the long table against the back wall of the dining area, with Sharkie and Arturo at other end, sat El Gato, Beltran, his "lady" friend, and J.R. Dobbs, the one called Bob, smoking his perennial pipe.

"Have you seen Blanca?" Migdala said as he put on his apron.

"Yes." He finished tying the apron and put himself next to her in front of the stove, adding diced potatoes next to the pile already on the grill.

She continued dishing food onto a plate. "Well? Where did you see her?"

He tilted his head in the direction of the bay. "On the schooner. They're heading out to sea."

"And you let her go?"

"Wasn't much I could do about it. I saw them heading out through the inlet. Besides, what the hell was I supposed to do? She's not my kid."

Migdala opened her mouth to say something but stopped and stood there, her face altering between hurt and anger. She lifted her apron to wipe her face with the reverse side and then went on with filling plates. "I need her here to help me."

"It's only for the day. I'm here to help. Let's get through this. Come on, it's a great day. Look at all these people. You're going to get rich."

She put down the plate she was holding and leaned in to hiss into his ear. "Do you see who's sitting over there?" She jerked her head toward Beltran and friends at the back table. "I'm sure they have brought Harding with them."

"I don't think so."

"Don't serve them." She picked up the plate and turned toward the counter with it, glaring across the room at Beltran. "But go out and take orders from the others."

He walked around the counter into the dining area, stopped at one table and wrote down two different orders that he took back to the counter. Arturo had just returned to the table with a fresh cup of coffee from the new Bunn coffee maker on the newly renovated sideboard. Scheutz walked over to talk with him and Sharkie, to see if they wanted to place a food order, and to tell them Tapon was on his way back as soon as he tied up his boat.

Arturo raised his cup. "Gringo espresso. Se gusto mucho." Arturo had lived in New York, in Queens, for several years before moving back to the island.

Sharkie pouted his lower lip at him with a sour look as if to say that all gringo coffee was no good. Their differing opinions quickly escalated into the kind of argument the two were known for. If Tapon were there he would take one side or the other, which had a tendency to shorten the argument with two overwhelming the third. Scheutz waited for the argument to subside so he could ask again whether they wanted to order. But their escalating vehemence made him laugh and he gave up and walked away.

As he passed the opposite end of the long table, Beltran leaned toward him and asked if he could take their order. With no more than a glance in his direction, Scheutz merely said, "No" and continued back toward the counter.

Well, that was fun. Snubbing someone to their face like that was certainly a lot more fun than smacking them. If you smack someone, you at least acknowledge their existence. Stepping away as he did conferred on them the wormhood they deserved. If only he could convince himself it was one of them who had killed Juaquin. After all, they were the bad guys. They were certainly capable of the deed. But Juaquin was one of their own. The only reason, probably, that El Gato did not inform the police of Asher's possible role in Juaquin's death was that they had an aversion to talking to the police about anything.

He smiled to Migdala as he approached the counter to pick up two plates of food. Despite the sinking feeling he had had since learning of Asher's part in Juaquin's death, he felt in such a good mood this morning. Why wouldn't he be in a good mood, what with the schooner afloat at last, and the restaurant back up and running. Great things were to be expected going forward from today. Both Samantha and Asher were hot to go to the South Pacific with the newly revived schooner. Maybe it would get Asher away from here before someone else learned about him and Juaquin.

Migdala was not yet finished with her sour looks for this morning. He was not working fast enough, obviously. And she blamed him for letting Blanca go out on that cruise. Did he really deserve to be treated like this? Lately, she'd been acting for all the world just like Samantha did for that year before she cut out for New Hampshire.

He was brought out of his thoughts by the heavy scent of perfume emanating from Beltran's secretary as she appeared next to him at the counter. Migdala transferred her nasty look from him to the secretary. "What do you want here?"

The secretary reacted as if she had been slapped. "I…we want to eat breakfast."

"Well, I want you and your two friends to leave here. Your kind are not wanted in here."

The secretary glared at Migdala. "My kind, as you say, paid to keep this little restaurant open for years while Juaquin was alive. You have no right to ask us to leave."

"Leave or I'll call the police."

"Uh…I wouldn't do that," Scheutz said.

"You keep out of this. I want those people out of here."

The secretary huffed away from the counter, colliding with Tapon who had just come in, almost knocking him down. Tapon turned to give Scheutz and Migdala a comical look. Sharkie and Arturo, at their end of the long table, thought the collision very funny, and stopped arguing long enough to lean in to hear what Tapon was saying as he stopped to talk to Beltran and his friends at the other end of the table. A lengthy discussion was now underway between Beltran and Tapon. Scheutz and Migdala went on with dishing up meals and delivering them to tables. Tapon finally left the group and came to the counter. "Those people say you won't feed them," he said to Migdala.

"That is true," she said, without turning from the stove. "Do you know who they are?" Tapon looked at Scheutz and shrugged.

"They were in business with your son," Scheutz said.

The old man frowned, turned to look at the four people at the back table and then turned back to Migdala. She continued her work, but Scheutz waited for the old man to reply. Tapon leaned his arms on the counter, turned to look at Beltran and company again and then back. The great sadness came over him again and his eyes filled once again with unshed tears. "But they did not kill him, did they?"

"No."

"Who did?"

"The police don't know." What good would it do at this point to tell him who did it? What good would it do to tell anyone? If Asher's confession was true, he surely must have done it either by accident or for some good reason. And Scheutz had not yet been able to talk with him about it.

"But it wasn't them?" Tapon said.

"No."

"Then why does Migdala not want them in here?"

"Because they are connected with Harding. Remember Harding?" The old man nodded. "Harding has already taken Blanca away once. Migdala is very afraid he will do it again. And she is afraid these people will help him."

Tapon pursed his lips and nodded again slowly. He walked to the table and sat down across from Sharkie, then stood and moved down the table to where the other three sat. After a few minutes of subdued conversation, Tapon stood and, in a loud voice, yelled at them, "Vayansen," flicking his fingers toward the door as if trying to shake bugs off them. "Esta restaurante se llama El Tapon. I am Tapon, and I tell you to go. Ahora mismo." Scheutz moved quickly through the restaurant to stand next to the old man.

"We do not have to leave." Beltran's voice came out prissy as he raised his chest to Tapon. "This is a public place and you cannot discriminate against us." El Gato glared at the old man with half-closed eyes while the secretary pursed his over-rouged lips. The words between Beltran and Tapon escalated in Spanish with the two men yelling into each other's face. Almost all the other breakfast patrons stopped eating and sat watching. Arturo and Sharkie seemed to think the whole thing was very funny, each slapping the table and laughing uproariously. Scheutz took Tapon's arm and tried gently to turn him away from the row while motioning for Beltran to pipe down. Finally, he pleaded with Sharkie to get the old man away from the table.

As Arturo and Sharkie led Tapon away, Migdala came to Scheutz's side. "I called the police." In a low and calm voice she said to Beltran, "I want you to leave. I will tell the police you caused a disturbance in here."

Beltran pointed at Tapon's back. "He caused it."

"I will tell the police you assaulted him. All these witnesses will back me up."

Beltran paused, staring at her silently. In a very low and private voice that Scheutz, standing next to her could overhear, he said, "We have come here only for the emeralds, nothing else. And we will haunt you until we get them." He stared into Migdala's eyes, waiting for a response.

She turned to Scheutz, giving him a questioning gaze as if she had no idea what Beltran was talking about. Scheutz shrugged and shook his head. She turned back to Beltran, spreading her hands and shrugging as if to say she had no idea what he was talking about. The outside door banged open and Otero stepped through like some comic book hero come to rescue the maiden.

J.R.Dobbs stood and removed his pipe. "I think we should leave. This kind of scene is not helping us at all." As Beltran passed Migdala, he said in his low, intimate but threatening voice, "Keep an eye on your daughter."

She yelled at Otero, "Arrest those people. They kidnapped my daughter."

Otero appeared to move from hero to policeman mode and held out his arm to block Beltran and his secretary. El Gato moved to go around them, and Otero pointed at him. "Stay where you are." Once again the patrons in the restaurant stopped their Sunday morning meal and turned to stare at the ruckus being made. Two men at a table near the door stood to block the doorway.

"Where is Blanca?" Otero said.

"I do not know who you mean," Beltran said.

Scheutz spoke up. "She's safe. She's out on my boat with people who are taking care of her." He flipped his thumb toward Beltran. "And he does know who you mean. We found her in his house in Rincon when we went looking for her."

Otero looked toward Migdala who nodded. Turning back to Beltran, he spread his hands and shrugged as if saying there was nothing he could do about it but they would have to leave. "Go. Vete."

"Pero..."

"Out. Para fuera."

"But..."

"Now." He took a handful of the front of Beltran's shirt and began leading him toward the door. El Gato made as if to step in and remove Otero's hand but Otero laid his other hand on the butt of his service pistol, glaring at El Gato until he fell into step behind Beltran and the secretary. Dobbs, walking behind them, gave Otero a placating smile as he passed. A man at the door stepped aside to make room. Once they had gone outside, conversation and the clink of silverware against china resumed. Tapon applauded and Arturo proclaimed Officer Otero to be un buen hombre.

Back behind the counter, Migdala drew Scheutz to the side of the room and through the door into the apartment hallway. "What are we going to do?"

"Obviously, the only thing we can do to get rid of those people is to give them the emeralds. I thought we could get away with it, but we can't. They'll never quit."

"I think you are right. We can tell them we will give them the emeralds if they never come back here." She stepped away from him, leaving a hand on his arm. "We better get back in there. Jesu Christe, I never thought we would get this busy."

The breakfast hour extended into lunch which did not let up until almost three in the afternoon. Word got around the island about the big argument with Beltran that morning and people came in making jokes about the new floorshow being offered. Otero came back for lunch and reported that he had asked Beltran and his friends to get on the ferry that day for the main island. But of course he could not make that official because they had not technically done anything wrong.

"They're a public nuisance, doesn't that count?" Scheutz said

"Well, so are you, but we haven't asked you to leave."

Arturo and Sharkie, both back for lunch and sitting at the rear table with Otero, thought that was the funniest thing they'd heard that day. "It is like a circus in here," Arturo said. "How does anyone get any eating done?"

Scheutz was in the middle of washing dishes when the last lunch patron left. Migdala announced they were closing for the rest of the day. There would be no Sunday supper hour. "Why not?" he asked. "Tonight could be a big crowd; second day open; and Sunday's always a lot of people."

"What time does your boat come back from its cruise?"

"I don't know. Before the sun goes down, certainly. Five or six o'clock. Why?"

"Those people from Rincon will see it come in the bay. And they will be waiting for it."

Scheutz pulled his hands up out of the sink. "You're right, I never thought of t hat. We should go out and meet the boat before Beltran gets to it."

"You still have the emeralds hidden on it, right?"

"Come on. Let's close the place up." He dried his hands while she put away whatever perishables still sat out behind the counter. They left everything else in the restaurant sitting just where it was and locked the front door, going out through the apartment in the back to her station wagon.

Driving into town they decided to go to Sharkie's place where Tapon's dory was tied up. On the way they stopped on the malecón to tell Tapon they were taking his boat out to meet the schooner. The old man waved his hand okay. Once outside the reefs, Scheutz turned south, both he and Migdala scanning the horizon for sails. Samantha ought to be bringing the schooner in by now. The ocean outside the bay moved in an animated chop with little white caps and a brisk northeast east wind typical of this time of year. They had not yet cleared the southern tip of Culebra before Migdala yelled and pointed to a set of tanbark sails off the eastern tip of Vieques, the island directly south. Scheutz steered for it.

Migdala knelt in the bow and waved to attract the attention of those on the schooner while Scheutz steered for the leeward side of the boat. When they were only about fifty yards off, Samantha at the helm apparently recognized them and hove to, heading the prow up into the wind. Scheutz eased the dory in against the port side of the schooner as Migdala stood to toss a painter line up to Asher leaning over the gunwale. He tied them off to a stanchion and dropped a rope ladder for them to board, the two boats pitching in the waves.

Asher gave first Migdala and then Scheutz a hand to step on board. Samantha maintained the widespread stance at the helm that Scheutz remembered so well. Blanca was nowhere to be seen. Migdala walked immediately aft to stand before the wheel, saying something to Samantha that the wind carried away. Samantha yelled something back at her and before Scheutz could intervene it looked as if the two of them might square off on each other and to hell with the pitching deck. Samantha held one spoke of the wheel while jabbing her forefinger at Migdala's face. Migdala, still facing her across the wheel, held both forefingers in the air until a particularly hefty upheaval of the boat pitched her to starboard, whereupon she grabbed two wheel spokes. With Samantha holding two spokes also, it looked like the two of them danced some high-spirited jig replete with yelling above the wind.

"You kidnapped my daughter."

"Your daughter stowed away on board."

"What have you done with her?"

"It's what am I going to do with you if you don't let go of the goddamned wheel."

"Where is Blanca?"

"Hiding from you."

"Where?"

"Below."

Migdala turned and grabbed the top of the doghouse to steady herself while she entered the gangway. Scheutz had reached the cockpit and followed her. Before going below, though, he stopped and said to Samantha, "Sorry about that. She's pretty overwrought."

Samantha nodded. "I can see that." She turned the wheel slowly, putting the schooner back on its course.

The boat heeled to port as Scheutz descended to the cabin. Migdala stood yelling at the closed door to the aft starboard side of the cabin. "Venga afuera. Come out here."

"No." Blanca's voice came from only a foot away on the other side of the door.

"Venga afuera."

"No. Tu vete."

Migdala turned to Scheutz. "What am I going to do? She won't come out."

He tried. "Blanca, come out of there, will you. Stop being silly. We have a big problem here, which we have to work out. Come on."

"No. I am going to run away to sea."

He had some difficulty keeping himself from laughing. "Well, not in my boat. So, get your ass out here." If Migdala were not taking this whole thing so seriously, he would not even pretend it meant anything. Here was a fifteen-year-old girl acting like a four-year-old, and a mother treating the fifteen-year-old like a four-year-old. True, there was some danger to her from those goons back at Punta Aloe, but as soon as he turned the emeralds over to them, that would go away. But all this mother-daughter angst going on in front of him had the entertainment value of an afternoon telenovela.

Migdala continued her yell-fest behind him. He let her have the grin he was having such a hard time holding back, bowed slightly from the waist, and gestured with his hands that it was now her turn to pound on the door once again. Leaving her to it, he climbed back up to the main deck.

Asher lounged against the starboard rail, his legs extended down the listing deck. Culebra was a beautiful sight off the port bow, the low gorse-clogged hills fronted by the Atlantic waves crashing against the extended reefs. Samantha had turned the bow westward slightly putting their tack on more of a broad reach. They had let the main and foresails out some and the staysails filled with the steady breeze. The old schooner skipped along at a good eight knots, just as smooth as she had always done before having her hull broken. He caught Asher's eye and they smiled at each other, each knowing what the other was thinking at the moment. Samantha paid them no mind, but alternated her glances between the luft of the sails and the silhouette of the island in front of them. From the play of that slight old smile on her lips he could tell she was once again back in trance that kept her returning to the sea.

He hated to interrupt her but they had to talk about why he and Migdala had come out here to meet them. When he moved to stand before Samantha at the helm she smiled at him. He stood in front of the wheel, his hand on the binnacle for balance on the pitching deck. "We've got to take Blanca off the boat."

"Why? She's having the time of her life. And we're almost there, anyhow."

"There are some bad people waiting for the boat to come back in and her mother wants to avoid her being exposed to them."

"Oh. Really? Why didn't she say so?"

"She's not handling this all too well. This thing with her daughter and those people has gotten a little out of hand."

"What d'you plan on doing?"

"I'd like to take her off into the dory, skirt the island to come in on the other side near the town, and then hide her somewhere till we can get rid of those people."

"How you going to get rid of them?"

"Actually, what they're really after is a cache of emeralds. We'll trade the emeralds for some peace of mind about the girl."

He and Samantha looked into each other's eyes, she waiting for him to say something more. He did not know what else to say her. She knew. Her eyes told him she knew that he and Migdala were now together. There was no longer any question. He had to turn away and looked up at the top of the main sail where it strained against the mast. When he looked back, her gaze had gone off toward the southwest.

"Let's talk about this tonight," he said.

He went back below. Migdala and her errant offspring were still at it. This was bullshit; they had to get her off this boat. He yelled at the door, "Blanca, back off from the door, I'm coming in." Without waiting for a reply, he pounded a foot against the wood exactly where he knew the hasp to be on the other side. Something splintered, Blanca let out a screech, and the door swung inward, banging against something, or someone, standing directly behind it. Blanca howled in pain as the door hit her head.

Before the howling stopped Migdala was in the cabin with her hand on Blanca's arm. "You are coming off this boat with us."

"No." Blanca, wearing a white t-shirt, shorts, and peaked baseball cap very much like Samantha's, broke away from her mother and lunged out through the cabin.

"Grab her, Clem."

Scheutz caught the girl from behind, pinning her arms to her side. He leaned his back against bulkhead to keep from being tossed off balance by the pitching boat. Literally growling between clenched teeth, Blanca squirmed mightily in his embrace but was no match for his strength.

"Let's go," Migdala shouted.

"Wait. We have to get the emeralds."

"Aye, Dios. Where the hell are they?"

The small hidey-hole holding the packet of emeralds had been built into the trim of the new rib he and Asher had sistered next to the one splintered by the hurricane. He could not let go of the girl and so described for Migdala how to slide out the piece of trim that had been dovetailed into the main body of the rib on the underside of the upper deck. This little piece of genius had been Asher's work. Migdala drew out the parcel and dropped it down the front of her shorts causing an odd-looking bulge. He let out a laugh, but both Blanca and Migdala were too seriously engaged, each in their own life-or-death struggle, to even notice.

Migdala grabbed Blanca's legs just above the knees and they dragged her upside-down up the steps onto the main deck. On deck, Asher hurried over to help. Samantha refused even to look at them; merely shook her head with that superior attitude she sometimes put on. Blanca stretched her arms in Samantha's direction screaming for her to save her.

"If you do not stop squirming, Blanca, we are going to tie you up," Migdala hissed at her.

They carried her to the port rail, screaming at the top of her lungs. Scheutz paused at the side of the boat. Getting down into the dory holding this screaming banshee with both the dory and the schooner pitching in this sea was going to be a chore. They could all end up in the drink. He asked Asher to haul out life vests for the three of them. He and Migdala held the struggling girl while Asher pulled a vest onto her torso and zipped it closed. She wrapped her arms around Asher's head and screamed for him to save her.

Asher grinned and patted her on the head. Scheutz slipped his own life vest on but could not zip it up the front. He clamped an arm around the girl's waist and climbed over the rail to the rope ladder. She screamed and flung her arms and legs wildly in every direction. It amazed him that their position on the outside of the boat did not paralyze the girl with fear. It certainly scared the shit out of him. He descended slowly, Asher holding onto his arm from above, until he could drop himself and his baggage into the bouncing dory. Migdala jumped into the boat right behind him.

He wrestled Blanca into the bottom of the dory and wedged the two of them between the seats. Migdala started the engine and signaled for Asher to let go the painter. As they had agreed on the way out from the bay, she turned the dory west toward the southern coast of the island. And headed west.

Chapter 30

"Blanca, sit still." Migdala yelled, still working the tiller as they rounded the southern tip of the island. Scheutz held the girl's shoulders tight against him as she writhed and swore. Blanca had whacked her mother in the back of the head and Scheutz reached to grab her wrist, hanging on as she tried over and over to wrench from his grasp.

They rounded Punto Tampico and headed in past the ferryboat pier to the tiny dock behind the guesthouse. The moment they nosed into the dock Blanca lurched forward to jump from the boat to the dock, but Scheutz held onto her arm. Migdala took hold of the other arm and began rapidly explaining to her again why they needed to stay hidden from Beltran, and especially El Gato.

Blanca finally settled down on the middle seat of the boat and began to cry. "I don't care. I want to get away from here."

"You want to get away from me?" Migdala asked..

"No, it is not you, Mami." Blanca reached out to touch her hand. "I just want to get away from this island."

"But not with them. They are bad people."

"I can take care of myself."

"Bullshit," Scheutz could not help but add.

Blanca looked at him, then dropped her head into her hands and sobbed harder. Migdala put her arms around the girl's shoulders and pulled her head to her own shoulder. She gave Scheutz a withering look that suggested he stay out of it.

Migdala stepped ashore, helping Blanca up behind her. She stooped to hold the bowline while Scheutz made his way forward and then up onto the dock. He took the line and tied the boat off while she led her daughter around the side of the building to the seaside. He passed them and stopped to look carefully up along the malecon before motioning for them to follow him.

"Let's go find Otereo," Migdala said. "He must help us keep her away from those people. She gathered Blanca, holding her by the arm and they walked through the town to the police station. If their guess was right, Beltran should be out there trying to intercept the schooner when it came in. So, hopefully, they did not have to worry about running into him and El Gato in town. The other two, Dobbs and the secretary; they both seemed harmless.

Inside the police station the chubby secretary sat at her desk doing paperwork. No, she did not know where Otero was, but she would contact him on his jeep radio. She gave Scheutz the same distrustful look she treated him with the day he had spent in their jail cell. To Blanca, she said, "Como estas, cariña?"

"Pretty shitty."

The secretary turned to give Scheutz another look, probably thinking her attitude was his fault. When Otero's voice came back over the radio in answer to her call, she explained that Migdala, her daughter, and the awful gringo were asking for him. He said he was out near the old Naval Station and he would come right down.

While they waited, the night deputy came in, an elderly man in a somewhat rumpled uniform. Scheutz recognized him as a regular customer at the restaurant in the morning. The secretary left and the deputy took up his post and duties that apparently involved reading a magazine.

Scheutz took a seat in Otero's desk chair, but Migdala and Blanca remained standing. The deputy waved his hand for Scheutz not to sit in that chair but Scheutz ignored him and he didn't seem to want to pursue the matter. Blanca fidgeted and Migdala held onto her arm. Scheutz amused himself watching the old deputy read with his feet up on the secretary's desk.

When Otero finally did come bustling through the door, the first thing he did was motion Scheutz away from his desk. He leveled his gaze at Migdala. "What is the problem?"

"We have a problem."

"I just asked, 'What is the problem?'"

"You have to arrest those three men and that woman you threw out of the restaurant this morning."

"I have been keeping my eye on them. What did they do to for me to arrest them?"

"They are after my daughter. They want to make her a whore."

Otero gave her a pained look. He shook his head. "I know what they want. They want those stones this man has." He pointed his finger aside at Scheutz. "The little fat guy says he stole them from him."

"Bullshit." Scheutz made no move to give up Otero's chair.

"It is not true." Migdala leaned in closer to Otero's face. Tears welled up in her eyes. "Those emeralds belonged to my uncle. Those people murdered him so they could steal them. That is why you should arrest them." She maintained her position, holding his eyes with hers.

Otero squinted and turned away to look at Scheutz. "I still think you killed her uncle."

"Don't be such an asshole."

"I'll show you who is an asshole. You see that little cell in the back of the room. If you do not get out of my chair, I will put you in it again. It is waiting for you."

"Stop it, both of you." Migdala leaned in closer to Otero. "What are you going to do about those people?"

"I'm going to keep watching them."

"They did kill my uncle, you know. That ugly one, El Gato, did."

"I don't have any proof of that."

"You don't have any proof of me doing it either," Scheutz said. "But I can see why you would choose to go after me; because you're afraid of someone like El Gato."

Otero leaned across his desk. "I am not afraid of anyone."

"Coward."

"STOP IT." Migdala slammed her hand onto the top of the desk.

Blanca giggled. The old deputy grinned widely but silently on the other side of the room.

Otero glared at Scheutz and then stood quiet looking at Migdala, apparently thinking the matter over. Finally, he said, "Since those people say that all they want is the emeralds, why don't you just give them up. Then they will go away and your problem is over."

"What if they do not go away then?"

"Then…I suppose I could arrest them."

"And, for what?"

"Let me see." He looked at the ceiling, then at the deputy, then at Blanca. "I could arrest them for attempted kidnapping. What they call sex-trafficking."

"Even if, as you say, you have no proof?"

Otero rested his eyes on Blanca. "There is always proof. Of anything."

Migdala reached for his hand and gave it a squeeze. "Can you find them now?"

Otero nodded his head. "When I left them just now, they were waiting for this gringo's boat to tie up at the mooring out near the Naval Station. They are probably still there."

"Go and get them. We will meet them here. We will give them the emeralds." She looked at Scheutz. "Right, Clement, we will give them the emeralds?"

He nodded.

Otero looked back and forth between Scheutz and Migdala and then Blanca. Finally he said to Blanca, "You are worth a lot, chiquita."

Blanca looked at her mother. "Too much."

"Esta bien." Otero stood. "You will wait here and I will come back with the band of outlaws."

Scheutz stood. "No, don't bring them here. Tell them I will bring the emeralds to the ferry dock first thing in the morning."

Otero nodded. "If that's what you want."

"And tell them I will only give them the emeralds just before they get on the ferry. No ferry, no stones."

"Okay."

"And I would like you to be with me."

"Okay, if that's what you want. If you are not worried I will arrest you before you get the chance to give up the emeralds."

Migdala poked him in the chest. "You better not. You will have to answer to me."

Otero gave her a big, phony grin and headed for the door. "Come on. I will drive you home."

They decided to leave Tapon's boat where it was and Scheutz could move it in the morning after dealing with Beltran. Otero drove them in the jeep to the restaurant, and planned to return to where the schooner lay to make sure Beltran and his friends made it home.

Scheutz needed to make sure of it himself and make sure they got the message about leaving in the morning. "I'll ride out to the boat with you," he said to Otero.

"No, no. You stay here."

Once Migdala and Blanca were inside, Scheutz took Migdala's Volvo back downtown, parked on the malecón and walked behind the guesthouse to untie Tapon's dory. It would be getting dark soon and halfway out he began looking for possible lights that might be on, both on the schooner and on the opposite shore at Punta Aloe. Nothing yet at either place, but he could see Otero's jeep making its way along the road across the little ridge that ran behind the water treatment plant and the old Naval Station.

When he reached the schooner he could see the dinghy was not there, was not attached to its stern davit nor tied up at the hull. He cut the outboard and drifted up to the side of the schooner next to the ladder that hung off the side. Once on the deck, a quick look and a shout told him that Samantha and Asher were not aboard. Back in the dory, he steered toward the shore where he could see Otero walking from his jeep.

"What are you doing here," Otero shouted. "I just left you off."

"Nobody's aboard. Did Beltran have a rental car?'

"Yes. A gray Toyota. It is not here."

Scheutz cut the engine and hopped ashore, tying the boat securely to a small overhanging tree next to the water. "I'll ride back with you. Let's go see if Migdala and Blanca are okay."

"That's what you were supposed to be doing anyhow."

Otero raced the jeep back along the dirt road onto the Escudero and up the hill. Sure enough, there sat the gray Toyota alongside the road next to the restaurant. Scheutz and Otero hurried inside. The apartment appeared to be empty, and they ran down the hall to the door to the restaurant. There they found Migdala and Blanca sitting at the long table nearest the counter with Beltran, looking like he was chairing a business meeting across from them. He was flanked on one side by his secretary and Dobbs, and on the other by El Gato. George, the secretary sat poised, smoking a cigarette while Dobbs lounged with his pipe. El Gato wore his menacing grin. Asher stood at El Gato's end of the table in a pose that Scheutz knew well, alert and quietly waiting. Samantha stood at the other end of the table, and even she wore a menacing look, her legs spread apart as if she stood at the helm of a boat, her arms folded across her chest. Tapon, Arturo, and Sharkie all sat together at a neighboring table, playing dominos. Otero went to stand by Migdala's chair and Scheutz stood next to Blanca's. No one said anything.

Finally Otero said, "What are you are all doing here?"

"We saw their rental car out there," Samantha said. "And Asher thought we ought to come in and make sure they were not in here waiting for Blanca to come back. I'm glad we did."

"We just came for supper," Sharkie said. Tapon eyed the Beltran group with the same alertness as Asher.

Scheutz worked up the most menacing gaze he could muster to glare at Beltran. Otero and El Gato, he noticed, had locked onto each other's eyes. Otero, in one of his macho poses, probably wanted to prove Scheutz wrong about his being afraid of El Gato, but if there were any immediate threat in the room it would come from him. Otero had nonchalantly laid his hand on the butt of the pistol at his side. Good for him. George, seemed to be wavering under the stress provided by all this company. She glanced around the group from one to another, Asher to Otero to Samantha to Scheutz and then the three old men at the other table. The only calm one in the room seemed to be Dobbs whose head tilted slightly to starboard as his fingers lightly touched the bowl of his pipe.

"We were just now discussing jewels," Beltran said, one eyebrow raised slightly.

"And I am the jewel," Blanca said.

Scheutz laid a hand on her shoulder. "This is not really the right time to be a smart-ass, babe."

"Do you have the emeralds?" Beltran asked Scheutz.

"Do you agree to the terms?" Migdala asked.

Beltran nodded. "We came here for the stones. Not the girl."

Otero bent forward, pointing his finger in Beltran's face. "So you admit you are a sex-trafficker."

"Por favor." Beltran waved his hand as if shooing a fly.

"Where are these damned emeralds," Sharkie said. "Let's get on with this; it's suppertime."

Where were they? He had been so concerned about hanging onto Blanca that he almost forgot about the stones. "Did you give them to me?' he asked Migdala.

"No, I have them." She took the small folded envelope that held the stones from the left pocket of her shorts and laid them on the table in front of her.

Beltran's and George's eyes locked onto the packet. El Gato reached across the table and folded his hand around it. The entire table, including Dobbs, tensed. Otero grabbed El Gato's wrist and twisted it, stiffening the arm in such a way as to turn the man's body away from the table. El Gato turned his face toward Otero, his lips snarled in an effort to wrestle his arm from the policeman's grasp. Otero had the advantage and he placed his other hand on El Gato's elbow, pushing it toward the table. El Gato's snarl turned to a grimace. His other hand appeared on the table-top holding a small automatic pistol.

Before anyone else at the table could react, Dobbs reached in front of Beltran and took the gun from El Gato's hand. "No. No. No," Dobbs said. "We do not do that." He put the gun away, somewhere below the table-top, then took his pipe from his mouth. "Put the package back on the table." El Gato dropped the envelope and Otero let go his wrist. Dobbs pointed at the packet with the stem of his pipe and said to Migdala. "Now let's see them"

Migdala unfolded the packet and, keeping both hands on the edges of the paper moved it closer to the center of the table. The entire circle moved their heads in simultaneously like a football huddle. Tapon, Sharkie, and Arturo stood and moved behind those sitting at the table.

"Turn on more lights," Arturo said. Sharkie ran to the overhead light switch next to the front door. Tapon went through the apartment door to return with a table lamp, which he plugged into a socket on the front of the counter, and then set the lamp next to the open packet of emeralds. They shone magnificently in the light.

Beltran brought a loupe to his eye and reached to pick up one of the larger emeralds, a stone of a about a half-inch width. He put the loupe to his eye and studied it, then put it down and picked up another. After a third stone, he raised his head to ask Scheutz, "And where did you get these stones?"

"Why? You know where I got them. From the Coastal Patrol captain in Cuba."

"They are not the right stones."

"They're the only ones I have."

"These are synthetic."

"What? Look how shiny they are."

Beltran pointed at the stones with the same hand that held the loupe. "Exactly. The synthetic emerald, what they call a Chatham emerald is always shinier than a natural emerald. And these, I don't even think these are Chatham."

"What are you talking about?" Tapon asked.

Beltran gave a sigh of exasperation, as if impatient about having to explain to a bunch of amateurs. "A man named Chatham discovered a way to enhance emeralds back in the 1930s. He used a flux process with natural beryl. The synthetics do not have little flaws in them the way naturals do, and they are shinier. But they are not worth as much as natural emeralds."

"But they are still worth money, no?" Migdala asked.

Beltran shrugged. "If they were Chathams, they would still bring a fair amount. But these are not even Chathams." He put his loupe to his eye, picked up another stone and showed it Dobbs.

Dobbs took the loupe that Beltran handed him. "You are right; these do not look like Chathams. I'm not sure but I think they are more like Birons. Or maybe even worse, Tairus." He looked up at Scheutz. "Tairus is a breed of synthetic that is made in Russia. You say these came from Cuba?"

"According to Harding, that's what Juaquin sent us to Cuba for," Scheutz said. "Supposedly, they made their way there from Columbia where they were supposed to have been mined."

"Well." Dobbs dropped the stone into the pile. "Somebody in Cuba switched them for these Russian ones."

"So where does that leave us?" Migdala asked.

"Disappointed."

"So they are not worth anything?"

"Oh, not so, not so, not so. They are certainly worth something. But about half of what we were expecting."

"So will you take them and go?"

Beltran asked, "How much do you want for these stones?"

"They're not mine," Migdala said. "I don't want anything for them. I only want you to go away."

Beltran raised his eyebrows and looked toward Dobbs.

"You two..." Dobbs waved his pipe stem back forth between Migdala and Blanca. "You two are the rightful heirs, I suppose, of Juaquin's estate. How much do you want for them?"

"A lot," Blanca blurted.

Migdala put a hand on Blanca's shoulder. "Callate. Just sit still and shut up, will you?" She said to Dobbs, "You are skipping my grandfather. As Tio Juaquin's father, he is the rightful heir to anything he owned."

Tapon moved around the table to stand behind Migdala and face Dobbs. "Oh, yo digo..." He stroked his chin. "Yo digo que...I say what Blanca says; they are worth a lot."

"I will tell you what they are worth," Beltran said. "And then we will offer you one quarter of that amount." He looked at each face across the table from him, pausing at each one in turn.

Dobbs took a pull from his pipe, looking off toward the far corner of the ceiling. Then he shrugged. "It is reasonable that we will offer one quarter of their worth. As Juaquin's partner, Señor Beltran already owns one half of these stones. He says he is prepared to offer you half of what belonged to Juaquin."

"Right here, right now," Beltran said.

"How much is that?" Tapon asked.

Beltran picked up the stones randomly and let them fall through his fingers, pursing his lips in thought. Finally, he said, "I will give you twenty-five thousand dollars in cash."

"How about fifty thousand?" Blanca began squirming again.

Beltran put his face in his hands and shook his head slowly. Then he raised his head and pointed a forefinger at Blanca. "I want to tell you something, chiquita. I am not a saint, but if I was, I could not ever put up with you. I am also not a sex-trafficker, as this policeman says, but even if I was I would never even think of trying to sell you to anyone."

"How about this?" Scheutz interrupted. "We will give them to you for thirty thousand."

"I have a better proposal for you," Beltran said. He paused, looked down at the stones and then raised his eyes slowly to Scheutz for dramatic affect. "Out there…" He pointed toward the bay. "Is a sailboat that belongs to Harding. He was working for Juaquin and should also be part owner of these emeralds. And you, Senor Scheutz, in my way of thinking, should also benefit from the sale of these gems since you brought them from Cuba and have kept them safe all this time. Why don't we say twenty-five thousand dollars plus that sailboat?"

"Where is Harding?" Otero wanted to know. "If you are harboring that murderer…"

"He is not a murderer and I am not harboring him. Stop acting like a stupid policeman."

Otero reached across the table to make a grab for Beltran, but El Gato took hold of his wrist, turned his arm and forced it down to the table directly on top of the emeralds. Otero let out a yelp and struggled to release his arm. Now El Gato had the advantage, turning Otero's hand back and forcing his wrist on the top of the stones.

Dobbs stood, placing his hands, one on Otero's arm and the other on El Gato's. "Stop this, both of you. You are both idiots." El Gato cautiously released Otero's arm, watching him, ready for him to try to

do something further. But Otero only lifted his wrist from the table, holding it like a broken wing. "Back away," Dobbs said to him.
Otero backed up from the table, glaring at El Gato while continuing to hold his hand in the air, like a child showing a booboo to his mommy. In the long silence that followed, all eyes were on Otero. Beltran broke the mood. "May we return to the price of the emeralds?"

Migdala came back to the table. "Why would we want that boat?"

"It's actually a pretty good boat," Scheutz said. "A thirty-foot fiberglass Cascade sloop. With a little work, it could be worth something."

Migdala turned from the table to look at him, then looked at Tapon and then Asher. Tapon shrugged. Asher nodded in agreement with Scheutz.

"How do we know," Scheutz asked. "whether Harding won't just show up over here and claim the boat? Or sail it away without saying anything to us at all?"

"He no longer has title to the boat," Dobbs said. "I do."

"Besides," Beltran said. He paused and then looked at Otero before fixing his eyes on Migdala. "You can be certain that Harding will not ever bother you ever again. He has given us his resignation and returned to where he came from."

Scheutz had the distinct impression that Beltran was trying to tell them something without actually saying it. Obviously, Harding had been terminated, but to what extent he was not about to let on. Not that he really cared, as long as the man was gone. He looked at Migdala, trying tp tell her it would be all right.

Migdala looked for a long moment into Scheutz's eyes. "We'll take the boat."

Beltran patted his hand on the table. "A deal?"

"As long as you four leave on the ferry tomorrow morning," Otero said, still glaring at El Gato.

"We cannot leave fast enough." George let out an exasperated breath.

Beltran pointed to his large black pocketbook. He lifted it to the table, removed a canvas envelope from which she counted out thirty thousand-dollar bills, laying them in piles of ten thousand each. Scheutz looked at Beltran to see if he caught the mistake made between the twenty-five thousand agreed upon and the thirty thousand George laid out. But Beltran seemed to have lost interest in the whole proceeding. No one said anything as Blanca recounted each pile and giggled, smiling at her mother. Migdala picked up each pile and handed the wad to her grandfather who folded it in half without looking at it, putting it away in his side pocket as if they were merely spending money.

No one seemed to have anything further to say until Dobbs suggested they leave. They all stood, including Migdala and Blanca. Before turning to go, Dobbs said to Migdala that he would make sure to send the sailboat's title to her.

Otero told them to go to their rental apartment at Punta Aloe and stay there until the next morning. He would be on duty tonight and did not want to see them near the restaurant. He suggested they buy food on the way back and eat in the apartment. When they left, he said he planned to follow them to make sure. Before he went out he asked Migdala if she would fix some supper for him when he came back.

"Well, I'm hungry, too," Sharkie said as the outer door closed behind Otero.

Migdala followed Asher to the kitchen. Arturo made for the cold drinks case and began dragging out beer for everyone. Tapon and Sharkie sat in their regular seats.

Samantha sat down next to Scheutz and Blanca and spoke for the first time since the meeting began.

"Blanca and I want to talk with you about something."

Blanca squirmed and leaned into him. "I want to go with you to the South Pacific."

"What?" he turned to Samantha. "Did you put her up to this?"

"She put me up to it. I think it would be a great idea."

"She's just a kid."

"She'll be sixteen in a couple of months. We've known a lot of ship crew members who were sixteen."

Blanca nudged him. "Come on, come on, say yes."

"Whoa. Hang on. What does your mother have to say about this?"

"I haven't told her yet."

"You mean you haven't asked her yet."

"Well, that too."

He looked over at Migdala where she stood behind the counter with Asher making supper for all of them. It would break his heart if one of his sons had announced at age fifteen that he wanted to run off to sea. He shook his head. "I can't say yes to that. She will never say yes. You can't break her heart like that."

Blanca slapped her hand across his upper arm. "Oh, you."

Samantha gave him a knowing smile and nodded. She knew his sons and what he was like when they lived with him in New Hampshire. To Blanca, she said, "I told you, he will never say yes to this. He won't try to convince your mother. You have to convince her."

Blanca made a face and slouched in her chair. Scheutz said to her, "Why don't you help your mother with supper? Let Samantha and I talk about this." She gave him her teenage glare, rose, and strode across the room to the counter. He and Samantha watched her go and then sat quietly. He did not know what to say to her.

"You can still go to the South Pacific, you know," she said.

The whole thing had originally been her idea back a year ago or so. It had been some kind of fantasy in his mind, mostly fueled by pictures and movies he'd seen of places like Bora Bora, and stories told by people sitting around the cockpit on some mooring off Virgin Gorda, drinking mai tais. After Samantha left to go back home to New Hampshire and then the ship got busted up in the hurricane, that fantasy went the way of all fantasies, remembered and occasionally mused upon. Recently, when she came back with half her father's inheritance in her pocket, and began talking about Bora Bora again, it had been like seeing a TV rerun of the movie that had once moved him. But it was still just a fantasy.

Chapter 31

Scheutz and Asher spent the morning going through Harding's sloop, below decks, the main cabin, the forward v-berth, the lockers. Dobbs had sent the title and registration showing that he had signed it over to

Migdala. They could not remember when they had seen Harding make improvements to this boat but somebody had partially restored it before they met him in St. Thomas. It had a three-cylinder diesel engine with low mileage on it. You could close down two cylinders, start it with a hand-crank on one cylinder, and then open up the other two. The bilge pump was new, as was the water-cooling system and the small refrigerator. Dobbs had spent some money on these things. Leaving it in Harding hands rendered the boat unfit to perform whatever little smuggling trips they had used it for. After the bowsprit got broken on the way over from St. Thomas, Harding just let it sit.

Where was Harding now, Scheutz wondered. He could see why the man didn't show up for their meeting about the emeralds. Between the police wanting to throw him in jail, Migdala wanting to cut his balls off, and Beltran wanting to exact some other kind of unspeakable disciplinary action upon him, Harding would do well to head back to the States, wherever he was from. Then again, knowing him, he was probably wanted by the police back there, which is probably why he ended up here in the Caribbean. Dobbs's remark about him back in the restaurant had a kind of finality to it, leading Scheutz to think it would be a cold day in Culebra before they saw him again.

But what a nice little boat. Scheutz had assumed that because Harding owned it that it must be a piece of crap. They were finding now that it wasn't. The hull had been formed years ago, probably right around the time the whole boating world was switching over from wood planks to fiberglass, back when they did not know for sure how thin a hull they could get away with, and so this hull was the thickness of a wooden plank. With a six-foot draft, the boat was meant for deep-water sailing. And the rigging, now that they had a closer look, was fairly new and in good shape, except of course for the broken bowsprit and the cable going to the mast. But, fix the bowsprit, scrape the hull, give it a coat of paint plus a coat of varnish on the wooden superstructure, and you'd have as pretty a little boat as you could find on the water.

It was certainly worth some money. He'd love to have this boat to fix up and mess around in, or take a trip down islands. This lovely little sloop helped weigh the argument toward staying right where he was. Migdala had said she would have no use for a boat like this and would give it entirely over to Scheutz if he stayed and helped her with the restaurant. This boat could go a long way to plug the hole that losing the love of his life, that wonderful schooner, was going to make.

But what a silly thing to think. Was this about boats, or about two different people, Samantha and Migdala? Or was it about two different styles of living, struggling here on this little island to help Migdala build up her restaurant, or idling out the rest of his days in some Club Med type resort, watching his brains slowly ooze out his ears onto a beautiful white sandy beach?

"You are not supposed to be there." The voice came from Otero, sitting in his jeep on the shore.

Scheutz snapped out of his reverie, realizing he'd been lost in staring at the ridge of the small hills across the bay, and turned to give the policeman a wave. "It's okay, I own the boat now."

Otero shouted back. "I don't care who owns the boat, that is still a crime scene. A man was murdered there."

"No, he wasn't."

"Yes, he was." Asher's voice came up through the gangway from below, too soft for Otero to hear.

"Yes, he was." Otero echoed from the shore. "Now get off."

Scheutz stood and spread his hands. "Okay, let me get my stuff from below."

"No, don't touch anything," Otero shouted.

"I just put it there."

Otero got out of the jeep and walked to the water's edge, standing with his fists on his hips. "Get it and get out."

"Be right up." Scheutz descended the steps to the main cabin as Asher stepped aside to let him pass. Scheutz shook his head. "I can't decide whether I like that guy or not."

"He's just doing what he thinks is right," Asher said.

Scheutz stood in the aisle in the cramped cabin, capturing Asher in as direct a gaze as he could muster. "So, you want to tell me what actually did happen here?"

Asher gave back the same stare, then broke away and glanced around the cabin. Finally, he nodded as if in resignation. "I came here looking for the girl."

"Why."

"Because I thought she might be here."

"Come on, man, don't give me a run-around."

Asher shrugged. "I got to tell you, I never liked that Harding. He's like…he smells bad. Not like sweat, you know, like bad juju."

"What does that have to do with it?"

"I see her from the schooner, swim out here and him pull her up the side and them go below. So, I come over in the dinghy."

"Where was I?"

"I don't know. The hurricane be coming and you in town, maybe at the restaurant. I be getting the schooner battened down. Anyhow, I go below and Harding be standing 'bout where you be now. He naked and he wanting to know what I was doing here. I say I came to get Blanca."

"And where was she?"

"I don't see her, so I guess she up in the v-berth; that little door is closed. Harding tell me to get off his boat. I yell to Blanca I be taking her back to her mother and she yell at me from behind the door. Harding try to push me up the ladder but I don't go. He yelling like he do. And then before I know it someone behind me, grabbing his arms around me and holding my arms. They be trying to carry me up to the deck. Then Blanca come out. With her clothes on, I am happy to see."

"So, there are four people in this little space?"

"Yes. Blanca up on the side bunk yelling, and Harding yelling, and the man behind me, who was Juaquin, he yelling."

Otero's shouts came through the gangway from the shore. "What are you doing in there? Get off the boat."

"So, how does the spear gun come into this mess?" Scheutz wanted to know.

"I don't know. It be on that ledge behind the side bunk. It come in my hand and I start jabbing Harding and when I turned to jab Juaquin it go off."

"I am on the radio," Otero shouted to them.

"We'd better get out of here before he calls in the Coast Guard."

They climbed to the deck and over the side into the dinghy. Asher grinned and waved at Otero who looked surprised. Scheutz steered across the bay toward town. If they went toward the schooner, Otero would surely show up there, but maybe if they went to the town they could avoid engaging in some further conversation with him. It was getting close to suppertime anyhow and they were due at work.

All through supper Scheutz could not get the scene on the boat out of his head. The restaurant was overly busy. The winter tourist season was definitely off to a brisk start, even with all the mess left over from the hurricane damage. Blanca did not show up, so Migdala asked Eusebio to wait tables for them. In the midst of it all, when Samantha came in, Scheutz waved her over to the counter and asked if she knew where Blanca was hiding.

Samantha looked around the restaurant as if expecting to see the girl, then shrugged and raised her eyebrows. "I haven't seen her all day. By the way, we have to talk. Can you come over to Chuck's tonight when you get off work?"

"About what?"

"About the schooner."

"What about it?"

"About whether it's ready for the trip. What else we need to do, what kind of supplies I need to lay in, who's going with us. I'm getting kind of anxious to get going. And now there's this other boat we have to do something with."

He stopped cutting the vegetables and stared at her. She raised her eyebrows the way she always did when asking an unspoken question. All he had to do was say yes, he would come to Chuck's that night, but nothing came out. She waited, her eyebrows dropping and her eyes narrowing with what looked like some more important question. Finally, he waved the hand with the vegetable knife in it and nodded that he would come. She squinted at him a moment longer and turned to go as he went back to cutting up vegetables.

Could Samantha sail that schooner to Bora Bora? Could Migdala continue to take care of Blanca and build up this restaurant without his help? Without his and Asher's help, he should say, because Asher was sure to go wherever the schooner went. Well, of course they could, both women could do exactly what they planned to do. That's the way they were, each of them. That ability to get done whatever they wanted to do was one of the things that had always attracted him to one woman over another. His children's mother had been like that, too. That look of concentration on her face alone could give him an erection.

No, in the long stretch it didn't really matter for each of these women which one he went with. All he'd do is make it easier for the one he chose. He was not a hero. He was born to be a helper, had been ever since he was a kid living in that apartment with his father and brothers. His older brother Hank ran the show and all he and his little brother Willi did was get by with as little effort as they could. That's even what his family name meant in German, *ein scheutzer,* a soldier. And that's why he and Asher got along so well; they were like alter-egos, helping out whoever was giving orders, except that he had always reserved the right to choose who was giving the orders.

Migdala stopped in the middle of piling food onto plates and yelling at Asher and Eusebio and came to stand for a short moment behind Scheutz so that he could feel her breasts pushing against his back. So that no one else could see, she reached down and pinched his ass and murmured "Mmm" into his spine. Before he could respond she returned to her place in front of the stove.

That was nice. She certainly was loading up her side of the equation. Nothing like a small sailboat and a pinch on the ass to get him leaning in her direction. Like he'd always said, "I'm no pushover, but I can be had."

By the time the last diners left, a little after ten, Blanca had still not shown her face. Migdala left Scheutz and Asher to clean up after telling Eusebio he could go home. She was off, she said, to find Otero, worried that maybe Harding, had shown up again. The girl did not necessarily need that kind of influence to take off somewhere, to some beach party on the other side of the island, but it had been a while since she had not shown up for work. He could hear the gears on the Volvo grinding in anger as she backed out onto the road.

Asher took off to meet some friends at the El Batey and left Scheutz to lock up. On his way out of the apartment, he heard a small noise in Blanca's bedroom and looked in. In the pitch dark a voice said, "Did Mama leave in the car?"

"Yes. You been in here all this time?"

"No. I snuck in about an hour ago."

"What the hell's going on? She's worried sick about you."

"I'm so sick about her worrying sick about me."

"Well, if it makes you happier, I'm not worried about you."

"Muchas gracias."

"Well, maybe a little."

"Stop it."

"No, seriously, turn the light on. What's going on?"

She switched on the lamp next to her bed and leaned back against the headboard. "Nothing's going on."

"Asher finally told me about what happened to Juaquin."

She flinched and seemed to shrink into the headboard, her eyes and her jaw dropped. "Wha…what did he say?"

"He told me how he had been poking Harding and Juaquin with the tip of the spear to get them off him and the spear gun went off and it was close enough to Juaquin's heart that it pierced him with all its force."

"Did he tell you what made the spear gun go off?"

"Said it was an accident."

She pulled her knees up to her chest and wrapped her arms around them, looking around the room but not at Scheutz. Then she began to cry. Tears flooded her face and she bent her head to her knees. He felt an urge to sit next to her and put his arms around the sobbing ball of her, but kept his ground. Whatever was causing her this pain, he sensed she needed to stand up with herself right now more than she needed comfort. She looked up at him and the cascade started afresh. "I…I did it."

"You did what?"

"I pulled the trigger."

"Do you mean you pulled the trigger on purpose?"

Sniff. "No. But I had my hand on it."

"So you can't say you know for sure. Four people wrestling around in that tiny space and one person picks up a spear gun that goes off. And you say you're the one caused it to go off. Sorry, Blanca, but you can't take all the blame for that."

"It was my fault they were in there wrestling, as you call it."

"Yeah."

Her head came up. "And it was Asher's fault; it was none of his business why I was on Harding's boat."

He had to admit she was right. It was none of Asher's business whether or not she was throwing herself away on a no-good like

Harding. But Scheutz could certainly not fault Asher for it. He might have done the same thing himself. And it really was not anybody's fault that Juaquin died on that boat. Unless, for some very reason, you might want to blame Juaquin himself for it. But they'd probably never know for sure what Juaquin was planning for Blanca. Maybe even Harding didn't know. Beltran would, but the hell with it, they were all better off just leaving the whole thing alone from now on.

"Listen, Blanca, I don't think you should blame yourself for what happened to Tio Juaquin. And don't blame Asher; he was just looking out for you, like he does with people he cares about."

The tears started again and Blanca stuck her palms into her eyes. "It was my fault for being on the boat with Harding. I wanted him to sail away from this place with me on it." She bent her head to her arms and blubbered. "I just can't stand it here any more. Being on this island feels like some judge sentenced me to twenty years in kindergarten."

"Did you talk with your mother about her letting you go on the boat with Samantha?"

"You mean with Samantha and you and Asher? Yes, I did."

"And what did she say?"

"She said she loved me and she wanted to keep me prisoner here in kindergarten till we got to be creaky old ladies together and could sit outside on the bench all day like Tapon and Sharkie and play with cats instead of Sharkie's dog."

"She didn't say that."

"Something like that."

"Come on. Why don't you wash your face and walk into town with me? I have to meet Samantha at Chuck's Pizza. And maybe we'll see your mother driving by and get her to come have a beer with us and we'll all talk about the South Pacific."

She sat with her wet face in her hands until he finally took one wrist and led her off the bed, out of the room and into the bathroom where she could wash her face.

Walking on the bay road, halfway into town, Otero stopped his jeep to tell them Migdala was looking everywhere for Blanca. Scheutz told him they were headed for Chuck's, and if Otero saw her he should tell her that's where Blanca would be.

"I am not your messenger." He drove on.

On the street near the bar Migdala stood outside glaring at them with her hands on her hips. As they drew close a couple of patrons sitting on the low wall across from the bar nursing their beers began razzing Blanca with things like, "You mama, she after you, man." and "You going to get it when you get home."

Blanca waved at her mother. "Here I am."

Migdala did not respond and the scowl never left her face. When they got near she ordered Blanca to the car, which was parked on the malecon.

"Let's go inside," Scheutz said to Migdala. "Samantha is waiting to talk to us."

"To me?"

"Yes. And to Blanca, and me. Come on."

The air inside Chuck's was hot, not helped much by the fan blowing from high on the wall at the end of the bar. It smelled of cigarettes and pizza and beer and, as usual at this time on a Friday night, was packed with people and the loud patter of conversation in both English and Spanish. Samantha sat at a table against the far wall of the ell that turned away from the bar. The German and a thin, middle-aged tourist with frizzy hair, a woman Scheutz had seen around town, sat with her. When they approached the table Samantha motioned for them to go with her back outside. On the street, they found a spot on the wall. Scheutz went back inside for beer for everyone. Blanca was underage so he got an extra glass into which they all, including her mother, could donate small dollops from their bottles.

"Where is Asher?" Samantha asked.

"He's over at El Batey. Meeting some people, he said."

"Well, I really wanted to talk with him and you. We need to get moving if we're to get out of here."

He looked at Migdala, tried looking into her eyes but couldn't. She sat very still, waiting. This was a last chance to change his mind. He looked at Samantha, tried looking into her eyes but couldn't. "I…" He took a gulp of beer and looked at Blanca, into her eyes. She, at least, had stood up today, grabbed herself by the nape of the neck and forced herself to confess to him her guilt about her actions in the death of her uncle Juaquin. She should be an inspiration to him to stand up himself and make up his goddamned mind. "I…I'm not going," he said.

Samantha stopped with her beer bottle half-way to her mouth. She lowered the bottle till her hand rested on her thigh and stared moved her head to take in both directions up and down the street. Then she nodded. "I knew it. I mean, I guessed it the way you been acting since I came back."

All four, Samantha and Blanca sitting on the wall and Scheutz and Migdala on the sidewalk in front of them, had nothing to say. Next to them a group of young men suddenly burst out in loud laughter at some story told in Spanish. Blanca sipped from her beer glass and Scheutz from his bottle.

"I wish you would come," Samantha said. Her tone sounded like she might be saying, "C'mon; it'll be fun." She smiled at him. He looked toward Migdala whose expressionless gaze said his going or not going meant a lot more to her than it did to Samantha. "No?" Samantha said. "I need a crew."

"Asher will go. I don't think he'd ever leave that boat." He flicked his thumb toward Blanca. "And she'd be a wonderful crew."

Blanca gulped last of her beer, set the glass on the stone wall, and draped her arm over her mother's shoulders. "How about it, mamacita? Can I go?"

Migdala slid her eyes sidewise to Blanca's and then turned her head toward Samantha.

Chapter 32

There goes that damned rooster again. The sound cut into whatever he was dreaming about—whatever anxiety that was—like a cawful bird beak pecking at his gizzard. What had he been dreaming about? Oh, yeah, like Prometheus he was bound to earth. He turned to lie on his back and found his right hand had been pinned by Migdala's body where she lay on her side facing away from him. He pulled the hand gently out from under her so as not to wake her; it began tingling, coming back to life. He shook it, imagining throttling that damned chicken in the neighbor's back yard.

Boy, what was that dream all about? He was not lately given to dreams of such intensity. His body tensed with anxiety, his breath came short. That's what the anxiety was all about; for the first time in many years he would become earth-bound. He should be looking forward to it, not having nightmares. Was he going to be able to do this? Did he really give a rat's ass about the restaurant business? No, but he did care about the woman lying next to him. And he had to admit he had longed for the feeling of home he had not experienced since leaving New Hampshire seven years ago.

So why did this all of a sudden feel so claustrophobic? Because there was no getting out, that's why. For so many years now, sailing around the Caribbean, if something went wrong or if a situation arose they didn't like, he and Samantha could just take off for some other island. And when they finally got the *Panacea* it was even easier. But the *Panacea* was no panacea. He had thought of it as a home, a moving home, but it wasn't really. It felt like something out of the fantasy world he and his little brother had conjured up when they were kids. They had sailed off on plenty of fantasy boats then, fighting off pirates or giving hell to German U boats and Japanese kamikaze planes. And, just like playtime when he was a child, messing about in boats in the Caribbean kept him safe from the real world. His childhood home felt claustrophobic because he had to stay there. But home in New Hampshire with his sons had been a happy time where he had to deal with the real world and he had proof he could deal with it. So, he should just get over all this anxiety.

At least for now. And just in case this arrangement with Migdala didn't work out, he could always leave. Truth was he really could not see himself tied in again with Samantha, especially in some far off alien environment like Tahiti or Bora Bora. And now with her inheritance from her father, if she was unhappy with their re-union, she had the wherewithal to take off and leave him to a Robinson Crusoe trip on some sandy atoll. The probability of that happening was pretty high. On the other hand, here he had Harding's sloop, a damned good, sea-worthy boat that needed only some cosmetic fixing-up. He could take off on his own. In fact, he could balance off the potential drudgery of working this restaurant with little trips to St. Croix or Haiti. And, if it got bad here, why couldn't he and Migdala take off on that sloop?

So it would be alright. He felt his body relax a little. The rooster had shut up but another a few houses over insisted on keeping up the chatter. He breathed easier and snuggled himself against Migdala who murmured without waking.

Friday was produce day at the ferry dock. Blanca, in her school uniform, helped set up for breakfast before catching a ride with Scheutz when he drove the Volvo down to meet the boat. Migdala and Asher kept up with the breakfast patrons. As he moved the car to the curb in front of the school, she asked if she could ride to the ferry dock instead. She had to meet someone and could still get to school on time. He drove on, and parked on the malecón just as the ferry, fifty yards offshore, and turned to back into the exit ramp.

Passengers were required to wait while the ferry's ramp lowered and vehicles drove onto the cobble-stoned ramp leading up to the malecon. The first vehicle off, as usual, was the produce truck. Scheutz was not in any big hurry to buy vegetables and get back to the restaurant. He tarried with Blanca watching the last vehicle, a tourist van, drive up from the water's edge. Behind it the pedestrian passengers left the boat and came ashore in no particular pattern. One woman, in bright-red pants suit stepped with great care from the boat ramp to the cobblestones, stopped and looked up at them. Blanca waved at her vigorously. Migdala's mother.

Blanca ran down the ramp to meet her and took the small traveling case from her hand. He waited for them to approach him. This was not, he was sure, a good sign. What was the woman doing here? That argument she and Migdala indulged in back in Mayaguez had been pretty nasty, the kind of argument that seemed to have been running for years. When they left Mayaguez that night he had asked her what the problem was between her and her mother, and Migdala had told him, coming close to spitting the words out, that it had always been like that between them. He remembered her beginning that story with, "We got off on the wrong foot right from the start." As if her mother's major bone of contention was Migdala's being born in the first place.

Blanca introduced her grandmother to him as Marisol. Oh yes, now he remembered her name. She acted as if she had never met him before, shook his hand and narrowed her eyes in what he took for recognition. She was shorter than Blanca, shorter than Scheutz had remembered, still a pretty woman even though small jowls had begun to form along her jaw line. She couldn't be much older than he was; probably became a mother, just like Migdala, at an early age. Her make-up had been precisely applied, the line of bright lipstick severe against the outline of her lips. Her hair of dark curls had obviously been recently tightly permed. With the carefully pressed pants suit, she looked very much out of place at this little tourist dock.

He turned to Blanca. "Well, chiquita, look what time it is. You better get yourself off to school before you're late."

"You have a car, I suppose," Marisol said. "We can drop her off on the way back."

"But I've got to shop for vegetables. The school is only a few blocks."

"And what am I supposed to do?"

"You can help me pick out the best tomatoes."

"I do not pick out vegetables."

"Okay. Well, why don't you hang out on the bench over there until I'm done and I'll give you a ride to the restaurant." She gave him no reaction. "Or wherever else you want to go." To Blanca who stood just behind her grandmother with a lightly bemused look on her face. "And you get yourself off to school, girl."

"Are you her father?" Marisol asked.

"No. Just a friend."

"Then you do not tell her what to do."

Whoa. That's where Migdala gets her bossy streak. That's why they don't get along. Basic law of physics; like particles repel each other. He swallowed the old adolescent urge to say something snotty, like "You'd probably be better at picking out vegetables than you are at picking out pants suits." But he pulled his eyes away from hers to Blanca who was having trouble stifling a grin. In lieu of comment he turned his back on the two of them and walked to the end of the malecón where the produce truck stood parked in its usual spot.

He brought the first batch of bags to the Volvo and knocked on the rear window for Blanca to come help him open the rear so he could stow them. She and her grandmother sat inside with the engine running and the air conditioner on, engaged in some deep conversation that involved a lot of hand waving. With Blanca in the front seat turned to

Marisol in the back, they did not look as if they were fighting; on the contrary, they looked conspiratorial.

He stowed the first bags and went back for the few boxes and other bags he had left at the produce truck. He had forgotten to bring the hand-truck from the restaurant. As he packed the second batch in the rear of the station wagon, the two women stopped their conversation. Blanca turned to smile at him while her grandmother faced forward in what felt like an air-conditioned silence. He closed up the back and got in the driver's seat, once again interrupting an excited exchange, excited at least on Blanca's part.

On the way back he stopped across from the school to let Blanca off and then continued to the restaurant. After parking behind, he went to open the rear while Marisol sat, possibly waiting for him to open the car door for her. Tough. He hoped she'd break a nail opening the door herself. He went inside to retrieve the hand-truck so he could pile everything on it in one trip.

Inside, the restaurant was still very busy. Asher ran back and forth with orders while Migdala cooked, the dishes piled high in the sink waiting for him. Before going back out through the door into the apartment with the hand-truck, he called out to her. "Hey, your mother's out here."

"¿Que dices? My mother?" She pulled her hand away just in time before cutting herself.

"I think she's waiting for you to come out and open the car door for her."

"She makes me crazy. What is she doing here?"

"I get the feeling Blanca had something to do with it."

She looked up toward where Tapon sat at his usual table with his friends. "I wonder if he is expecting her."

"I'll ask her." He let the door swing closed and pushed the hand truck down the hall to the rear door and out into the yard. At the Volvo, he lifted the rear and hauled the nearest box of vegetables out and onto the hand truck. Marisol still sat in the back seat. "Your father is in the restaurant," he called to her. "In case you're looking for him."

"I do not want to see him. Tell Migdala to come out here."

He finished piling the boxes and bags of vegetables onto the hand truck, closed the station wagon and wheeled around to the front of the restaurant. There he knocked on the screen door and Asher held it open while he wheeled the hand truck inside. As he went past the counter he mimicked the old sixties Latin rock tune, "Hey, Chiquita, you Mama, she callin' you, man."

Migdala banged a plate of food on the counter for Asher. "Up yours. And hers."

When he returned from storing the vegetables into their various holding units, nothing seemed to have changed. Migdala filled orders, Asher carried them to tables and brought more orders, and the conversation among Tapon and friends continued unabated. He could only assume the mother was still in the car. He went outside to see and, yes, she was still there, but now the engine was running, probably to keep the air conditioner on. What a weird lady.

He was tempted to ask her what he might do to help, but thought better of it. She reminded him of the nuns in grade school, the kind of people he had spent his life being snotty to whenever he couldn't avoid them. That had been a real problem over the last few years whenever he and Samantha would hire out on some yacht owned by some imperious woman. For some reason that kind of attitude coming from a man was not as hard for him to deal with. There had been a few problems in the army and some with logging bosses in New Hampshire, but coping with them felt sort of natural. When he encountered it in a woman, it just left him frustrated, not able to get in and mix it up with her the way he might with a man. And what about a future with Migdala, who occasionally treated herself to bouts of bossiness? Could he deal with that?

Well, screw it; her mother was not any of his business. He went back inside where the breakfast rush had settled down, got himself a cup of coffee and went to stand at Tapon's table. "Did you know your daughter is outside in the car?" he said to the old man.

"I do not have a daughter."

"Well, Migdala's mother is outside."

Tapon turned away from him and asked Sharkie something about his boat. Scheutz went back to the counter and made preparations to start in on the pile of dishes in the sink. Migdala had just finished the last order. "Why don't you go see about your mother?" Scheutz said to her. Bossy bitch or not, having her sit out there in the car like that just bugged him.

Before Migdala could say anything, the apartment door opened and Marisol entered. She looked around, stopped to take a long look at Tapon in the back of the room, and settled her gaze on Migdala. Scheutz rattled the dishes in the sink with increased enthusiasm. Migdala stopped what she was doing at the stove and locked eyes with her mother. At the back table, Tapon stopped talking and arguing with Arturo, dropped the finger he was pointing in his friends face, and paused with a long look at Marisol before continuing.

Marisol turned away from her daughter to gaze around the large room, taking in the tables, the décor, the kitchen area. This would be all new to her, especially with the restoration done after the hurricane. What looked like positive appraisal in her eyes did not seem to change the stern set of her mouth and chin. Her eyes narrowed again as she took another gander at Tapon, and stayed narrowed as it passed over Asher and Scheutz back to Migdala. "I want to talk to you," she said to Migdala.

"Have a seat. I've got to put this food away so it doesn't spoil."

"I will be in the living room." She turned and went back through the door to the apartment.

Migdala continued calmly putting things away. Finally, she stopped next to Scheutz. "Will you come in and talk to my mother with me?"

"Why me? It's none of my business."

"Yes it is."

"How so? What does she want to talk about?"

"I don't know. I just know I cannot deal with her. Please come. Whatever it is, I know it's going to be a fight, and I just…I don't know."

"So, what am I, the knight in shining armor here to save you from the fiery dragon?"

She laid a hand on his arm in that way she had. "You have no idea how close to the truth that is."

He dried his hands and took off his apron. She called Asher over and asked him to mind the restaurant for a while, since things had slowed down to almost nothing. Scheutz followed her into the apartment where her mother sat on one end of the sofa, her feet placed primly together on the floor.

"Can you please leave us?' she said to Scheutz.

"He must stay," Migdala said.

"This doesn't concern him."

"Whatever it has to do with me concerns him."

Marisol looked back and forth between him and her daughter without changing expression, and then relaxed everything, face and body, but just a little. "I need to talk to you about Blanca."

"What about Blanca?"

"You know that she was doing very well in school when she lived with me. Before you came back from whatever you were doing in New York all that time and brought her here to this place."

"I don't need to remind you that you grew up in this place."

"That is why I know how bad it is, and for Blanca es muy mal."

"I can't imagine how you could know that."

"She told me."

Migdala sat silent for a long moment, her eyes brimming with tears. She brushed them with the back of her hand. "And so you have come to tell me to make it better for her."

"No, I have come to take her back with me. Your uncle left me with pretty much money. I intend to use some of it to send Blanca to a private high school."

"Where?"

"In Mayaguez. She can live with me in the big house there."

"I do not want my daughter to live with you. She will become too much like you."

Now it was Marisol's turn to sit silent with tears brimming in her eyes. She dabbed at them with a handkerchief she took from her purse. Finally, she raised her head and set her jaw. "Blanca is sixteen. She can decide what she wants to do."

"What Blanca wants to do is to go off to the South Pacific in a big sailboat."

"You cannot let her do that."

"It doesn't seem like I have much say in what my daughter does."

"The same as I was left with nothing to say about what you did at that age."

Scheutz had about enough of listening to these two women saying things to purposefully hurt the other. The mother was right, this was none of his business. The mother was also right in saying that this small island could not contain the energy of that girl. Whatever was going to happen to her, it would make a lot of sense for it to happen somewhere else.

Chapter 33

The sun peeked just over the low ridge at the eastern tip of the island, sending rays skittering across the waves of the inlet and bouncing off the small surf that crashed over the reefs.

"Nothing else to say." Scheutz gave Samantha a hug.

"Guess not." She gave him one last squeeze but did not look up to meet his eyes. "I'll see you when we come back."

He waited for her to say something more. She merely pursed her lips and turned away, the tension tight in her shoulders the way he had come to recognize when she had a lot more to say but wasn't saying it. Just for the sake of their last moments together he tried to summon up the old feeling he had carried around for her these last seven years, but all that crept in was that image in the last few years of her standing stern-lipped at the helm of some boat not speaking to him because she was pissed about something or other. Here she was now being stern-lipped and tight-shouldered because she was majorly pissed off at him for choosing not to come with her.

But there really was nothing left for him to say. And, even though she might have wanted to say more, what good would it do? His mind was made up. His mind was made up months ago, after the hurricane, after that phone call from her parents' house in New Hampshire. Yeah, he was down for a while after that, but it surprised him even now how quickly he had gotten over it. Nothing like when Gerry left with the kids all those years ago. That took years, this took only a few months. And for that he had Migdala to thank.

Why had he even put himself through all that crap about making up his mind whether he was going with Samantha or staying here with Migdala? Probably just because he was too chicken to actually come out and tell Samantha it was truly over between them. And, as a result, like many acts of cowardice, he had put both Migdala and Samantha through unnecessary hassle.

But whether he had decided to go or to stay, Migdala was destined to loose Blanca to this trip. It was just as well. He and Migdala had sat up for hours talking about whether or not to let the girl go with Marisol. If she didn't let her go, she would have been gone anyhow, run away, inside of a week. And, at least this way they were sure she wouldn't end up back in Rincon with Harding and Beltran, or in Mayaguez with her grandmother. And that would give Harding and Beltran access to her. No matter what kind of problems Scheutz had had with Samantha, he had to admit, the woman had a lot of class, a lot of personal dignity. With her as a mentor Blanca stood an excellent chance of learning to take care of herself the same way.

Asher stood amidship fussing with the tie-downs on the new Avon inflatable dinghy Samantha had just bought a few days before. Scheutz went to stand next to him and laid a hand on his shoulder. "Take care of that girl."

"Don't have to tell me, mon. I'm on it."

"I'll see you when you bring the boat back."

"Yah. It been good, boss. Good time."

Scheutz put his arms around the man's wiry body and Asher patted him on the back until he let go. He had hoped Asher would refuse to go on this trip to the South Pacific, venturing into totally foreign waters. But no, Asher went with the boat. Asher had told him once that sailors were not travelers, the boat was their home and they tried never to leave home. All that other stuff outside the boat was just the neighborhood changing.

Below them the teak deck began to vibrate slightly with the sound of the engine turning over until it caught, and then responded to the steady low rumble of the 671 diesel. Samantha called something that Scheutz didn't catch but Asher turned aft, waved at her and shouted "Yah." He then walked forward to where Blanca and Migdala stood in the prow, both of them with the early morning sun glinting off the tears streaming down their faces. "Help with the anchor," Asher said to Blanca, and she turned away from her mother.

Migdala came to Scheutz and buried her face in his chest, her tears wetting his t-shirt. "We better go," he said to her. She nodded without moving away. He led her to the starboard rail where she finally let go of him and they climbed down to the work raft still anchored in the shallow water.

The schooner's anchor came up out of the water and Asher leaned over to fetch it aboard as the boat moved slowly forward away from the work raft and into the morning breeze. Blanca leaned over the rail and waved, shouting, "Adios, Tio Clemente. Adios, Mamma. Te quiero mucho."

Migdala waved vigorously. "Te quiero. Me llamas."

They watched as the boat advanced slowly toward the inlet. Asher and Blanca could be seen raising first one jib then another, and then the foresail. Just before reaching the inlet, the mainsail went up and then, with a strong morning sun backlighting the tanbark sails, the Panacea fell off the wind and turned to starboard, leaning gently toward them on a broad reach.

The End

CPSIA information can be obtained at www.ICGtesting.com
Printed in the USA
BVOW04s1141131013

333536BV00007B/43/P

9 780982 073285